A Scent of Seduction

An Unlikely Husband Series: Book 4

by
Mary Campisi

Dedication

To my readers... Whether you are new to my work or have been following me for years, this book is for you, with heartfelt gratitude.

English noblewoman Julia Langford wants nothing more than to escape the constraints of a society that demands she turn in her breeches and secure a husband. She cares nothing about men or love until she encounters daring sea captain Jon Remmington, a man who steals her heart and her innocence with searing kisses and bold touches.

Jon Remmington sails the sea avoiding anything that resembles commitment—until he meets the golden-haired temptress with a will to match his own. One night of passion binds them together, but a debt of honor forces Jon to abandon his bride. When he discovers that Julia is caught in a dangerous game of intrigue, Jon devises a secret plan to return to her side, where he will risk his life to protect her, and earn the chance to rekindle the greatest love either has ever known.

AUTHOR NOTE: *A Scent of Seduction* was previously published as *Innocent Betrayal*. Edits have been made to ensure continuity between the books, including character names.

An Unlikely Husband Series:

Book One: *The Seduction of Sophie Seacrest* (Sophie & Holt's story)

Book Two: *A Taste of Seduction* (Francie & Alexander's story)

Book Three: *A Touch of Seduction*: a novella (Ariana & Jason's story)

Book Four: *A Scent of Seduction* (Julia & Jon's story)

Included in this ebook is the first chapter of *The Redemption of Madeline Munrove*, The Model Wife series, Book 1.

This book was previously published as *Innocent Betrayal* in 2000 by Kensington Publishing and in 2012 by The Wild Rose Press (First English Tea Rose). It has been updated, edited, and re-titled as *A Scent of Seduction*, Book Four of An Unlikely Husband series.

Chapter 1

"Be damned! He's done it again," Jon Remmington muttered under his breath. He'd been watching the boy for a full ten minutes. If his count was correct, the little ruffian had just pickpocketed his third victim. Not that lifting coin from this group would be a difficult task. Many of them, especially his own men, were plunging into various stages of drunkenness with the same gritty determination they employed while manning his ship. They deserved this night of reckless abandon after weeks at sea, and Jon planned to let them have it. But he was not about to sit by and watch some scrawny urchin steal from them.

He peered through the gray haze, trying to concentrate on the boy's actions. The Fox's Tail was crowded and smoky, making it difficult to see clearly, but Jon thought he had figured out the boy's game. Each time the little tough edged up to an unsuspecting victim, he would lean in close, whisper in his ear, and then depart, shaking hands as he faded away, taking his booty with him. Jon eased back in his chair and took a long draft of ale. He was a patient man. Odds were that soon enough the boy would approach one of his men, and then Jon would teach him a lesson.

He scanned the pub, taking in the scene around him. The Fox's Tail attracted all breed of man, from sailor to nobleman, oddly bound together by the port and ale that flowed freely through the establishment, loosening their tongues and their purses. Its walls housed the latest whispers of scandal, whether they be social or political, and it was no secret the rooms upstairs were frequented by customers wanting a quick tumble with one of the pub's well-endowed barmaids.

It was all available for the right price. Rumors abounded regarding the illegal trade pushing up and down the coast. Silks, lace, spices. A half smile played about Jon's lips as he thought of the crafty merchants who bought their wares straight off the boats only to sell them to unsuspecting noblemen for nearly three times their worth.

The boy hadn't moved from his spot. He seemed to be waiting for something or someone. Was he a Bow Street Runner?

"Will ye 'ave another?" A blond barmaid leaned over, her huge breasts spilling out of the peasant's top she wore. When she smiled at him, he recognized the invitation in her brown eyes.

"Is there anything else ye be wantin'?" Her voice was low and husky.

Jon's gaze swept the length of her full figure and settled on her breasts. "Later."

"Me name's Hazel," she murmured, running her tongue slowly over parted lips.

He smiled at her.

"Later," she repeated before picking up her tray and disappearing amidst a group of raucous seamen.

"I see the women are flocking to you, as always," a voice boomed from behind.

Jon turned to see his first mate, Mac Judson, settling his bulky frame into a nearby chair. He grinned at the old man, then shrugged and closed his eyes. "I know, Mac, but what's a man to do?"

"Hah!" the older man bellowed in laughter. "You've a way with the women, that's for sure." He paused only long enough to take a healthy swallow of ale before he continued. "They all love you, from England to the Orient, princess to barmaid, but not a one of 'em has ever been able to catch you."

Jon's smile stretched, his eyes still closed. "Oh, they catch me when I want them to, Mac, but keeping me, now that's a different story."

Mac chuckled and slapped Jon on the back. "One day, boy, one of them will. You'll see or my name isn't Mac Judson."

Jon's eyes snapped open as he remembered the pickpocket. The boy had edged closer to a group of scruffy seamen, two of whom were Jon's deckhands. "Mac, look at that boy standing over by Amos and Jeremy." He pointed toward the group of five.

Mac squinted. "The scrawny thing in the black cap?"

"That's the one. He's been fleecing unsuspecting victims all night, and I'm about to teach him a lesson."

"You sure he's stealing?" Mac's bushy white eyebrows drew together as he studied the boy. "He looks like the same one that's been asking around for Gerald Thackery."

"The *Matilda*'s captain?"

Mac nodded and rubbed his white beard. "The lad's been quizzing everybody in the place, looking for the captain. Said he wanted to sign on as a cabin boy." Mac's faded blue eyes twinkled. "We pretended we didn't know where he was." He leaned his big bulk toward Jon and whispered, "We didn't have the heart to tell him the good captain was taking his pleasure upstairs."

Jon frowned. "I don't believe it. It's just a ruse to cover what he's really been doing, and that's stealing."

"Why would a body bent on stealing strike up a conversation with the person he's about to rob? Especially an urchin like that one. From what I heard and what I can see, he's no more than fifteen or so and so scared, he can't even give a straight look in the eye to ask a question."

Jon said nothing as he watched the boy sneak up to one of his men.

"I know you find it hard to believe a person would want to go to America," Mac continued. "But there's many a man who believes it's the land of opportunity."

Jon ignored the comment. "Did you see that? Did you see him brush up against Amos?" He stood, towering over Mac. "That's the last coin he'll steal tonight," he muttered, pushing away from the table as he moved with steady purpose through the crowd.

A glass broke behind him, crashing to the floor, followed by yelling and the sound of fists connecting. Jon turned just in time to avoid the blunt edge of a bottle hurled in the air by some drunken sod. It landed squarely on the head of the man next to him, toppling him to the ground. Within seconds, an all-out brawl exploded. Jon pushed his way toward the boy, grabbing and hauling him up and over his shoulder toward the stairs that were a few feet away. He ignored the kicking legs and squirming body on his shoulder as he took the stairs two at a time. Flinging the first door open, he thrust the boy inside and almost laughed when the boy scurried to the furthest corner of the room.

"Unless you're planning to jump out that window, you have no other means of escape." Jon leaned against the door, blocking the only other exit.

The would-be thief scanned the entire room quickly, then scanned it once more. "What ye be wantin' from me?"

"Now there's a question." Jon laughed and pushed away from the door. "What I be wantin' from ye," he drawled, "is to see how much coin you stole downstairs." He advanced on the boy, pinning him against the wall with one hand. "We'll see how much booty you collected tonight," he said, working his free hand inside the boy's oversized pockets. Empty. He opened the front of the jacket and looked for hidden pockets. "Did you steal this jacket, too?" he asked, fingering the fine silk lining. He received no answer, not that he expected one, though he had expected to find pockets filled with money.

"Where's the money?" he demanded. "I know it's here somewhere." Ignoring the panic in the boy's eyes, Jon ran his hands slowly along the oversized shirtfront and encountered two soft mounds. "What the devil—!" He grabbed the shirt and jerked the buttons open to reveal full, lush breasts straining against the confines of their heavy cotton binding. *A woman!* She tried to cover herself, but Jon caught her small hands and forced them to her side. The shirt fell open to reveal the creamy swell of her bosom, and for a second he wished he could have a peek beneath the layers of cotton binding.

He looked away and gazed up into a pair of gray eyes. They

were soft and shimmering, surrounded by a thick fringe of lash. How had he missed those eyes?

"So," he said in a soft voice. "The he is a she." She tried to bolt but he clamped down on her arm and closed in until they were noses apart. They stared at one another—the predator and the prey. Before she could protest, he jerked the stocking cap from her head and a mass of golden locks tumbled about her shoulders.

She was beautiful, of that he was certain. Her full lips trembled with what seemed like fear. What would she taste like? Sweet and fresh would be his guess. Of course, there was one way to find out, but that wasn't why he'd brought her up here. Until a moment ago, he'd thought her a thieving "he," and whether female or male, beautiful or not, she remained a thief.

"I saw you stealing."

"I did no such thing!" she protested, all trace of the cockney accent she'd used a moment before gone.

He frowned. "Who are you?"

She didn't answer for the longest time, and when she did it wasn't really an answer at all. "I'm looking for Captain Gerald Thackery. He's sailing his ship to America."

"What do you want with that scoundrel?" Jon held little respect for a man who cheated his men out of honest wages and spent the better part of his life in drunken excess.

"I..." She hesitated a moment. "I'm trying to secure passage to America and thought I might travel as a cabin boy."

"Oh," Jon scoffed. "More deceit. Exactly how did you plan to carry it off?" His gaze lingered on her breasts, taking perverse pleasure in the crimson color spreading across her cheeks.

She yanked her jacket closed. "I'd planned to disguise myself as a cabin boy."

Jon laughed outright. "With Thackery as captain? He'd sniff you out a mile away." He leaned in close, the scent of lilac filling his nostrils. "Listen," he whispered. Grunting moans and soft sighs traveled through the walls. A man's voice, deep and commanding, rasped out words of pleasure that made her flush ten shades deeper than a moment before. "Sail with him and that's how you'll be passing your time."

He paused a moment. "If you want to get to America, there are legitimate ways to go about it. You wouldn't need to come to a dockside pub dressed as a boy looking for a man you know nothing about."

"I had no choice," she spat out.

"There's always a choice." Jon turned from the woman and tried to sort out her deceit. From the corner of his eye, he saw her reach two fingers inside the heavy binding that covered her breasts. *What the devil was she up to?* He swung around and hauled her to the narrow bed in the corner.

She kicked him with her booted foot, just missing his groin.

"Damn you!" Jon stilled her squirming body with one arm as he thrust his free hand inside the binding and pulled out a crumpled scrap of paper.

He stared at it a long time, barely noticing Gerald Thackery's name scrawled on the fine linen stationery. It was the name on the letterhead that gave him pause.

Holt Langford.

How in the devil had she gotten hold of his best friend's stationery? Before he could question her, a sharp blow struck his temple. "Aghh," he moaned, clutching his head in pain. He doubled over, crouching onto the wooden floor among shards of glass as a fine stream of blood oozed from his right temple. He lifted his aching head just in time to see the woman flee.

Moments later, Jon hurtled the steps two at a time, racing out the door in pursuit of his quarry. He ignored the dull throbbing in his head as he scanned the darkness. She was out there somewhere, but the docks of London could hide a person for days.

There were no signs of life in the area, save a lone elegant carriage traveling several yards ahead of him. She was gone. *Damn her.* Jon turned back toward the pub and swiped at the wetness on his cheek. Blood smeared his fingers as he cursed all women, but one in particular, to everlasting hell.

***

The carriage rolled away from The Fox's Tail and toward the comfortable familiarity of the Gregorys' drawing room as Julia Langford squeezed her eyes shut and lay back against the burgundy velvet squabs. If she kept her eyes firmly shut, perhaps the last hour would fade into the vagueness of a bad dream.

"Julia?" Isabelle Fleming's concern was evident from the quiver in her voice. "Something's happened, hasn't it? It's finally gone too far."

"Let me rest a moment, Belle. Just a moment and I'll be fine."

Julia tried to make the vision disappear but the events of the evening were too powerful to whisk away with the brush of a hand or blink of an eye. He kept coming for her, a bronzed warrior, towering over her, blocking all thoughts of escape. What would he do when he caught her? A stray lock of chestnut hair fell over his forehead while the rest trailed to his shoulders in wavy disarray. His nose was slightly crooked, his jaw too square. Eyes, deeply set, were a rich brown, like fine French chocolate, smooth and decadent. Those eyes bore into her as he closed the distance between them.

The man backed her against a wall. She inhaled his male scent, felt his warm breath on her hair, watched his firm mouth moving closer. She pressed her palms against the wall, bracing for the onslaught of his kiss. There was no escape. His mouth descended, stopped mere inches from hers. Fear warred with anticipation as she waited. Could he hear the wild beating of her heart? He spoke in a whisper-soft voice. "Liar." His voice grew louder. "Thief."

Julia's eyes flew open. She blinked twice and rubbed her temples. What if the man knew Holt? She'd seen the way he stared at the paper. Had he recognized the name? She thrust the possibility aside. Highly unlikely. The monster wasn't even an

Englishman.

"I had a bit of trouble tonight, Belle." Julia avoided her friend's watchful gaze and grabbed one of the boxes that held a carefully wrapped rose gown and various layers of undergarments.

"What happened?"

"I wasn't careful enough. I couldn't think of anything but meeting Captain Thackery, and I let my guard down." Julia shook her head and reached for her camisole. "There was a man—"

"And?"

"He accused me of stealing. And he found the piece of paper with Captain Thackery's name on it." Shimmying out of the gray breeches, she pointed her toe into a rose-colored stocking.

"Well, that would tell him nothing."

Julia busied herself with the stocking. "It was on Holt's letterhead."

"Oh." And then, "Let's remain calm. Holt doesn't frequent such places and our families only travel to London a few times a year. This man couldn't possibly know your brother." She shook out a frilly petticoat and laid it across her lap.

Julia sighed. "I'm sure you're right. If Holt ever knew we were masquerading as boys in taverns, he'd have our heads."

A twinkle of mischief lit Belle's eyes. "We did it all last Season, and he never found out."

"But this is the first time at The Fox's Tail. It's nothing like the quaint taverns we're used to frequenting." A vision of a fierce warrior intruded on her thoughts. "It's seedy and wild, with all sorts of untamed characters milling about. You wouldn't have liked it at all."

"I'd choose that any day over dance cards and demure smiles with silly introductions and the latest *on dit*." She sighed. "Why can't our families accept the fact that we don't want to marry?"

"Duty." Julia gathered the rose gown and worked it over her

head. "We've been born to it, Belle. My brother's an earl; your father's a duke. It's expected."

Belle helped Julia pull the gown into place, smoothing wrinkles with her small hands. "Expected perhaps, but accepted, never. I'll not conform to it."

"Nor will I, which is why I'm determined to go to America. I'll have the freedom to make my own choices without societal constraints." She paused. "And I'll be with Jason and his family."

Belle laughed. "Of course. The brother who permits you to ignore societal constraints."

Julia wrinkled her nose. "You needn't be so blunt about it. Need I remind you he was the only member of my family who didn't desert me?" The only image she had of her dead mother was a small locket with her picture in it. As for her father, Edward Langford had found little time for family, spending most of his hours in other women's company. Or their beds, as she had heard.

And then, there was her oldest brother, Holt, the current Earl of Westover. He'd been gone twelve years—and while she loved him, he was a stranger.

"It certainly was much easier to get Jason to do your bidding."

Julia rolled her eyes. "There's no comparison. Holt wants to see me settled in a manner befitting a woman of my station, and to him that means marriage. He absolutely refused to let me travel with Jason and his family to America. Why, even Caroline was permitted to go, but not me. And why? Because, I must look for a husband."

"He means well. Maybe he's trying to make up for all the years he was gone." Belle reached for the silver brush in Julia's hand. "He might never say it, but Holt does love you."

"Of course, he loves me." That was not the point. Freedom. That was the point.

"He's quite noble, too."

"To a fault."

"Jason let you get away with outrageous antics."

Julia threw up her hands and turned to Belle. "He teased me about being too outspoken and independent, but he also encouraged me to be that way. Holt wants me to 'repress my forward behavior and adopt a more demure air,'" she mimicked. "I won't do it."

"There's certainly not a lot about you that's demure."

"Exactly. And now, because of some meddling man, I've most probably missed my opportunity to meet Captain Thackery, who was my last hope of gaining passage to America."

"Well, you can't go back there after what happened tonight. You'll have to speak with Holt again."

"And hear him lecture me for the twenty-eighth time about how I am a young woman of proper breeding who needs to think about a husband and children rather than traipse to an uncivilized country? No, thank you. And of course—" Julia rattled on as heat rose to her face "—my dear brother would never miss an opportunity to tell me that I am not really a *young* woman anymore."

"Ah, yes, I do see a smattering of gray amongst all this gold," Belle said as she wound Julia's hair high atop her head, securing the locks with small pins. "What an old creature you are." When she spoke next, all traces of humor vanished. "Try speaking with him once more. Ask him under what terms he would consider letting you travel to America."

"The effort will prove futile." Her friend did not know Holt the way she did.

Belle sighed. "If I thought one of my brothers would secure passage for you and not inform Father, I'd have made the arrangements long ago. Unfortunately, they would tell the Duke straightaway, and he would not be pleased."

Before they could consider their predicament further, the carriage ground to a halt. "Oh no," Julia groaned. "We're at the Gregorys' and I've not finished dressing." She reached for her rose slippers. "What's our story tonight?"

Belle tapped a finger to her chin and said, "We told Holt we were coming with my aunt and vice versa. Then Auntie got sick midway to the Gregorys', and we had to return her to her residence, thus the lapse in time. We weren't concerned about chaperones, because we knew Holt and Sophie would be here." Her eyes narrowed. "As long as your brother doesn't talk to my aunt, our honor will be safe."

"And Higgins?" Julia inclined her head toward the front where the ancient driver sat. Their usual driver on such nights of adventure had taken ill, and Belle had intruded upon Higgins to fill in.

"Higgins is my friend," Belle assured her. "You have nothing to fear from him." Her voice lowered to a whisper. "I've got him wrapped around my little finger, just like the rest of my family." She grinned. "Being the youngest child with five older brothers does have its advantages."

"So you've said." Belle's brothers were giants, with quick tongues and ferocious snarls that dissipated the moment their little sister entered the room. She could cajole, scold, and tease them and receive no further retribution than a hearty laugh or lift in the air. Julia could not begin to fathom such a relationship with Holt.

Belle grabbed the sapphire-encrusted combs from the tissue and placed them in Julia's hair. "Perfect. If only we weren't off to a night of sheer boredom. I wish I'd been the one to have your adventure in The Fox's Tail tonight. At least I'd have something exciting to think about while I danced with my latest would-be suitor."

The image of her dark abductor flashed through Julia's mind. "No," she said in a shaky voice. "Do not wish that, Belle. Above all things, do not wish that."

Chapter 2

Julia gave up watching the clock sometime after two in the morning. Her mind kept racing with what she would say in the morning. It was her last attempt to convince Holt to let her follow her heart's desire. If she could only make him understand how much she wanted this, she could set sail for America within a fortnight. On the other hand, if this meeting ended in her oldest brother's staunch refusal as all the others had, then she would be forced to resort to desperate measures, though at the moment, she was not quite certain what those would be. From the moment Jason told her he was heading to America with his new family and their sister, Caroline, Julia had planned to join them.

One obstacle stood in the way of her freedom. Actually, it was a very big obstacle, mountainous to be exact, with a will to match her own. It had a name, too, Holt Langford, Earl of Westover. Her eldest brother was not a man to trifle with. *Drat and double drat!* Julia punched her pillow and settled on her stomach to plan one final attack. If this one failed, she was doomed.

***

Julia awoke to the sound of a horse's whinny. She scurried out of bed, rushed to the window, and threw back the heavy velvet curtain. Holt sat astride a huge stallion; Sophie accompanied him on a sleek, chestnut mount. What an attractive and perfectly matched couple they were!

She watched as her brother lifted a hand to caress Sophie's neck, trailing it over her bosom. *Goodness!* Julia stepped away from the window and let the curtain fall back into place. What would it feel like to be touched in such a manner? Visions of the stranger's hands roaming her body invaded her. Drat, drat, *drat!*

A short while later, Julia ventured into the dining room where she fixed a quick cup of tea. She would sample Mrs. Florence's scrumptious sausage and biscuits after she spoke with Holt—unless he rejected her request again. Then she would be too depressed to eat. Chiding herself for already anticipating defeat, she pasted a smile on her face and headed for the study. When she reached the heavy oak door, she hesitated a moment, then knocked.

"Come in." Holt disliked interruptions and the tone of his voice indicated such, but this interruption was necessary. He glanced up when she entered and the irritation faded from his voice. Perhaps that was a good sign. "Good morning, Julia. Did you enjoy the ball last night?"

"As much as I do those sorts of things." She shrugged and sat on the gold and burgundy sofa.

"I see." Holt leaned back in his chair, clasped his large hands behind his head. "Too many suitors vying for your affections, all of them dandies living off of their fathers' money."

Julia smiled at her brother's very accurate assessment of her steadfast opinion of the ton. "Something like that," she said.

"No wonder you've got them all falling over your skirts. You're beautiful, witty, and intelligent—a rare commodity in a woman." He laughed at her sour expression. "That Barton fellow has asked me for the third time if he may call on you. I can't put him off much longer."

Julia rolled her eyes, letting Holt know what she thought of Andrew J. Barton, Viscount Arondale.

He laughed again. "My thoughts exactly. You'd be miserable with that sniveling creature." He leaned forward and jotted a note to himself.

Who would have believed the scrawny, fearful boy he'd once been would turn into the man seated before her? He'd returned to England a few years ago, and after several "complications," he'd married and taken on the title of earl. She loved her eldest brother, had shared many a meal with him, accompanied him to balls and soirées, and engaged in thought-provoking conversation. But he'd always remained a bit aloof.

And he was not Jason. Nobody was Jason. Oh, how she

missed him. The two brothers did not even look alike. Holt was a big man, standing well over six feet with a body of bronze and muscle, honed from years at sea. He possessed none of the conventional looks deemed handsome by England's standards, but that didn't stop women from seeking him out. He had high cheekbones, a straight nose, a square jaw, and the most arresting pair of navy eyes. His jet-black hair hung several inches past his shoulders, definitely longer than the current fashion. And the small golden hoop he still wore in his left ear served as a reminder of his years at sea. Whether he'd sailed as merchant or pirate, no one really knew and he never said. The very fact of *not* knowing only added to the alluring enigma of the man. She met those watchful eyes and willed herself to be strong.

"Julia?" Holt prodded. "Is something wrong?" *She must be strong.* When she didn't answer, he rounded the desk and sat beside her. "Tell me, what is it?"

It was the gentleness in his voice that spilled the first tear. Her brother hated tears but that knowledge did not make them stop as the second and third fell. "I don't fit in here," she sniffed. "And I can't be something I'm not. I've tried."

Holt frowned. "Jason did you no favor letting you believe it would be equally acceptable to walk into a room of crowded people wearing breeches instead of a gown."

"He only wanted to make up for our lack of family." As soon as the words were out, Julia wished she could take them back. Holt tensed but his expression remained unreadable. "I'm sorry. I didn't mean you."

A full minute passed in silence, save the ticking of the oak clock resting on the mantel. How could she have been so thoughtless? Hadn't Belle told her just last evening that Holt was overprotective because he'd been away for so long?

His navy eyes darkened, then gentled. "Expectations are different for a woman, Julia," he said, taking her hands in his. "Women aren't given the freedom a man enjoys. Unfair as it may seem to you, that's the way of it."

"But why?" she insisted. "We come to London so you may display me on the marriage mart, but I don't want to get married. Marriage will make me some man's chattel and no matter what you say, I know that's what happens." Holt raised a dark brow and Julia rushed on. "Except in your case. You and Sophie love each other and you treat her like a queen. She's the one person you can't intimidate." When she saw the muscles in his jaw twitch, she said, "Don't deny it. You share something rare and beautiful, and I'm very happy for you but I'm not willing to risk loving someone who doesn't love me. The pain would be too deep to watch him cast me aside for his mistresses."

"And what do you know of such things?"

Julia shrugged. "Gossipmongers abound, whether in London or the country. I heard enough whispered tales about Father and his women to make me vow never to marry." She concentrated on the soft muslin fabric of her gown. "So you see, there's really no reason to refuse my trip to America."

"Not all men are like Father."

"But too many are. Besides, it's more than just the idea of marriage. I'm a Langford. Adventure is in our blood." She would try one more time. "Can't I please have the freedom to make my own choice?"

She could almost see Holt's mind, thinking, studying, and assessing. He ran a hand through his hair and sighed. "I know I've fought your traveling to America, but there are several reasons I don't want you to go. Some of them are selfish. I want my children to know their Aunt Julia as a person, not just a bedtime story, and I would miss you very much; so would Sophie." He paused, then added, "But aside from my own selfish reasons for wanting you to remain here, I'm concerned for you. I've traveled the world and it isn't always a kind place." He tightened his hold on her. "You've led a very sheltered existence with only occasional trips to London, like now. Granted, it's been said if one survives London, one can survive anything, but I'm talking about foreign lands with different and sometimes unfriendly people. Not to mention the basic backward elements of living in an undeveloped land."

"But that's part of the excitement, is it not?"

"And danger," Holt said in a tight voice.

"Jason is there, so there's no need to worry." Holt's stern look told her he did not agree. Julia pushed on, determined to change his mind. "Despite what you may think, I am quite capable of adjusting to a different lifestyle. Why, I could even perform housekeeping duties if necessary."

"Hah. I doubt you'd be able to find your way to the kitchen."

"But I could," she persisted.

"Julia," Holt began in that placating manner he often used with her. "To my knowledge, you've never been in a kitchen other than to steal a tart. And, if the rumor is true, you'd be buried alive under your clothing if it weren't for your personal maid. I dread to consider what might happen if you tried to mop a floor."

"Just because I haven't done any of those things doesn't mean I can't."

"It would be a disaster."

A wonderful thought struck her. "If I could do all of those things you mentioned, would you permit me to go?"

"Cooking and cleaning?"

"Why not?"

"That's ridiculous. You're a woman of quality. Even in America, you'd not be expected to perform such manual labor. You would lead a privileged lifestyle, much as you do here."

"Yes, I know, but what I'm asking is if I can prove you wrong by doing something you're certain I can't, such as learning housekeeping, then will you admit you could be wrong about America?"

"And let you go?"

"And let me go." She held her breath. Perhaps he might agree.

Holt said nothing for what seemed like ages but Julia knew

better than to interrupt him. He would make his decision when he was ready and no amount of prompting or impatient urgings would hurry him. She leaned against the cushions of the sofa, closed her eyes, and thought of the books she'd been reading about America. New lands, new people. Endless possibilities.

"I'll agree on one condition." Her brother's words sliced through her thoughts. "For a period of three weeks, we'll remain in London and you will become a servant here. You will dress the part, work with the servants, and not socialize with any of your friends."

"That's all?" *Was he truly giving her a chance to earn her way to America?*

"You will cook, polish, and scrub as directed."

"Fine. Is that all?" *Yes, indeed he was.*

He hesitated, obviously surprised by her rapid consent. "You will wear serviceable gowns. No more silks or satins."

Julia smiled.

"And no soirées or balls either," he spat out.

"That should not pose a problem." She lowered her head to hide another smile. This servant business had her brother in a major huff. He certainly didn't seem to like the idea, which made her all the more determined to succeed.

"Are you positive you wish to go through with this charade?" he asked, rubbing the back of his neck as though he could not wait to be done with this conversation.

"If it is the only way I can obtain passage to America, then yes, it's what I want."

"Before you give me your final answer, there is one more small condition we must agree upon."

"Yes?" She'd agree to any condition as long as it got her on a ship bound for America.

"If you fail to carry off this little ruse, fail in any way to meet the terms, then all talk of America will cease." He placed his hands over hers. "Then you will accept your fate and remain in England."

Julia bit her lip. If she failed, he'd prohibit her from

traveling to America. Ever. She'd be forced to stay in England and whether or not he spoke the words, she knew he would eventually attempt to coerce her into a marriage match.

"Julia?"

"I agree," she blurted out. "If I fail, I won't mention America again. You have my word."

Holt smiled then and squeezed her hand. He thought he'd beat her at this game of wills. In truth, he probably didn't think she'd make it past a day or two but she'd show him. She would succeed. She quickly amended that thought; she *must* succeed.

Chapter 3

Julia heard the companionable chatter of dinner conversation as she approached the dining room, laden with a tureen of creamed asparagus soup. Holt's hearty laughter echoed to her.

She approved of their dinner guest, Jon Remmington, though she had yet to meet him. Anyone who could lighten her brother's somber countenance and make him laugh in earnest was someone she would hold in high esteem. And he was from America, which meant he could prove a valuable resource to her in some capacity once she won her wager with Holt.

She turned her thoughts to the scant tidbits she knew about their guest. He was an American, though a displaced one, having fallen out with his father several years ago. Jon Remmington had met Holt at sea but the conditions of their first encounter remained unknown. They'd been adversaries, two men of equal strength and power who later became best friends, sailing the sea together, exploring distant, exotic lands. Julia was more than a little curious to meet the man who could challenge her brother and gain his friendship.

"Are you all set to bring in the soup, Julia?" Mrs. Florence grinned, barely able to control her mirth. Julia smiled back at the plump cook who had been preparing delectable dishes for the Langford household for almost twenty years.

"I believe so, Mrs. Florence. I only regret that I won't be feasting on your roast pork and spiced apples."

"The earl said this was to be a special dinner for his good friend, Mr. Remmington, so I fixed one of the family's favorites." She bent her gray head toward Julia and whispered, "I'll save you some in the kitchen, Lady Julia."

"You're a dear. It will be scrumptious, as usual." Julia lifted the tureen of asparagus soup, noting it was much heavier than she expected. "How on earth do you manage these things?"

Mrs. Florence let out a booming laugh. Behind her, Julia heard the soft tittering of two young maids as they watched her wrestle with the huge bowl. She grinned at them, knowing her transition from noblewoman to servant had created quite a stir. There were even whispered rumors that bets had been taken as to whether or not she'd succeed in her mission.

"Good luck to you," Mrs. Florence whispered, her kind blue eyes twinkling as she opened the door for Julia. Concentrating on the creamy, green liquid in front of her, Julia took slow, careful steps toward the dining room where her family entertained their honored guest. As she entered the ornate elegance of the dining room, her gaze shot to an empty spot on the linen tablecloth. Just large enough, with a little room to spare. She edged closer to the table…

"I wish I'd had the opportunity to meet your brother and his family." A very deep, very familiar voice spoke to the right of her.

The tureen clattered onto the table, sloshing asparagus soup on the pristine tablecloth. Julia withdrew quickly, her gaze riveted on the man who'd just spoken. *It was him!* Dark eyes sliced over her, widened in recognition seconds before he looked away.

"Julia!" Holt glared at her. "You're staring at our guest. And look what you've done to his shirt." Her brother motioned toward Jon Remmington's white shirt. Pale green spots splattered the front in a random pattern.

"Julia, why don't you see if you can find something to clean up this little accident? I'm sure Mr. Remmington bears you no ill will." Sophie's soft voice cut the tension clinging to the room. "As we all know, accidents do happen." She shot her husband a murderous look but he ignored the warning, piercing Julia with his navy stare.

"Sophie is quite right." Jon Remmington drawled. "It's nothing, Holt, really. Best to let it just be forgotten."

***

Best to let it just be forgotten. Those had been Jon's own words, but he'd spent the rest of the supper hour anticipating the return of the maid named Julia. But she did not return and he wasn't at all surprised. Still, he waited, more than a little curious about this maid who dressed in boy's clothes and frequented taverns. What had she been after? More to the point, did it have anything to do with Holt? Jon had to find out, had to be certain Holt was safe from his past, for God knew, Jon wasn't.

He recalled the conversation he and Holt had in the library after supper. They'd been enjoying a very fine brandy and reminiscing about the old days at sea.

"How much have you told Sophie?" Jon asked, eager to allay his own concerns.

Holt's jaw tensed. "She only knows I was a merchant tradesman."

Hmm. How to broach the subject they'd both vowed never to speak of again? "Nothing else?"

"Of course not."

"Good." Jon crossed one booted leg over the other and stared into his snifter. "He saw me, you know." There. Finally, after seven years, he'd said it.

"Impossible."

"No," Jon corrected. "Most definitely possible." Silence followed, filling the room with memories, dark, ugly images of men lying in pools of blood, gasping for one last breath as the life oozed out of them. Jon was the first to speak. "I didn't leave right away. I had to be certain the files were destroyed." He paused. "I pulled off my mask, the damn thing was so hot, and watched the building go up in flames. And then, I saw someone at the window, staring straight at me. A few seconds later, the fire took over and he was gone."

"Damn," Holt said. "The building was empty; we checked it."

Jon shrugged. "He could have been hiding or even entered once the fire started."

"Peter Crowlton stood to become a very wealthy man but only if he had the files."

"The bastard was willing to sacrifice all of us," Jon bit out, thinking of the brutal murders of twelve fellow espionage agents. Crowlton had sold their files and exposed his own kind, for money and power.

"But we stopped him," Holt said. "The files were destroyed, our mission complete. The Crown was satisfied."

"They never found a body." Jon tried to keep his voice casual. "Not even in all the charred ashes of the building. Don't you find that odd?"

"It's been seven years. The man's dead."

"Logic says you're right, but every once in a while, something out of the ordinary happens, say, for instance, a stranger taking an unusual interest in me, asking a lot of personal questions about my past. Or a person who seems out of place in a particular situation. It makes me think about Crowlton and the fact that his body was never found."

Holt laughed. "Nonsense. That life is behind us now. I'm a respectable businessman, titled no less, with a wife and children. And you're a philandering, wealthy merchant who roams the world in search of excitement."

Jon smiled. "You forgot to include British-born American. Makes me sound more interesting. Like an unsolvable puzzle." He swirled the brandy in his snifter and took another drink.

"That's because you *are* an unsolvable puzzle, my man," Holt said. "And you like it that way. It makes you irresistible to all those women who trail after you and your American accent with that Virginia drawl. If they only knew you were as British as I am, they'd be very disappointed."

"But they'll never know, will they?"

"Not from me they won't."

"I knew I could count on my best friend." Jon paused a moment, his brow furrowed, his smile gone. "You're probably right about Crowlton. Most likely he's dead. But, if he were alive, we both know he'd be hunting me." He looked up from his snifter to see Holt give a slight nod of agreement. "Part of me wants nothing more than to meet him, face to face, so I can repay him for killing his own."

"Nothing's worse than a traitor," Holt agreed.

"If by some crazy stretch, the bastard were still alive, he'd only be after me." Jon measured his next words. "Or those I care about. I don't have to tell you what to look for."

"Is there some particular reason you're telling me this now? Has something happened?"

Well, there it was. Time to confess. "I don't trust your new maid."

"Which one?"

"The woman who spilled the asparagus soup on me. Julia, I believe."

"Julia?" Holt's lips curved up a bit. Was he hiding a smile?

"There's something about her. She's not what she appears." *Even when she wasn't dressed in a boy's clothes.*

"Really?"

"She dresses in maid's clothing, but carries herself with the grace and elegance of a well-bred lady. Her speech tells of education, unless she's an awfully good imitator." Jon frowned. "And she was quite flippant, with little regard for social class, which is unseemly in a maid, but actually quite refreshing in a woman."

"Julia is a maid, I assure you."

"And her skin is too soft," Jon said, recalling the velvety swell of her bosom...

"Her skin? What in the hell do you know of her skin?"

Jon cleared his throat. "Why, nothing other than what my observant eye relays to me."

"You think Julia is hiding something?" Holt's expression was blank, his voice cautious, as though he were trying very hard to show no emotion.

"Perhaps. How long has she been in your employ?"

Holt's eyes narrowed on him. "She's been here less than a week."

Why did he look away and take a sudden interest in the papers on his desk? "Where was she previously employed?" References would be easy enough to check.

"She said she'd been taking care of an ailing grandmother in the country for the past two years." Holt shoved the papers aside, leaned back in his chair, and strummed his fingers on the massive oak desk.

"So there are no other employers to vouch for her work?"

"None."

Not the kind who would admit it anyway. A blurred image of Peter Crowlton swam before him. Was it his imagination, or was Holt avoiding the subject of his new maid?

"Judging from the skills she's displayed, it's hard to believe she's really a maid. There was more asparagus soup splattered all over the place after she cleaned up than when she actually spilled the stuff." Jon twirled the brandy snifter between his fingers and waited for his friend's reply.

"Out with it, man. What are you saying?"

"Maybe she's here on a mission."

"To do what? Steal Mrs. Florence's lemon tart recipe?"

"Maybe she's spying on you. Maybe Crowlton is still alive. Admit it. It is a possibility."

Holt laughed and reached for the brandy decanter. "It is most definitely not a possibility. Julia. A spy."

The whole idea was beginning to sound ridiculous, even to Jon. But what if Holt knew about her escapades as a boy? Would he feel differently? Something told him not to divulge Julia's secret just yet. If there were proof to be found, he'd find it. Then he'd go to Holt and expose her. Jon took a drink, savoring the burning sensation. Maybe tonight he'd get drunk and forget all the nagging, unanswered questions banging about in his head.

Holt interrupted his thoughts. "If Crowlton weren't dead, which I'm certain he is, planting a spy in my house would be his style. He'd use a go-between to gather information for him, someone nonthreatening—" he filled his glass and then added "—like a beautiful woman."

Holt's words stayed with Jon, nagging him with uncertainty. Was Julia a spy, sent by a half-crazed maniac bent on revenge? Did she have a rendezvous with Crowlton at The Fox's Tail the other night?

The evening ended a short while later with Julia's image shrouded in mystery, a tantalizing enigma wrapped in a dangerous cloak of lies and deceit. Jon paced his room for the better part of an hour, his thoughts on the beautiful servant who spoke with more refinement than many of his titled acquaintances.

There were too many unanswered questions. He planned to seek Julia out himself and question her. And she would talk. He'd give her no choice. He had to know if Peter Crowlton had sent her. Was The Serpent still alive, slithering back into his life for one final attack? He clenched his fists, his thoughts on the golden-haired beauty who might well prove to be the link between past and present, good and evil, life and death.

***

Julia rushed about the guestroom, plumping pillows and folding fresh linens. She'd secured the heavy emerald draperies with thick, golden tassels and thrown open the window to admit light and fresh air.

A faint breeze swirled throughout the room. The late afternoon sun peeked through, casting its warmth on the objects within, illuminating them with its gentle radiance. The fragrance of fresh-cut honeysuckle in a glass vase on the bureau wafted through the air. She stood in the center of the room, drinking it all in, eyes closed, senses alive as the touch, feel, and smell of summer blanketed her.

Times like these brought her such peace she could almost pretend Jon Remmington did not exist. Unfortunately, they were short lived because the man seemed to be everywhere, watching her with his slow, steady gaze, and now thanks to her hard-headed brother, she'd have to face Jon Remmington daily because Holt had invited him to spend the remainder of his visit with them.

How would she possibly tolerate the man for another three weeks? She'd considered seeking out Sophie and beseeching her to change Holt's mind and make that dreadful man go away. But what reason could she possibly give? None, without revealing the incident at The Fox's Tail and she'd die before admitting to that. It also seemed Jon Remmington possessed a few scruples, and had decided to remain quiet on the matter as well.

Julia sighed. It was bad enough he haunted her dreams at night, but now she'd have to tolerate him during her waking hours as well. And a living, breathing Jon Remmington was just plain dangerous.

When the door opened, she whirled around to stand face to face with her tormentor. Jon Remmington's dark eyes pinned her, stripping away her defenses with their intensity. His lips thinned to a tight line, the brackets at the side deep. He reached her in four long strides. "Looking for something?"

She stepped back, trying to distance herself from him. "I—I came to prepare your room." The admission sounded weak, even to her and she knew it to be true.

He scanned the room, then patted his vest pocket. "I keep my purse with me."

Miserable man. "I had no intention of taking your belongings."

"Indeed?"

"Yes, indeed. I had duties to attend in this room now that you're staying at the Langfords' townhouse." She didn't try to hide the bitterness that crept into her words. Why couldn't he just go away? She feared he might tell Holt about the incident at The Fox's Tail. It had been bad enough seeing him in the dining room last evening, but the thought of him underfoot as a resident did strange things to her insides, leaving her a little breathless, a sensation she did not relish.

She searched for an escape and seconds later, leapt toward the bed. A large forearm snatched her in midair and slammed her onto the emerald counterpane. Jon Remmington threw one long leg over both of hers, blocking any thoughts of escape. Julia struggled to free herself, pushing and squirming against his harsh grip. She struck out at him, clawing his jaw and neck, drawing blood.

"Stop it, damn you." He caught her wrists with one hand and forced them above her head. He pushed her further into the bed, shifting his weight to rest more fully on her.

He was going to crush her into the counterpane! "Let me up, you beast," she gasped, as she lay breathless and panting beneath him.

His eyes burned with quiet intensity as they moved from her face to her neck and settled on her breasts. That look made her tingle and her heart pounded against her rib cage. Surely, he heard it. How could he not, when it beat in such loud cadence?

Her gaze settled on his face, strong and formidable one moment, yet warm and gentle the next. His rich brown eyes remained fixed on her chest as though lulled into a trance by the rise and fall of her breasts. Julia's nipples hardened into small peaks and she prayed he would not notice but when he lifted his head, the small smile playing about his full lips told her the thin muslin had shielded nothing from his view.

He held her gaze as he trailed his free hand up her rib cage, his fingers nearly brushing her breast. She wanted him to put his hand on the swollen peak of her breast and soothe the ache he'd created with that one heated look. With great effort, she forced her body to be still, giving herself up to the unknown pleasure of his feather-soft touch. The pads of his fingers circled the hollow of her neck in a slow, gentle rhythm. Her body grew light and heavy at the same time as she turned toward his touch.

He smiled again, this time a slow smile, revealing white teeth and wrinkle lines at the corner of his eyes. He was devastating when he smiled. He still held her hands above her head, but his hold gentled as he rubbed one of her wrists with the pad of his thumb. Were the small shivers tingling through her from his touch, or had they happened with a mere smile?

He stroked her hair, pulled out a pin, and tossed it on the counterpane. Then he reached for another and another, until her unbound hair spilled into his hand. He closed his fingers about a jumble of hair and lowered his head to breathe in her scent.

"Lilac," he whispered.

"I prefer lilac over rose," she blurted out, wondering at his fascination with her hair. She'd always thought it to be something of a nuisance, a big unruly mass that refused to stay in place.

"I definitely prefer lilac," he murmured. "Especially on you."

Her heart skipped two beats as his words washed over her, smooth and seductive, like fine sherry on a winter night. He eased his grip on her hands, and she reached up to stroke his cheek.

He lifted his head and moved closer to her, so close she could see golden flecks in his brown eyes. She hadn't noticed them before. Or the small scar above his right eyebrow. Her gaze roamed his face, settled on his mouth...

Holt's voice on the other side of the door startled her. "I'll just check with Jon and see if he'd care to take an afternoon ride with us."

"That's a splendid idea." This from Sophie. "I do so wish your sister could go along with us."

"Absolutely not."

"But I think they would get along quite well."

"No, Sophie, they certainly would not. Jon's not husband material and despite what my sister says, she *will* settle down one day."

"Perhaps it could be with Jon. She might tame him," Sophie said in a low voice. "Look what happened to you." There was a very long pause, followed by a giggle. "Stop it, Holt. Stop it now. Not in the middle of the hall," she whispered, giggling again.

"That's not what you said last night." There was laughter in his voice and another long pause followed by a loud rap on the door.

"Jon?"

Julia met Jon's gaze. *Would he expose her?*

"Yes?"

"Sophie and I are going for a ride and thought you might like to accompany us."

There was a brief pause and then, "Give me a few moments to change and I'll meet you at the stables."

Julia kept her eyes trained on the door long after their voices faded away. Jon eased himself off her and leaned against the mahogany bedpost.

"Who are you?" he demanded, his voice low and quiet.

She refused to look at him, certain if she did he'd see the vulnerability there and take full advantage of her weakness. Jon Remmington mustn't learn her identity or America would be nothing but a broken dream, forever lost. Gathering her courage, she pushed herself from the wrinkled counterpane and began collecting the pins that lay scattered before her.

"My name is Julia Barry. I'm a servant here." She must not reveal too much.

"And before you were employed by Lord and Lady Westover?" His tone was stiff and impersonal now, all trace of gentleness gone.

"Why, I was employed elsewhere." Why must he be so persistent? And so cold? How could he pretend nothing had passed between them?

"As what?"

"What does that mean?" If she feigned ignorance, he might ease up on his questions. Then again, he seemed to be the persistent type.

"It means," he bit out, "I intend to find out who the hell you are and what you're really doing here. I find you at a seedy tavern dressed as a boy one day, and in the home of my best friend wearing maid's clothes the next. How is it that a simple servant has the speech and grace of a well-bred lady?" He leaned toward her, his face mere inches from hers. "I don't expect an answer from you because whatever comes from your lips will most likely be another lie."

"I am not a thief, nor a liar. My goal hasn't changed. I plan to find passage to America. I'm working here to earn that right."

Jon's eyes narrowed. "I'll be watching every move you make, Julia Barry." He spat out her name as though he'd tasted sour milk. As though he thought it wasn't her real name at all. "When you think you're alone, turn around, and I'll be there. Watching you. If I find you're involved in a scheme to harm Holt Langford, as I suspect you may well be, I will personally cart you off to Newgate."

"I would never hurt Holt!"

"Holt? My, how familiar you are. Even a wayward American like me knows a servant does not address nobility in such a manner." Jon rose from the bed and headed for the door. When he reached it, he turned to face her with a smile that didn't quite reach his eyes. "Just remember, I'll be watching you." Then he was gone, closing the door behind him.

***

"Now, Julia, I'll tell you my secret to making a meat pie." Mrs. Florence leaned over, her round body crowding out the work area, and whispered, "It's all in the crust."

"The crust," Julia repeated, knowing there was much more to making a meat pie than those simple words. In the last few days, she'd gained a whole new perspective on food that had nothing to do with eating it. She hadn't known it could be chopped, shredded, sautéed, broiled, fried, and steamed. Never again would she look at a plate of food as a simple means to fill an empty stomach.

"Now, you add the water to the flour, like this," Mrs. Florence said, pouring a healthy amount into a big bowl. "Then you add butter and start to mix, using two forks. Don't be afraid to get the dough on your hands, it washes right off." She worked the two forks into the big lump, cutting and slashing with her pudgy fingers until the pastry resembled hundreds of small peas.

"And that's our crust?" Julia had eaten Mrs. Florence's

meat pies for years, but she had serious doubts about the mass of tiny, shredded lumps in front of her. It didn't resemble anything she'd eaten before, nor did it look like it had any chance of turning into a flaky, mouth-watering crust.

"Of course it's our crust, child. But it won't be suitable to eat unless it's properly cut up," Mrs. Florence said, turning the pastry over with her forks.

"Cut up," Julia repeated, adding that term to her list of food activities. One could also cut up something.

"Now you give it a try. Go ahead." Mrs. Florence pushed the bowl toward Julia, handing over the long forks. "That's a girl." She chuckled as Julia struggled with the utensils. After several more attempts and a few kind words from her mentor, Julia got the knack of using the forks and cutting the pastry. "You've cut it up but good." She chuckled again, slicing a hunk of pastry and placing it on the floured counter. "I like to make pastries when I'm troubled about something." She winked. "I can cut to my heart's desire and nobody gets hurt."

"Like Mr. Florence?" Julia teased, thinking of the wizened stableman who was several inches shorter and many pounds lighter than his wife.

Mrs. Florence let out a hoot of laughter, shaking her rolling pin at Julia. "When I'm mad at Mr. Florence, child, I make bread."

***

Julia balled her fists and struck at the big lump. She left an imprint where her knuckles collided with the dough. Laughing, she punched again. Soon her fists were moving in earnest, attacking the dough with a vengeance.

Punching the dough one last time, she poked a finger in the middle to test for softness. It bounced back slowly, not unlike Mrs. Florence's upper arms had done a little while ago when Julia accidentally bumped into her.

Mrs. Florence had pointed to the huge sack of flour that morning and announced that today was bread-making day, which meant she must have had a tiff with her husband. Julia's suspicions were confirmed when the cook growled at the flour mixture and pummeled it with such force that a fine spattering of white landed everywhere—the counter, floor, her apron, Julia's nose. When she'd exhausted her frustrations, she pushed the bowl to Julia and encouraged her to have a go at it.

Julia spent several minutes punching the dough. She understood why Mrs. Florence did this when she was angry. The technique proved quite effective to relieve stress and required only minor instruction before a person was ready to attempt the process alone. Julia didn't even need an imaginary villain to pound on. A face appeared each time she punched. Dark and brooding with brown eyes flecked in gold. *Bam!* She struck his already crooked nose. *Pow!* Her knuckles connected with his square jaw. *Whack!* Wiped that crooked grin off his mouth. *Bam! Pow! Whack!*

A fleshy hand stilled her arm. "That's enough, child." Mrs. Florence's kind voice dragged her away from the taunting image of Jon Remmington.

Julia grasped the edges of the large bowl to still her shaking hands. She'd actually imagined she was doing all of those nasty things to his face—and thoroughly enjoying herself.

The kitchen door swung open and two rosy-cheeked young girls entered, giggling behind their hands.

"All right, you two," Mrs. Florence said, a hint of amusement in her voice. "Out with it. What are you both up to this early in the morning?"

"Oh, Mum, 'e certainly is a beauty." Bridgett, the shorter of the two maids, twirled about and ended on a sigh. "With 'is deep accent an' 'is slow smile, I was all tied up in knots."

"And those eyes," Heather, the other maid, piped in. "I thought 'e could see right through me. They was the same color as the shavings we put on Lady Julia's hot chocolate."

Julia looked down at her dough-crusted hands and began rubbing at the sticky stuff. She would not get into a discussion about *him*. She would not do it.

"Strange though," Bridgett said, her voice dipping. "'E

complimented us on the meal and the like, but then 'e asked where you was this morning, Lady, I mean, Julia."

"Why would he say something like that?" She shrugged and tried to make light of the inquiry.

"Wouldn't you want to know where the she-devil was that spilled asparagus soup on your shirt, cream in your lap, and tea on your shoulder?" Bridgett asked.

The two girls clamped their hands to their mouths, trying to suppress another round of giggles. Mrs. Florence hid a smile. "Out with the two of you now. There's plenty to be done. Shoo."

Bridgett and Heather scurried out of the kitchen, giggling as they left. Julia bent to the task of removing the rest of the drying dough from her fingers. It had begun to itch and would soon be unbearable if she didn't get it all off.

"Come, child. There's an easier way to get your hands clean," Mrs. Florence said. "If you keep up with what you're doing, your hands will be raw." She guided Julia to a large basin of warm water, where she handed her a bar of soap and a towel.

"Mr. Remmington is quite a looker, don't you think?"

"I hadn't noticed." Julia lathered her hands and concentrated on the tiny bubbles the soap made.

"That's odd. I thought you'd be particularly interested in him, seeing as he's an American and all. And we all know how much you want to join up with Master Jason and his family."

Mrs. Florence was no fool. "I don't need him. I've got my own plan." She pulled at the globs of dough, watching them float in the water a moment and then sink. Too bad she couldn't get rid of Jon Remmington that easily.

When Mrs. Florence clucked her tongue, Julia knew a lecture was about to follow. "Everybody needs somebody at one time or another, usually when we fight it the hardest." Julia hazarded a glance at her and knew she was thinking of Mr. Florence.

"Well, I certainly don't need Jon Remmington for business

or otherwise." She grabbed the towel and began drying her chapped hands.

"Do you mean to tell me you haven't felt those blue eyes following you around the room?"

A vision of deep, rich chocolate swirled before her. "His eyes aren't blue. They're dark brown with tiny golden flecks." No sooner were the words out of her mouth than Julia realized her error.

"You haven't noticed him, eh?" The older woman threw back her head and laughed, jiggling the extra flesh on her ample chin.

Julia rubbed her hands on the towel in swift, jerky movements, trying to gather her thoughts. "Well, perhaps I *have* noticed those eagle eyes on me," she admitted. "But only because I know he's just waiting for me to mess up again. The man unsettles me, and the harder I try to concentrate on the task, the more I seem to make an absolute muddle of things."

"He *was* a tad upset when you spilled that cream on him."

"I tried to wipe it up right away."

Mrs. Florence chuckled. "Lesson number one child: never wipe anything that's fallen on a man's lap."

Julia recalled Jon's stunned face and the sudden viselike grip of his hand, stilling her actions. He hadn't spoken for several moments and when he finally did, his voice was low and gruff, commanding her to get out. Immediately. Thank the heavens there were no other witnesses to the disastrous event save Mrs. Florence who stood by in shocked horror.

"Your wager will be over soon enough and then you may present yourself to Mr. Remmington as Julia Langford."

"Never!" If he found out she was Holt's sister, Jon would waste little time exposing her escapades, and all chances of traveling to America would sink as quickly as the dough had a few moments ago. Holt would see her little jaunt to The Fox's Tail as a betrayal and would marry her off posthaste. She must protect her identity at all costs until Jon Remmington was safely away from them, sailing off to another adventure.

Chapter 4

The next six days passed with relative ease. Of course, there were a few minor mishaps where Jon Remmington was concerned, but nothing so severe that a careful laundering wouldn't remove—though Julia did wonder if the cranberry juice stain on his shirt cuff would be permanent. Well, she wouldn't feel guilty about that or the claret spill on his trousers either. He should not have tried to grab the silver pitcher or glass carafe from her as though she were an incapable goose. She knew how to serve refreshments, had even acted as Jason's hostess on occasion.

It wasn't her fault that Jon Remmington unnerved her to the point she lost her wits around him. His steady stare, following her every movement, was enough to make her spill, drop, bobble, or overturn most everything she got her hands on. Things would progress quite smoothly if he would just leave her alone and not watch her every move like a cat about to pounce.

One more week and she could bid good riddance to Julia Barry, wearer of scratchy, dyed muslin and cotton hose. One more week and she'd win her wager with Holt and could begin making plans for America. It might even be possible to commence her journey the next week, if she were fortunate enough. Belle had told her about a ship setting sail in three weeks' time. Certainly, she needn't wait any longer than that. Julia hummed a light tune as she placed the warm biscuits in a serving dish.

One more week. Seven more days of Jon Remmington's dark gaze taunting her. She closed her hand around a biscuit, squashed it. He'd be leaving soon for his ship. Was it seven or eight days? Not that she cared. The sooner he was gone, the better. Another biscuit crumbled between her fingers.

How dare he accuse her of scheming to harm Holt? The man was a beast. Very soon, she'd never have to see him again. A third biscuit suffered the fate of the others, bits and pieces falling through her fingers onto the floor. Then another and another.

"Good heavens, child—" Mrs. Florence grabbed Julia's arm "—what are you doing?"

Julia looked down at the half-crumbled biscuit in her hand. Tiny crumbs clung to her fingers, larger ones were strewn everywhere—on her apron, the table, the floor. "Oh my goodness!" There were only four biscuits remaining in the serving dish. She'd destroyed twelve without even knowing it! Julia scooped up crumbs and large chunks of biscuit into her apron, hurried to the rubbish pail, and shook out its contents. When she finished, a small mountain of white heaped from the pail, threatening to spill onto the floor.

"It's all right, child." Mrs. Florence's voice was soft and soothing. "I'll serve for you tonight."

"No!" The word flew out of Julia's mouth with more force than she intended. "No, Mrs. Florence," she repeated on a quieter note. "I'm fine. Really." Patting the cook's fleshy forearm, Julia offered a weak smile. "I don't know what came over me."

"Well, I do, and I say it's about enough of the two of you going at each other." Mrs. Florence nodded her gray head. "Why, a body's got to be blind not to see it. Plain and simple blind, if you ask me." She crossed her arms over her ample breasts and snorted.

"See what?" The look Mrs. Florence gave Julia said she was no fool even if Julia thought she was.

"Hmmph. Why do you think you've been so clumsy lately? Have you thought about it? And you've only blundered about around one certain person. Don't you find that odd?"

"He makes me nervous."

"Does he now?"

"He's always watching me." Julia brushed the remaining crumbs from her apron. "Everywhere I turn, he's looking at me with those dark eyes. It's like he sees something I don't, and it unsettles me." She paced around the kitchen table. "*He* unsettles me. When I'm near him, I can't think straight. And I get all fluttery inside."

"It makes you a mite angry," Mrs. Florence said knowingly.

"Furious," Julia admitted.

"Well, that about sums it up, I guess," the older woman said, clucking her tongue.

"It does? How so?" Sometimes Mrs. Florence could be very confusing.

"You've taken a fancy to him and he to you."

"Never!"

Mrs. Florence smiled.

"I don't even like him." How *could* she think such a thing? The cook's smile turned into a wide grin.

"He's a mean, selfish bully." *Even if his touch is as gentle as a summer rain.*

This time, Mrs. Florence actually threw back her head and laughed.

"And he detests me." But she had noticed the heat in those brown eyes when he thought she wasn't looking.

Pushing her large frame from the table, Mrs. Florence stood and reached for Julia's hand. Her kind, blue eyes misted with tears as she said, "Oh, child, you've so much to learn." She let out a deep sigh that puffed out the apron covering her bosom. "The man may glare at you, bully or ignore you, but one thing is for certain. He wants you like a man wants a woman or my name isn't Gertrude Florence." Julia swallowed and looked away. "Now don't go getting all embarrassed on me. I don't imagine anyone has ever talked about such things with you. You could do worse than a gent like Jon Remmington."

"Holt would never permit such a match," Julia said. But would *she?* Of course not, she'd have to be crazy to consider a match with a man like him. Or any man for that matter.

"No, I don't suppose he would. More's the pity, if you ask me. You'd make a fine match. Fine children, too, with your golden hair and his brown eyes." She sighed again. "Aye, more's the pity."

A vision of a golden-haired little boy floated before Julia. He was no more than four or five with a smattering of freckles across the bridge of his nose. He was laughing, a musical, joyous sound that filled the air. But it was his eyes that made her breath catch. They were as deep and rich as fine French chocolate.

"Ah, well," Mrs. Florence continued, "supper needs to be served. Why don't you plead a headache and go to your room? I'll explain it all to the earl."

"I can't," Julia said, smoothing her apron and wiping off a few stray crumbs. "I won't give him any reason to go back on our wager." She forced a smile, pretending a confidence she didn't quite feel. "It's only one more week. What else could possibly go wrong?"

Twenty minutes later, Julia carried a tray laden with roast duck and potatoes into the dining room. She kept her eyes trained on the platter in front of her, determined to ignore Jon Remmington. The low murmur of voices drifted to her as she edged closer, Sophie's soft tone mixed with Holt's deep one.

"We're going to miss you, Jon," Sophie said.

Not everyone. Julia eyed a large space of white tablecloth. Perfect. She leaned over, the platter balanced in her hands.

"I'm sorry I won't be meeting your sister," Jon said.

The platter landed on the table with a loud thud. A few small potatoes rolled off the side, followed by several slices of duck and a healthy measure of juice that slopped onto the pristine tablecloth. Julia closed her eyes, dreading Jon Remmington's smug expression more than Holt's reprimand, which would be forthcoming. Silence filled the room, so much so that Julia hazarded a glance in her brother's direction to make sure he hadn't keeled over with anger.

Sophie's sweet voice sliced through the tenseness in the room. "It's fine, Julia. I'll call Mrs. Florence to help clean up this little accident." She set her napkin aside and rose from her chair, squeezing Holt's hand. He sat there, staring at Julia, his jaw working back and forth, a small muscle twitching on the left side.

Oh, dear Lord, he was going to string her by her feet.

Jon's soft laughter broke the silence. "At least the duck and potatoes landed on the table and not me." His eyes filled with humor as he sought Julia's gaze. "As you must know, Miss Barry, I can ill afford to lose any more shirts."

"They were honest accidents, all of them." How dare he be so indelicate as to bring up her past mistakes? Couldn't he tell Holt was fuming?

Jon lifted a dark brow. "I should hope so. I would hate to think you were intentionally dumping food and drink on me." He grinned at her, seeming to take pleasure in her obvious discomfort. "Though I must admit, the thought had crossed my mind."

Julia wanted to tell him what he could do with his thoughts, but Holt would never forgive her, and the closest she'd get to America would be in her dreams. She bit the inside of her cheek to keep quiet.

"I apologize for Miss Barry's clumsiness," Holt said. "I think she might be better suited as a scullery maid. Permanently." He leaned back in his chair and took a sip of wine, his gaze trained on her. She stared back, the silent threat dangling between them, permeating the room with heated anger and unspoken accusations.

He wanted her to apologize to his guest.

Julia looked away first. Drat and double drat! There was no squirming out of an apology, so she turned toward her nemesis and focused on his cravat. "I apologize for my accident." *I wish the potatoes had landed in your lap.* "I did not intend to disrupt your meal." *But I am truly delighted I did.*

"Apology accepted." His gaze moved over her like a warm summer breeze. Julia tried to concentrate on the perfect folds of his cravat but good heavens, the man was doing it to her again! He was making her forget her anger, making her all hot and cold at the same time. And jittery—like a hundred butterflies fluttering about in her stomach. It was his eyes that did it, dark and rich and full of heat.

She would not look at those eyes. She would not. Under no circumstances. She strained to find the most minute fold in Jon Remmington's pristine cravat.

Mrs. Florence chose that precise moment to enter the dining room in a flurry of starch and white muslin, cleaning towels draped over one arm and a fresh platter of potatoes and roast duck in her hands.

"Oh dear me, I do apologize, my lord," she gushed, bustling forth, her plump cheeks puffed out and rosy. "Lady Sophie told me about the little…er…accident." She shot a sympathetic glance in Julia's direction before setting the new platter down and scurrying to clean up the soggy mess that sat congealing in the middle of the table.

"Accidents do happen," Sophie inserted, laying a hand on her husband's shoulder as she brushed past him to take her seat. Holt grunted in response, but his eyes warmed at her touch.

"There you go, good as new." Mrs. Florence inspected the white linen she'd placed over the gravy-soaked spot. The errant potatoes and slices of duck had been disposed of and the new platter wafted delectable aromas about the room.

"Thank you, Mrs. Florence," Holt said. He stared at Julia. "I'd like you to have Miss Barry report to Mrs. Bloomfield in the morning. Let's hope she shows a greater aptitude for polishing than she did for serving." With that comment, he stabbed a hunk of roast duck, and said, "That will be all for this evening, Miss Barry. You may be dismissed."

Dismissed like so much baggage? Humiliation warred with outrage as Julia squared her shoulders and left the room. Oh, how she wanted to tell Holt exactly what she thought of his high-handed manner. She wanted to turn around and run back to him, screaming and yelling. And kicking. She moved toward her small room in the servants' quarters, cursing her situation.

Holt wanted her to fly at him in a fit of rage. Then she would lose the wager and there would be no more talk of

America. She would not allow it to happen. She *could not* allow it, not when she was one week away from winning her freedom. If it meant pasting a sweet smile on her face and gritting her teeth for the next seven days, she would do it.

No one would draw her off course, not even that arrogant American who crept into her dreams at night. As she fell into bed, she vowed to push Jon Remmington so far from her mind that by morning he'd be no more than a vague memory.

***

Eunice Bloomfield took her duties as head housekeeper very seriously. Julia had never met a person with so many rules and restrictions concerning the proper way to do things. Not even Miss Fielding's *Proper Comportment for a Lady* contained as many "thou shall nots."

Mrs. Bloomfield had a very particular method for accomplishing every task, down to the minutest detail, and seemed intent on making certain Julia followed in her footsteps.

"Now, this very useful apparatus is called a feather duster." She held up a wooden-handled contraption with thousands of black feathers protruding from it. "It is a wonderful tool for reaching high places, brushing off ornately carved objects, and ridding a room of a fine film of dust."

Julia watched in amazement as Mrs. Bloomfield glided about the room, flitting from candlestick to mantel to windowsill, whirling the feather duster before her. She reminded Julia of a ballet dancer, albeit a gray-haired one, bending and swaying her tall frame like a young sapling. "The key to proper feather dusting is movement," she said, flicking the duster over a crystal vase in several short, quick motions.

Rumor had it she'd worked in the queen's court years ago as head housekeeper. Julia didn't doubt it. She'd never met a servant with a vocabulary or diction like Mrs. Bloomfield.

"And then one must twist and bend," Mrs. Bloomfield continued, aiming the duster at the clawed legs of a green velvet sofa. "Now flick, twirl, flick, twirl, like this."

Julia hid a smile. She liked Mrs. Bloomfield, despite her bending, twisting, and twirling idiosyncrasies, of which there were many.

"Now, dear," Mrs. Bloomfield said, handing over the feather duster. "Let's see you work your way toward the side table, beginning at this chair. And don't forget to twist."

***

Jon stifled another laugh. He'd been watching Julia whirl about the green salon, bending and twisting as she swatted the oak furniture with her huge feather duster. First a dip and a swipe at a chair leg, then a turn and a bow toward a side table. On and on it went, the dips and curtsies, twists and turns, until Jon grew dizzy from watching her.

And to top it all off, she was singing. *Singing!* The melody couldn't reach him from his vantage point on the other side of the wide French doors, but he could see her lips moving in rapid animation.

The woman was mad. Absolutely mad. She looked ridiculous dancing around the room, slicing the feather duster through the air as though it were a mighty sword and she a great warrior heading to battle.

He watched her for several more minutes, concluding that Holt had been right. Julia was no spy. How he'd entertained such an idea, even for a scant moment, was absurd, especially now as she scooped up the duster and batted it over her head, flicking a brass sconce so hard it almost fell off the wall.

Julia Barry was too clumsy, pure and simple. A man as precise as Peter Crowlton wouldn't risk involvement with someone as unpredictable and uncoordinated as Julia Barry, even if she were utterly beautiful. He breathed a small sigh of relief. She wasn't a spy. Thank God.

He frowned. If she weren't a spy, then that left only one other option—thief. Jon frowned again, not pleased with that possibility.

Peering through the small, white pane, he watched Julia turn abruptly and run toward him. For a brief moment he thought he'd been discovered, but she stopped several feet from the glass doors and dug her heels into the Aubusson carpet. Bending down, she untied the laces of her heavy, black shoes and kicked them off, one at a time, giggling as they sailed in opposite directions.

What was the woman up to now? He soon found out as she lifted the feather duster high above her head, then brought it down in a grand arc and sweep, hurling it back and forth between her hands, faster and faster until in one final motion, she flung the duster in the air and caught it behind her back.

Jon shook his head. He must have been mad to think this woman might be a spy. Now a candidate for Bedlam, that was something he could visualize for Miss Julia Barry. His thoughts were cemented to certainty when she leapt in the air, landed squarely on both feet, and began spinning, head thrust back, arms outstretched, duster in hand. Round and round she went, faster and faster until at last she collapsed on the wheat-colored rug.

Jon slipped through the French doors and edged his way toward her. She lay flat on her back, arms and legs outstretched, chest heaving from her latest acrobatics. And the damn duster was still in her hand!

"Would you care to dance?" He stood over her, trying his damnedest not to smile.

Julia's eyes popped open. "You! Where did you come from?" She tried to straighten into a sitting position, but her last ten spins must have been too much for her, and she fell back against the rug. "I'm dizzy."

"I'm not surprised," Jon said. "I was just trying to figure out if you belong in the ballet—or the circus."

"You're despicable," she muttered.

"And you are—" he tapped his forefinger to his chin "—outrageous and crazy. Put the two together and there you have it. Outrageously crazy." He frowned and then smiled. "Or is it crazily outrageous?"

Julia giggled. "Which one is it, Mr. Remmington? Am I

crazy or just outrageous?"

She'd moved into a semi-sitting position, with her elbows supporting her upper body. Her gray dress bunched around her legs, revealing their firm shape. He glimpsed a good deal of ankle clad in a heavy stocking material. Wisps of golden hair swirled about her neck and trailed down her back. Her pink lips were slightly open.

Julia was too beautiful to be wrapped in such common trappings, tucked away in servant's garb with nothing better to look forward to than marrying some commoner and having a brood of whiny brats.

She belonged in silks and satins, not broadcloth and muslin. Her horizon should span the Orient and West Indies, Egypt and Africa, not just a city and country home in England. She should be waited on, attended to, and looked after.

Julia Barry should be his mistress.

He gasped for breath, blinking his eyes to refocus on anything but the vision of Julia, golden and beautiful, lying beneath him.

"Jon?"

Her voice reached him, moved over him without lifting a finger. He stood mesmerized as Julia's small tongue darted out to run over her full pink lips. Oh, but he could get lost considering the numerous possibilities of that delectable mouth.

"Jon? Are you all right?" She scrambled to stand beside him, but not before he glimpsed an ample amount of leg and thigh. What was wrong with him, practically peeping under a woman's skirt?

She reached out to touch his arm, but he flung it away.

"Have you no sense of decency, sprawling before me like that?" he spat out. "If you've got an itch that needs satisfying, then just say so and dispense with the coquetry."

Her hand moved too fast. Actually, he hadn't thought she'd have the nerve to slap him. But she did, hard and square on the cheek. "Stay away from me."

"As you wish." Jon bowed, low and deep, his voice hard.

Julia backed away, her face pale, her lower lip trembling. But he didn't see fear in those gray eyes that never left his face. Determination, wariness, perhaps even a bit of well-placed rage. But fear? Definitely not.

Men twice her size feared him. Always had. But that was during wartime when his reputation as The Chameleon spanned the continent. It was a lifetime ago yet he found it ironic that this slip of a girl should meet him face to face and not be afraid. He hid a smile as he watched her slowly edge toward the great oak doors. The woman was no fool. She knew when to cut her losses and make her exit. He waited until her hand touched the doorknob. She was inches from escaping. Jon couldn't resist.

"Julia," he called. "Just remember, if you're…feeling…ah…restless…you know where to find me."

"Beast," she hissed, throwing open the door and running into the hall.

Good, let her think him a swine. That way she'd stay out of his way. If he didn't see her, maybe he'd stop wanting her.

Or maybe it was already too late.

Julia Barry was working her way under his carefully constructed facade, and he didn't like it. Not one bit. He found himself actually caring that he might have hurt her feelings. No one got that close to him. Ever.

Jon looked down at the Aubusson carpet and remembered Julia lying there, a vision of innocence and seduction. Innocent? Julia? Now that was a real laugh, though suddenly, he found nothing remotely amusing about the situation.

***

"I never thought you'd pull it off." Holt's lips curved into a half-smile as he gazed down at Julia. They stood in the green salon, surrounded by afternoon sunlight and heavy brocades.

She'd won! Julia twirled around in her simple muslin gown and heavy, black shoes, laughter tinkling from her. "I can't believe it." She twirled around again and ended in a *plié*. "I'm

45

actually going to America. Oh, Holt, isn't this just grand?"

Whatever melancholy had possessed her the last several evenings was gone now. She was going to America!

Holt stood with his back to her, staring out the window. Perhaps he hadn't heard her or was engrossed with something outside. She moved next to him to peer out the window. Nothing but bustling carriages and cobblestone.

"What's got you in such a dither?" she asked. "Are you upset because I beat you at your own game? Admit it, you expected me to muddle it up and quit somewhere around the second day."

"You're right. I did."

She chose to ignore the possibility that his dissatisfaction had anything to do with her. "I knew I could do it. Of course, my hands will never be the same." She surveyed her chapped knuckles with a frown. "And my feet ache from wearing these heavy shoes. I think we should redesign the servants' garb. It's actually quite uncomfortable what with the scratchy underthings that rub against your leg. And the stockings are simply dreadful." Lifting her gown to her ankle, she studied the heavy cotton stockings and made a face. "But it was all worth it."

Holt sighed and turned to face her. "Julia." She knew that tone. It meant he was about to tell her something disappointing. Something she did not want to hear. But what? Last night he'd agreed she'd won their wager, so what could have happened between last evening and this morning to dampen his mood? "I need to speak with you."

There it was again, that same tone with just a hint of sympathy thrown in. "Holt, forgive my boldness, but what could possibly be more important at this moment than making plans for my trip to America?"

He cleared his throat, took a deep breath, and cleared his throat again. "Actually, it's about your trip." His jaw twitched and his black brows knitted into a straight line.

That definitely meant trouble. Had he somehow heard about

the creamer incident with Jon? Dear God, she didn't want a silly thing like that to ruin her chances of traveling to America.

"The first available ship that meets my standards isn't leaving for another six months."

Julia spun around so he wouldn't see her tears. He *knew* she hadn't meant to wait six months to sail to America and yet, he'd never promised it would be any shorter. Deep down, he probably never planned on her winning the wager. "How can that be?"

"I'm sorry." His hands settled on her shoulders.

She could not give up. Desperation caused her to burst out, "What about Jon Remmington? Is he not sailing in a few days?"

"No." The harshness of her brother's response surprised her. His voice leveled. "Jon can't take you."

Julia turned. "Not even if his best friend asks him?"

"Absolutely not."

"I see," she said, though she did not see at all.

She couldn't wait six months, six weeks, or even six days. She had to make her own plans, choose her own destiny, here and now, because America loomed farther away every day. But one thing was certain; she would get there, no matter what it took.

***

"I'd hoped you might consider extending your visit," Holt said as he handed Jon a snifter of brandy.

"Sorry, old man, but you know I don't like to settle in one place for too long. Besides, it's time I sailed home for a little while and checked on my lands."

"Are you certain that's the only reason you're going back? There wouldn't happen to be a special *someone* waiting for you? Maybe one of those beauties from the Far East?"

Jon shook his head and sipped his brandy. "There are always many *someones* as you well know, but never that *special* someone." He shrugged. "I prefer it that way. Less complicated."

Holt's laughter rang out beyond the closed study door and into the hallway where Julia had her ear bent to the door. She ignored the slight twinge she experienced when Jon referred to his limitless supply of female companionship. Why should she care when she detested the man?

And she did detest him. *Didn't she?*

She'd spent the better part of another long night driving the beast from her thoughts and had finally convinced herself of her success when she'd heard his name announced. No longer under the guise of servant garb, Julia had raced up the stairs and hidden in the nursery for the remainder of the evening.

Unfortunately, her stomach got the better of her a few hours later, and she decided to sneak into the kitchen for a glass of warm milk and a raspberry scone. As she tiptoed past the library door, Jon's drawl reached her. Though she didn't believe in spying, she had to admit there were times when it proved quite useful, such as now. Jon Remmington was going home to America! Would Holt reconsider and give her an opportunity to leave in a few days' time? Somehow, she didn't think so, not that it mattered because she'd just figured out the perfect plan.

***

"I don't understand why you can't wait and go to America with Holt's blessing," Belle whispered from the darkened interior of the carriage. As arranged, at precisely midnight, the Fleming carriage had quietly rolled past the Langfords' townhouse, stopping only long enough to pick up a darkly clad youth dressed in breeches and a stocking cap.

"Don't you see, Belle, this is the perfect opportunity." Julia pulled off the black cap and shook out her hair. "Jon Remmington is going to America. I heard him say so with my own two ears. Who knows when and if Holt will truly permit me to go there? It could be six months or never. He wouldn't deliberately deceive me, but my oldest brother has a way of making things work to his advantage."

"But he told you if you won the wager you could go, did he

not?"

Julia scowled. "Of course that's what he said because he never thought I'd win. Now that I have, I find there's a caveat and more time involved. I think he's hoping I'll secure a husband and forget about it."

Belle smiled. "We both know that won't happen."

"Absolutely not, which is why I must leave now when I have the perfect opportunity."

Belle gnawed her bottom lip. "But what do you know of Jon Remmington?"

"He's Holt's best friend." Heat spread from Julia's neck to her cheeks and she was grateful the darkened carriage saved her from an explanation.

"Holt will be furious when he finds out. But what of this Mr. Remmington? How do you think he'll react when he discovers his best friend's sister has stowed away on his ship?"

"He'll be more than furious. He'll want to shoot me at the very least, but by the time he finds me, we'll be well on our way to America." She hesitated a moment, placing her hand over Belle's. "I have a small confession to make."

"What have you done now?" Belle asked, sounding like a mother hen about to scold her chick for a misdeed.

"Remember the man I told you about at The Fox's Tail?"

"The one who caught you and accused you of stealing?"

Julia nodded. "It was Jon Remmington." She winced at the colorful expletive that flew out of Belle's mouth. "I know what you're thinking, but he's my last chance. If the man knew I was Holt's sister, he'd march me to him posthaste. Can you imagine what would happen to me then?"

Belle sighed. "Probably nothing you don't deserve at the moment. If I thought it would do any good, I'd try to dissuade you from this scheme of yours. But I know you'll do it with or without my help and I'd rather know what you were up to."

"Thank you, Belle. You're a true friend."

"A foolish friend is more like it." Belle shook her head and sighed again. "All right, Julia, tell me what you want me to do."

Chapter 5

Jon Remmington watched the black conveyance drive away from the townhouse. He knew it was the same carriage that had been at The Fox's Tail the night he'd met Julia and he'd lay odds the figure hurrying into it clad in boy's clothes was Julia as well. Interesting. Although the carriage remained a fair distance away, it was obvious it belonged to someone of wealth.

Was Julia Barry a thief? Or could she be a rich man's whore? He hadn't considered that possibility. The question nagged at him, pounding in his head as loud as a star percussionist. He had to know if she was bartering her delectable body or stolen goods to the slimy bastard in the black carriage.

Jon stood in the shadows of Holt's brick townhouse, hidden from the occasional passerby. Damn it, where had she gone? What was she doing? And who the hell was she doing it with?

Julia was a beautiful woman. His jaded thoughts turned to the obvious. She was being used as a plaything by some wealthy nobleman. But dressed as a boy? He'd seen more bizarre behavior over the years and had long since stopped thinking about the sexual appetites and preferences that abounded in society. But perhaps she really *was* a thief. He almost wished she were. For some obscure reason, thievery seemed more palatable than the other possibility.

One half hour later, the same black carriage halted a few hundred feet away, and a lone figure emerged. Jon stamped out his cheroot and trained his eyes on the carriage. The absence of a family crest or other marking that would signify the owner disturbed him. The conveyance was new and sleek, its fancy design speaking of wealth and privilege. As it rolled by, he was almost certain one of the curtains moved. Then the conveyance disappeared into the night, and his thoughts turned back to Julia.

He recognized her soft swaying walk, despite the bulky

clothes she wore. She waited for the carriage to move on before she cut down a side alley leading to the back entry of the townhouse. Jon raced down the other alley and crouched behind a row of rubbish bins. In a matter of minutes, Julia emerged, whistling softly as she moved toward the iron door of the townhouse.

She took no more than a few steps toward the door before Jon grabbed her, hauled her against his chest, and clamped a hand across her mouth. "What have we here? If it isn't the little she-boy."

Julia struggled against his grasp, but he pinned her arms to her sides with scarce effort and backed her against the old brick of the building, content to let her exhaust herself with useless struggles. When she quieted, he leaned over, his voice a mere whisper in her ear, "Behave yourself and I'll remove my hand from your mouth."

The stocking cap bobbed up and down in silent agreement. Jon eased his hand away, releasing his hold on her. They stood mere inches apart, locked in silent battle.

"Don't even try it," he warned, guessing at her next move. "I can read that devious little mind of yours, but you're not going anywhere without my consent."

Her mouth flattened, seconds before she spat out, "What do you want?"

"For starters, I'd like to know where the hell you went in that black carriage dressed like a boy."

The moon cast a faint light on her face, making it easy to detect the slight flaring of her nostrils and the momentary widening of her gray eyes. She was scheming. In his short acquaintance with Julia Barry, he knew that much of what came out of her mouth was untrue. He also knew she was a terrible liar and one look at her face usually proved enough to distinguish truth from untruth.

"I do not see where my affairs are any of your concern." Her voice held all of the haughty grandeur of a lady and not for the first time, Jon wondered at how easily she slipped into the role of the upper crust—as though it were second nature.

"I see you're employing the speech of a lady this evening. Where might you have acquired that fine skill?"

She fixed her gaze on an old tomcat that sat perched on one of the rubbish bins. "Sophie...I mean, Lady Westover has set a wonderful example and encourages proper speech and etiquette, even among the servants."

"But that's not where you learned those things, is it?"

"Of course it is," she shot back. "Where else would I have learned them?"

"Where else indeed," he said, letting the unspoken accusation that she was lying hang between them.

"What is it you want from me?"

Jon let out a short, humorless laugh. "In case you've forgotten our last chat, I have every intention of getting to the bottom of whatever little scheme you're involved in." He grabbed her small chin, forced her to look at him. "Were you thieving or whoring?"

Julia's hand flew up to slap his face, but he caught her wrist. "You might have gotten away with that once, but don't try it again," he said through clenched teeth.

"You're hurting me," she hissed.

He loosened his grip on her wrist and tried a different tactic. "Did you steal something from Lord Westover?"

"No!"

"Or anyone in that household?"

"Absolutely not."

"Hmm." She'd looked very uncomfortable with that last question. What could she have taken? Jewels? Coin? He had to find out. "Then you won't mind if I check for myself? Just to make certain you aren't harboring any stolen goods or money? We've done this before, remember?"

Ignoring the shocked look on her face, he parted her large jacket. His hands traveled down the front of the oversized shirt, moving over her curves in a brisk, businesslike manner. He tried not to think of the soft swell of her breasts or the smooth skin beneath the shirt. His hands slowed. He wanted to remain apart from the touch and feel of this woman, apart from the rapid, little breaths and the swollen peaks he'd brushed a second ago.

"Nothing yet," he said, his voice ragged. *God, but she felt good.* He should stop this game now before it got out of hand but he feared it was already too late, and in some ways had been since the first time he'd laid eyes on her. His hands shook as he stroked her breasts through the thin cotton of her shirt, grazed the taut peaks with his knuckles. When she whimpered, he forgot about searching for stolen property.

This woman was in his blood, and there was no use denying it any longer. His hands worked their way to her ribs, trailed back to her breasts, brushing the swollen nipples with the pads of his fingers. She moaned. He cursed and pulled her to him. "Julia," he breathed. He placed a soft kiss behind her ear and when she didn't fight him, he planted light kisses along her jaw until he was but a breath from her lips. "Give me your mouth."

He wanted her, wanted all of her. When their lips met, the kiss was not gentle, but demanding and possessive. He ran his tongue along her lower lip, urging her mouth open. Her lips parted and he dove into the sweetness, touching, tasting, wanting. The thought of sinking into her warm flesh with her legs wrapped high around him had him hot and throbbing.

"Tell me where you went tonight," he whispered into her mouth. He had to know, had to hear her admit her treachery and lies. Then he could forgive her and lose himself in her sweet, hot body. "Tell me, Julia," he coaxed, sliding his fingers down the length of her body, pressing his palm between her legs.

"I can't."

"Can't? Or won't?"

She jerked involuntarily toward his hand. "Can't," she murmured in a ragged voice.

Jon's fingers stilled again. *She'd lie even in the heat of passion.* He released her, disgusted with his lack of control.

Taking a step back, he reached in his pocket and pulled out a cheroot. His hand shook as he struggled with the light. *Damn her!* She wasn't going to tell him.

"It's not what it looked like."

"Oh? What exactly did it *look* like?" He would not make this easy for her.

Julia winced. "Perhaps it looked like I was somewhere I should not have been."

"Perhaps?" He tossed his cheroot to the ground, smashed it with his booted heel. Why in the hell was he so upset over this girl when it looked like she was up to no more wrong doing than meeting her lover for a midnight tryst? "Do you want to know what I think you were doing?" Without waiting for her reply, he continued. "I don't think you're a thief because I found no evidence of such and God knows, I looked." To hell with her tender sensibilities. "That only leaves one unexplored possibility."

He waited for her to respond as the blackness of night engulfed them. Finally, she spoke. "What do you think I am?"

Jon did not hesitate with his response. "A rich man's whore."

She gasped and balled her hands into fists but remained silent, neither admitting nor refuting the accusation.

"What else could you be?" he flung back. "You leave in the middle of the night dressed as a boy, which is strange, even by my standards. Who knows? Maybe your nobleman lover likes to pretend you're a street urchin until he deflowers you to discover the beautiful woman underneath." Jon paused as the image of Julia, trapped and naked beneath some fat, old noble settled in his brain and tore at his guts. "That's it, isn't it?" he bit out. "That's what excites him."

She wouldn't answer. Instead, she huddled against the brick, turning away from him as though to shield herself from his hurtful words. Truth was often an ugly bedfellow, and Julia Barry might do well to accept that fact.

"I do have one question."

She turned further into the wall. Why did it bother him so much to discover she was a whore? He'd been with a few in his day. More than a few. But she'd seemed different. As annoying, mouthy, and frustratingly impossible as the woman was, she'd touched him deep inside where his real feelings lay, lost and hidden.

"I just want to know—" he tried to keep his voice calm and unaffected "—why you were so hot for me when you'd obviously just been with your lover? Or are you like that with any man?"

She whirled on him like a she-cat. "Yes, I lie with every man who appeals to me. Whenever, wherever, however, from nobleman to stable boy. It doesn't matter and neither do you. You were just one more face." She paused, her breath coming in harsh, heavy rasps and added, "Or should I say one more body among a string of countless others?" She pushed away from the wall, planted her feet squarely, and pointed a finger at him. "But you're not worth the trouble." With that, she turned and walked away, head held high, steps graceful, almost regal.

And for the hundredth time since he'd first set eyes on her, he asked himself the same question.

Who is Julia Barry?

***

Slightly before dawn, three days later, two small figures darted about one of the most popular docks in London. The morning was cool, the dock mostly deserted, save for a lone sailor or two. Conditions were perfect.

"Are you certain you won't reconsider and do this whole thing in a more civilized manner?" Belle whispered from her crouched position behind an old wooden barrel.

Julia shook her stocking-capped head, her eyes glued on the deck of *The Falcon*. She'd seen movement a moment before, a dark-clad, round figure ambling about. Where had he gone? "I can't."

"But a stowaway aboard a ship full of men? That's extremely dangerous."

Julia let out a low snort. "So is a room full of marriage-hunting 'gentlemen' in London." She leaned in close and whispered, "And most show no mercy or discretion when vying for the largest purse."

Belle sighed. "I know, but I wish you were on better terms with Mr. Remmington." She gnawed her lower lip. "It would make things so much easier."

"Nothing would ever be easy with that man," Julia said, her head pounding at the mention of him. She'd battled a ferocious headache since she decided to stow away on *The Falcon*.

A tall, dark figure came into view aboard the ship. From the distance, Julia noted the proprietary stance of his well-muscled frame. She sipped in tiny breaths as she watched him.

"Is that Jon Remmington?" Belle whispered.

"That's him." Julia tried to control the jumpiness in her body. What would he do to her if he found her hiding on his ship? Kill her? Certainly not. Have her thrown in Newgate? Possibly. Take her back to Holt? Most definitely. Well, it wouldn't be an issue because she was not going to get caught. She hadn't figured out how to manage it, but she'd come up with a plan.

"We'd better get you on board while the crew is still light," Belle said as a few straggling crewmen headed across the wooden planking toward the massive ship.

Julia squeezed Belle's hands. "Remember our plan. Holt thinks we're shopping for the day. He'll find the note I left him in his study and will be so thrilled we're decorating ourselves for the duke's ball, he won't question a thing."

Belle nodded. "And at exactly seven o'clock, I shall present him with this note." She patted her pocket.

"Then he'll know I've taken off to America with my unwilling host, and it will be too late for him to stop me." She tried to keep the triumphant note from her voice, but it was difficult.

"I'll miss you, Julia," Belle said, her eyes bright.

"And I, you. I'll never be able to thank you enough." Why

did she suddenly feel like she was deserting everyone who cared about her and loved her? She thought of Holt, proud, unbending, fiercely loyal, and the victory she'd felt a moment before faded.

"Go. Now," Belle said, giving her friend a quick hug.

"I'll write as soon as I am settled. I promise."

"I know you will," Belle whispered.

"I'll work on a plan," Julia sniffed. "A plan to get you to America." She tried to smile. "You know me, I always have a plan."

"Take care of yourself."

"I will." Julia hugged her friend one last time, straightened, and headed toward the ship. She flung her canvas bag over one shoulder and concentrated on imitating the purposeful swagger of the sailor in front of her. Unfortunately, he was several inches taller and many pounds heavier, making her attempts more comical than serious.

A slap across the shoulders almost sent her flying over the roped railing. "Wot ye got in yer trousers, mate?" came a deep, gravelly voice from behind. "Is it bugs or a slithery snake?" Julia kept her eyes down, ignoring the loud guffaws and hoots that followed.

"Aw, now, I didna' mean ta hurt yer feelins'," the old sailor said, draping his burly arm about her shoulders. "Wot's yer name, boy?" he asked, skewering his face so close that Julia was forced to stop. Stealing a quick glance in the sailor's direction revealed more than she wanted to see. Or smell. His black, beady eyes scrunched almost closed as they studied her. A long scar ran from his forehead to the left side of his jaw. He had several teeth missing and when he smiled, which he was doing now, she could see great black gaps in his mouth.

Julia couldn't tell if the foul odor emanating from the man came from his mouth or his body. Either way, the result was a sour, garlic-onion smell, mixed with rotten cabbage.

"Ease up, Big Tom. Ease up." A jovial voice rang out to the right of her. Julia hazarded a glance in the direction of her savior. He was a short, robust man with a ruddy face and long white hair and beard to match. With his bright blue eyes, he reminded her of St. Nicholas.

"Ah, Mac, I didna mean no harm," the giant said.

"We're traveling light as it is this trip, Tom, and we can't have you scaring off the new crew now, can we?" the man named Mac said.

"No, sir," Big Tom said, bowing his head low like an over-playful puppy who'd just been caught with his owner's shoe.

"No harm done," the older man said, walking alongside Julia. "What's your name, boy?"

Julia hesitated, cleared her throat, and squeaked out a small reply, "Simon."

"Ah, Simon," Mac repeated. "Fine name. My uncle's name was Simon."

Julia nodded, not knowing what else to do. "You'll like the captain," Mac continued in his soothing voice. "He's fair and decent. A true gentleman." He paused, then pointed a stubby finger. "There he is. Look. Over there."

"Hmm," Julia mumbled, darting a quick look. It was Jon Remmington all right. Proud, arrogant, in command. She dipped her head, kept her eyes to the ground lest he spot her and recognize her from the fear in her eyes. And it was there, enveloping her whole body, squeezing the breath from her chest, filling her nostrils with its scent. She was so close. She could not fail. She *would* not fail.

"Be damned. Where's he got himself off to now?" Mac said in a puzzled voice. "Ah well, no matter. You'll meet the captain soon enough."

Julia darted a glance toward the spot where she'd last seen Jon. It was empty. Jon Remmington was gone.

***

She was going to die. Julia was certain of it. And right now death would be a welcome relief from the endless rocking of the ship. She'd decided that hours ago when the ship first left port and encountered choppy waters, but her sentiments had increased tenfold with the lurching of the ship. Her quarters were dark and cramped and she could barely feel her legs anymore.

What could she expect when she was stowed away in Jon Remmington's armoire? How long had she been in here? Three hours? Four? There'd been no time to seek out a safe haven, what with all the crew moving about, shouting commands, readying to set sail. Then she'd heard *his* voice and panicked, stealing into the first cabin she saw. Not until she lay crouched in the armoire did she smell Jon's spicy cologne and realize her mistake.

The ship rolled again, sending Julia's stomach somersaulting. If she could only get fresh air, a breath, perhaps, of something other than the spicy cologne and stale cigar smoke that filled her nostrils. Then maybe her insides would settle and cease their continuous flips and turns.

She struggled to her knees, burrowing her way through the pile of clothing, seeking a different, less offensive scent. Her fingers landed on a swatch of silk material. Odd that silk should be in Jon's chambers. Julia pressed the fabric to her nose and sniffed the sweet, overpowering fragrance that emanated from the material. A woman's perfume? It certainly smelled like it, but it wasn't anything like the lilac water Julia preferred. This was more of a compelling, exotic blend, demanding and bold, like the wearer would be.

Unable to contain her curiosity, Julia ran her fingers over the silk again. Behind it were other garments, definitely a woman's, made of filmy fabrics. The last one she touched was but a wisp of satin with gaping holes where they shouldn't be. Julia withdrew her hand quickly.

Damn Jon Remmington. Damn him for accusing her of something he himself was doing. And damn him for making her care.

The ship pitched again and Julia flew against the side of the armoire. At least everything was bolted down so there was no fear of toppling over. Unfortunately, the same could not be said of Julia's stomach. At any moment she was going to lose the few biscuits she'd stolen from Mrs. Florence's pantry.

She sipped in a breath and tried to ignore the sour taste in her mouth as she thought of Holt and Sophie. Soon, Belle would deliver the letter, a single sheet of scented lilac paper, informing them only that she was sailing to America aboard Jon Remmington's ship and would stay with Jason and Ariana.

She prayed they would understand and forgive her. Perhaps not right away, but in time. Very soon it would all be over thanks to the help of her friend, and though she hated to admit it, thanks to Jon Remmington as well.

The very thought of the man unsettled her. She refused to dwell on what his reaction would be if he discovered her aboard his ship. He would not find out, he simply would not. Her stomach did another flip-flop. Squeezing her eyes shut, she huddled into a small ball, rested her head on her knees and drifted into a troubled sleep.

***

"What the hell!"

Julia jumped, fully awake. Her eyes flew open to find a furious Jon Remmington glaring down at her. He towered over her, drenched from head to toe, looking as wild and untamed as the storm outside. Tiny droplets of water fell in a steady stream from his wavy hair, which, when wet, looked almost black. His broad arms crossed over his chest, revealing a mass of dark hair above a half-opened shirt that clung to his well-muscled body. His breeches could have been a second skin. She tried to scoot farther back into the armoire, but there was nowhere to go.

"You!" Jon grabbed her arm, pinned her with eyes as dark and unfathomable as the storm outside. "What in God's name are *you* doing on my ship?"

"I can explain." But of course, she couldn't.

"Get out of there," he demanded. "Get out now, before I drag you out."

Julia tried to move but her limbs refused to cooperate. They were weak and lifeless after so many hours scrunched in a corner. She searched for something to hang onto so she could pull herself up, but she was weary and disoriented.

The ship pitched and flung her back, slamming the doors to the armoire shut. Julia flailed about inside as dizziness overtook her.

A few seconds later, Jon crashed the armoire open, almost ripping the doors from their hinges. He flung aside several garments trying to reach Julia. She hit at his face and kicked with her feet, squirming and yelling as he grabbed for her arm. She would not go down without a fight, she vowed, as he half lifted, half dragged her out of the closet. Hoisting her into his arms, he carried her across the swaying room toward the bed, mindless of the wet spots he made on her shirt and breeches. Julia turned her head toward his shoulder and bit. Hard.

"Witch!" Jon tossed her onto the bed. Julia hit the firm surface with such force her teeth rattled and her stomach jumped like a bouncing ball. She eased onto her side, moving slowly in an effort to settle the queasy feeling and taste of bile and biscuit.

It would not do to disgrace herself. Not now, in front of this odious man. She closed her eyes, concentrated on her breathing and tried to ignore the man standing over her.

Go away. Please go away and do not come back.

A door closed and she relaxed, sinking her head deeper into the pillow. It smelled of Jon's cologne. She shoved it away and glanced toward the door. She gasped, surprised to see *him* standing there, the frown on his face more threatening than before. The shivers that ran through her had nothing to do with her damp clothes. Jon Remmington looked like he wanted to throttle her. Should she be afraid?

He pushed away from the door and closed the distance between them. She looked at him again, noting the flaring nostrils and twitching jaw. Maybe she ought to be afraid.

But he was a gentleman, wasn't he? Mac, the older crewman with the white beard, had even said so. And after all,

Jon *was* her brother's best friend. Certainly, that counted for something, didn't it? Of course it did.

But he was *not* an Englishman.

No, he was an American. Would he revert to some primitive behavior, like she'd read the savages did when they went on a warpath? They liked blond hair. She fingered her curls. Curly, long, blond hair. She scooted further back toward the wall of the berth.

"Get back here."

Julia crept forward a few inches, taking deep breaths to calm herself and her stomach.

"Now tell me what in the devil you're doing here."

She opened her mouth to speak. Her stomach lurched with the ship. *She was not going to make it.*

"Talk, damn you," he said through clenched teeth. "Now."

Her stomach rolled again. Sweat broke out on her upper lip. "I'm going to be sick."

"Don't think I'll fall for another one of your tricks," Jon barked. "Now talk."

Julia didn't hear his words, didn't hear anything but the sound of her own rapid breathing as she willed herself not to be sick all over Jon Remmington's bed. But it was too late. Clapping a hand over her mouth, she jumped from the bed, frantic and wild-eyed, searching for a chamber pot.

She must have looked as dreadful as she felt, because Jon's demands ceased as he clasped her arm and guided her to the far end of the cabin where, within seconds, she proceeded to relieve herself of her breakfast. When she was certain there was nothing left in her stomach, she rinsed her mouth with the glass of water Jon handed her and allowed him to help her back to bed.

Too weak to protest, Julia allowed him to remove her shoes and pull a blanket over her chilled body. He remained silent as he placed a cool cloth on her forehead and smoothed back her hair.

"We'll talk in the morning." His voice was gruff. He

touched her cheek gently before he drew his hand away. She closed her eyes and let sleep take her.

***

Julia yawned, stretched her arms over her head, and luxuriated in the early morning quiet. All was silent save for a gentle swishing of water and the distant cry of a bird. She extended her arms the full length of the berth and hit upon a hard, unmoving object.

Her eyes flew open to find Jon Remmington's large frame settled at the end of the bed. He appeared relaxed, his broad shoulders resting against the wall with one booted leg crossed over his knee, his muscular arms folded across his chest. But there was no calmness in the brooding eyes that followed her every move. "Talk."

Julia scooted to the top of the berth placing what little distance between them she could. What to tell him? She supposed it was time to own up to the truth, at least some of it.

"And a good morning to you, too, sir," she replied, stalling as she decided what and exactly how much to tell. *Drat* but that dark look said he knew her ruse and it wasn't going to work. "Well," she began, toying with the blanket, "I suppose I owe you an explanation." She tried a feeble attempt at a laugh, which flopped miserably. "I must have given you a bit of a start when you found me in your armoire." She glanced at him.

His stare grew harsher.

"Things aren't quite what they seem. You were right about that, but I do have a very good explanation." She paused a moment, hoping he would help her along, just a little, but that obviously wasn't going to happen, not if the rapid twitching of his jaw or the further narrowing of his eyes were any indication.

"Your little game is up," Jon ground out. "You've got exactly one minute to talk and it had better be a damn good explanation."

"Oh, all right." Julia frowned at him. "You needn't be so nasty about it."

"Julia," he warned.

She fidgeted with the blanket again, glanced around the cabin twice, and finally settled her gaze on his stern face. "I'm not really a maid, if you haven't guessed. My name is Julia Elizabeth Barry and my brother is an earl." Well, that was a part truth. Barry *was* her mother's maiden name and her brother *was* an earl. "What exactly do you find so amusing?" The man could be most annoying.

He laughed once more and shook his head. "You really should be on the stage. Have you ever considered that as a profession?"

"But I am a woman of quality. The Langfords are friends and the maid act was just a ruse, a silly game. Nothing more." Could he really not tell she was of noble blood?

Before she could glean an answer, he leapt toward her and grabbed her forearms, his face mere inches from hers. "I tire of your games. You've insinuated yourself upon me since the day we met. Now, you will tell me who you are and what you are about."

She looked at his face and wondered again if he were capable of bodily harm. Upper lip curling, eyebrows pulled together in an unforgiving line, eyes black with anger, he reminded her of a wild animal. At the moment, there was nothing civilized about the man. Or human, for that matter.

Yes, she feared he could cause her much harm if he chose to. "My name is Julia Elizabeth Barry." *Langford.* She could not tell him her real last name, not with him snarling at her like that. He might decide to snap her neck in two. She eyed his huge hands. He could squeeze the very life out of her. He'd probably do just that if she told him she was Holt's sister. Correction. His best friend's sister.

Jon let out a string of curses and rose to pace the small cabin. He moved to the desk and retrieved her satchel, then returned to dump its contents in her lap. "I suppose these are yours as well?"

Sparkling jewels winked back at her in a colorful array of

dazzling brilliance. She grasped a ruby necklace and an emerald hairpin. "These were my mother's," she said softly. "Now they are mine."

"Like hell they are," Jon growled, snatching them from her and thrusting the pieces back into the burgundy satchel. "This jewelry belongs to the Langfords and you stole it from them."

"But—"

"Enough! Do not tell me you are a member of the nobility one more time, or I swear I'll be forced to use extreme measures." The murderous look in his eyes kept her from challenging him. "Now, you will speak and tell me why you are on board my ship."

"I'm on my way to America. To see my brother and his family." She ignored the warning look he gave her and plunged forward. "Holt Langford and I had a wager. I've known the Langfords forever and am especially good friends with Sophie. They're like family to me, more so than my own. Holt agreed to help me get to America if I proved I could survive there. You see," she rushed on, relieved that Jon appeared to be listening, "he didn't think I would do well there, being a woman of quality such as I am. Each time I broached the subject of America, he put me off with one excuse or another. Then, he came up with the wager: if I could survive as a servant for three weeks, performing all of the duties required, he would arrange passage for me."

"So why are you on board *this* ship?"

"Holt told me there wouldn't be a ship suitable to take me for another six months." She sighed. "I couldn't wait. I won the wager, fair and square. When you said you were going home—" she shrugged "—well, you seemed like the logical choice."

"When did I say I was going *home?*"

"In the study, when you were talking to Holt one night."

"So we may add eavesdropping to your list of crimes." He smiled then, a cold, ruthless smile. "I must say, you are resourceful. Unfortunately for you, your duplicity has caught you in quite a predicament."

"What do you mean?"

"The last time I consulted my map," he said, pinning her with a dark stare, "we were headed for the West Indies."

"What?"

He scowled at her. "You heard me, you little minx."

"But I must get to America."

"Then you have a problem."

"I don't understand. You said you were going *home.*"

"I am. To the West Indies." His smile turned brutal. "It's been my home for more years than I can remember."

Fear wrapped itself around her, choking her ability to reason. "Take me to America," she pleaded. "My jewelry's worth a small fortune. You can have it all."

"I can have the jewelry you stole from my best friend's family? No, thank you."

"Then Jason will pay you when we get to America." Jon raised a brow in response. "All right, I don't blame you for not trusting me, but I have no other way to pay you."

He stared at her a long time until silence grew thick and heavy between them. "I can think of a way," Jon said, his expression unreadable.

"You can?" *He was going to help her. But how?*

His bold gaze roamed her body, caressing her with his eyes, lingering on her breasts and stomach. Heat crept up her neck, spread to her cheeks as his words sunk in.

"You want me to barter my body?" she asked as embarrassment turned to fury.

He shrugged. "I seriously doubt it's the first time."

"You beast!" Julia sprang from the bed and lunged at him, but Jon was too quick. He was on the other side of the door, the heavy key rustling in the lock, before she'd taken more than three steps.

She banged on the old wooden door, screaming and cursing him to the devil. *How dare he? How dare he!*

Chapter 6

Jon tried to ignore the blasphemous curses screeching from his cabin, the ones that wished him to perdition in the form of a two-headed goat. When the door banging and crashing glass started, he acted as though it were an everyday occurrence. His men tried to do the same, but it was difficult pretending not to hear a crazy woman likening him to a particular part of a horse's anatomy.

He'd wring her neck and take great pleasure in it. At least then, she'd be quiet. He rubbed the back of his neck, cursing the day he first laid eyes on Julia Barry.

"Jon." Mac Judson placed his hand on the rail and stared out to sea. "It might not be any of my business, but you seem to be in somewhat of a predicament."

"You're right, Mac," Jon watched the gray waves lap after one another. "It's none of your business."

Julia chose that moment to let out another wail. He should have gagged her. Next, metal crashed against metal. And tied her up. To the bed. Spread-eagle. That would have given her something to think about.

"It does seem rather odd, if I do say so myself," Mac commented, stuffing his pipe with tobacco.

"What does?" Jon scanned the dark clouds looming overhead. He wished for a storm, loud enough to drown out all manner of sound.

"Well," Mac said, puffing on his pipe. "I can't recall a time when any of your women raised their voice to you, let alone hauled out a string of curses like that little miss in your cabin. I'd say she's downright hostile."

"She had a little upset. She'll be fine," Jon said, frowning. "And she isn't my woman."

"Oh?"

"It's difficult to explain." He kept his eyes on the water, which calmed him, even at its fiercest moments. "I found her in my armoire."

Mac threw back his head and let out a rich, hearty laugh that filled the air and drowned out Julia's blasphemous tongue. "Found her? In your armoire?" Another wave of laughter rolled over him.

Jon shot him a warning look. "She was hiding there."

"Hiding?" Mac's round face scrunched up. "She's a stowaway?"

"She thought I was going to America." He laughed, but the sound held no warmth. "Can you imagine that," he said, turning to face the older man. "*Me*, going to America?"

Mac puffed on his pipe a moment before answering. "No, I can't say as where I can actually picture you setting foot in America again, at least not yet."

"Not until I receive word that my bastard of a father is dead and buried."

Mac said nothing. A loud screech came from below deck, followed by another and another. "What are you going to do with her?" he asked, inclining his white head toward the sound.

"I know what I'd like to do with her," Jon said, shooting a quick glance at the choppy water before them.

Mac grinned. "You're too much of a gentleman to hoist a female overboard."

"She's no lady; of that you can be sure." Nobility indeed. And he was the king's uncle. "I've been debating my situation for the better part of the night." *When I wasn't getting hard listening to the little witch's soft moans and long sighs.*

"And?"

"We're too far out to take her back now, so we'll continue to the West Indies, and I'll ship her back once we arrive." A loud piercing howl filled the air and he winced, followed by a string of curses that could match his men's. Jon closed his eyes, trying to gather his patience. "If she'll just shut up," he bit out, enunciating one word at a time, "I'll promise to send her to America."

Mac let out a long sigh, relief evident on his round face. "That's the best idea I've heard in a long time."

***

Two hours later, Jon turned the key in the lock and entered the cabin. Julia had been quiet for a full fifteen minutes, and he hoped she was asleep. No matter, the situation between them must be dealt with and the sooner the better.

She sat in a corner on the far end of the bunk. There were no curse words, no blasphemies, nothing. Only a cold, steady stare. What was she up to now? Did she have a weapon hidden under her shirt? He tried to remember if the pistol he kept in his desk drawer was loaded.

Jon moved toward her. If she had found the pistol, he'd be on her before she got a shot off. He reached the berth and towered over her. If the woman had any sense, she'd be afraid of him.

Julia lifted her head slightly, her gray eyes watching him. She sat cross-legged on the bed, her golden locks falling freely about her shoulders to curl just under the swell of her breast. He cast a quick glance in that direction. Fatal error. Was that the outline of a nipple he'd just seen? He shook his head to clear his thoughts. It couldn't be, unless she wore only a light chemise. Or nothing at all.

He cleared his throat. He must get his thoughts back on course. After all, he was in charge of the situation. Julia Barry should be cowering in a corner, begging forgiveness for her treachery. "I've been thinking…" She had the most beautiful neck. Long and slender.

"I accept your proposal."

What proposal?

"I'll come to your bed if you take me to America."

Her words struck him more forcefully than his own pistol would have. "You would sell your own body to get to America?" The very thought infuriated him, which made him even angrier.

"If there were no gentlemen available to honor other forms of payment."

Her words stung. *She* was acting the wounded victim, the

same woman who'd told him nothing but lies from the moment he'd set eyes on her. Julia Barry was a common thief and a manipulator.

"I haven't decided what to do with you yet," Jon lied, unwilling to give her the satisfaction of letting her think she'd gotten her way. Let her stew for a bit, think she had to barter that delectable body of hers.

Julia glared at him. "So now you're withdrawing your offer? It would appear you are untrustworthy as well as unscrupulous, and I, unfortunately, am currently at your mercy."

"So it would appear." The woman's tongue was more deadly than any weapon he owned.

"When you decide my fate, would you be so kind as to inform me?"

He leaned forward, his face mere inches from hers. "My dear, sweet Julia, you will be the first to know." He bestowed a dazzling smile on her. "In the meantime," he said, his voice dropping to a husky drawl, "you might try to be a bit more congenial. You used words today that made my men blush and that won't do." He lifted a lock of hair from her shoulders, fingering its silken texture. "You see, I've never had a problem with the ladies, and your behavior today makes it seem as though you don't hold me in high regard."

"Because I don't," she bit out.

"Hmm." He let her hair glide through his fingers in a shimmering cascade. She tried to move away, backing up until she hit the wall of the cabin. He leaned closer. "You know my crew might even think you don't like me."

Julia didn't answer. Jon tipped her chin up with his finger. Still, she remained silent. It must be killing her not to open that pretty little mouth and begin spouting all manner of blasphemies at him.

"But that can't possibly be true, can it, Julia? You do like me, don't you?" Jon paused to gauge her reaction. As anticipated, her face flushed crimson, her eyes narrowed, and her nostrils flared.

She was furious.

He continued. "It's imperative that you treat me with great affection during the remainder of the trip." His fingers tightened on her hair.

"Go to hell." Her chin flew up but she couldn't release herself from his grip.

"And deep admiration." He wound her hair around his hand, forcing her closer.

"Rakehell."

He opened his hand and her hair spilled about her shoulders. "And utmost respect." Their faces were almost touching.

"Incorrigible wastrel."

He turned his head slightly to hide a smile. He'd never enjoyed a woman so much out of bed as he did this one with her quick, saucy tongue. She proved an exhilarating challenge for him, much different from the simpering females he'd known who were content to bat their lashes and agree with everything he said, no matter how outrageous.

"Fool. Idiot. Bully," she spat out.

"Enough."

"Lecher."

"Lecher?" He laughed. "I have never been called a lecher in my life. My men believe women swoon at my touch. I would hate to ruin that fantasy for them." He released his grasp on her shoulders and tipped her chin up to look at him. "Women aboard this ship have always been with *me,* which means hands off to the crew. You might want to consider a bit of play acting."

She frowned and spat out, "Play acting?"

"Indeed. As lovers. But we must be believable."

He leaned closer and whispered, "We must give the impression we have been intimate."

She scowled and turned away from him.

"What do you say? Are you up for a bit of play acting?"

"I'll do it." Her words were empty, void of emotion. Jon

would not feel sorry for her, would not feel anything for her. She was a schemer, a master manipulator, and a grand liar, and he would do well to remember that.

***

Morning dawned bright and clear. Julia was still abed though she'd been awake for hours, pondering her current dilemma. She knew from his constant tossing and turning last night that Jon hadn't slept much either. She'd worried for a moment he would demand to share the bed, but he'd done nothing more than scowl at her and toss his bedroll in the corner.

But what would happen today? Would he demand the use of her body in exchange for safe passage to America? The very thought of his crude proposal made her cheeks burn. He wouldn't go through with it. Would he? He was Holt's friend. He was a man of honor. Wasn't he?

Julia's head pounded with unanswered questions. What a mess she'd gotten herself into. She had to think, had to reason her way out of this horrible situation.

A raucous yell above board caught her attention and reminded her of Jon's warnings. *We must give the impression we have been intimate.* How on earth was she supposed to do that? Well, she was not about to ask him.

Barbarians, the whole bloody lot of them.

The cabin door opened, and Jon entered carrying a tray laden with food. He glanced in her direction and appeared surprised to find her awake.

"It's early. I thought you'd still be asleep," he said, setting the tray on the bed.

"I...had a rather restless night, I guess." Julia propped herself up, suddenly awkward with the intimacy of the moment.

His strong hands spread strawberry jam on a biscuit. "I doubt you've ever slept on a ship before."

Or in the same room with a man. "No, this is a new experience for me." *One I'd just as soon forget.*

He poured a steaming brew from an old metal pot and said, "My crew's not English and none of them are tea drinkers. I brought you coffee, but it may not be to your liking."

What was he up to now? He was being too polite. She inched away until her back hit the headboard.

"Coffee is fine, thank you." She reached for the mug and their fingers touched, a feather-light brushing, nothing more. He pulled his hand away, snatched a biscuit from the tray, and tore into it. They ate the rest of their meal in silence, save the occasional clatter of silverware and the muted voices of the crew.

When Julia could stand the tension no longer, she ventured to speak. "Would it be possible to get a little sunshine today?"

"Perhaps," Jon replied, spearing a piece of bacon.

"Thank you."

His head shot up, his eyes narrowing on her face. "Stop acting like a damn scared rabbit." He threw down his napkin and stood. "I'm not going to throw you overboard!" Muttering an oath under his breath, he strode to the door. "I'll be back in fifteen minutes to take you on deck."

Once he'd left, she scurried out of bed and performed her morning ablutions as best she could. It only took ten minutes to don a blue day gown as she was minus most of her undergarments. What a difference it made not to have to worry about petticoats and the like. Thankfully, packing had prohibited such items. She'd wondered what American women wore and prayed the encumbrances were less and not more.

America. She closed her eyes to recreate the pictures she'd seen in her books. She must continue to believe that one way or another, she was going to America. Even if it was by way of the West Indies. Her eyes flew open. The note she left Holt said she was sailing with Jon to America, but he knew Jon was headed for the West Indies. Oh dear Lord, would he follow her and attempt to force her back to England?

A brisk rap on the door brought her out of her dark reverie.

"Come in."

The key rattled in the lock, and the heavy wooden door opened. Jon's presence filled the room. "Where are the rest of your clothes?"

"Excuse me?"

"Your undergarments," he said impatiently. "I can see the entire shape of your legs and your—" he stopped midsentence, eyed her bosom "—and the rest of your person. It's indecent."

"It's all I have except for a few pair of breeches."

"Worse yet," he muttered in disgust. "I've seen you in breeches and let me assure you, they leave little to the imagination." He strode past her to the armoire, flung open the doors, and pulled out a pale pink sateen gown with black, frilly lace. He thrust the gown at her. "Put this on."

"I will not."

"Julia," he warned.

"I refuse to wear that gown," she said peevishly. "It will make me look like a courtesan."

"Which is a step up," Jon ground out. "Because right now you look like a street-side doxy."

"I will not wear that gown. Besides, it's too big." There, she'd see what he had to say about that. She sounded petty, but the very idea of wearing a gown that belonged to one of his mistresses was too much.

"I see what you mean," he commented, his eyes trained on her breasts. "You are rather small."

"Why, you crude—"

"Time to go," Jon said, grabbing her arm. "And remember, my sweet Julia, you love me more than the air you breathe."

***

"Will you 'ave another bowl 'a soup, Miss Julia?"

"Why, thank you, Amos, but I couldn't eat another bite." She smiled at the grizzled old man, her gaze drawn to his gapped grin. He reminded her of the color gray—gray hair, gray eyes, a gray beard, gray complexion, gray shirt, and breeches. Even the five teeth left in his mouth were gray.

"More ale, Miss Julia?" Jeremy asked, his face turning as

red as the ruffled mop of hair on his head. He couldn't have been more than fifteen. How had he landed aboard *The Falcon?* Perhaps she could talk to him later but first, she had to get him past blushing every time he looked her way.

"I've had one and that's really my limit, Jeremy. But thank you for asking."

"Where'd ya say ya come from?" Big Tom bellowed, ripping off a hunk of bread and stuffing half of it into his mouth.

"That's wot I'd like ta know," Amos chimed in. "Us men sees all the cap'n's visit'rs, 'specially the women." He scrunched up his faded gray eyes and scratched his head. "But we nev'r seen the likes 'a you."

Julia ignored the heat rushing to her face. "Well, no, you might not have seen me," she hesitated. "Or rather, *recognized* me, because, you see—" she let out a nervous laugh "—I didn't look exactly like I do now. As a matter of fact—"

"She was with me in my cabin and hardly wearing appropriate attire to greet my men," Jon cut in. "Isn't that right, my dear?"

Julia wished she could sink through the wooden planks into the deep, dark waters of anonymity, never to be seen again. Jon had just confirmed their suspicions. She was his whore. It was one thing for them to speculate they were lovers and quite another to hear their captain admit to the liaison in such a crude manner.

"Julia?" Jon's deep drawl pushed through her thoughts, pulling her back. How she wanted to jump from her seat and claw that smug look off his face. She balled her hands into fists and raised her head to meet his intense gaze.

The table fell silent as all eyes settled on their captain. The wooden floorboards creaked back and forth in rhythm with the waves beating against the ship. "Well, now, it doesn't matter how Miss Julia got aboard or that none of you sorry men saw her," Mac Judson said, breaking the silence. His blue eyes twinkled with sympathy and encouragement as he smiled at

Julia. "I for one am just happy we'll be sharing company with such a beautiful, charming young woman. Makes for a much shorter trip."

Amos lifted his mug. "Hear, hear. Miss Julia's a mite bett'r-look'n' than any 'a you old cusses."

"She's the most beautiful woman I've ever seen," Jeremy said, his blush deepening.

"She sure is purty," Big Tom grinned, making the scar on his forehead crinkle.

Jon slammed his fist on the wooden table. "Enough!"

"Captain?" Mac Judson asked. "Is something wrong? The men were just trying to make your guest feel welcome, like you always tell them to do when you have a *visitor* aboard."

Julia lowered her head to hide her smile. Jon was not pleased that his men had come to her rescue and saved her from further humiliation. Despite their outward appearances and obvious lack of manners, they possessed good intentions and kind hearts—unlike their captain, who was nothing more than a blackguard and a boor.

Yet, he'd led her to believe they were not to be trusted where a woman was concerned. In truth, she was probably safer with these men than with their captain.

The meal proceeded with the entire crew, minus Jon, exchanging delightful antics about life at sea and traveling the world. Julia listened with an eager ear as she heard tales of Istanbul, Greece, and Peking.

With the meal finished, the men scurried off, leaving Julia alone. Jon stood in the distance, gazing out to sea, his hair windblown and tousled from the steady breeze, his dark features set against the brilliant backdrop of the afternoon sun, like a fierce warrior returning from battle. He seemed troubled, and it surprised her she could discern that fact. When two people spent vast quantities of time together, wasn't it to be expected they would learn each other's likes and dislikes? The notion seemed plausible but it was the very *knowing* that disturbed her.

She'd begun to sense his moods from a look or word, even the quirk of an eyebrow. It scared her to acknowledge she might be interested in scratching the surface of that hard exterior to find the real man beneath. And, Julia *knew* there was a very different man behind the cold exterior Jon showed her.

Unfortunately, only a fool would open herself up to the pain and heartache of caring about Jon Remmington, and she was no fool.

"Miss Julia, if ye don't go below deck or put a hat on soon, ye'll be as red as a lobster come sunset."

Julia turned to the old, grizzled sailor who'd just spoken. "Why, thank you for reminding me, Amos. I was so enjoying this fine weather I didn't even consider my skin." She frowned. "Unfortunately, I find myself without a hat or bonnet, which means I suppose I should return to the cabin until the sun sets."

"But the cap'n has one o' them big straw 'uns he wears in the Indies," Amos said.

"The captain's not in a mood to be disturbed right now," Mac Judson said, casting a look in Jon's direction. "We'd best call it a day for now. I'll escort Miss Julia to her cabin."

She hazarded another glance at Jon. He was staring straight at her, and the fierceness of his expression frightened her. She turned quickly, clasped Mac Judson's arm, and followed him below deck.

"Is he always like that?" she whispered as they reached the cabin door.

Mac shook his head and smiled. "He's *never* like that, Miss Julia. Leastwise, not unless the subject of his family comes up, which it rarely does." His blue eyes twinkled. "Jon's as carefree and easygoing as they come. He's always had a way with the ladies, a real charmer that one, with his sweet words and that big smile. Women go crazy over him."

Julia snorted indelicately. "Pardon my rudeness, Mr. Judson, but that description does not fit the man on the deck. That man is crude and overbearing."

Mac's smile spread. "I'm seeing that, Miss Julia, and I

couldn't agree with you more." He paused a moment, before adding, "If I were a betting man, I'd say he's got it bad, real bad, and it's about time."

"Got what bad, Mr. Judson?"

Mac's smile only deepened as he pushed open the door for her. "You'll find out soon enough. Rest assured, you'll find out soon enough."

Chapter 7

No one seemed to notice that Jon was silent through supper the next evening. He and Julia were sitting among his crew, eating barley soup and hard rolls with chunks of ham. He'd had to get out of that damned cabin. She was too close, too accessible, insinuating herself upon him minute by minute, hour by hour, making him crazy with wanting her.

Wherever he turned, he saw her fresh beauty, her tantalizing smile. The sound of her voice called to him with whispered promises as he listened to the velvety notes of humming or, God pardon his sick mind, her sighs of sleep. Even her anger drew him in, the spark in her gray eyes, captivating him as no other woman had. He dared not think of that luscious body, though, even the thought of *not* thinking about it made him want her.

Damn it, *why her?* Why did just the thought of her make him ache? She drove him crazy, and he didn't even think he liked her, with her waspish tongue and shrewish ways. Oh, but he wanted her; there was no denying that any longer. He bit into a chunk of hard bread and tried to convince himself it was because he hadn't bedded her yet, and once he had, she'd be relegated to the scores of other women who'd come before. But there was this gnawing feeling deep in his gut that told him she might just be different from all the rest. That angered him most of all.

"Jon, tell Miss Julia about the silks we brought back from the Orient," Jeremy said, interrupting Jon's dark musings.

"I doubt Miss Julia has much to do with silks," he responded, his gaze settling on the plain muslin gown she wore.

Julia gasped. His men fell silent. Jon cursed his foolish behavior. Even loud, burly men like these knew a direct cut when they heard one. What was the matter with him? He'd always had a reputation with the ladies, young and old alike. They all loved him, loved his carefree, debonair style and rakish grin. But not this one. She would just as soon throw daggers at him if the opportunity presented itself.

He glanced at her. She had a smile pasted on her face, but he didn't miss the flaring nostrils or the wide-eyed stare. He'd bet she wanted to strangle him for his rude behavior, and he couldn't blame her. He *had* been ill-mannered and inconsiderate toward her. He just wished to hell he knew why.

She was looking at him now, her gray gaze intent on his mouth as she leaned toward him, her pink lips stopping a breath from his own. He stared in stunned silence as she placed the softest of kisses on his lips.

Though he expected the contact, even yearned for it, when her warm mouth touched his, the union startled him, sending shards of raw sensation through his body. He jerked away, wiped his mouth with the back of his hand, and spat out, "What the hell are you doing?"

The smile she gave him was sweet and innocent and totally unlike the Julia Barry he knew. Damn her, but she was taking great pleasure making a fool out of him in front of his men. She leaned closer, whispering in his ear, "You told me specifically that I was to show you great affection in front of your men." Her small teeth nipped his earlobe. "That's all I'm trying to do, Jon. Honestly." She fingered the curls at the nape of his neck.

"Damn you!" he muttered through clenched teeth seconds before he rose from the table and stalked off, spewing a string of oaths under his breath.

All eyes followed their captain's retreating back. When he was out of sight, they turned back to their bowls in silence, sopping up broth with chunks of bread. Several minutes passed without a word. Jeremy snickered first, a low snorting sound, followed by Amos's high-pitched howl that matched the piercing cry of the sea gulls overhead. Within seconds, the whole lot of them broke into gales of laughter, deep, full-bellied laughs that started and ended with hoots and hollers.

Julia laughed, too, though she really didn't know why. The last few days had proved more than a little trying, but she refused to examine the motive behind her sudden giddiness, other than to acknowledge that Jon Remmington was nowhere in sight and she was relieved.

A large hand covered hers and squeezed gently. Julia turned to look into the twinkling blue eyes of Mac Judson. She liked this kindly man with his shock of white hair and even disposition. He smiled as though he'd sensed her false bravado and was proud of it, nonetheless. "Care to take a walk in the setting sun with an old man?"

"I'd be honored."

They made their way to the stern of *The Falcon* and stood side by side gazing out over the dark, endless water. How could these men find chartered lands with only a map and compass? They were brave, fearless souls with passion in their veins and purpose in their hearts. Men like Mac Judson and Holt and— she hesitated a moment—Jon. They sought and found their destiny with a single-mindedness she admired. Thinking about them renewed her determination to see her destiny fulfilled.

"Don't be too harsh on him, Miss Julia," Mac said, breaking into her thoughts. "Jon will come around soon enough."

Julia leaned close to the older man. "No, he won't." Wisps of hair escaped from her braid, whipped across her face. She brushed them aside and said, "He's not happy I'm here." She paused, added, "I stowed away in his cabin."

Mac winked at her and grinned. "That's what I heard. Well done, young lady. Well done indeed."

"Did you hear what I said? I stowed away, hidden in his armoire."

"I heard you well enough, Miss Julia, and I applaud you. Jon needs a woman who will stand up to him instead of those frilly, gushy dress-ups that swoon when he looks their way and would never dare let him know they have an opinion."

"But you have it all wrong. I'm not his woman."

Mac raised a bushy white brow but said nothing.

"Truly, I'm not. He wants us to act like a couple for appearance's sake. He said it would ruin his image if I didn't fawn all over him," she finished, rolling her eyes to show him what she thought of the whole idea.

Mac let out another laugh. "The truth will come out soon enough, Miss Julia. It always does, whether we like it or not."

She wanted to argue the point further but held her tongue. Mac would believe what he wished, no matter how strongly she and Jon denied it.

"Jon told me you were headed for America."

She nodded. "Mac," she began, choosing her next words with great care. "Why doesn't he consider America his home?"

A small frown played about his usually cheerful face "Now what do you know about that?"

"He said he considers the West Indies his home." She pressed on. "Did something happen in America?"

Mac sighed, leaned back against the ship's railing, and crossed his arms over his rounded middle. When he spoke, his voice was quiet, his bushy brows pulled together in thought. "I've been sailing the seas for some thirty plus years. Met a lot of men in my day—most of them running from something— usually their past." He paused and stroked his white beard. "Jon's a good sort. It was his father's doing. The old man drove him away. Jon comes from a long line of Remmingtons, each one of them prouder than the one before. They own hundreds of acres of tobacco and cotton in Virginia. As the oldest son, his father expected him to remain at Willow Oaks and carry on the family tradition. Of course, Jon wanted none of it, not even the little rich girl his father picked out for him. He couldn't ignore the wanderlust in his blood but his father would hear none of it, threatened to disown him if he left. That didn't stop Jon; he took off anyway, barely sixteen at the time."

"And he's never returned?" A dull ache started in the middle of her chest. The pain of being left behind.

"He went back once, seven years ago." Mac's blue eyes darkened. "It turned out badly. The old man started on him again, tried to foist the Willow Oaks legacy back on him. I was there, and it was not a pretty sight. Jon swore he'd never return as long as the old man was alive and frankly, I can't say I blame him."

Julia fell silent, sifting through this new knowledge of Jon Remmington. She could see why he and Holt were such good friends. They'd both suffered similar circumstances as the eldest sons of powerful families, duty thrust upon them at a young age, twisting and imprisoning them in its harmful grips.

"Does he have any brothers or sisters?" she asked, suddenly needing to know if others had suffered as she had.

"He's got a younger brother and twin sisters." Mac cleared his throat and turned to her. "I've spoken more than I should have." He touched her arm gently, smiling into her upturned face. "When the time is right, Jon will tell you," he said, patting her arm. "Now, we best get you back to your cabin."

***

Julia sat cross-legged on the bunk, combing out her hair. When she'd bid Mac good-night and entered the cabin, it had been dark save for a pale light shimmering in the corner. Jon's obvious absence had brought her equal amounts relief and disappointment, though she couldn't say why. Actually, she'd been hoping to prod him into talking about his home life and family.

Did he plan to return to America after his father's death? Would he stay? What of the brother and twin sisters? Were they old enough to remember him? And the pretty, little rich girl he was to marry? The questions raced through her brain, one after the other, in such a furious jumble she didn't hear the rap on her door.

"Miss Julia?" Jeremy's young voice called out to her.

Julia scurried off the bed and pulled open the door. "Yes?"

She stood dumbfounded, as Jeremy and Amos entered the cabin carrying a huge wooden tub. "Captain thought you might enjoy a bath," Jeremy said, blushing. "We've been collecting this water." He motioned to several steaming buckets behind him. "But it's been a devil to heat." He and Amos set the tub in the middle of the room and proceeded to empty the buckets into it.

Such a tender gesture initiated by the man who was fast becoming more of a mystery with each passing minute. He confused and angered her with his high-handed manner and sarcastic tongue, but he also beckoned her with his heated gaze and soft caress.

"Enjoy your bath, Miss Julia." Amos grinned at her, and she smiled back, curious if the old sailor had ever seen bath water. Doubtful.

"I thank you fine gentlemen for thinking of me. I shall most certainly enjoy my bath."

"It weren't nothing, Miss Julia," Jeremy piped in. "It was all the captain's doing. You might want to thank him."

"Yes, well..." She hesitated a moment. "I most certainly will."

As soon as the two men left, Julia hurried to the armoire and pulled out her travel bag. She ruffled through its rumpled contents until she located a small bottle of lilac water. Unscrewing the top, she poured an ample amount into the tub and luxuriated in the heady fragrance. She unlaced her gown with lightning speed, and seconds later sank into the steamy water of her own private heaven.

An hour later, she sat on the bed, dressed in a batiste nightgown that covered her from head to toe. "Ouch," she snapped, pulling at a large knot of wet hair. No wonder her lady's maid mouthed curse words and dropped subtle hints about opting for a more fashionable, shorter style whenever the poor girl had the task of combing Julia's hair. She bent forward and began the painstaking chore of untangling the matted mess.

When the door clicked open, Julia glanced up. Jon stood in the doorway, tall and dark against the evening shadows. "Thank you for the bath," she said softly. "It was most enjoyable."

He shrugged but didn't look at her. "You're welcome." He moved to the tub and stared into the water as though it contained something of great interest.

Was he really as cold and heartless as he wanted her to think? She was beginning to wonder.

"I was thinking of a bath myself," Jon said, turning toward her, his expression unreadable. "Would you mind?"

The thought of him naked made her hot and cold all at once. When she could find her voice, she stammered, "Why no," with as much matter-of-factness as she could muster. If he could appear so nonchalant about his nakedness, then why couldn't she? The truth smacked against her bravado; she'd never in her entire life seen a man naked. The very idea was petrifying—and intriguing. "I wish I'd known," she mumbled, grabbing for something to say, "I wouldn't have put the lilac water in the tub."

He smiled tightly. "Consider it one more step in our ruse."

"I don't understand."

"Don't you? When my men smell your scent on me, they'll have no doubt that we're lovers. That's our plan, isn't it?" he asked, his voice soft and mesmerizing. "To pretend to be lovers?" Without waiting for her response, he turned and began unbuttoning his shirt.

Julia hesitated a moment, unable to look away as he pulled off his shirt to reveal a darkly tanned, well-muscled back. When he bent to remove his boots, his tightly clad breeches stretched to expose the finely carved muscles of his thighs and buttocks, leaving Julia a vision of what his unclothed body would look like.

She swallowed and fanned herself. Good heavens, the room had grown stuffy. It grew even stuffier when Jon bent his head to unfasten the buttons on his breeches. Julia sipped in tiny breaths as his strong hands worked the fabric over his slim hips. He stopped and jerked his head around, his dark eyes boring into her.

"Unless you'd like to help, you'd better turn around now."

Julia gasped and buried her head in the pillow, but no matter how deep she burrowed, she couldn't block out the rich sound of Jon's laughter or the sight of his perfect body.

***

Jon stood over Julia, entranced by the slow, even movements of her breathing. Every so often she made a small mewling sound followed by a sigh. He'd counted ten in the last fifteen minutes. That's how long he'd been standing over her, filled with desire, close to bursting. He'd been without a woman too long, and that's why the need pulsing in him right now was so great—that damn need had *nothing* to do with Julia Barry.

He let out a muffled curse and moved to leave her but remembered the reason he'd approached the bed. He'd meant to place her under the covers to protect her from the night's chill. He tried to nudge the blanket from under her sleeping body. She let out a soft moan and shifted position, exposing a long, slender leg. His gaze stripped her of the thin material that covered her exquisite curves and envisioned supple flesh, warm and inviting. Damn, but the woman was bewitching him, even in her sleep! He pulled at the blanket again, but with no success. After three more attempts, he decided there was no way to get her under the covers without lifting her, which meant touching her body, which meant torturing himself with her forbidden sweetness, which meant—

Damn it, he should just leave her. He hesitated. She could catch a chill and perhaps a fever. Then what? He cursed again, scooped her into his arms, and froze when she snuggled against his bare chest, making a mewling sound, not unlike a contented cat. "Julia," he choked out. "Stop it."

"Mmm," she murmured, nuzzling against his chest.

Jon let out a strangled sound as he flung back the covers and laid her on the bed as quickly as possible. She snaked her arms around his neck before he could straighten and pulled him toward her. Her actions caught him by surprise, and he lost his balance and tumbled on top of her. Her throaty laughter pumped through his veins as she tightened her arms and shifted her body beneath his. "Julia." He tried to ignore the throbbing in his breeches and bit out, "Stop this. I'm no saint."

She smiled, her eyes still closed and moved again, rubbing herself against him. "I've dreamed this a thousand times with you." She'd dreamed this intimate act a thousand times with *him*, a man she clearly loathed and fought with at every turn? Hardly. A sickening feeling settled in his gut. She was still sleeping, dreaming about someone else.

"A thousand times and more," she moaned in a breathy voice, her fingers trailing along his shoulders. "Oh, Jon."

His head snapped up. "Julia, wake up," his harsh command startled her out of her slumber, and her eyes flew open. "You were dreaming."

"Was I?" She stared at his mouth.

"Don't," he said. She ignored his words and lifted a shaky hand to trace his lips with her fingertips. God, she was killing him, one sweet touch at a time. His tongue shot out to trace a pattern over the pads of her fingers. "If you want me to leave, say so right now," he rasped. "Because in another minute I won't be able to."

She traced his lips again. "Stay."

He groaned and captured her mouth, releasing all the pent-up passion and longing he'd harbored since the first time he saw her. She returned the kiss with a fire of her own, her tongue seeking and mating with his, tracing his lips, sucking his tongue, exploring his mouth. She moaned, holding him to her as he shifted his weight and settled between her thighs.

"I can't wait any longer." He would go slowly next time. Or the time after that. Right now, he had to have her, hard and deep. He skimmed her thigh, grabbed the hem of her nightgown, and yanked it to her waist. He stroked her creamy flesh, his fingers brushing her woman's heat with feather-light touches. Her low, pleading moans unraveled the last shreds of his control. "I've got to have you now," he ground out as he tore at the buttons of his breeches, releasing himself in one swift movement. Jon grabbed her buttocks, lifting her off the bed and positioned himself over her. For one brief moment their gazes locked, and then he thrust into her.

She screamed as he tore through the resistance of her untried body and his mind registered the truth: she was a virgin.

"You're killing me!" Julia yelled, beating her fists against his chest. "Get off of me, you beast!" She wiggled and squirmed, trying to dislodge him.

"Be still!" he spat out. He was near to bursting and couldn't think when each small movement of her luscious body took him to the edge of sanity. One more little wiggle and he'd forget her tender sensibilities and pump into her until he spilled his seed deep inside her warmth.

She stopped moving. Sweat beaded Jon's face, the muscles in his neck straining, his forearms tight in their effort to support the bulk of his weight. Be damned! He had to get control. One little jerk, one little movement or sigh and he'd be pounding into her like a madman. If he could maintain control for another moment, he'd be in command again. Then he could ignore Julia's exquisite tightness and withdraw from her.

"Are you in pain?" she asked, her voice little more than a breath.

Jon refused to look at her. He almost had it, his mind almost blocked out the feel of her body. Just a few more seconds.

"Jon?"

He would not look at her. He did not want to see those big, gray eyes because that would only make him want to look at her mouth. That luscious mouth with those full, pink lips.

"I'm sorry if I overreacted," she said shyly. "It...it...you're not hurting me anymore."

He couldn't speak.

"I just feel this kind of fullness...down there," she continued.

Why wouldn't she just be quiet?

"It's actually not unpleasant."

Jon groaned. If she kept talking, he was going to show her what real fullness felt like.

"So if you'd like to proceed..."

His control burst, and he plunged into her, deeply, wildly, wanting all of her. "God forgive me," he groaned, burying his face in her neck. "I can't help myself." Julia responded with a heat of her own, wrapping her legs around his waist, pulling him closer. She met each thrust with a powerful need of her own, bucking off the bed, moaning his name, pleading for release. Jon worked his fingers between their bodies and stroked her swollen flesh with his fingertips. Five little strokes were all it took as Julia's climax came with a rush and a cry of pleasure, followed by a long, satisfied sigh. Jon pumped into her once more, shouted her name, and spilled his seed deep inside her womb.

***

"Julia?" Jon was the first to speak. He lay on his side, studying her as she pretended to sleep. It was evident from her uneven breathing and squinting eyes she was not sleeping, but merely avoiding this inevitable confrontation. "Julia, give over." Jon tried not to sound exasperated but it was damned difficult. "I know you're awake."

Her eyes inched open.

"And you're naked," he said, enjoying the shocked look on her face as she tried to cover herself with the rumpled sheet. She'd have to work a little harder if she wanted the damned thing since most of it lay nestled between his legs.

"Don't." He lifted her hands from their feeble attempt to cover her breasts. "Your body is beautiful. And I've seen it all. Every delectable inch." She blushed darker than a beet. He traced small circles on her palm and admitted, "I've been undressing you in my mind, practically from the moment we met."

"You have?"

He smiled. "But reality is so much better." He planted a chaste kiss on her lips. "Why didn't you tell me you were a virgin?"

"Would it have made a difference?"

"Of course it would have made a difference." The woman could be impossible. Even in bed. "I'm not in the habit of seducing young virgins."

"Well, now you've made an exception."

"Because—" he continued as though she hadn't spoken "—I've always been able to tell the difference." He regretted the words as soon as he spoke them. Shock flashed across her face, but it disappeared so quickly he thought he might have imagined it. She turned her face away, lips in a straight line, eyes glued to the ceiling.

"I'm sorry." Jon stumbled with the word; he wasn't in the habit of apologizing to a woman, especially in his bed.

"We had a deal. I've kept my part." Her eyes grew bright and shiny.

"A deal? What deal?" The woman would make a saint lose his patience. She continued to stare at the ceiling, blinking several times. *Trying to keep the tears at bay, no doubt. Bold, proud Julia.*

Her lips barely moved as she said, "You told me you'd take me to America if I came to your bed."

"You thought I'd actually do that? What kind of a beast do you think I am?" He grasped her chin and forced her to look at him. "I intended to send you to America once we reached the West Indies. Bedding you was never part of that plan."

Her lower lip trembled. "It wasn't?"

"Of course not," he growled, angered she should think so little of him. "I've wanted you in my bed since the first time I saw you, and it had nothing to do with any bargain."

She smiled then, a small, faint tilting of her lips that made him think she was pleased with what he'd just admitted. That made him angry. She'd gotten him to admit a weakness for her. Damn the woman, and damn her to hell for sleeping with *him* as part of a bargain.

"You, on the other hand, believed that sharing my bed would ensure your passage to America."

"No! What happened between us has nothing to do with my

getting to America."

His gaze narrowed. "Is that the truth or another lie? I'm beginning to think the only truths we've shared lie right here in this bed." He reached for a lock of golden hair, fingered its silky texture, and brushed it against her nipple.

She pushed his hand away. "Why do you always believe the worst of me? First you thought me a thief, then a whore, and now a conniver who would sleep with you to obtain what I wanted. Perhaps I am simply a passionate lover of adventure; can you not consider that?"

The notion was inconceivable because he had never met a woman whose determination did not begin and end with ulterior motives centered on increasing wealth or trapping a man, usually him. To entertain the very idea that Julia was different from other women would make her unique. Damn, it would make her *irresistible,* and that would be a huge problem.

For him.

The man who enjoyed his own harem might fall prey to the charms of one woman alone. Julia. He fought the churning in his gut and pushed the ridiculous notion aside. It was much safer to remain suspicious of her motives. Perhaps he'd test her. "I won't marry you." That got her attention. Her head whipped back around and she stared at him as though he'd just claimed an association with the devil.

"And I *won't* marry you."

Had she just said she *wouldn't* marry him? He must have heard wrong. Women from all over the world wanted to marry him. Of course she *wanted* to marry him; she was just being coy because he'd said he wouldn't marry *her*. Or maybe it was a trap to make him want her. "Oh, come now, Julia, you know if I offered for you, you'd accept."

"No, I would not."

That sounded like a definite no. Merely an angle to lure him in and get him to offer marriage. "No?" he asked again.

"No," she repeated, her voice rising.

"What if your father demanded it?"

"My father's dead."

"A brother then. What if he forced the issue?" This was becoming a matter of pride.

She paled. "I tire of this game, Jon. We're both in agreement. There will be no marriage."

Something was amiss; he sensed it. "Tell me why the mention of a brother made you look as though you'd seen a ghost."

Her eyes widened with concern and perhaps a little fear. "If my brother finds me, he'll drag me back to London by my hair."

"Not if I have anything to say about it," Jon vowed, surprised by his fierce need to protect her. "No one will harm you, Julia. I'll get you to America, if that's where you truly wish to go."

"Unless my brother finds me first," she murmured, turning on her side.

"What did you say?"

"Nothing." Her words trailed off, but he didn't miss the concern in her voice. Did she think he would not protect her?

He stroked her hair and trailed a hand along her hip. Such exquisite beauty drenched in lilac. She turned to him and met his gaze as passion flared between them, full and hot and explosive.

Jon wanted her with a fierceness that was foreign to him. How could this woman make him burn with anger one moment and drown in desire the next? How could she be so different from any woman he'd known before? He refused to dwell on this, not with Julia's sweetness so close to him. She was his tonight, and tonight was all that mattered. Tomorrow was too far away to consider.

***

Several hours later, Jeremy summoned Mac Judson above board. "I think you might wanta take a look at who's approachin', sir," he said, barely able to contain his excitement.

"It had better be worthwhile, my boy." Mac grabbed the

spyglass and squinted through it. "You know I'm a sight older than you young bucks and I don't appreciate being roused in the middle of the night for no good reason."

"You'll see, sir," Jeremy said. "'E's the stuff of legends."

Mac grumbled, adjusting the glass. "What did that overactive imagination of yours conjure up this time?"

Jeremy laughed. "It's the real thing. I swear."

"Well, I'll be damned," Mac murmured. "If it isn't *The Raven.*"

"Should I call the captain?"

Mac shook his head. "No need to wake him yet. He's got nothing to fear from his best friend."

***

Twenty minutes later, Holt Langford stood before Mac Judson, fists clenched, gaze narrowed. "Where is he, Mac? Where's that bastard hiding?"

"Holt, in God's name, what's happened?"

He ignored the old man's question and bit out, "Is there a girl on board, blond hair, gray eyes?"

Mac nodded. "Yes, that's Miss Julia."

"Where is she?"

"Holt, let's talk."

"The time for talking is done. If he touched her, he'll wish he were dead." He turned and strode toward Jon Remmington's cabin and pounded on the door.

The loud banging startled Jon awake. He hurried out of bed, grabbed his breeches, and threw them on. "What the—" He flung the door open and was met with a right cross to the chin, followed by a left. He stumbled backward, careening against the bed. His attacker stormed after him, pummeling him with both fists. A right, then a left connected with Jon's left eye, then his right cheek. He staggered to the desk, blood oozing from his face as he tried to get his bearings to deliver his own blow, but the man charged at him, sinking his fist in Jon's belly, doubling him over. He must get in a punch…he must… Waves of dizziness passed over him. Damn, but he'd been blindsided and now he couldn't catch a breath. Two monstrous hands grabbed him by the shoulders and dragged him to the ground, followed by a direct blow to the nose. A sick crack filled the air as blood spurted everywhere.

There was a scream. "No! Please don't kill him!" The assailant looked up and Jon recognized Holt Langford. *What the hell? Why had his best friend practically beaten him to a bloody pulp?* Jon fell to the wooden floor, clutching his head as he tried to still the pain.

"Julia, for God's sake, cover yourself," Holt commanded.

With great effort, Jon looked toward the bed. Out of the corner of his left eye he saw Julia, crying, covered in nothing more than a thin sheet. She looked so helpless, so alone. He watched as she yanked a blanket from the bed, threw it over her shoulders, and scurried toward him.

"Julia! Do not take one more step," Holt warned. She hesitated a moment before letting out a small cry and rushing to Jon's side. She kneeled beside him, placed her arms over his chest as though to protect him. Jon winced. Even her touch hurt. If he weren't in such pain, he'd find it comical that this slip of a girl thought to keep him safe. A bit late for that now. Blood oozed down his cheek, his right eye was almost swollen shut, and his left seemed blurry. He knew his nose was broken. Again. Maybe he'd even cracked a rib or two.

"Julia, get out of the way. Now!" Holt grabbed her arm and hauled her back to the bed. "Stay there," he warned. He strode back to Jon and demanded, "Fight me, you bastard."

Jon tried to focus on Holt, but he was nothing more than a dark blur towering over him. He opened his mouth to speak and tasted blood. "Holt...what the hell is this about?" God, but it hurt to speak. Maybe his jaw was broken, too.

"You ruined my sister, you bastard!"

"Your—" the word stuck in his throat "—sister." It was more statement than question. A sick dread crept through his beaten body. She couldn't be his sister. *She couldn't be.*

"Please, Holt," Julia begged, scrambling off the bed again,

the blanket trailing behind her as she ran to Jon's side. "Please leave him be. He didn't know, I swear." The small room filled with silence, save her tearful pleading. "Jon, I'm so sorry for what I've done," she whispered. "I lied to you and you suffered because of it. Please forgive me."

Jon closed his eyes, blocking out the golden beauty beside him. He didn't want to see her tears or the anguish on her face. She was to blame for this bloody mess. Julia could have told him who she was days ago, when he first discovered her on his ship, but then he would have returned her to her brother. Immediately. She knew that. Her lies and deceit had placed the noose around his neck. Her silence had tightened it.

"Please, Jon," she begged. He turned away. Julia sniffed and cleared her throat. "Holt, are you taking me back to England?"

Jon heard the dread in her voice, thick and heavy with loathing.

"On the morrow," he replied.

"And then?" she asked, though Jon knew she already suspected the answer.

"Then it will be up to your new husband to decide what becomes of you," he said. Jon opened his left eye and met Holt's harsh stare.

"Husband? What husband?"

"Of course, how remiss of me. You haven't been properly introduced," Holt said, his voice cold and brittle. "My dear, meet your betrothed, Jon Remmington. Jon, meet your betrothed, Lady Julia Langford. *My sister.*"

Chapter 8

Julia rested her head against the rough wall of Holt's cabin and tried to still the pounding in her head. The last few hours had been a nightmare she would just as soon forget, but the memories flooded back, taunting and pulling, driving her mad with remembering. Her last vision of Jon flashed through her mind as he stood on board *The Falcon*, staring out to sea like a fierce, angry warrior. Cold. Hard. Unforgiving.

There had been no wistful looks or hushed words between them. No tender good-byes. No good-byes at all. He hadn't looked at or spoken a word to her since Holt's ruthless attack. Nor had he argued when Holt announced they were to be married. Jon had remained impassive, as though the decision were of little consequence.

Julia was the one who fought the announcement, begging Holt not to force the issue. His only reply had been marriage or a duel, which left Julia no real choice at all.

How had she gotten herself into such a mess? She was to be married posthaste to a man she had repeatedly deceived, one who would never forgive her and most certainly never love her. Or permit her to travel to America. These were sad and depressing thoughts, but the realization that she'd fallen in love with such a man was the most depressing of all.

***

Jon knew Holt would search him out once Julia was gone. There were matters to be settled, things that needed said. He had not looked at Julia as she boarded *The Raven*, not even when he felt her sorrowful eyes on him, begging for some kind of sign. Some kind of forgiveness. He slammed his hand against the wooden railing. Well, he'd be damned if she'd get absolution from him. Because of her lying, scheming ways, his whole life was about to turn upside down and there wasn't a damn thing he could do about it.

"We need to talk." Holt spoke from behind him. Jon turned away from the black, curling waves of the sea. Even the water provided no solace for him this day. He led Holt below deck, to his cabin and the bottle of whisky waiting for him. He needed a drink. He needed several drinks to ease the pain in his body. And several more to dull his brain into accepting the inevitable.

He poured two whiskies, handed one to Holt, and downed the other. It burned his throat and the second felt even better. After the third, he set down his glass and waited.

"You *will* marry her," Holt said, his words cold and stiff.

Jon poured another whisky. He felt like hell and probably looked worse. The whisky had begun to ease the dull aching in his battered body, but his brain pounded in his skull whenever he thought of Julia Langford.

Marriage! He knew she was trouble the first time he laid eyes on her, even before he discovered she was a woman. He would have to marry her. There would be no alternative with Holt. Trapped. He hated that feeling. If only she hadn't lied to him about her identity, none of this would have happened. He never would have touched her. But even as the words ran through his head, he doubted their truth and that sickened him even more.

"Jon? Did you hear me?"

"Of course I heard you," he said, making no attempt to hide the bitterness in his voice. "You want me to marry your sister and provide her with the luxuries befitting a woman of her station." His fingers tightened around his empty glass. "A grand estate, diamonds and rubies, silks and satins. She and I will then settle into a comfortable married existence in the country and raise a passel of children." He forced a smile. "In short, my life will be over."

Holt's smile was equally forced, his voice deceptively soft. "Not exactly." His eyes turned the color of the turbulent waters they sailed. "Julia needs the protection of your name because you've compromised her. Once she has that, you may consider your obligation fulfilled."

The man made no sense. "Perhaps you would care to explain."

"I'll be quite clear about your responsibilities, lest you get confused at some point and try to change them. You *will* marry Julia and give her your name. Period. That's the only requirement necessary to be her husband. You'll not provide a home, clothing, jewels, or any other possession. You'll be free to sail the seas and visit your exotic lands and pursue your other—" he paused to press the point "—pleasures. But my sister will not be one of those pleasures."

"And if Julia disagrees with your plan?" He refused to acknowledge the tightness in his gut or the ache in his chest. Holt was granting him as much freedom as any man in these circumstances could hope for and that's what Jon wanted, wasn't it? *Why in the hell didn't he feel relieved?*

"She won't disagree. Not when I tell her you only agreed to marry her if you would be granted freedom to roam the world, free of husbandly duties and the burden of a family. If that fails—" Holt shrugged "—I'll tell her about all the women you're bedding while she pines for you at home."

"And if she happens to be with child?" *Pregnant. With his child.* His anger lessened.

Holt's expression grew fierce. "It won't be your problem," he said, his voice colder than the battering gusts of wind outside.

"Why are you set on doing this?"

Holt rounded on him, fists clenched, the cords of his neck strained and pulsing. "If you weren't my best friend, I'd dispense with all this unpleasantness and just shoot you for what you did. I have to protect Julia. You can't love her." His voice shook. "You're incapable of love, we both know that. You'll use her until you tire of her, then toss her aside. I've seen you do it too many times. But Julia will fall in love with you, if she hasn't already. She'll wait for you to return from one trip or another until finally you won't return at all. I will not let you destroy her."

Jon stiffened at the cruelty of the words. "And if I refuse?"

"You won't. Remember Istanbul? I saved you from getting

a knife in your back. You owe me, and I'm calling in your marker."

"Bastard." Of course, he remembered Istanbul. The Serpent and his greed had almost landed Jon dead and would have, had Holt not saved his life.

"Maybe I am a bastard, but I protect what's mine."

Jon squeezed his eyes shut, willing the pounding in his head to still. *Julia needs the protection of your name because you have compromised her. Once she has that, you may consider your obligation fulfilled. Obligation fulfilled...obligation fulfilled. And if she's with child? It won't be your problem...won't be your problem.*

"Do you agree?" Holt asked, cutting into Jon's thoughts.

The movement was so minute, nothing more than a slight dip of his head, but he knew Holt had seen his response. Jon turned away, grabbed the bottle of whisky, and poured two fingers into his glass. He needed a good drunk right now. He'd lost too much this day—his friend, his freedom.

Julia.

He was not going to lose the blissful numbness that waited for him in the depths of the amber liquid. It couldn't heal him, but it sure as hell could make him forget for a while and that's what he needed right now. To forget. The pain in his bruised body would heal eventually, though his nose might have another crook to it. But the regret? Now that's what would eat at him long after the alcohol wore off.

Regret that he'd ever met *her*. He'd tasted her, touched her, made love to her and somehow, without his mind's knowledge or his heart's consent, opened up to her. There was no use denying it. She was inside of him now, a living, breathing part of him, and there wasn't a damn thing he could do about it. What did it matter? Their marriage would be a sham. And perhaps, one day, he would regret that most of all.

***

"He should've been here by now," Holt ground out, stabbing a piece of roast beef with his fork.

"It's only been a week. Besides, the wedding isn't for another four days. He'll be here," Sophie said, sympathy coating her words.

Julia kept her head bent but her eyes darted between her brother and sister-in-law and the small mountain of peas in front of her. *He wasn't coming. He hated her for what happened.* She dug her left hand into the fold of her gown.

"Two more days," Holt muttered. "Two more days and I'm going after him."

He couldn't even look at her when she left.

"He'll be here, darling," Sophie said. "Mmm," she murmured. "Aren't these peas delicious? So sweet and tender."

"If he doesn't show, I swear to God, I'll call the blackguard out."

"They really are quite good," Sophie went on as though Holt hadn't spoken.

"I'll find him," Holt vowed.

"With just a hint of crunchiness."

"He'll do his duty."

Sophie shoved a forkful of peas into her husband's open mouth. "Taste them, Holt," she ground out.

"Aggh," he choked, spewing several peas onto the white tablecloth. Sophie jumped from her chair and whacked him several times between the shoulder blades. "Sophie," he managed, "what the hell are you trying to do? Kill me?"

"Of course not, dear," she said, giving him one last whack. "But you've been so busy *talking,* you've barely touched your dinner."

Holt scowled and grabbed his water goblet. "Who would know where he's hiding?" he murmured.

Sophie let out an exasperated sigh.

Julia jabbed at the peas on her plate, smashing them into a pile of green mush. *Probably gone to the West Indies to be with one of his mistresses.* She picked up her knife and began shredding her roast beef. *She wished she could hate him.*

"He's still got four days. He'll be here," Sophie said, laying her hand on his arm and nodding toward Julia.

He ignored her silent plea and plowed forward, "He's got two days, Sophie. Two days to show himself." His hand shook as he grabbed a glass of claret and emptied it.

Julia studied the design on her plate. An array of smashed peas and shredded beef adorned the setting, creating a pattern of color and contrast. Interesting. She used her fork to trace a path through the green and brown concoction, swirling it around, mixing it together. Only a small spot of white and gold pattern remained visible on the plate, where three small boiled potatoes sat. Her fork attacked the little white balls, flattening them with quick, sure strokes. *Gone. Gone. Gone. And she didn't care*, she told herself, even as the lump in her throat grew larger.

"Julia!"

Her head snapped up.

"What in God's name are you doing?" Holt demanded.

Julia blinked. What had she been doing?

Thinking of Jon Remmington. She looked at the fork in her hand as though it belonged to someone else. She glanced at her plate and gasped at the brown heaps of chunky mush covering it.

Holt and Sophie stared at her as though she'd gone mad. She stared back at them, scooped up a forkful of the brown muck that resembled the contents of a chamber pot, and took a bite, pretending it was one of Mrs. Florence's finest preparations. Scooping another forkful, she smiled at her brother and sister-in-law and extended the fork. "Care to try any? It's actually quite tasty."

They shook their heads, eyes trained on her fork. Julia waved the utensil toward them and plopped its contents in her mouth.

"Mmm," she said as though it were a great delicacy.

Maybe she really was going crazy. Crazy wouldn't be so bad. At least then, she wouldn't *feel* anything. No disgrace over being considered "ruined." No humiliation when Jon didn't show up for their wedding. No despair over her lost dream of America. No sorrow for what might have been. But most of all, no pain for loving a man who would never love her.

* * *

There was no way out. Three bottles and four sleepless nights later, Jon accepted his fate. He had to marry Julia Langford. And then he had to leave her. Strangely enough, the latter part bothered him more.

He would have to walk away from her golden beauty, quick wit, and sunny smile. Forget those clear, gray eyes and full, pink lips. Pretend he'd never sampled the secret treasures of her delectable body, touched her silken curves, lost himself in her sweetness. He would have to erase her throaty laugh and gentle touch from his memory.

He would have to forget her. Jon berated himself for letting the little temptress break down his defenses. How had she done it? No one ever got close enough to cause him pain or grief, and yet, Julia had done both. Quickly. Thoroughly. Curse the witch. He needed another drink.

A knock at the door stilled his hand on the bottle.

"Come in," he rasped, his voice hoarse from too much drink.

That would be the maid, delivering another bottle. He listened as the footsteps crossed the plush golden carpet of the huge apartment he'd rented a few days before.

"Just put it on the sideboard next to the other one." Jon's words slurred and spilled over one another. He was slouched on the sofa, head flung back, eyes closed. The footsteps stopped directly in front of him. *Damn it, why couldn't he be left in peace?*

"Jon, my boy," Mac Judson said, his voice laced with equal amounts of concern and disgust. "What are you doing to yourself?"

Jon worked his left eye open and recognized the portly form of his longtime friend. "Celebrating my nuptials, Mac." His mouth turned up slightly at the corners. *Damn, but it hurt to*

103

smile. He really needed another drink. "And…and…" His mind blanked a second while he grasped for the word. "Recuperating. That's it," he drawled, the words moving over his tongue like tiny pebbles. "Re-cu-per-a-ting."

Mac shook his head and wrested the bottle from Jon's grasp. He set it on the table beside them and said, "Give it up, Jon. No more whisky."

"Just one more, Mac," Jon slurred. "Have one with me." He waved a hand at the bottle, then dropped it with a thump to his side. His head fell back farther into the cushions.

"No more." Mac's voice was firm. "You've got to pull yourself together. You haven't bathed or shaved since…" He hesitated. "Since Miss Julia left."

Jon jerked his head off the cushions, ignoring the splintering pain that shot through his brain. His good eye narrowed to a dark slit. "This has nothing to do with her," he lied. Not that he was willing to admit to anyone, anyway.

"It sure as hell does," Mac said, plopping down next to him. The force of his weight hitting the sofa jarred Jon's aching body and made him wince.

"Mac," he said on a ragged sigh. "My body's been beaten and bruised. My nose is most likely broken, and my right eye's almost swollen shut. Whisky eases the pain."

"To my way of thinking," Mac continued as though Jon hadn't spoken, "you could do a lot worse than Miss Julia. She's pretty, well spoken—"

"Mac," Jon warned.

"Charming, witty, graceful—"

"Enough."

"Sincere, caring—"

"Stop!"

Mac smiled, his blue eyes crinkling at the corners. "But you already know all that, don't you?"

Jon said nothing.

"Marry the girl and settle down. Raise a bunch of little ones." His smile disappeared. "Don't make the same mistake as me. The sea is a tempting mistress when you're a young buck like yourself, but time passes too quickly. In the blink of an eye, you're an old man with nothing but a hard bunk for a bed partner and a lifetime of regrets."

In all the years they'd been together, this was the first time Mac had ever hinted at regret. The tears in his eyes, the furrowed brow, the slumped shoulders spoke of loss. A woman was the cause of it. Damn all women.

"You don't understand." Jon rubbed the stubble on his chin. How long had it been since his last shave? Two days? Three?

"What's to understand?" Mac shot back, all traces of his earlier moroseness gone. "You bedded your best friend's sister. You marry her. Period." Jon's lack of response seemed to irk him. "I know you never wanted to get married, boy. But, like I said, you could have done worse. Remember that sheik's daughter a few years back? The one who hid in your bed? We were lucky to get out of there alive."

"I never touched her."

"Didn't matter," Mac said, pulling out his pipe and tobacco. "Point is, we all know you *did* touch Miss Julia. Holt just wants you to do right by her." He lit his pipe and took a puff. "So marry her." He puffed again. "Have a passel of kids. Golden-haired ones with big gray eyes." Another puff. "Be happy." Puff. Puff.

"Enough!" Jon slammed his hand on the sofa. He didn't want to hear any more about what he should or shouldn't do. "I never said I wasn't going to marry her."

Mac blinked. "So." He paused. "You are going to marry her." It was as much a statement as a question.

Jon nodded once, keeping his eyes fixed on a small gold vase in the corner of the room.

"Good." Mac puffed on his pipe again. "And that's the problem?" he guessed.

"She'll be mine in name only," Jon said, refusing to meet Mac's questioning gaze. "After the wedding, I disappear from her life. Holt's got it all worked out." The words came out brittle as old bones. "He saved my life. I owe him." He raked a hand through his hair. "She'll think I deserted her."

"Jesus," Mac whispered, his pipe resting on his knee, long forgotten. He spied the whisky bottle sitting on the table and grabbed it, throwing his head back for a long, healthy swallow. When he was finished, he wiped his mouth with the back of his hand and thrust the bottle at Jon.

Jon brought the bottle to his lips and savored the burn traveling down his throat. It was his cure, albeit temporary, from the pain that festered and swelled inside. One day, it would ooze out, but not now. Not today.

"Jon?" Mac accepted the proffered bottle and took another swallow. "Are you saying you *want* to marry Miss Julia?"

Jon looked away.

"Sweet Jesus, you *do* want to marry her," Mac whispered, tilting his head back and chugging more amber liquid.

"It doesn't matter," Jon spat out, a muscle twitching in his jaw. God, but the whisky wasn't working fast enough. "I've given my word. After the wedding, Julia will never see me again."

***

Two days and several bottles of whisky later, Jon sent a message to Holt, confirming their *meeting* two days hence. He couldn't bring himself to say *wedding*. Probably because it wasn't really a wedding. It was more of a farce than anything else. A great big facade to protect Julia Langford's reputation. As though she cared what polite society might say.

Jon smiled at that. She'd begged her brother not to force the marriage. His smile disappeared as he recalled her mournful words and the incessant pleading. His mouth curved downward. She really *didn't* want to marry him. That fact amazed him, considering the bevy of females around the world who would do anything to become Mrs. Jon Remmington—lie, cheat, play the whore or the sophisticate—whatever it took to trap him.

But not Julia. What would she say when she discovered she

had a husband in name only? After Holt told her his twisted version of Jon's wedding terms, she'd feel hurt and betrayed. Anger would set in, red-hot, searing anger, wrapping itself around her, tighter and tighter, choking out all feeling except one. Hatred for the husband who deserted her.

An unbidden thought crept into his mind, clutched his gut, tore at his soul. Did Julia harbor any tender feelings toward him at all? Affection? Warmth? Perhaps a hint of love? He cursed and called himself a thousand kinds of fool. What good would it do to torment himself with games and guessing?

He'd given his word, and he meant to honor it. There were a few minor details to take care of, and then he'd leave. Glenview Manor, the country estate he'd inherited from his uncle ten years ago, sat in readiness, awaiting its new mistress. It was nestled in a small village about two hours' riding distance from Holt and would afford Julia a certain amount of independence.

Jon's man, Billington, had overseen the tidying up of the place, and his last report two days ago indicated the staff was eager and ready to meet the new Mrs. Remmington. Jon and the tall, lanky Englishman had been conducting business for more years than he could remember. Billington was a most discreet man who rarely smiled or showed emotion of any kind. He hadn't even batted an eye when Jon gave him his latest assignment: spy on the future Mrs. Remmington.

It would be easy enough. Billington would pose as the butler of Glenview Manor and track Julia's comings and goings. Once a month, he'd send a report to Jon at his last known address. If there was any threat to Julia's health or welfare, Billington was to enlist a special messenger to locate Jon. Immediately. Not that Jon thought it would be necessary. The most upheaval he expected to disturb the quiet, staid existence at Glenview Manor would be a stray animal on the grounds. Perhaps a deer or fox.

Or a Serpent. A dark, faceless form emerged, shattering his thoughts into hundreds of fragmented, terrifying possibilities.

Peter Crowlton. If he were still alive, Julia would be in grave danger. Jon yanked at his cravat, trying to loosen it, but the folds of cloth wrapped around him like a snake.

Why did Jon continue to drive himself mad with a mission that was over years ago? God help him, he'd even thought for a time Julia might be a spy. Which showed how cloudy his judgment had become. She was no more capable of spying than Holt's cook.

Holt believed Peter Crowlton was dead. He'd been fairly adamant about it. The Crown thought so, too. Why after seven years could Jon still not accept the traitor's death and let go of the past?

Because there had been no body.

Jon squeezed his eyes shut, trying to still the clamoring in his head. Crowlton had always been the reason Jon never announced his arrival when he made his periodic visits to Glenview Manor. He came in the night and left the same way, shrouded in a cloud of mystery and intrigue. The servants at the manor were loyal and dedicated carryovers from his uncle's days, their families having served generations of Remmingtons. They never questioned their master's odd comings and goings, nor did they share gossip with the neighboring estates. It was one of Jon's few demands and for all of his generosity, that request seemed a meager exchange.

Soon, he would entrust Julia into the capable hands of his staff. He would not let his mind torment him with visions of Peter Crowlton slithering into his thoughts any longer. The Serpent was dead, most likely a bag of bones lying in an unmarked grave. In seven years, there had been no sign of the man other than in the dark imaginings of Jon's brain. It was time to move out of the shadows of his life, time to stop looking behind him at every turn. He would slay The Serpent in his mind—swiftly, surely. Permanently.

The vision of a faceless Peter Crowlton, clad in black, glided toward him, stopping mere inches from him. Jon raised his sword, wielding the shiny blade high over his head as he prepared the blow. The Serpent struck out, wrapped his hands around Jon's neck, and squeezed. The sword came down with a loud thwack, splitting open the back of Crowlton's skull. Blood spurted everywhere; The Serpent fell back, his hands sliding from Jon's neck as he slithered to the ground.

Jon smiled and opened his eyes. He'd slain his worst nightmare; The Serpent was dead.

***

Julia stood before the full-length mirror staring at a woman who seemed more ready for a funeral than a wedding. She might be dressed in an empire-cut satin gown with rows and rows of tiny seed pearls adorning it and more pearls scattered in her upswept hair, but her face held no joy. No sparkle. No smile.

A slight rap at the door interrupted her thoughts.

"Come in."

Sophie entered in a swirl of gold and mauve brilliance. Julia glanced at her sister-in-law through the mirror and managed a weak smile. She looked beautiful as usual, in her elegant gown, with her auburn hair piled high atop her head and her emerald eyes sparkling. Holt was very lucky to have her for a wife, and he treated her like a queen.

But of course, *they* loved each other. She blinked several times.

"Julia, are you all right? Is something in your eye?"

Julia blinked again and sniffed. *Yes,* she wanted to scream. *Something was in her eye! And in her heart, and in her soul, and in her very being. And it was called pain. Pure pain, so deep and real, it knocked the breath from her. And it was all because she loved a man who did not love her, who would never love her.* Instead of uttering the unbearable truth, she murmured, "I think I may have gotten something in my eye, but I'll be fine." She placed her fingertips to the corners of her eyes and pressed gently. "There. All better."

"You look beautiful."

"Thank you."

"I wish you had consented to a real wedding dress, not just an elaborate ball gown."

They'd been through this before. "It wasn't necessary to go to all the trouble."

"But it's your *wedding,*" Sophie said, sounding so sad that Julia wanted to comfort *her*.

"A gown doesn't make a wedding. Nor does a vow make a marriage."

"Give him a chance. Jon's a wonderful man. He's just in a bit of a shock right now."

"He hates me. I lied and deceived him and because of it, he's forced to marry me." Her bottom lip quivered. "When I tried to tell him how sorry I was, he wouldn't even look at me."

Sophie placed her hands on Julia's shoulders and said in a soft voice, "Things *will* work out. Look at Holt and me. If you recall, we didn't exactly have a smooth go of it early on." Her emerald eyes darkened as though remembering less pleasant times.

"You're being too kind to my brother. He was an utter fool, and I thought he'd never come to his senses."

"At least he had sense enough to get rid of that odious man I was supposed to marry."

"And conveniently fill in as the groom," Julia added, recalling Sophie's wedding day.

"Yes, well, that was convenient of him, I must say. But I would have much preferred to discover my future husband's identity *before* I walked down the aisle."

Julia smiled.

"There's a girl," Sophie whispered. "Things will work out. Truly."

"I wish I could believe that." She turned to her sister-in-law. "Sometimes I think it would almost be better if I were marrying someone who'd been..." She hesitated over the word. "*Selected* for me." Seeing the surprised look on Sophie's face, Julia pressed on, before she lost her nerve. "That way, both parties would know the rules; there would be no expectations or disappointments. Everything would be understood. With Jon, nothing is understood."

"You love him, don't you?"

"Is it that obvious?"

"To me it is. You once said you never wanted to marry. Yet your whole concern these past several days has been for Jon. Would he blame you for the forced marriage? Would he forgive you? Would he hate you? Would he ever love you? Not once did you say, I don't want to marry the man."

"But I really didn't want to—before," Julia said, puzzled at Sophie's words. There was truth in what she said. Julia hadn't fought the marriage since she left Jon's ship. Why? The question floated through her mind, slowly at first, then faster, gathering momentum and spinning like a top before crashing with a loud thud. Out of the wreckage emerged the answer, clear and true.

She loved him, loved the glimpses of honesty and vulnerability he'd shown. No man, not even Holt, had ever forced her to accept responsibility for her actions the way Jon had. He understood her.

"But you want to marry him now?" Sophie prompted in a soft voice, clasping Julia's cold hands.

"Yes," Julia admitted, full of equal parts awe and despair. "Yes, I do, despite our differences." A tiny shred of hope unraveled with her words. "Oh, Sophie, do you really think we could have a chance?"

"Absolutely," Sophie assured her, squeezing her hand. "Who knows, one day he may even take you to America."

***

"Damn you, Jon, that was an underhanded thing to do," Holt barked.

Jon took care to keep his expression blank. It wouldn't do to let Holt see how important this was to him. "I'm a man of means. My wealth at least equals yours and I want to provide for my 'wife' as befits a Remmington. That includes setting up a household."

Holt stood. "That wasn't part of the deal."

"It wasn't part of *your* deal," Jon corrected. "I always intended to provide for Julia." He shoved his hands in the pockets of his black trousers. "It's the very least I can do."

"I want her to remain with us," Holt said, his voice rising. "She'll need time to adjust."

"Exactly," Jon cut in, his tone sharper than he'd intended. "And exactly how will she adjust when she's a married woman, with an absent husband, living in her brother's home?" Jon shot him a look of disgust. "It's a pathetic situation and don't think Julia won't feel it the first time the gossipmongers come around to get a glimpse of *Mr*. Remmington. What are you going to do? Fight off each one single-handedly until the last old lady lies in a heap at your feet, with your sword through her heart?"

Holt's cold look would have made a lesser man cower. Jon squared his shoulders and said, "She deserves some independence. Let her go." When Holt didn't respond, Jon forgot his vow to hold his emotions in check. "How can you be that insensitive to the woman? Can't you leave her some measure of pride? She'll have a household to run in the country. Great expanses of land to roam and garden and ride her horse." He stopped a moment to catch his breath. "She'll be free of both of us. We've got to let her go," he finished quietly. He shifted his weight from one leg to the other, avoiding those watchful eyes that saw too much. He hadn't meant to give Holt any reason to become suspicious of his true feelings for Julia. Hell, he hadn't meant to act as though he cared so much—but he did care.

And it was becoming increasingly difficult to pretend he didn't.

"Let her go, Holt," Jon repeated, his words a soft command.

Holt opened his mouth to speak, hesitated, then closed it. Had he guessed his friend's true feelings? Small beads of sweat popped out on Jon's forehead. He was hot, too hot with all these formal clothes on. Wedding clothes. His wedding.

"She may go," Holt said, then turned and walked to the oak sideboard to pour a whisky.

Jon let out a long breath, unaware he'd even been holding it. Had Holt noticed? It wouldn't do to let him think he had the upper hand where Julia was concerned. Jon pulled a gold watch piece from his pocket and glanced at the time. In fifteen minutes, he'd meet his bride. He snapped the lid shut and stuffed the piece back in his vest pocket.

Fifteen more minutes. The tiny box containing Julia's wedding ring shifted in his right trouser pocket. The ring had been in the Remmington family for years, a gift given him by his grandmother on his last visit to Virginia. Would Julia wear it after he was gone?

Anxious for a few minutes alone, Jon headed for the doors. He'd wait in the green salon until the ceremony began. He wanted quiet and a reprieve from Holt's watchful eyes.

His hand was on the knob when Holt's voice reached him.

"Jon?"

"Yes?" He paused but didn't turn around. *Here it comes.*

"Forget about Julia. You can't have her."

"I know." Jon tried to ignore the tightness in his chest. *But would he ever stop wanting her?*

"Tomorrow, you'll sail out of here and into the arms of Monique or Isabel or even Desiree, and Julia will be less than a memory," Holt said matter-of-factly.

"And if she isn't?" Jon asked, unable to stop himself.

"A vague memory at best." Holt continued as though Jon hadn't spoken.

"And what do I do," Jon asked, clutching the doorknob until his knuckles turned white, "when that memory haunts me, day and night, until it becomes more real than life itself? When the only peace I find will be in and through that memory? When nothing and no one will soothe me but that memory?"

Jon didn't wait for a reply. Instead, he flung open the oak door and strode down the hallway and toward the green salon, leaving his future brother-in-law staring after him.

Chapter 9

"And do you, Julia Elizabeth Langford, take this man, Jon Alexander Remmington…"

Julia wished Jon would look at her, acknowledge her presence at least, but other than a brief nod when she'd first entered the room, he'd said nothing. "Julia?" Father Gerard's gentle voice reached her through her distress.

"I do," she said, hazarding a quick glance at Jon. He stood tall and proud, looking straight ahead, much like a soldier doing his duty.

It had seemed a lifetime ago since they'd been together. She feasted her eyes on him, from his blackened eye and broken nose to the sleek lines of his cutaway jacket and polished shoes. She wanted to place soft kisses all over his battered and bruised face, clasp his strong hands to her heart, brush that ever-errant lock of dark hair from his forehead.

She wanted to be his wife. Sophie had said to be patient. Jon would come around. Julia hoped that was true.

"Jon Alexander Remmington," Father Gerard continued, "do you take this woman, Julia Elizabeth Langford…"

When Father Gerard finished, Julia held her breath.

"I do," Jon said, his voice strong and steady. Almost as though he meant it. *Had* he meant those two little words that possessed the power to change their lives forever?

Father Gerard smiled. "You may place the ring on her finger." Julia held out her hand as Jon pulled a small velvet box from his pocket and flipped the top open.

The priest continued. "Now place the ring on Julia's finger and repeat after me…"

Jon removed the sapphire and diamond band from its case and grasped Julia's hand. A tingle ran along her skin where his warm fingers touched hers. He looked at her then, his dark eyes burning into her, through her, marking her with their heat. His grip on her hand tightened, pulling her closer, their bodies almost touching.

Holt cleared his throat and the spell shattered. Jon tore his gaze away and placed the ring on her finger. "With this ring, I thee wed," he repeated, his voice hard and distant. His grip loosened and he stepped away, leaving a respectable distance between them. Gone was the man with the hungry eyes of a moment ago, replaced once again with the polite stranger.

"I now pronounce you man and wife." Father Gerard smiled. "You may kiss the bride."

Will he choose a peck on the cheek or a kiss on the hand? Jon faced her and stepped forward, his dark eyes locking with hers. He placed his hands on either side of her face and leaned forward slowly. It seemed an eternity before his lips touched hers, feather-soft at first and then deeper, with more urgency. Julia opened her mouth under his gentle coaxing, meshed her tongue with his and gloried in the low groan that escaped from him. He pulled her close, their bodies molded to one another, his arousal pressing hard and urgent against her belly. She moaned. *He wanted her.*

Her moan turned to a shocked gasp as strong arms thrust her away, breaking the kiss. Her eyes flew open to find Jon staring at her, his breathing deep and uneven. He'd pushed her away? It would have been less humiliating if Holt had been the one to pull them apart. Or even Father Gerard, though the stout, old priest would have been hard-pressed to complete the task. But Jon? Nothing could be more humiliating than to be tossed aside by one's husband, at one's own wedding ceremony, no less.

How dare he make her want him so and then cast her aside like a bit of useless baggage? Anger seethed through her, as hot and pulsing as the desire had been moments before. She would show him what real humiliation felt like.

Father Gerard cleared his throat. "We need only sign the register and everything will be official."

"Fine," Jon said, motioning Julia to follow the priest.

"Fine," Julia huffed. "And when we're through, I'd like a word with you." She squared her shoulders. "In private."

If she weren't so furious, she might have laughed. The look

on his face was truly priceless. One might have thought she'd asked him to lay a golden egg. He was avoiding her and she was determined to find out why.

"Oh, Julia," Sophie crooned, coming up behind her as Julia turned away from the register. "You make such a beautiful bride. Doesn't she, Jon?" she asked, gracing him with a dazzling smile.

"Yes, she's beautiful," Jon said cautiously, as though the words were dragged from him, one letter at a time. Why did his acknowledgment sound more like a confession than a compliment?

"And so are you, my dear," Holt cut in, draping an arm over his wife's shoulders.

"If you'll both excuse us," Julia said, clasping Jon's arm. "My husband and I have some very pressing, private matters to discuss."

Holt raised a brow. "Oh?"

"Yes, Holt, you heard me correctly. I haven't seen him in days." She tapped her foot with growing impatience. "Eleven to be exact and we have much that needs to be discussed." Julia turned to leave, attempting to tug Jon with her. It would have been easier to move a mountain.

"I think it would be rude to desert family right now," Jon said, his voice cold and impersonal.

"Really? Then is it not also rude to desert one's betrothed until the wedding day, arriving mere minutes before the ceremony is to begin?" A dull flush crept up Jon's face, blending with the purple and blue bruises that already marked it. Was that a flush of embarrassment or anger?

"I was detained," Jon said, flashing a look at Holt.

Oh. Detained. As with a mistress, no doubt. She wanted to blacken his other eye. Well, there would be no more mistresses. She clenched her hand in the folds of her gown. She didn't care if mistresses were widely accepted among her class; she would not share her husband with anyone.

"Go with her, Jon," Sophie coaxed. "We'll see you at seven

for supper."

Jon and Holt exchanged looks and Julia swore Holt shook his head. Before she could think on it further, Jon turned and headed for the doorway, practically dragging her behind him.

***

"Now, madame wife," Jon said, closing Julia's bedroom door. "What is so pressing that you require my immediate attention?" He turned the lock. In less than five minutes, he'd have her running from the room. "Or is it that you can't wait to lie beneath me again?" Make that four minutes.

"How did you guess?" She moved toward him and ran her slender fingers down his arms.

"What do you think you're doing?" He stepped back. She followed him, reaching for his neck cloth, loosening the folds. Jon grabbed her hands. "Stop it, Julia."

She offered him a siren's smile full of sensual promise. Did she know what she was doing to him?

"I've missed you," she whispered, pressing her body close. He took another step back, trying to get away from her softness, and bumped into a large mahogany dresser. Julia raised her head and ran her tongue slowly along her upper lip. "Why have you been ignoring me?" she purred.

"Stop it." He grabbed her arms and set her away from him. Didn't she understand he *couldn't* look at her, not without wanting her in a most primitive, elemental way? Right now, he wanted nothing more than to throw her on the bed, toss up her skirts, and bury himself deep in her woman's heat. One more joining with her, hot and explosive, to carry him through the long, cold nights ahead. But it wouldn't be enough. It would never be enough.

The scent of lilac smothered him and thoughts of Julia floated through his mind, teasing and taunting him with her golden beauty and soft laughter. But the living, breathing Julia was something else altogether. She made his pulse quicken and his body throb.

"Make love to me," she whispered.

Her breath tickled his neck. Dear God, but he wanted her. Badly. When she placed her hand on the bulge in his pants, he almost exploded. "No!" He pulled back and turned away, his breath coming in great gulps as he tried to steady himself. *Control. Stay in control.* "I'm sorry," he said quietly, turning to face her.

"No," she whispered, shaking her head, her shoulders slumping forward. "I'm the one who should apologize. I tried to tempt you, make you want me as I've wanted you every night since you left." Her gaze slipped to the carpet. "Then I was going to reject you."

"Why?" He had to know.

"I wanted you to feel the pain of wanting and not having." She sniffed. "But it doesn't matter now. The joke was on me all along." Another sniff. "You have to care about something in order to want it, and it's more than obvious you don't."

"Don't what?" Jon asked, stalling. He wanted nothing more than to gather her in his arms and comfort her, but he couldn't. He thrust his hands in his pockets.

His response irritated her. She squared her shoulders like an angry golden goddess and bit out, "Don't care about or want *me*."

"I can't want you." He willed her to understand something he himself did not.

"Hah," she said. "You were too busy with your mistresses to even think about wanting me. That's it, isn't it?" She balled her fists, placing them on her hips. "Of course," she rushed on. "You went straight into the arms of Desiree or Monique or whatever her name is and—" She stopped midsentence. "It's Desiree *and* Monique, isn't it?"

"There've been no other women," Jon said quietly.

"You have two mistresses!"

"No one since you."

"Or do you have more than two?" Her eyes narrowed. "I heard your men talking. They mentioned more than one name." She crossed her arms and tapped her foot. Was she waiting for an *explanation?* Jon sighed. The woman was acting the shrew already, and they hadn't even been married an hour. He'd love to tell her she was spilling out of her gown with her arms crossed that way but thought better of it. This was the woman who'd toppled him with a pitcher at The Fox's Tail.

"I want to know their names," she demanded.

Jon's curiosity got the better of him. "For what purpose?"

"So I may pen them each a note and tell them their services are no longer required."

Jon stifled a laugh. If she were going to pen each of his women a note, she had better begin immediately and perhaps in three weeks' time she'd complete the task. He smiled. Julia would kill him if he mentioned that fact.

"I should like a meeting with Mac Judson. He can provide me with details such as addresses and the like."

"I'll be sure to mention that to him." Mac would roar with laughter.

"And," she added peevishly, "you may discard those items of women's clothing in your cabin. They are much too large for me and in extremely poor taste."

"Yes, m'lady." He liked Julia better naked, anyway.

"Good," she finished, cocking her head to one side. "I think you should know I'll not share you with other women."

"Oh?" He was enjoying this game. Too bad it wasn't for real. A sharp pain stabbed his gut. He'd even tolerate the shrewish part. Anything, if he could be with her.

"No. I will not," she said, her full lips pulling into a straight line.

"Julia," Jon said, his smile fading. Every minute that ticked away brought him closer to leaving her. "There have been no women since I met you."

"No one?"

He shook his head.

"Why?"

"Why?"

"Yes," she said, tapping her foot again. "Why have there

been no other women? It's obvious that you're a very—" her eyes darted to his groin "—virile man."

Jon's lips twitched. "Thank you."

A crimson flush spread slowly from her neck to the roots of her golden hair. "You have quite a reputation with women. It would not be out of character for you to have seen one of them at some point during the last eleven days."

Jon fought to keep a smile from his face. His expression remained bland as he responded, "Perhaps none of them appealed to me."

"None of them?" she asked, looking astonished.

"Perhaps none compared to you, fair wife." The words slipped out, but the truth had a way of doing that sometimes.

"Must you make fun of me? Can't you see I am humiliated enough having to ask about your mistresses?" Julia's chin flew up two notches.

He sobered. "I spoke the truth."

"But you don't want me. You said so yourself." Her voice held a mixture of confusion and irritation.

"I said I *couldn't* want you. Not that I didn't want you." His gentle words reached out to her, offering a soothing balm for all the words he couldn't speak. "I know it makes little sense to you, but believe this, Julia," he said, grasping her hands. "I have *wanted* you since the day I first laid eyes on you and I've never stopped wanting you. I have been fighting with myself since you walked into the salon today, trying not to touch you." He stepped closer, unaware he'd moved. "Trying not to want you." He touched her hair, silky and soft, shining like spun gold laced with pearls.

"But why?"

He frowned. "Because I would only hurt you and I'd do anything to spare you that." A surge of protectiveness shot through him, startling him in its intensity. *He would protect his wife. Even from himself.* "No matter what happens or how circumstances may indicate otherwise, I will always want you." He stroked her cheek, willing her to understand. "Always," he repeated. "Remember that."

"Oh, Jon," she murmured, "I love you." She smiled, a little shy smile, like a child giving a homemade gift, uncertain if the receiver will accept it. "I have loved you for so very long."

Jon touched her cheek, his insides raw and aching as her words pierced him deeper than Holt's blows. "No, Julia. You can't love me."

"But I do," she said, smiling again, tears glistening in her large eyes. "Love me, Jon," she whispered, rising on tiptoe to brush a kiss across his lips.

He would always love her. He was losing the battle with his conscience. All the reinforcements were turning into casualties, along with his first line of defense that had been good intentions and honor. Jon slipped fast into the abyss of love and desire. He wanted Julia with a depth of feeling that left him breathless and shaking. One more attempt. Integrity emerged from the reserves to make one final valiant effort.

"You'll hate me tomorrow," Jon said, his voice low and ragged as he tried to fight the butterfly kisses landing on his lips, his chin, his neck.

"I could never hate you," Julia whispered. She ran her tongue along his neck, sucking gently. Integrity fell to its knees, shattered by an explosion of desire.

"God, help me, I can't fight you anymore." Jon crushed his mouth to hers, plunging his tongue inside, stroking, sucking, mating with hers. His hands moved over her body like a starving man, feeding on the satin skin against his callused fingers. He lifted her gown, grazing his fingertips along her thigh, kneading and stroking her buttocks, trying to absorb all of her.

It had to last him a lifetime. He worked his way to the bed, worshipping her mouth with his tongue, her body with his hands. He followed her onto the counterpane, pressing his body against hers.

He was moving too fast. He should savor the sensations, but she felt so damn good. He burned where she touched him, leaving a hot trail of aching need where her fingers had been. If he didn't slow down soon, he'd spill his seed before he got his clothes off.

Julia moaned, a pure sound of pleasure as her fingers explored beneath his shirt. She stroked his back with her nails, exciting him with her touch. Her hands played over his buttocks, grabbing and kneading, pulling him closer.

She jerked her hips up, a pure involuntary reaction, Jon was certain, but a silent plea to join their bodies. *Patience. Think of Julia.* His sex throbbed. *No, don't think of Julia. Think of her pleasure.* He almost exploded. *Correction. Think of anything but Julia.*

She moved again. This time, the movement was slow, determined, and damned exciting. Too exciting. The little witch knew what she was doing now.

"Jon," she whispered. "Love me." Her throaty words hurled him to a place where nothing remained but sensation. Pure sensation, wild and primitive. He wanted to lose himself in the touch of her satin skin beneath his fingertips, the sound of her low moans dying in his mouth. He wanted to revel in her innocent beauty as she reached her woman's pleasure, bury himself in the lilac scent that covered her body.

He wanted her and, God forgive him, he had to have her. Now. He eased himself off of her, lifted her gown to her hips, and pulled down her pantaloons. She lay before him, bare, exposed, and beautiful. He tore at the buttons on his trousers and his sex sprang free.

Bending over Julia, he spread her legs wide and stroked her silky thighs, easing them farther apart. She lay like a goddess, half clothed in golden beauty. He climbed onto the bed and knelt between her legs, lifting them high, placing them on his shoulders. Her eyes widened in confusion but when he stroked the back of her legs, the confusion turned to delight. She moaned and he thrust into her, burying himself deep inside.

She raised her hips to meet his driving need, clutched his forearms, and breathed his name. Her face shone with pure pleasure as he worked her body, fast then slow, then faster still.

"Julia," Jon rasped, unable to bear much more of the sweet agony. He plunged into her twice more, deep and hard, reaching for the very center of her. Julia cried out as her body convulsed against him. He drove into her one more time, groaning her name as he poured himself into her.

Julia evoked the need in him to protect, to cherish, to love. He pulled her close and drifted off to sleep as one final thought flitted through his brain. *Julia Remmington. His wife.* He smiled.

***

A short while later, Jon stood, fully dressed, looking down at his wife's sleeping form. She lay curled on her side, cocooned in the mauve counterpane, golden hair tangled and loose, a slim ankle peeking from beneath the heavy material. A sleeping beauty in wanton disarray. If only she could stay nestled in dreams and ignorance, she'd never discover the heartache that awaited when her slumber ended.

Jon frowned. He would not regret what happened between them in this bed. She'd touched him as no woman had ever touched him before. He'd needed to feel that closeness, if only one more time. Damn honor. Damn integrity. Damn Holt Langford.

He leaned over to touch the cascade of golden hair fanning her head like a crown. The scent of lilac drew him in, tantalizing him with memories. Jon's hand hovered mere inches from her head before he withdrew it.

"I love you," he whispered to her sleeping form. "I love you, Julia Remmington."

Then he was gone.

***

Julia emerged from slumber, stretching like a cat basking in the sun on a lazy afternoon. Twilight filtered through the half-drawn ivory curtains, casting shadows on the bed.

The bed. Heat rushed over her face as she recalled what had transpired there. With Jon. Her body tingled in response.

Where was he? Probably downstairs with Holt and Sophie. Holt hadn't looked too pleased earlier when she'd announced she wanted a private word with her husband. Actually, his expression was rather fierce, almost downright hostile. She sighed and tossed back the counterpane. The two of them had better settle their differences because Jon was her husband now and would be for a long while. She smiled at the thought as she sat up and began brushing at the wrinkles in her gown, suddenly very anxious to see him again.

***

A quarter of an hour later, Julia emerged from her bedchamber and descended the staircase. She forced herself to slow her step. It wouldn't do to let her new husband know how much she wanted to see him. Or Holt, for that matter. Her brother might have forced the marriage, but he wasn't overly thrilled with his best friend marrying his sister.

"Lady Julia, may I help you?" someone squeaked out behind her.

Julia whirled around to find Pierce, the butler, staring down at her. All six-foot-five of his lanky self. Julia liked the new butler and not just because he happened to be Mrs. Florence's nephew. Matthew Pierce was about her age, well-mannered and very serious about his position. She sent him a smile that turned his pale face ten different shades of red.

"Actually, I'm looking for Mr. Remmington. Could you tell me where he might be?"

Pierce turned redder still. Magenta? Yes, that was the color, spreading from his long neck to his ears.

"M-M-Mister Remmington isn't here," he managed, as though someone were choking the words out of him.

"Oh." Disappointment clouded her good mood. Where had he gone? When would he be back? It wouldn't do to quiz poor Pierce. Next he'd pass out in front of her and that wouldn't bode well for him. A vision of Pierce's lanky form thudding to the ground came to mind. He would block a good portion of the hallway and the dining room door, depending on how he landed. Julia stifled a giggle. His arms and legs would flail out, navy waistcoat askew. Holt would find no humor in the young man's body sprawled on the floor; of that she was certain. Her brother could be such a stickler at times and she didn't want to do anything to jeopardize Pierce's new position with the family.

"B-b-but," he stammered, "the earl and Lady Sophie are in the dining room."

"Excellent." She patted him on the arm and smiled again, hoping the gestures wouldn't send him into a fit of apoplexy.

Pierce cleared his throat once. Twice. Three times. "Will there be anything else, Lady Julia?" he asked, his blue eyes darting around the room, fixing on a sight directly behind her right ear. Why wasn't he looking at her? The color in his face had settled to a dusty rose. Thank goodness for that. Poor Pierce seemed quite undone tonight.

"No, thank you, Pierce. That will be all." Julia turned toward the dining room door. She breezed into the room with a smile. This day had turned out far better than she could have hoped. A new husband, a new beginning. Now, all she had to do was find that husband.

"Julia."

She shook herself out of her musings and threw her sister-in-law a bright smile. "Hello, Sophie. Hello, Holt." Her eyes lit on the roast duck sitting amidst bowls of peas and potatoes and corn pudding. And asparagus soup. Her heart did a little flip when she spotted the tureen of green soup.

"I'm famished," she announced, plopping herself in the seat next to Holt. "Asparagus soup. My favorite." She giggled and cast a sideways glance at Sophie.

Apparently, Sophie found no humor in her words, for her sister-in-law sat very still, staring at her plate, her beautiful face as stoic as a soldier heading to battle.

Perhaps she'd forgotten the incident with Jon and the asparagus soup. Well, Julia would never forget it, not the shocked look on his face or the splattered green on his white shirt. She stifled another giggle and glanced in Holt's direction. What was the matter now? His eyes were on her, hard and cool as ice. She was tempted to stick out her tongue or cross her eyes, anything to get a reaction from him. He was not going to ruin her wedding day. Oh, no, she would not let him be an old spoilsport about this marriage business. The sooner he got used to the idea that Jon was her husband, the better for all of them.

"I must thank you, Holt," she said casually, filling her bowl. "If it hadn't been for your insistence, I never would have married Jon." Julia picked up her spoon. "I do believe it will all work out for the best," she added, leaning over to nibble on a tiny piece of asparagus.

"Julia." Holt's deep voice washed over her with its intensity. "There's something I need to tell you."

Tiny alarms rang in her brain, signaling a warning, but she refused to heed them. Holt never failed to lecture her about something, feed her some bad piece of news, and then offer his advice. She scooped more soup into her mouth. Like an oldest brother, or an earl, or head of the household, of which he was all three. Well, not this time. Her spoon scraped the bottom of the bowl. He would not ruin this day for her because she vowed not to listen to his dismal, doomsayer voice again.

"It concerns Jon."

There was that voice again but she was not listening to it. She grabbed a golden biscuit and took a big bite.

"He's gone."

She stuffed more biscuit into her mouth, heedless of the crumbs tumbling onto her lap. *Gone?* She refused to listen to that voice because it had just said her husband, the man she loved, was gone. Something wet touched her cheeks. Tears. Why was she crying? She didn't believe those horrible words Holt had just spoken. Another tear slipped down her cheek.

"I'm sorry, Julia. It will be better this way." Holt touched her shoulder and she jumped. How had he gotten there? When had he moved?

"Oh, Julia," Sophie sobbed. "I'm so sorry." Weeping swept

through the background like music to a play with a tragic ending.

"Damn him," Holt muttered, under his breath. "I thought he told you. I thought you knew."

His words kept coming, pounding against her brain like a crazed messenger demanding entry. Slowly, against her will, meaning penetrated her body, seeped through her veins. Jon was gone. When? Where? *Why?* The questions spun in her head like a child's top, twirling aimlessly. Squeezing her eyes shut, she willed away the questions, willed away the soft sobs of her sister-in-law and the cold words of her brother. *Jon had planned to leave? It was part of an agreement?*

That couldn't be true. The man who'd looked at her so tenderly, touched her so deeply, loved her so passionately, could not have done so knowing he would leave her forever when he left her bed.

Julia tasted blood and lifted her hand to her lips. She stared at the faint red splotches on her fingertips. Blood. The blood was real. The tears that streamed down her face were real. Holt's words were real. Everything about this whole horrible scene was real.

She bent her head and let grief invade her body, fill her with the pain of betrayal and love lost as understanding stamped out denial. Her cries echoed a soulful mourning over hopes and dreams, lying like burnt offerings in the charred ashes of deceit. A huge gaping hole lay in the middle of her heart. A gift from her husband.

Strong arms tried to pull her from the pain of her grief but it was too late. As welcoming darkness called her, she gave herself up to its bliss and drifted into blackness.

Chapter 10

"I've had it, Sophie. I'm calling the doctor." Holt's words floated to Julia through her bedroom door in sharp, angry tones.

What had she done now?

"Give her a little more time. It's only been a day," Sophie said.

"One day too long if she's mourning over that good-for-nothing bastard."

Who were they talking about?

"Holt! How can you speak that way about a man who has been your best friend for years?"

A heaviness settled in the middle of Julia's chest as she realized who they were discussing.

"He's no longer my friend."

A brooding face with eyes the color of French chocolate floated through Julia's mind. She stamped out the vision.

"People make mistakes. Have you forgotten the early days of our relationship?" Sophie asked. "You left me as well."

Julia squeezed her eyes shut.

"That was different," Holt pointed out. "I loved you."

A tear trickled down Julia's cheek.

"Hah!" she scoffed. "I see your memory has failed you, dear husband."

"Sophie," Holt warned.

"One day, you *will* need to settle things with Jon," Sophie said. "If for no one else's sake than your own."

There was that name she was trying so hard to forget.

"And if he never returns? What then?" The challenge of her brother's words smothered Julia and she burrowed deeper under the covers, blocking out Sophie's response, blocking out the world as she descended once again into darkness.

***

Julia's room was awash with light. She sensed it, even though her eyes remained closed. Why was she still abed when the sun peeking through the draperies hinted it must be late morning? She should have been up by now, roaming the hills and enjoying the countryside with her mare.

"Julia?" a voice called from the other side of the bed.

She moved her head with the speed of a tortoise, her body weighted down by some inexplicable force that seeped energy from her bones. With great effort, she opened her eyes.

"Oh, thank God," Sophie cried, clasping Julia's hands. "Thank God you're finally awake."

"Julia? Are you all right?" Holt rose from his chair to stand beside the bed. His handsome face, always so calm and unperturbed, was lined with shadows of fatigue that matched the rough edges of concern in his voice.

"How long have I been asleep?"

"Two days."

"What—" She stopped midsentence as memories flooded her brain. Jon had deserted her after less than a day of marriage. *She would not cry again.* He'd made his choice and it had not been her. She would not let that knowledge destroy her.

"What exactly did he say?" She barely recognized the cold, empty voice as her own.

"What do you mean?" Holt's words were equally void of emotion.

"How do you know he won't be back?"

Holt's eyes narrowed slightly. "He told me."

"What were his exact words?" She had to know. Every minute detail. It was the only hope she had of exorcising Jon Remmington.

Holt cleared his throat, hesitated a moment, then said, "There was an agreement between us. It was to be a marriage in name only. Jon would marry you, give you his name, and then he'd leave, free to sail the sea without any—" he paused, seeming to search for the proper word "—encumbrances."

Encumbrances? That's what she had been to him? Not a wife, not a friend. Not even a lover. She'd been an encumbrance. The word pierced her heart like a dagger, drawing forth the blood of her pain and grief.

"I see."

"He won't be back." The dagger twisted.

"But he's set you up with a very fine country house in Bath," Sophie rushed in, wringing her hands. "There is a full house of servants waiting to see to your needs. And I heard Jon say Allegra is to be transported as well."

Holt glared at his wife, as though silently chastising her for saying too much, but Sophie seemed unaware of his dark mood as she continued to smile at Julia, offering hope where none existed.

"Holt?" Julia asked. "Is this true?"

Her brother shoved his hands in his pockets. "You don't have to go, Julia," he said, frowning. "Bath is at least two hours from Ellswood. You're a woman alone. You should stay with us, where you will be cared for."

A woman alone. The words sank into Julia's brain. In that moment, she knew she would leave, *must* leave. Jon might have bound her to him in marriage, but he'd freed her as well. Now she could move about as a married woman without threat of disgrace or ruination. She could roam the countryside, dance barefoot in fields of sweet-smelling grass, ride bareback at sunrise, the wind rifling through her unbound hair. Freedom. At last. A vision of Jon flashed before her, his dark eyes boring into her soul. She frowned. He'd given her the gift of freedom but had stolen her dream of America as well as her heart, locking her in a prison where he held the only key. One day, perhaps, she'd be able to forgive him. But not today.

"I have much to do," Julia announced, throwing back the covers. "I'm leaving in the morning."

***

"Oh, Holt, why didn't you tell her about the letter?" Sophie dabbed at a stray tear with her lace handkerchief as she watched the carriages roll away.

"There was no point."

"No point?"

"He'll never change. Jon has probably sent hundreds of missives to hundreds of women telling them how much he missed them and regretted having to leave them, from Istanbul to France. Julia is just one more even if she is his wife. I won't let him dally with her any longer."

"But what if he's sincere? What if he really does miss her? What if he's in love with her?" Sophie persisted.

Holt pulled his wife to him and said, "Jon? In love? Impossible."

***

The sun climbed over the horizon, nudging its way past the somber tones of night. Julia raced down the hill on Allegra, the feel of the wind in her face, the sound of the horse's hooves beating the ground in rapid staccato. Freedom. Freedom. Freedom. She threw back her head and laughed, a rich, glorious sound that filled the morning air.

Horse and rider reached the bottom of the hill, panting and gasping for breath. "Good girl," Julia whispered, stroking Allegra's neck. The horse nickered and threw her head up, nostrils flaring from the early morning exercise. Julia laughed again, basking in the pure enjoyment of the morning. She slid from her mount, brushed off her breeches and gave silent thanks that Holt was miles away. He never tired of chastising her for dressing like a man.

"There you go," she said, dropping Allegra's reins. "Enjoy your breakfast." The horse snorted twice, and then sank her nose in the sweet clover.

It had been one week since her arrival at Glenview Manor and already it felt like home. She loved her new residence, from the great expanses of old ivy crawling along the aging brick walls to the twenty rows of red rosebushes centered in the front lawn. The area stretched out, clipped and manicured in such green splendor, she wondered if the gardener lay hidden in the boxwoods, shears open and ready, waiting for the next glossy leaf to sprout so he could trim it posthaste.

Rows of privet blended into one another, making it

impossible to tell where one stopped and the other began. They wound around in a square pattern, forming a green maze that led to a center where a large white fountain sat. A stone angel perched atop the fountain, its wings suspended in the air, a steady stream of water spouting from its pursed lips.

But the land to the rear of the house was what captured Julia's eye. There were several small and not-so-small garden areas, randomly placed in the back lawn. One was for herbs, one for wildflowers, and one for vegetables. The scent of lavender and honeysuckle filled the air to the west, while a patch of vibrant pink and purple coneflowers called one's vision to the east.

Oh, how Francie Bishop would love these gardens. Perhaps one day Julia would invite the Bishops for a visit. But what would she say when Francie asked about her missing husband? What to say indeed. Julia sighed. Perhaps she would not invite them after all.

The manor itself drew her in with its simple yet elegant furnishings. The rooms echoed pale green and creams with hints of gold. No dark, brooding colors here. Julia especially loved her bedroom with the ivory walls and thick, cream counterpane bordered with thin, pale green piping and the rich cream draperies, held back with golden tassels. White vases carved with golden dragons adorned the dressing table and nightstand and reminded Julia of a vase Holt had given her. It had been a remembrance of his past excursions to the Orient. Had *someone else* been with him during that trip, perhaps even touched that same vase, and brought back a few of his own?

She would not dwell on *him.* Julia drew in a deep breath and let the fresh air fill her lungs and cleanse her mind. At that very moment, Allegra lifted her head and whinnied, her ears pricked up and alert. "What is it, girl?" Julia followed the horse's gaze toward the hilltop marking the perimeter of Remmington property.

A lone figure sat astride a massive white horse, so still that horse and rider appeared as one. Julia's heart skipped two beats. Could it be Jon? She shielded her eyes from the sun, trying to get a better view. Was it him? Had he returned? What would she say? The rider lifted a hand in greeting and galloped toward her. The sun shifted and Julia's heart sank when she noticed the rider's golden hair. The man brought his mount to a halt several feet from her. "Good day, my lady."

"Good day, sir," Julia replied, calculating the distance to the house. The intensity of the man's stare unnerved her. Could she jump on Allegra and outrun him?

The stranger smiled and laughed, the sound rolling over her like the summer breeze that blew his golden hair about his shoulders. "There's no need to fear me." His expression softened, revealing a dimple on the right side of his cheek. He was a handsome man of medium height and slight build. Almost too handsome, with his high cheekbones and sky-blue eyes. She guessed his age to be somewhere in the mid-thirties.

"You startled me sir, nothing more," Julia replied, determined that this stranger should not think her a ninny. She was a grown woman now, married as well, and needed to learn how to handle such situations. After all, there would be no husband to rescue her.

"Forgive me." He smiled again, revealing an even row of very white teeth. He patted his horse and dismounted in one fluid motion, amazing Julia with his grace and form. Taking a step forward, he bowed and extended a hand, covered in fine kid leather. "Allow me to introduce myself. I am Andrew Kleeton. I own the property to the west of Glenview Manor."

Julia smiled and placed her hand in his. "I'm pleased to meet you. I'm Lady Julia Remmington, mistress of Glenview Manor."

"Ahh," Andrew Kleeton said. "Finally, we meet a member of the Remmington family." He paused a moment. "And where pray might Mr. Remmington be?"

She wanted to tell him she had no idea where Mr. Remmington was at the moment, nor did she know where he would be next week, or next month. Or next year for that matter. And she had no idea what he was doing or with whom. She forced back the anger that threatened to escape in the form of blasphemous words and pasted a smile on her face as she withdrew her hand. "Mr. Remmington was called away on business." *Business indeed!*

Andrew Kleeton lifted a golden brow. "He left his new bride to attend business? When do you expect his return?"

They were innocent words, spoken as a mere formality, she was certain, with perhaps a hint of curiosity, but they magnified Jon's absence tenfold. "He'll return when his business is complete." She tried to keep the sharpness from her voice but it pierced every word like a screeching bird.

"Ah," he said. "He should take care not to leave his beautiful young bride alone for too long." His blue eyes narrowed the tiniest bit as though the man knew she was lying, knew also she had no idea where her husband was or when he would return.

She cleared her throat and looked away. "Yes, well, when I do see him, I shall pass along your regards." She smoothed back her hair and gathered Allegra's reins. "It's been a pleasure to meet you, Mr. Kleeton."

"The pleasure has truly been all mine, Lady Remmington." Casting his reins over the pommel of his black saddle, he stepped forward, stopping mere inches from her. "A woman who rides bareback is rare indeed," he murmured.

Julia blushed, taken aback by his bold candor. "I'm certain there are not many who would share your opinion."

"Then they are fools. Forcing people to fit into society's mold is a travesty that begets nothing but boring, self-righteous men and simpering, sniveling women."

She stifled a giggle. "I do happen to know quite a few men and women who fit that description."

A slow smile broke out on Andrew Kleeton's handsome face. He leaned forward and whispered, "As do I." The blue in his eyes deepened to match the morning sky.

Julia smiled back, enjoying the quiet camaraderie of the

moment.

"Allow me to serve as your footman," he said, bending down and lacing his hands. She placed a booted foot into the makeshift stirrup and swung her other leg over the saddle, thankful she'd worn breeches this morning.

Andrew Kleeton stepped back and dusted his gloved hands on his breeches. "Has anyone informed you, Lady Remmington, that your current manner of dress would appall the ton?"

"You don't think they would appreciate these as the height of fashion?" She pointed to her black breeches. "Why ever not, Mr. Kleeton?" She placed both hands on her hips in mock indignation.

He tilted his head and studied her attire. Then he shrugged and said, "I have no idea. Some people can be quite narrow-minded."

Julia threw back her head and laughed. "My thoughts exactly."

***

The ride back to the stables took no more than fifteen minutes. As she dismounted and rubbed down Allegra, Julia's thoughts returned to her new acquaintance. Andrew Kleeton was charming and handsome. In some ways, he reminded her of Jason, with his quick wit and easy smile. She hoped the rest of her neighbors possessed equally pleasant dispositions. Time would indeed tell.

"You don't trust me to walk your horse down for you?" a gruff voice called out from behind her.

She turned to find the groomsman, Henry Barnes, standing several feet behind her and Allegra, his wizened old face scrunched up and disapproving.

"Of course not, Mr. Barnes. I'm just used to taking care of Allegra myself."

The old man moved closer, crossed his arms over his thin chest, and grunted. His beady, black eyes moved from her to Allegra and back again. "I promised the master I'd take good care of you and see to yer horse's needs and I aim to do just that."

"Master?"

Henry Barnes nodded. "Yup. The master hisself came to see me 'bout you and yer horse. Asked me to give you both special attention, seein' as ye're such a horse lover and all." He uncrossed his arms and scratched his gray head.

"Mr. Barnes, are you speaking of my husband?"

The old man looked at her like she'd gone mad. "Beggin' yer pardon, Lady Remmington, but there ain't no other master here. Hasn't been one since 'is uncle died ten years back."

"Glenview Manor is a family estate?" She'd assumed her new home was just that. A new home. Certainly not one inhabited by Jon's ancestors.

"Sure is. Been in the family for ages."

"And was his uncle an Englishman?" Jon was an American. Wasn't he?

"'Course he was. They all was a bunch of blue bloods, earls and dukes and the like. 'Til the master's father up and moved 'em all to America." Barnes's thin lips turned into a frown as he shook his head. "If that didn't cause quite a stir. Yes sirree. Quite a stir." He rubbed the gray and white stubble on his chin with a scrawny hand.

"Jon's English?"

Henry Barnes's head bobbed up and down. "Not only is 'e English," he whispered, "but when 'is old man dies, 'e'll be a duke as well. Don't claim it though and none of us is 'sposed to talk about it. 'E wants us to call 'im Jon, but it just don't seem right."

Jon was English? English nobility, no less! Henry Barnes's words swam in her head, swirling around until they made her dizzy. "I thought he was an American," she said, as much to herself as to the old man beside her.

"'E's both, in a way. 'is father is as mean as sin. I remember 'im. Always jealous of his older brother, the duke. One day, there was this big falling-out and the master's father scurried 'em all to America." He snapped his bony fingers. "Just like that. Overnight. The master weren't more'n eight years old. It tore the duke apart to see 'em gone. He never married, never had no kids and they was all like 'is own, 'specially the master. 'E looked just like the duke."

"But he came back?" Julia asked.

"When 'e was about fifteen, he jest appeared one day. Still don't know how he got 'ere, exactly. Never did say. Only thing he told 'is uncle was that 'e weren't never goin' back to America while 'is father was alive. 'E went to school 'ere. You know, all them fancy ones, and then 'e joined the Royal Navy for a while."

"But he didn't stay with them." She knew he and Holt met at sea and traveled the world together.

Henry Barnes screwed up his face a minute, tapping his finger on his temple. "Nah, he didn't stay too long. Couple years, maybe. But 'e always kept in touch with 'is uncle and when the old man died, this all became 'is." Barnes set his beady gaze on Julia. "'E coulda' thrown us all out on our ears back then. But 'e didn't. No sirree. 'E kep' us all on, ev'ry last one of us, paid us full wages and not a soul livin' in the big house."

Jon? The same man who'd walked out of their marriage without a backward glance had provided jobs and homes for an entire household that housed no master? For ten years? It was incredible. Almost unbelievable.

"I don't mean to sound uncaring, Mr. Barnes, but why would he do such a thing?"

"Ah, there's the question," the old man said smiling. It was a knowing smile, a smile that intimated she didn't know much about the man. His master. Her husband. Henry Barnes was right. She didn't know much about him, and she knew less as the minutes ticked by.

"'E said we was like family to 'im when 'e lost 'is own in Virginia. That's where 'e lived in America." Julia nodded. That much she did know. "'E jest wanted to repay us for takin' care o' 'im and 'is uncle." He paused. "Like family. That boy's like family to me. To all of us."

"Did he visit often?" She'd always pictured Jon aboard a ship or in some exotic land with a beautiful woman, not on his family's estate, conversing with an aging, wiry groomsman.

Henry Barnes shrugged his bony shoulders. "Not as often as we woulda liked. 'E came at night and left at night. Never wanted nobody to know 'e was 'ere. Kinda like he was tryin' to be secretive. Always brought us lots a presents though. I got a silver statue of a horse and a Chinese vase with a wild stallion carved on it."

Why would Jon want to keep his whereabouts a secret? She would ponder that tidbit in the privacy of her bedroom this evening for heaven knew, there would be little else happening in that room.

***

"Lady Remmington, you wished to have a word with me?" Edward Billington, Glenview Manor's butler, approached the rose-covered sofa Julia sat on and stopped a few feet away. He towered over her, his tall, lanky frame standing at attention as he awaited his mistress's bidding.

"Why yes, Mr. Billington, there is something I wish to discuss with you." She looked up at the man and doubted her neck would stand much more straining to converse with him. "First, you must do me the favor of having a seat." When she noticed his hesitancy, she insisted. "Please. If nothing else, you will ease the crook in my neck. You are quite a tall man," she said, smiling up at him.

Edward Billington did not return the smile as he lowered himself onto the sofa. He sat with his hands folded in his lap, watching her. Julia poured him a cup of tea without asking if he'd like any. She knew he would have refused had she given him the opportunity to do so. Tea calmed her, and she hoped it would do the same for Mr. Billington, though she'd not offered the occasional shot of brandy Jason used to put in hers; that would be her own little soother, after the meeting.

"You appear to know quite a bit about Glenview Manor," she said, handing him his cup of tea. He accepted the proffered brew, but Julia could have sworn his gray eyes turned cold just a moment, as though he wanted to refuse. Of course, they both knew it would be extremely rude to do so and Edward Billington was anything but rude.

He nodded, but offered nothing more.

"I've been here a week and know little more than I did when I first arrived. Perhaps you could tell me a bit about the history of Glenview Manor, the inhabitants, that sort of thing." *She'd had to find out from the groomsman that her husband was British? And a nobleman, no less!*

The butler cleared his throat. "I assumed Mr. Remmington had discussed these matters with you," he said, studying the steam rising from the tea. Why wouldn't he look at her? He'd shifted positions at least five times in the two minutes since he'd taken a seat. Julia noted he sat ramrod straight, several inches from the back of the sofa. What was making him so uncomfortable?

"Unfortunately, no. Mr. Remmington left before I could become familiar with his estate or his employees. I hoped you'd be able to provide me with that information." There, she'd thrown the gauntlet. He could not refuse.

Edward Billington cleared his throat. "What exactly would you like to know?"

No, he couldn't be rude, but he could be very difficult.

"Tell me about yourself. How long have you been employed here?"

"I'm a relatively new member to Glenview Manor," he said.

That told her nothing. "How new?" she prodded.

He pursed his lips, as though he didn't want to let out the words. "Two weeks."

"Two weeks?" He knew too much to be here for such a short time. And the other members of the staff held him in very high regard. Whenever she questioned one of them about their master or his comings and goings, they deferred the questions to Billington. All except Henry Barnes. He'd told her more about her husband in ten minutes than the whole lot of them had in a week's time. What power did Edward Billington hold over the staff? Had Jon bestowed some special authority to him during his absence?

She studied the man as he sat on the edge of the sofa, motionless yet waiting. Like a big cat about to pounce, or perhaps, retreat. His cold gray eyes gave away nothing as he stared at her. He was hiding something; she sensed it. This man was more than a middle-aged butler with thinning hair.

"Excuse me for being bold, Mr. Billington, but I find it quite odd that you've been employed by Mr. Remmington for a mere two weeks and yet the entire staff defers to you." She gave him a small smile. "Why, if I didn't know better, I'd say you wielded more power than I do where the staff is concerned."

He cleared his throat and set his teacup down on the mahogany table in front of him. "I said I have been at Glenview Manor for two weeks. I have been in Mr. Remmington's employ for much longer than that."

"Oh? How long and in what capacity?"

"Years. I've had various duties, depending on the need at the time."

The man was deliberately avoiding her questions. "Mr. Billington, it's becoming quite clear you do not wish to answer my questions." She clenched her fingers around the delicate china cup as she waited for his answer.

A full minute passed before Edward Billington opened his mouth and spoke. "It is not that I refuse to answer your questions, Lady Remmington, but I am employed by Mr. Remmington and cannot divulge information without his permission."

"Oh. How exactly do you obtain permission, Mr. Billington, when my husband isn't here? No, don't bother to answer that, because I know you won't anyway." She set the teacup on the table before she crushed it between her hands. "Henry Barnes said my husband was here recently. Is that true?"

"Mr. Barnes speaks out of turn."

"At least he speaks."

"Fools speak all of the time and rarely say anything."

"Where is my husband?" Julia threw the question at him like a volley from a cannon. He looked surprised but recovered within seconds, the mask of indifference back in place so quickly she almost thought she'd imagined the look. But it had been real. *Edward Billington knew where Jon was.*

"Lady Remmington," the words were stiff and very precise, "you are his wife, whereas I am only the butler. Certainly, if anyone knew Mr. Remmington's whereabouts, it would be you."

He was a smooth one, she'd grant him that. He knew how to turn and twist a phrase to make her question her own words. Almost. Julia leaned against the sofa and pasted a smile of serenity on her face. "One would most certainly think so, Mr. Billington. Unfortunately, that is not the case in this instance, as we are both well aware. I think you know my husband doesn't plan to return, and I also think you know where he is and how to contact him. But, since, as you say, you cannot speak on this matter without his permission, we will pretend that he is 'unavailable' for an indefinite period of time." Julia leaned forward, attempting to close the distance between them. Edward Billington inched toward the edge of the sofa. "Therefore," she continued, her words strong and steady, "until further notice, I will be in charge of running Glenview Manor. All questions and decisions will be handled by me."

"Certainly you do not wish to be bothered with such a tedious chore, Lady Remmington. Mr. Remmington left very specific instructions as to how the house should be run so as not to interfere with whatever pursuits you may entertain."

Julia noticed the slight twitch in his jaw. He wasn't happy with her announcement but he was making a very good show at remaining indifferent.

"Why, it's no bother at all. I look forward to working with

the staff and learning all about Glenview Manor. Since my husband left *specific* instructions as to how his home should be run in his absence, I will be most anxious to review the list as soon as possible."

Edward Billington remained silent, his bony fingers crossed at the knee. Julia noted his knuckles were white. A dull flush crept up his neck, stained his face and ears. He was either very angry or embarrassed at getting caught in a lie of his own making. Julia was fairly certain the *specific instructions* he referred to were mere fabrication. "Well, I believe that will be all for the moment, Mr. Billington," she said, rising.

"Yes, Lady Remmington," he replied, unfolding his lanky form into a standing position. He nodded once and turned toward the door.

"Ah, Mr. Billington?"

"Yes, Lady Remmington?" He'd reached the door in less than ten strides and had his hand on the knob, ready to bolt. His gaze remained on the oak door in front of him.

"I'll expect that list no later than tomorrow morning." There. Let him stew over that.

"Yes, Lady Remmington." The door opened and he disappeared before she could take another breath. Or give another command.

Edward Billington could try one's nerves with his cold stares and one-word responses. She knew no more about Jon's whereabouts now than she had before her meeting. She moved to the sideboard, grabbed a crystal decanter, and headed for the sofa. She could use a nice hot cup of tea, with just a hint of something stronger to relax her. Then again, she thought as she poured a healthy measure of amber liquid into her cup, perhaps she'd skip the tea this time.

Chapter 11

Jon called himself a hundred kinds of fool for the note he'd sent Julia confessing how much he missed her. It had been almost two weeks, and he'd gotten no response. Not a word. What had he expected? Even if she had received the letter, which was uncertain with a brother like Holt, she might well have torn it to shreds without reading it. Or, she might have read it first, and then torn it to shreds. She probably considered him among the lowest vermin crawling the earth after the way he'd married her, bedded her, and deserted her. He'd had no business trying to contact her.

So, why in the hell had he? He told himself he hadn't broken his promise to Holt by sending the note; it was simply his way of trying to ease the pain he'd caused Julia and a feeble attempt to appear less of a cad. He must have failed miserably, though, because every hour that dragged on without a response from her told him she wasn't pining for him anymore. That was one thing he'd learned about his wife: the woman could carry a grudge, especially if she had a reason.

It had been a stupid thing to do. Even if she'd received the letter and responded in a positive manner, what could he have offered her? He'd given Holt his word and short of challenging him to a duel, Jon had to stay out of Julia's life. A small part of him had hoped Holt would read the letter, take pity on the miserable, besotted fool he'd become, and relieve Jon of his vow. Of course, it was a ridiculous, unfounded hope. His emotions were getting the best of him. He was moody and in a bad temper most days. He'd tried to take his mind off his wife by concentrating on his spice and silk business, setting up meetings, and arranging shipments with various merchants. Filling in time, passing the hours, that's what he'd been doing, but he couldn't wait any longer for a message that wasn't coming, a message he had no business waiting for.

Tomorrow he'd leave England and head for the Indies. Billington would serve as his eyes and ears, sending him detailed reports on his wife. But Billington wouldn't be able to describe the way Julia's gray eyes sparkled when she laughed, or how the golden highlights danced through her hair when the sun shone on it a certain way. His account would not mention the faint scent of lilac that drifted about her or the soft murmur of her voice in the night.

It would only contain facts. Details. Appointments. Jon would have to settle for this. As long as she was safe, he would save the rest for his dreams and lose himself in the sweetness of remembering each night as sleep took him. As long as she was safe, he would stay away. But if anyone or anything threatened that safety, nothing would keep him from his wife. Not a brother, not a best friend, not a vow, not a duel. He would die to keep her safe.

***

"Mr. Billington, I'm going riding. I expect to return in time for afternoon tea." Julia stood in the middle of the oak hallway, adjusting the gold trim on the sleeve of her riding habit.

"If I might say, Lady Remmington, this is certainly a departure from your usual riding attire."

"Indeed it is." She knew he was referring to the customary white shirt and breeches she wore every day for her early morning ride with Allegra.

"Is there, ah, any particular reason you're dressed in such a fashion?"

How nosy of him. At least he did have the good grace to be hesitant about it, which meant he knew it was none of his business but wanted to know anyway. Why? So he could check it off on his list of *specific instructions?* Was checking up on his wife Jon's unwritten request? That whole ordeal had been a laugh. When Billington presented her with a list the following morning, there had been six handwritten directives, beginning and ending with "do not overburden Lady Remmington with mundane details." The handwriting was bold, sloppy, and totally unfamiliar.

Julia had accepted the proffered list without a word. How

could she dispute anything when she couldn't identify the handwriting as her husband's? After all, the only writing she'd ever witnessed was his signature in the marriage register. She'd not considered that little obstacle the day before when she'd been so adamant about obtaining the list. Of course, Jon could have written the list but Edward Billington could have penned it also. Or, perhaps it had been the cook, or the scullery maid. Fact was, it could have been written by anyone. There'd been no choice but to let the matter drop with a curt nod and a murmured thank-you.

"Lady Julia?" Mr. Billington closed the distance between them. "Might someone be joining you today?" He asked the question as though he had a right to a response—even expected one. She wondered for the third time in as many days what his relationship to her husband might be that he should assume such an attitude.

"Why, yes, as a matter of fact, I am riding with a friend today." *The nosy man would have to pry the rest of the information from her.* She headed for the door but had taken no more than three steps before his very precise voice reached her.

"I was not aware you had made any acquaintances since your arrival at Glenview Manor."

He was dying to know what she was up to. Hiding a smile, Julia pulled the heavy oak door open and glanced over her shoulder. "Well, I have, Mr. Billington." She stepped outside, still holding the door open. "And he's quite a handsome acquaintance at that." With those parting words, she pulled the door shut and hurried down the steps, breaking into a run as soon as her booted foot reached the ground.

The stables were several hundred feet from the main house and Julia's riding habit made running any distance quite difficult. Oh, how she wished she'd worn breeches! She tried to move faster as the steady, forceful steps of Edward Billington closed in on her, but her skirt was too constricting to break away from him.

"Lady Remmington! Why are you running from me? Please

stop!"

"I can't, Mr. Billington," she called back to him. "I'm already late."

He huffed behind her. "If you'll hold up a moment."

The man had begun to annoy her with his persistence. What right did he have to question her? After all, he was only the butler. Wasn't he?

Edward Billington rounded on her, face flushed, breathing heavy. "You are—" he drew in a deep breath "—riding with a gentleman?"

"If that is any of your concern, Mr. Billington, which I seriously doubt, then yes, I am riding with a gentleman."

"Who is the gentleman?"

She pressed her lips together before a blasphemous word escaped. "It really is none of your business."

"But it is Mr. Remmington's."

"How dare you? If Mr. Remmington were concerned, he would be here, wouldn't he?"

Edward Billington's gaze shifted to a point beyond her. He remained silent.

"Exactly." She tried to ignore the hurt his silence caused. Even the butler knew Jon didn't care about her.

"He would want to know."

Those simple words ignited a fire in her. She clenched her fists and spat out, "If he wants to know, then he'll have to ask me himself."

***

"How long have you lived at Penworth?" Julia asked.

"I purchased the property two years ago but have only been living there for the last six months." Andrew Kleeton smiled at Julia, revealing two deep-set dimples on either side of his mouth. "Please, call me Andrew. Mr. Kleeton reminds me of my father."

Julia smiled back at him. "All right. Andrew," she said, testing his name on her lips. "Then you must call me Julia."

"Fair enough."

They sat in an open meadow on the north side of Glenview Manor. Finch and starlings danced around them, with an occasional blue jay darting into the path. The melodies they created were gentle, soothing notes carried along with the early afternoon breeze. Julia closed her eyes, trying to block out her confrontation with Mr. Billington.

"There's nothing quite so beautiful as nature in all of its naked glory." Andrew's words reached her as she basked in the warm rays of sunshine on her upturned face.

"I've always preferred the country to city life," she confessed.

"So, you did not go to London during the Season?"

"I went, kicking and screaming," she said.

Andrew laughed. "Well, I was there and I did not notice anyone kicking or screaming. Wait a moment. I take that back. There were a few confirmed bachelors who got snagged by determined future mothers-in-law. Right into the marriage mart, with their heads still spinning."

Julia laughed, opening her eyes to see his grin. He looked like a Greek god, his longish blond hair bathed in sunlight, his skin a deep honeyed tone reflected by the rays. His handsome face was unmarred—no scars, bumps, or bruises. No crooks in his nose. A vision of Jon's battered face the last time she'd seen him popped before her eyes. Her smile faded.

"Julia?"

She pushed the vision of her husband away and said, "Tell me, Andrew, how did you avoid being snagged by some young girl's mother? Did you hide in a closet?"

He pretended outrage. "Of course not! Do you think me a coward? Not I," he vowed. "When I spotted some willful mother approaching me with her simpering daughter, I merely pulled the nearest old woman into my arms and began dancing with her. It drove the mothers mad and made my dance partners giggle like young schoolgirls. Quite a civilized way to avoid capture, I might add."

Julia laughed, forgetting about the shadow that had

dampened her high spirits a few moments before. "You're incorrigible."

"Thank you, m'lady." He bowed his head in mock sincerity. "I wish I'd met you last Season. I might have swept you off your feet before Remmington got to it."

His words might be light and teasing, but there was no humor in the blue gaze that settled over her. It was dark, intense, deadly serious. Julia shifted, uncomfortable with the way he looked at her. "You say that now that I am a married woman, but I'll wager had I looked at you twice, you would have dragged *two* old ladies onto the floor."

"Perhaps," he said. "Then again," he sighed, all seriousness gone, "perhaps not."

She shook her head and laughed. He did indeed remind her of Jason with his intelligence, wit, and sense of humor.

"I suppose we should be getting back," Andrew said as he stood to brush bits of tall grass from his clothes. He held out his hand to Julia and she accepted the gesture as her eyes drifted to the soft leather that covered his right hand. And his left.

He followed her gaze. "A war injury."

"I'm sorry," she said, looking away.

"Don't be. It happened a long time ago. I grew tired of women fainting at the sight of all the scars, so I bought gloves. Boxes and boxes of them. Different colors, styles, textures."

"How clever." Julia slipped her hand from his and moved toward Allegra. The sun was high above them now, indicating they'd been out at least a few hours. Time to head back to Glenview Manor and the inquisitive Mr. Billington.

The horses chomped the tall grass, filling their bellies as they trimmed a path for her. Julia patted Allegra's neck and reached for the reins. She mounted and turned toward Andrew who stood quite still, his hand shielding the hot sun from his eyes as he stared off into the distance at a lone figure on a horse.

"Andrew, do you know who that is?"

"He's too far away to tell much."

"Why would anyone be—" The words hung in mid-sentence. Billington! It had to be him. She couldn't wait to get back to the house to give him a piece of her mind. Spying, indeed! "I know who the culprit is, Andrew."

He kept his gaze trained on the horse and rider. "Who is it?"

"My overzealous, overprotective butler." She tapped her riding crop in her hand, beating a rapid staccato. "I'll take care of the situation as soon as I return to Glenview Manor."

***

Julia left Andrew at the corner of their properties, apologizing again for her butler's rude behavior. Andrew seemed quite bothered by the whole incident, almost outraged, vowing to intervene if Julia deemed it necessary. He insisted someone had to look out for her welfare in her husband's absence, and she didn't have the heart to tell him that was exactly what Billington thought he was doing by spying on her. Nor would she tell him her husband might well have been the one encouraging such behavior.

When she reached the stables, she dismounted and went in search of Henry Barnes. She found him in one of the stalls, tending to a huge black stallion. She guessed it was Jon's from the untamed look about him, as though he tolerated civilization, but barely. Like his master.

"Mr. Barnes," Julia began, trying to control the anger burning in her gut, "did Mr. Billington leave about two hours ago with one of the horses?"

The old man scratched his scraggly gray head. "No, ma'am."

He had to have taken one of the horses. Julia tried again. "He didn't come to you and request you saddle a mount for him?"

That got a laugh from Henry Barnes. "No, ma'am. That old bag o' bones can't ride no horse. Hah!"

"Well, then, did *anyone* come to you and request one of the horses?" she asked.

"That'd be Jack," he said, nodding his head.

"Jack?"

"Jack, the stable boy," he said, as though that should mean something to her.

"Jack, the stable boy," she repeated, nodding her head in total confusion.

"Yup." He rubbed the gray stubble on his chin. "I sent 'im out after you."

"*You* did?"

"Sure. When I sees you all dressed up like one o' them fair ladies from town, I got to wonderin' wot was wot. An' since I promised the master ta make sure you was safe, I sent young Jack out."

"Jon—I mean, Mr. Remmington asked you to watch out for me?" This was incredible. Did the man have the whole staff on alert? If he cared so much, why did he not just come home?

"Sure did. 'E knew I was good ta my word, or me name's not 'enry Barnes."

"But, Mr. Barnes, you had no right to have Jack follow me." Did none of these people understand their positions?

"Had to. Yer the master's wife. Have ta keep you safe fer 'im."

"I see," Julia said. But she didn't. The whole lot of them were crazy, including their master. Correction. Especially their master. What were they keeping her safe from? The only harm that had come to her since marrying Jon was a broken heart and he'd been the cause of it.

"Heard ya went out with a man." He shook his head. "Shouldna' done that. The master ain't gonna like it."

"Who did you hear that from?" She had a sneaking suspicion she already knew.

"Ol' Billington. Crusty lot, ain't 'e?"

"Among other things."

Henry Barnes laughed again, a full-bellied laugh that turned into a dry wheeze. "Ya shoulda seen ol' Billington run out 'ere, hollerin' up a storm ta git a body ta follow you. I done told 'im

I already had Jack saddlin' up."

"Mr. Barnes, why were the two of you so concerned? I went riding with a neighbor. Mr. Kleeton is a nice man. It was all perfectly innocent."

The old man cocked his head to the side and rubbed his chin again. "In all my years, I learn'd one thing. Nothin' is ev'r perfectly innocent." He nodded his head, his black eyes narrowing on her. "Jest you remember that."

***

Julia wanted nothing more than to take a nap. It had been a trying afternoon and she was bone-tired. A warm bed sounded much more appealing than afternoon tea. Halfway up the winding staircase, she heard Edward Billington's voice.

"Did you have a nice ride today, Lady Julia?" She whirled around to find him standing two steps behind her. Where had he come from? She must be so tired, it was affecting her senses, for she hadn't heard him at all.

"Why yes, I did have a most enjoyable time today, Mr. Billington." She put special emphasis on her next words. "With the exception of the spy you and Mr. Barnes sent after me."

Edward Billington's lips twitched. It was the closest thing to a smile she'd ever seen on him. "Don't consider him a spy, Lady Julia. He was more of an...observer."

"An observer? What exactly was he supposed to observe?" Julia gripped the oak railing, willing her nerves to settle.

"Your safety. He was sent to make certain you were in no threat of danger."

Julia threw her hands in the air. "Danger? What sort of danger could possibly overtake me in the middle of the country? There is nothing, I repeat, *nothing* here to cause me danger! The only thing jeopardizing my safety is the way you're treating me. It's enough to make me crazy!"

He looked at her as though she'd already gone mad. It was then Julia remembered where they were—on the staircase, in plain view and certainly shouting distance for the rest of the household to observe their little confrontation. She peeked over the railing and spotted several pairs of eyes staring back. They must have feared they'd be the next targets of their mistress's wrath, for they scattered like dust.

"Now, Mr. Billington," she said, turning back to the butler with as much dignity as she could muster, considering she'd just created a scene in front of the entire household. "I would like this foolishness to cease at once. I am not a child, and do not expect to be treated as one. If, as you say, you're only following my husband's instructions, then I apologize for directing my anger toward you, but unless Mr. Remmington relays his wishes to me directly and the reasons for them, this behavior must end immediately." *And since they both knew he wasn't coming back, this was a very polite way of telling him she'd take charge of her own life, thank you very much.* "Do we understand one another?"

"I understand what you are saying, Lady Remmington."

Ah yes, he understood but he hadn't *agreed* to her terms. Clever. Very clever, indeed. "And you will agree?" she persisted. *She'd get him to say yes if she had to pull the words out of those thin lips.*

Edward Billington stood ramrod straight and shook his balding head. "Unfortunately, I cannot abide by your wishes, Lady Remmington. I have Mr. Remmington's orders."

"To treat me as though I'm in prison?" She tried to control her anger, but it proved a difficult task. "I'm not permitted to ride my horse with a neighbor unless a spy is sent along? Will you be sending someone to watch me sleep as well to be certain I don't try to escape in the night?"

"The neighbor—"

"Is a very nice, harmless man," Julia finished for him. "His name is Andrew Kleeton. He has resided at Penworth for the last six months, though he purchased the place over two years ago. His manners are impeccable. He behaved the perfect gentleman." She held out her hand and began ticking off his attributes on her fingers. "Mr. Kleeton has blond hair, blue eyes, medium build. Let's see, what else? Ah, yes. He's an excellent horseman and, I believe, a confirmed bachelor, though he did travel to London for the Season. He's also a superb dresser who wears gloves because of his scars."

"Scars?"

"Yes. Scars. It seems he suffered a terrible accident that left his hands bad off. His solution was to purchase gloves in every style and color. Clever of him, wasn't it?"

"Very clever."

"Fortunately for him, the accident did not impair the use of his hands." She reached into the side pocket of her skirt and pulled out a card. "He sent me his card." She thrust it at him. "The penmanship is perfect, don't you agree?"

The butler didn't answer. He stared at the crisp white paper, his eye narrowed to mere slits.

"Mr. Billington? What is it?" Julia peered at the card lying open in his hand. Then she laughed. "I told you he was clever. Who would have thought to put that in there," she said, pointing to a silver embossed design at the bottom of the card. "What is that little creature anyway? A snake?"

"Or a serpent. Either way, just as deadly."

***

Jon banged on the door again. He knew that two in the morning was well past the sociable hour to be calling, but this was urgent business and Holt had damn well better be home. He raised his fist to pound on the door again when it swung open. A startled young man dressed in a dark blue robe held a lantern before him, terror written on his face. The butler. Jon remembered him and the way he used to gawk after Julia. He sympathized with the poor boy. Julia could tie him in knots and he was a grown man.

"M-m-may I help you, Mr. Remmington?" he asked, not moving from the door.

"You could help me by letting me in," Jon said.

"C-c-certainly, Mr. Remmington." Was the boy afraid of him? What had Holt told everyone about him? That he was a no-good rakehell who deserted his wife and beat children?

Jon pushed past the butler and stepped inside, shrugging out of his greatcoat. He was bone-weary. That's what traveling nonstop for three days straight did to a man. No, that's what being married to Julia did to a man. He'd been mad with worry since the second he opened Billington's missive marked *Urgent*. Twenty minutes later, Jon was on his way back to England. Fortunately, they were in port along the coast and *The Falcon* had not been difficult to locate. Billington had been with Jon long enough to know exactly where to look.

"I could use a drink," Jon said.

"C-c-certainly, sir," the boy stumbled over his words. "W-would you like coffee? Tea?"

"I was thinking more along the lines of whisky."

The butler turned a deep rose. "O-o-of course. F-f-follow me, sir." He turned on his heel and headed down the long hall. The only sounds of night were the shuffling of the butler's slippers and Jon's booted feet following behind.

Once inside the study, the young man lit another lamp and watched as Jon poured a whisky. "Come here, boy." Jon tilted his head and threw back the whisky in one gulp. He poured another.

The butler inched forward.

"For God's sake, I'm not going to hurt you. What's your name?" Why was everybody always afraid of him?

"P-P-Pierce, sir. Matthew Pierce."

"Well then, Pierce, come here." He poured a second glass of whisky and offered it to the butler. "Drink this."

"B-b-begging your pardon, Mr. Remmington, but I don't drink." Now his face looked purple. How could one face change colors so many times?

"Well, Pierce, tonight's an exception because as soon as you finish that drink, I'm going to ask you to wake Lord Westover. Now, come on, boy," he coaxed, nudging the glass into his hands, "drink up." Pierce eyed the amber liquid once more as though it might be a brew from the devil himself before he raised it to his lips, squeezed his eyes shut, and swallowed. He coughed, sputtered, and gasped for a full minute. When he finished, Jon saluted him with his own glass and downed his drink with a deliberate smoothness that came from years of practice.

"Well done, Pierce. Now, it's time to go get him." Pierce disappeared, stumbling a little in his hurry to obey. Or did he stumble in his hurry to be rid of Jon? Perhaps he really did instill fear in men, even when it was not his intention to do so.

Why then hadn't it worked on his wife?

God, how he missed her. Billington's report had concentrated on this Kleeton fellow and his note. There'd been very little mention of Julia, other than to say she seemed quite upset by his absence. Good. He hoped she missed him half as much as he missed her. If he had his way, it wouldn't be long before he'd see her again.

"What the hell are you doing here?"

Jon turned and nodded. "Nice to see you again, too, brother-in-law."

"Damn you, Jon, why are you here?"

"Unfortunately, it's not a social call," he said, rubbing the back of his neck. Damn, but at this moment, he felt every one of his thirty-one years. "Close the door."

Holt flung the door shut and reached him in six long strides. "Talk. Now. You've got ten minutes." He folded his arms over his chest and stared.

Holt would never listen to him in his current mood, which was darker than black. Jon had to ease the tension between them. "Do you really wear all those clothes to bed?" he asked, gesturing to the blue silk pajamas and burgundy robe.

"Nine minutes."

Maybe that sort of humor couldn't be appreciated at this hour of the morning. He'd try another tactic. "If you're thinking of hitting me again, could you please avoid the nose area? You broke it last time, and it still smarts."

"Eight."

Forget trying to change his mood. He always was

something of a spoilsport. Stubborn spoilsport. "It's about Julia."

"Six."

"What happened to seven?"

"You lost two minutes when you mentioned her name."

Jon took a deep breath and looked down at his whisky glass. Empty. His gaze clashed with Holt's. "It's about Julia *Remmington. My wife.*" He paused between each word, letting the silence heighten their meaning.

"One."

Jon ignored him. "She's been seeing one of her new neighbors." He hated the sound of that. It bothered him to think she might be interested in someone else when he couldn't get her out of his mind, day or night.

"Sounds like you've got a problem." Holt's tone grew smug and not in the least sympathetic.

"His name is Andrew Kleeton. He's been at Penworth about six months. Obviously, I've never met him or heard about him until now, which concerns me."

"So he prefers beautiful women over men," Holt said in his usual dry manner.

Jon shook his head. "If it were only that simple. He sent Julia his card the other day inviting her to go riding with him. Do you know what was on the card?" Without waiting for Holt to respond, Jon plowed forward, "It was an embossed drawing of a serpent."

"And?" He seemed nonplussed by the revelation.

"A *serpent*, Holt."

"Are you trying to tell me you think it's Crowlton?"

Jon shrugged. "I don't know. But I damn well intend to find out."

"This all sounds very speculative and quite premature. The man's apparent fondness for reptiles does not make him a killer."

"My man Billington also told me Kleeton wears gloves all the time. Seems he was in a bad accident some time ago that left his hands scarred."

That got Holt's attention. "A fire?"

"Possibly. Julia may be in danger. If he is The Serpent, he'll try to use her to get to me."

Holt let out a long breath. "I need a drink." He walked to the side table and poured a whisky.

"I want to go to her," Jon said.

"Impossible." He lifted the glass and drained it in one swallow. Then he poured another.

"She needs protection. Someone to watch over her and keep an eye on Kleeton."

"I can do that. I'll bring her back here," he said matter-of-factly.

"Do you really think she'll go with you? She's just settled into a new home. She won't let you haul her back for no good reason, and you can't tell her the truth without putting her in more jeopardy." He joined Holt at the side table and poured another whisky. "What would you tell her?"

"I'll think of something. She might not like it, but she'll listen."

"Even if she does agree, you can't put the rest of your family at risk. Every one of you would be targets, including Sophie and the children."

Holt remained silent for several minutes, and Jon waited while his friend turned over possibilities and weighed obstacles as he determined the best course of action. Holt had always been a great tactician, which had made him a great spy. "I'll hire a bodyguard to stay with her at Glenview Manor."

"Who?" Desperation washed over Jon, rendering him powerless. "Who but you and I would know how to handle a man like The Serpent?" He was going to Julia, with or without Holt's permission.

"We could contact The Crown and tell them of our suspicions," Holt said.

"What would we tell them? I found a man living next to me who uses embossed serpents on his calling cards and wears gloves at all times? They'd call us mad. Probably tell us we'd been on one too many missions." He rifled a hand through his hair. "It's not enough for them to bother with and you know it."

"You're probably right."

"I'm going to her." There. He'd said those same words over and over in his head since the moment he'd read Billington's missive.

Holt's gaze narrowed on him. "What did you say?"

"I'm going to her."

"Why?"

Jon stared at him. "Damn it, man, do you have to ask me that? I haven't slept in three days for worrying about her. Thinking I might get there too late. I *need* to see her and make certain she's safe. I'll go crazy if I'm not there. I have to protect her."

"Why couldn't you have displayed such honor a few weeks ago? *Before* you seduced her? Then she wouldn't be in this predicament."

The words stung, like salt in a wound. An open, bleeding, raw wound. Jon had tormented himself with those same thoughts for the past three days. He opened his mouth and let the truth spill out. "I love her."

"Does she know?"

Jon shook his head.

"If I do agree that you should go, how do you plan to keep her safe? Obviously you can't present yourself as you are. If Kleeton didn't shoot you, Julia would."

"I've got it all planned out. I wasn't known as The Chameleon for nothing," he said, referring to the code name he used during his espionage days. His specialty had been transformation, walking into a building as a young man and hobbling out an old one. With the right makeup and props, he could turn into anything.

"You'll go in disguise." Holt said, a hint of a smile on his face.

"The name's Cyrus Mandrey," Jon replied, lowering his

voice to a raspy imitation of his character. "I'll have bushy brown hair and a beard and mustache," he continued in that same voice, "with glasses this thick." His fingers extended an inch. "And nobody, but nobody's going to touch Lady Remmington."

"Even her husband?" Holt asked, raising a dark brow.

Jon dropped the guise. "About that promise. Would you consider releasing me from it?" He prepared for the worst but prayed for the best.

Holt rubbed his jaw, sighed. "I never thought you'd fall in love and certainly not with my little sister. I don't think it's my decision any longer. Now, it's up to Julia."

"I want to know that when this is all over, I can try to win my wife back without worrying you'll show up with a pistol."

"Agreed."

"Or a strong left hook."

Holt laughed, a full deep sound that echoed in the quiet room. "Let's have a drink and settle the details. If that bastard is still alive, I want him exposed as soon as possible."

Chapter 12

"Holt!" Julia ran across the room and into her brother's arms. "I've missed you."

He held her close and said, "And I've missed you. Actually, it's almost boring without you. There's no one running around the house, screaming and yelling, getting into mischief." He hugged her tighter. "I take that back. The children have done a rather nice job filling in for you."

Julia laughed. "How are my little darlings?"

"Excellent and getting bigger every day." He released her but kept hold of her hands. "Let me have a look at you." His smile deepened as he studied her through navy eyes the color of an evening sky. She still thought him the most handsome man she'd ever met—handsome and exasperating. The last time they'd argued, he'd insisted she stay with him and Sophie. Of course, she hadn't listened.

"Are you happy here, Julia?"

How to answer that? "As happy as a woman can be under these circumstances." She took a seat and poured herself a cup of tea. Next came two lumps of sugar and a drop of cream. As she stirred the hot brew, she studied the swirling designs the spoon made as the cream blended into the tea. Blended and disappeared, leaving only a trace behind, just like her husband, who'd worked his way into her heart, marked her forever, and then disappeared. "Living as a married woman without a husband is not a situation I ever considered," she said.

"You could be a married woman living with a husband you detest," Holt offered.

Julia smiled at her brother over the rim of her cup. Dear Holt. Situations of the heart always made him uncomfortable. "Yes, well, there is that to be thankful for."

"Speaking of that situation, there is something I wish to discuss with you."

Her hand jerked and a small spot of tea sloshed onto her lilac gown. "What situation?" Holt was going to discuss *Jon* with her?

"I'm concerned Jon might try to return to Glenview Manor."

"Ridiculous." He would never return. He'd made his choice and it hadn't been her.

"I have reason to believe he might try," Holt said. "For a time, anyway."

"He wouldn't dare," Julia said through clenched teeth.

"He sent me a letter, telling me he would like to see you again," Holt said, his eyes trained on her.

"He did?" She swallowed hard. He wanted to see her again? "Well, does he plan to come alone or would he be bringing Desiree and Monique with him?"

Holt coughed and sputtered, "What do you know of Desiree and Monique?"

"They're his mistresses." She waved a hand in the air, as though it were of no consequence to her. Inside she seethed, furious with Jon for being such a worthless scoundrel and with herself for the tears she'd wasted over him.

"They'll be available, I'm sure."

When he tires of his wife. Damn the man. Did he think he could walk back into her life without so much as an apology or an explanation, and she would accept him with open arms and a smile? Well, he could think again.

"Of course, I told him it was out of the question. I said you had no desire to see him, but Jon never has been a gentleman. He'll do what he wants. Or try to, anyway. That's why I've taken certain precautions to ensure your safety." Holt stood and walked toward the door. "I'll be back in a moment." He opened the door and murmured something to Billington, who must have been standing right outside. Spying on her, no doubt. Julia knew firsthand how easy it was to "overhear" a conversation through a door.

Julia heard a soft, raspy voice a moment before a tall, burly man entered. Her gaze riveted to his hair. There was so much of it. Everywhere. It covered his head like a brown, bushy nest, falling to just below his shoulders. His eyebrows formed a straight, thick line and his mustache flowed into a full beard that extended a good two inches below where she thought his chin might be. He wore thick spectacles that distorted the shape of his eyes and she was much too far away to discern their color. It appeared there were no more than a few inches of skin on his face that weren't covered with hair or spectacles.

"Julia, I'd like you to meet Cyrus Mandrey," Holt said. "Your protector."

The bushy-haired man nodded and said, "It's a pleasure to meet you, Lady Remmington."

"My protector?" she echoed, darting a puzzled look at Holt.

"Mr. Mandrey is going to make *certain* Jon doesn't bother you," Holt said.

"But that's absurd. And totally unnecessary." A hired protector? Ridiculous.

"Julia," Holt said in that tone that told her he tired of their bantering. "The only way I will allow you to remain at Glenview Manor is if Mr. Mandrey stays with you."

"But—"

He cut her off before she could say more. "Or else I will take you back with me in the morning."

Julia searched for a way to reason with her brother. She had no need of a protector. Especially not one who looked more animal than human. "I don't mean to be difficult," she began, keeping her voice level so he wouldn't detect her growing irritation, "but I don't need a protector. Jon may be a lot of things, but he would never harm me."

"I'm not talking about physical violence. I'm concerned with the emotional wreckage he'd leave behind," Holt said, his voice rising with every word. "With his *inevitable* departure. And he would leave, Julia. It's in his blood. Maybe not right away; it might take several weeks or months. Perhaps even a year. But one day, when you've just come to believe he'll be with you forever, he'll be gone. You'll wake one morning to find a note on your pillow. No apologies, no excuses. You'll live each day after that wondering if you'll ever see him again. Do you really want to live that kind of life?"

Julia closed her eyes and shook her head. She couldn't speak for the lump in her throat, stuck there like one of Mrs. Florence's biscuits. Holt was right, of course. Seeing Jon again would only spell disaster.

He stepped forward and clasped her cold hands in his. "I don't want you to go through what you did last time," he said in a gentle voice. "It was much too painful. For all of us."

Cyrus Mandrey cleared his throat. "If I may be so bold as to speak, Lady Remmington, perhaps your husband regrets his actions and wishes to make honest retribution. Perhaps he wishes nothing more than to see his wife again and grow into old age with her."

Julia stared at the bushy half-animal, half-man figure standing before her. How dare he speak of Jon's possible intentions. He knew nothing about Jon other than what Holt had told him. "If you believe that, even as a *remote* possibility," she said, her words as cold as a winter storm, "then you're implying my husband has a heart and a conscience. I know firsthand he possesses neither." Dismissing him, she turned to Holt. "I accept your proposal. At least until we're certain there are no attempts to return. Please discuss the details with Mr. Mandrey and provide background information he might deem necessary. Make it perfectly clear I do not wish to hear any further speculations from him as to why my husband may be trying to contact me."

Holt nodded. "It's for the best, Julia."

She chose not to respond. "If you'll excuse me, I feel a headache coming on."

"Oh course." Holt gave her a brief hug. Julia ignored Cyrus Mandrey as she brushed past him on her way to the door, but she felt his eyes following her every move.

When the door closed, Jon dropped the guise of Cyrus Mandrey and his words rushed out in low, fierce tones. "Did you have to paint such a black picture of me? She hates me!

Did you see the look in her eyes when you mentioned my name?"

Holt laughed, not trying to hide his amusement. "I told you that you'd have to win her back."

"But you didn't tell me you were going to make it so difficult," Jon said, scowling.

"I had to make her realize the danger of letting Jon back into her life," Holt said, all traces of humor gone. "It was the only way I could get her to accept the presence of Cyrus Mandrey. We need him to protect Julia and investigate Kleeton."

"I can't wait to meet the man," Jon said, slipping back into Cyrus Mandrey's raspy voice.

"I'm certain you will soon enough, my man. Soon enough."

***

Jon sat at a small table in one of the guest bedrooms. He would have preferred sleeping in the master suite. Right next door to his wife. Or, better yet, *with* his wife, in his bed. But that would have to wait. The success of this mission depended largely on his ability to convince Julia he was nothing more than a bodyguard with absolutely no resemblance to her husband.

He'd changed his physical appearance as much as possible. The bushy hair on his head, the full mustache and beard, thick glasses, and extra padding in his shirt were attempts to achieve that goal. A slow, shuffling gait replaced his usual, purposeful stride. When he spoke, the smooth, sensual tone that turned many a woman's knees to jelly shifted to Cyrus Mandrey's gravelly voice, not unlike the sound of sand rubbing on paper.

He leaned toward Edward Billington and whispered, "I want you to tell me everything you know about Andrew Kleeton." He remembered his wife's uncontrollable penchant for eavesdropping, and for all he knew, she could be on the other side of the door right now.

"Most of what I know I included in the missive I sent you." Edward Billington sat in a companion chair of cream and pale-green brocade, his lanky form bent toward Jon. "Apparently, Penworth belonged to the Duke and Duchess of Tindale until their death two years ago. Kleeton purchased the property at that time but did not take up residence until six months ago. As for the man himself," Billington continued, placing one long, bony finger on his chin, "he is of medium build, longish blond hair, light-blue eyes, dimples on either side of his mouth, perfect unblemished face. One might consider him quite handsome if one were interested in that sort of thing."

Jon rubbed his nose. His crooked, twice-broken nose. "Does Lady Julia seem interested in that sort of thing?" He shouldn't have asked the question because he didn't really want to know the answer.

Billington's long face showed no surprise over the strange question. "No, I wouldn't say she seemed interested."

Jon breathed a small sigh of relief. When this whole ordeal was over, he was going to have a difficult enough time winning Julia over without any outside complications.

"Though it's hard to tell."

Billington's words struck him in the gut like a lead ball. "Oh?"

"Well, sir, I've only observed them together on one occasion and that was yesterday when Mr. Kleeton arrived to take Lady Julia riding. It's difficult to formulate an opinion based on such limited information."

He should have known better than to ask Billington a question involving emotions.

"Forget I asked," Jon said, annoyed with himself for asking the question in the first place. "Let's move on. What about his hands?"

"Gloved. To somewhere above the wrist, but I couldn't determine how far."

"Well, we'll have to find a way to get them off, won't we?" Jon asked, crossing his arms behind his head and stretching his booted feet in front of him.

Billington's lips twitched. "My thoughts exactly, sir."

"Good. Are there any other matters we need to discuss?"

Billington's mouth puckered as though he'd just bitten into a lemon. "There is one small situation I'd like to discuss."

"Yes?"

Billington cleared his throat and said in a very low, precise voice, "It's about your wife, sir."

"My wife?"

His lips puckered again. He hesitated a moment, and then the words flew out like a cannonball. "She's quite willful, sir."

Jon tried not to smile. "Ah, I see. She's given you a mighty chase, hasn't she?" He could just imagine the two of them; they were about as compatible as oil and water.

Billington pulled out a handkerchief and mopped his balding head. "She's always questioning me, sir. Not in the demure manner of a woman befitting her station, but boldly, *brazenly*, like a man might do."

"Are you calling my wife masculine, Billington?" Jon asked, raising a bushy eyebrow. Too bad Billington couldn't see his lips twitching beneath all this hair.

"Oh no, sir. Not at all." He sat very straight in his chair. "It's just that, at times, she can be quite…undisciplined." A small bead of sweat trickled down his right temple.

"A hoyden?" Jon supplied, cocking his head to one side.

"No! No sir." He shook his head several times to press the point.

Be damned. The man had actually raised his voice and shown emotion. That was a first. Amazing. Edward Billington, the shrewd, no-nonsense, proper man who never lost his composure, had come undone because of Julia. Somehow, she'd found a way beneath Billington's carefully honed exterior and chipped away, no doubt with one argumentative word at a time, to release the emotions in the man. Negative, unfortunately, but emotions nonetheless.

Jon guessed it was time to stop tormenting the poor man. Julia had most likely tortured him enough with her obstinate questioning. "How would you like it, Billington, if Cyrus

Mandrey took over Lady Julia's comings and goings? You wouldn't have to be responsible for her. No more questioning, no more following her around, no more being *responsible* for her?"

Billington let out a long sigh and slumped in his chair. "I would be most appreciative of that, sir," he said, mopping his forehead again. "Most appreciative indeed."

***

Cyrus Mandrey took another sip of claret. Julia hadn't spoken five words since they'd sat down to supper fifteen minutes ago, and he'd had to practically drag them out of her. But he hadn't missed the furtive glances she threw his way when she thought he wasn't looking. She studied every movement, down to the way he buttered his roll and chewed his pork.

Enough was enough. He set down his fork and knife, sat back in his chair, and folded his hands over his stomach.

Julia glanced in his direction, a forkful of mashed potatoes poised midair. "Is the food not to your liking?" she asked, plopping the potatoes into her mouth.

"The food is fine."

She raised a golden eyebrow and swallowed. "You're not much of an eater," she commented, glancing over his half-full plate.

"On the contrary, I love food."

She nodded and took a small bite of pork, chewing thoughtfully. "If the food is fine and you love to eat, then why aren't you eating?"

"It's the company," he said.

A crimson flush inched up her neck and spread to her cheeks. Had the color spread downward, toward those lush, ripe breasts? He forced the thought away.

"I beg your pardon?" she said, her voice a mere squeak.

He shrugged and said, "You've been staring at me since we sat down."

She glared at him. "I have not been staring at you."

"You have. I know it's not because you're entranced with my good looks," he said, gesturing to himself. "Obviously, you're puzzled about something. What is it?"

The flush deepened and she stared at her plate. "Lady Julia, we'll be spending countless hours together. It's best if we're honest with each other from the start." Surprisingly, a bolt of lightning didn't shoot from the sky and strike him. Honesty, indeed. If she knew the truth right now, she'd fly across the table and scratch his eyes out.

"I was just wondering," she began, her eyes remaining on the plate in front of her. "Why did my brother select you, Mr. Mandrey?"

"I was the most qualified candidate."

Her head shot up. She opened her mouth to speak, then clamped it shut.

"You were about to say something," Cyrus prodded.

She shook her bent head, so the only thing he could see was a golden crown of ringlets bobbing back and forth. "Come now, Lady Julia, confess."

"It's nothing, Mr. Mandrey."

He admired the shimmering brilliance of her hair as the light danced over it. She'd worn it pulled back in a loose twist at the nape of her neck, a few tendrils escaping their confinement to trail about her shoulders. Compelling. Seductive. Like the woman. He shook his head and concentrated on the task at hand. "Honesty, Lady Julia."

The golden tendrils floated back and forth as she shook her head. "I can't be honest at the risk of being cruel."

Ah. So that was it. She doubted his ability to protect her but didn't want to hurt his feelings. A hint of a smile appeared beneath his beard. "You're concerned I might not be an adequate protector," he ventured.

She didn't answer.

"You think I might not be able to run very fast if need be due to the, ah, somewhat impaired movement in my legs." At least he'd played the part well.

Her head dipped lower.

"And I might not see the suspect or could possibly apprehend the wrong one, due to these spectacles." He fingered the thick glass. "Or perhaps this has nothing at all to do with my ability." He sipped his claret before speaking. "Perhaps you are so repelled by my homeliness, you can do nothing but stare at me in pity and disgust."

That got a reaction. Her head shot up, fire in her eyes, as she declared, "That is not true! I do not think you're ugly."

"Nor do I. I merely said homely." He smiled. "There is a difference you know."

She looked at him as though he'd gone mad. Then a giggle escaped her, followed by another. "A man with a sense of humor. How unique," she said, giggling again.

He raised his glass to salute her and took another drink. "Now, why don't you tell me what's bothering you."

A pink tinge washed over her cheeks. "I guess I do have some doubts as to your ability to protect me," she admitted. Her gray eyes seemed so contrite, so full of sympathy and concern, he almost wanted to tear away the disguise and show her who he really was.

"Please, don't apologize for your thoughts, Lady Julia. They're perfectly normal, considering the circumstances. Would an army feel comforted to learn their weapons were butter knives? How would an expert horseman feel if he were expected to show his skill on a wooden rocking horse?"

"Why do you make fun of yourself so, Mr. Mandrey?"

"I've learned to look beyond what appears to be, to find what is. Appearances are of no consequence to me. They rarely tell the true story. I was hired for my skill as a strategist and my cunning as a tactician. If I deploy these using the proper methods, brawn and speed will not be necessary."

"I see. And you feel you will be able to avoid an actual confrontation?"

"I do."

Julia picked up her fork and began toying with her food. "I

feel compelled to warn you that my husband may be equally skilled in such maneuvers."

Why would she say a thing like that? "Has he ever displayed certain capabilities that would lead you to believe this?"

"No, not exactly. But there's something about the way he moves, it's almost catlike, as though he could sneak up on a person when they least expected it."

She'd noticed that? He'd have to start walking with a heavier foot when this was all over. Trudge, that's what he'd do.

"And he has a very keen intelligence. I've seen him giving his full attention to one person and then turn and answer another before they've asked the question." She swirled her mashed potatoes in a circle. "I can't explain it. I just feel it."

Perhaps Julia should be the one in the espionage business after all. She could ferret out everyone with a hidden agenda, starting with Andrew Kleeton.

"Thank you for your concern, but I have been well trained," he said.

She smiled and nodded, slicing off a piece of roast pork.

Time to do a little prying. "What are your plans for tomorrow?" he asked.

"My plans?"

"Plans for the day. Your agenda. What will you be doing all day?" Dear God, he hoped her plans didn't include shopping or attending a tea, though the choices in the area for either diversion were limited.

"Nothing much. I plan to go riding with Mr. Kleeton in the morning, then I'll return for lunch and work in the garden until tea. I hadn't thought much past that. Why do you ask?"

He ignored the question. "Who is Andrew Kleeton?" He'd get her version of the suspect. She smiled. A rather large, happy smile, as though the thought of him made her warm inside. Cyrus clenched his fist under the table.

"He's a neighbor. We go riding together every morning."

Every morning! Billington had neglected to mention the

frequency of Julia's contact with Andrew Kleeton.

"Every morning," he repeated, when he had control of his temper.

"Yes," she nodded, scooping a spoonful of peas into her mouth and chewing. "He's an avid horseman and enjoys the ride." She smiled again. "He's also been quite insistent about escorting me about the area so I won't have to ride alone."

Like the fox escorting the hens to the hen house. Tomorrow couldn't come soon enough. "How thoughtful of him," he said in a dry, raspy voice.

"Yes, it really is quite thoughtful, isn't it? He's such a gentleman."

He didn't comment. "I look forward to meeting Mr. Kleeton tomorrow."

"You do? Why?"

She really hadn't figured it out yet. Sighing, he looked at her through his spectacles, which were nothing more than cut glass. He could see everything in minute detail. The distortion came from the side of the onlooker and the illusion that contorted his eyes, making them appear much smaller than they actually were.

"I have a job to do, Lady Julia. Where you go, I go. Everywhere. With a few minor exceptions, that is. If you have difficulty figuring out what those might be—" he gave her a little half smile that he doubted she could see beneath his beard "—I'll be happy to spell them out for you."

She sat there, huffing and puffing, getting indignant over his words and the way he'd said them. "Mr. Kleeton is hardly a suspect. Nor am I. I don't see why you have to follow us as though we're prisoners." She started tapping her knife on her plate.

If she only knew that her Mr. Kleeton was the number one suspect, who could well be a murderer *and* a traitor, she'd run so fast she'd wear out the bottoms of her slippers. "You'll have to ask your brother. Those were his instructions."

"I will," she said. "I most definitely will." She lifted her head and thrust out her chin. Cyrus almost laughed. Nobody was more mercurial than Julia. One minute she was weeping and the next she was ready to poke someone's eyes out. Probably his.

Best to let her stew about it for a while. Like it or not, he would accompany her with Kleeton tomorrow. He pushed back his chair and stood. Julia remained seated, staring at her plate. "What time will you be riding in the morning?"

She looked up and blurted out, "Early." She paused and gave him a sly little smile. "Very early."

The woman was up to something; he could almost see the wheels turning in her beautiful head. "How early?"

"I'll be leaving at six."

He hadn't pictured her to be an early morning person. He'd bet his last coin she was merely goading him. "I'll see you then." He nodded and prepared to leave. He should just walk out the door, but he couldn't resist the temptation to best her right now. "One more thing," he said, resting his hands on the back of his chair, "please extend my compliments to the cook."

"I will."

She was back to speaking in monosyllables again. "Might I request a meal of my choosing sometime in the near future?" he asked.

"Of course."

His gaze met hers. "I'd like to start off with cream of asparagus soup." She gasped. "For the main dish, I'd like roast duck." She turned white. "And red potatoes." Her eyes grew wide, as though she'd seen a ghost. From the past, he thought, stifling a chuckle. He nodded again and said, "You pick the dessert." With that, he shuffled out of the room, leaving Julia staring after him.

Chapter 13

At five forty-five the next morning, Cyrus Mandrey knocked on Lady Julia's door.

It creaked open a few inches and a half-asleep Julia peered at him from beneath heavy lids. Her hair fell like a golden cloak over her shoulders. It was obvious she'd just crawled out of bed.

"Are you ready?" he asked, tapping his riding crop.

"Ready?" Her voice was low and throaty, heavy with sleep. The sound washed over him, stirring his desire for her. A few more inches and he could be inside her room. A few more feet and he could be in her bed. A few more lifetimes and he might stand a chance. Patience was the key to all treasures, including his beautiful wife.

"I believe you told me you were riding with Mr. Kleeton at six o'clock this morning." Cyrus placed his hand on the door. If he could just inch it open a bit more, he might be able to see what she was wearing. No harm in looking. It was probably one of those virginal white gowns, like she'd worn on the ship, though with Julia's curves, it had looked anything but innocent.

He pushed the door forward just a hint.

She didn't seem to notice as her eyes drifted shut. He could see a few more inches. More than enough as he caught a glimpse of her splendid breasts and full hips, swathed in a light, filmy material. The gown clung to her curves in a gentle swirl, lending an ethereal quality to the whole creation. Had this been part of her trousseau? He leaned forward, and the faint scent of lilac drifted over him. Just one more inch.

Julia chose that precise moment to fall against the door, hit her head on the wood, and come awake with a shriek.

"Julia, are you all right?" Cyrus stepped forward and touched her arm.

"Your voice," she whispered. She no longer seemed aware that she'd shrieked in pain, or that she'd hit her head, or now stood before a veritable stranger, half clothed.

"My voice?" he repeated, dropping it a full two octaves to reach Cyrus Mandrey's level.

"You called me, Julia," she said, unable to take her eyes from him.

"I apologize," Cyrus said. "In my concern for your safety, I forgot my manners." *And he'd forgotten his senses because he'd been too busy ogling her body.*

"But your voice," she said again. "It sounded just like—" She closed her eyes a moment and when she opened them again, he saw the faint shimmering of unshed tears. "It was nothing," she said, pressing her fingers to the sides of her eyes. "If you give me ten minutes, I'll meet you at the stables."

"Of course. Are you certain you're all right?"

"I'm fine," she managed.

He backed out of the room. "I'll see you in ten minutes." He pulled the door shut. As he walked down the hall, he thought he heard a sniff and a sob from Julia's room.

What a damnable mess!

He hurried down the stairs and out the door. The morning air was fresh and brisk, reminding him summer would soon blend into fall. He smiled as the stable came into view and along with it, thoughts of seeing Henry Barnes and Flash.

"Mr. Barnes," he called out, entering the stable.

"In 'ere," the old man hollered from one of the stalls. Cyrus figured it would be Flash's. Old Henry had a penchant for the stallion, said their spirits were alike—wild and free.

"Hello, Mr. Barnes," Cyrus said, stepping up to Flash's stall. The horse whinnied at the sound of another voice and jerked his head up.

"'Ow are you?" The man's beady eyes scrunched up to get a better look at the stranger before him. Henry didn't like strangers, said they couldn't be trusted. He believed in two things. Family. And the Remmingtons.

"Name's Cyrus Mandrey, Mr. Barnes."

"Wot are you doin' 'ere?" He'd gone back to brushing Flash.

"I've been hired to protect Lady Julia," he said. That got his attention. His old, withered hand stilled on Flash's back.

"Be damned. I knew it! I told the little miss, the mast'r wouldna' like it if she went all ov'r the countryside with anoth'r man." He grinned, and the lines on his forehead and cheeks deepened. "Hah!"

Cyrus cleared his throat and hid a smile. "Actually, Mr. Barnes, I've been hired to protect Lady Julia *from* her husband."

"What?" Flash whinnied again and threw his head up, tossing it from side to side. "There boy, it's a'right," Henry said, stroking the stallion's black coat. "It's a'right." The horse calmed under his gentle touch. "That don't make no sense, mister. No sense a'tall."

Cyrus shrugged.

"Why a'body can see the master would nev'r do no 'arm to 'is wife. 'E loves 'er."

The conviction in Henry's words took Cyrus aback. "Why do you say that?"

"Plain simple as the nose on yer face," Henry said. "When 'e talked to me 'bout 'er comin' 'ere, 'e was all concerned 'bout her. Wanted the best fer 'er. But it was the way 'e talked 'bout 'er. 'Is voice got all soft and cozy like. I could tell. Plain simple."

Had it been that obvious that he was totally besotted with his wife? Apparently so. To everyone but the one person who should have seen it. His wife. But then he'd made every attempt to hide it from her. When this was all over, he'd make certain Julia never had reason to doubt him or his love again.

"If'n you ask me, ya oughta be protectin' her from that pretty boy, Kleeton."

"What do you know about Andrew Kleeton?"

"Enough to know I don' like 'im." Henry pointed a bony finger at Cyrus. "Keep yer eye on 'im. 'E's the one to watch."

Before Cyrus could ask any more questions, Julia entered the stables. "Mr. Mandrey?"

"Over here," Cyrus called out, glancing at his pocket watch. They were already fifteen minutes late. Julia had said they were to meet at the north end of the property at six o'clock. It would take a solid ten minutes to get there if they left now, and Henry still had to saddle the horses. They would be at least thirty minutes late. Would Kleeton wait? Cyrus had a feeling he would. If Kleeton *were* The Serpent, he'd use any opportunity to see Julia to further his quest for her husband. If he weren't, Cyrus believed he'd still wait for her in an attempt to coax her into becoming his own personal conquest. Both thoughts sickened and enraged him.

"I'm ready. I must have overslept."

Cyrus turned to greet her, but the words he'd planned to say stuck in his throat. Julia stood before him, dressed in a royal blue riding habit trimmed in gold. She wore her hair in one long braid that reminded him of nautical rope. He still wasn't used to seeing her in regal attire. Most of his memories had her garbed as a boy in breeches and an oversized jacket. Or, as a servant in thick muslin and sackcloth. Or, as a temptress on *The Falcon* in a gown sans underclothes. Or, and this was his fondest memory, as a full-blooded woman, warm and naked beneath him.

"A little early fer you ta'day, ain't it, Lady Julia?" Henry Barnes said with a grin.

She avoided looking at Cyrus. "Is it?"

Henry Barnes laughed and shook his head. "'Less my clock is off, I don' see you fer anoth'r three hours."

Julia picked at something on her jacket. "Don't mind him," she whispered. "He tends to get confused."

Cyrus stifled a laugh. Julia had a penchant for getting caught in traps of her own making. "Now for a mount. Would there be any objection if I took this one?" he asked, pointing to Flash.

"No," Julia said, so quickly he wondered if she'd heard the question.

"No?" Why would Flash matter to her?

"He's quite spirited," she said, clenching her gloves.

"I'm a superb horseman," he countered. And Flash was *his* horse.

"You might get hurt." She twisted the gloves between her hands.

"I'm a superb horseman," he repeated. What was the matter with her?

Julia threw a desperate look at Henry Barnes who stood off to one side, a huge grin on his face. She waited for him to say something to bail her out of her predicament. He lifted his shoulders and shrugged.

"He's only ever had one rider." There she went with those gloves again.

"He'll get used to me," Cyrus said, more curious by the moment.

"*One rider*," she emphasized the words.

"And?"

"My husband," she said, her voice a mere whisper. "Jon is the only person who's ever ridden Flash. He's his horse. No one else rides him."

For a second, he was so dumbfounded, he couldn't speak. For whatever reason, Julia had protected something that was his, and she'd been quite adamant about it. It wasn't exactly a profession of love, but it was a start.

"Fine. You should have said so in the first place." He turned to Henry Barnes, who was still grinning. "I'll take the chestnut in the corner."

Ten minutes later, they were saddled and ready to head out. Henry Barnes caught up to Cyrus and motioned him aside with a bony hand. "Jest thought I'd tell ya, case you didna' notice, I think she's in love with 'im too." With that, he stepped back, crossing his wiry arms over his chest, and laughed.

Cyrus saluted Henry as he left the stables. He had little time to ponder Henry's comment because Julia was several paces ahead of him. Was she in that much of a hurry to meet Kleeton? The thought did not sit well.

He caught up to her with his mount, Speed Demon, and they made their way to the north point of the property. Cyrus spotted a lone figure atop a huge, white stallion. Blood rushed to his head and anticipation pumped through him. In seconds he would face the man who might be the treacherous traitor and ruthless killer he'd exposed seven years ago. If he were, the man would be Peter Crowlton. The Serpent. And Crowlton would want revenge.

Cyrus gripped his reins tighter and followed Julia's lead, breaking into a full gallop, shortening the distance to the rider and the answers to the questions pounding in his brain. Within a matter of minutes, they pulled their mounts up, stopping several feet from the man Cyrus knew must be Andrew Kleeton. Billington had always been accurate with his descriptions and he'd not failed in this instance. Andrew Kleeton's features were fine-boned and delicate, his hair blond, his eyes blue, his nose thin and straight. Nothing like Jon Remmington. And unlike Jon, who could intimidate with a mere look, this man seemed incapable of frowning, much less killing.

But looks could be most deceiving.

"Hello, Lady Julia. As always, it's a pleasure to see you again." The man's voice slipped out like a caress. "Somewhat earlier than usual, but I was happy to accommodate your note and was pleased to receive it last evening."

Julia cleared her throat and said, "Yes, well, thank you. I would like to introduce you to Mr. Cyrus Mandrey. Mr. Mandrey, this is Mr. Andrew Kleeton."

Both men nodded.

"Mr. Mandrey is staying at Glenview Manor for a time," Julia said.

"How nice," Andrew murmured, his gaze scanning Cyrus's shaggy head and thick glasses. "Are you a relative? A cousin perhaps?" The small smile playing about Kleeton's well-curved lips told Cyrus he thought him a buffoon, no matter who he was.

"Not exactly." Julia shifted in her saddle and cast a sideways glance at Cyrus.

An uncomfortable silence settled over the trio as the men waited for Julia to speak again. She fumbled with her reins and almost dropped them.

Allegra sensed her mistress's discomfort and lifted her head, snorting and pawing the ground. The stallions eyed one another, nickering and blowing until Cyrus placed a hand on Speed Demon's mane and the horse stilled.

"Forgive me," Kleeton said, his words directed at Julia. "It was not my intention to embarrass you, yet it seems I've done exactly that. I was merely being polite, nothing more."

Julia was quick to ease the man's concern. "You have nothing to apologize for. It's just that the circumstances surrounding Mr. Mandrey's presence are a little...embarrassing."

"Then we needn't discuss it," Andrew said simply.

"I want to." Julia pushed back a stray lock of hair as Cyrus watched the byplay with growing irritation. Kleeton had her eating right out of his hand. He knew what to say and how to say it to get exactly what he wanted and make it look as though he had no part in it.

"It really isn't necessary," Kleeton said.

Julia smiled. A sweet, innocent smile just for Kleeton. Smiles like that should be reserved for her husband.

"Mr. Mandrey has been hired as my protector." She laughed. "The whole thing is quite ridiculous really. He's supposed to guard me from my husband."

That remark got a reaction from Kleeton. It was subtle, nothing more than a slight flinch of his left hand, but Cyrus noticed it as well as the gray leather covering that hand.

Kleeton recovered quickly. "Guard you from your husband? I'm afraid I don't understand."

"Nor do I. I tried to tell my brother it wasn't necessary, but he refused to listen. He gave me two choices, one of which was Mr. Mandrey. Had I chosen the other, I would have been back in his home last evening."

"Then I shall be indebted to Mr. Mandrey for keeping you here," Kleeton said, giving a slight nod in Cyrus's direction.

"I've only been at Glenview Manor a short time, but it feels like home already." Her eyes sparkled as she scanned the fields and rolling hills peppered with elm trees and several hundred feet away, clumps of orange and yellow daylilies. "It's breathtaking."

"Yes, it is," Kleeton agreed, but his eyes were on Julia. He thought *she* was exquisite. Cyrus balled his hands into fists, wishing he could sink one of them into Kleeton's perfect nose. Then it wouldn't be so perfect anymore. The man had nerve, trying to seduce his wife right in front of him. Of course, he didn't know that Jon Remmington was within ten feet of him, disguised under a brown wig and beard.

"Let's race," Julia said, a glimmer of excitement in her voice. "Mr. Mandrey is an accomplished horseman, too."

"Bravo," Kleeton said, but his words sounded flat.

"Hah!" Julia yelled, digging her booted heels into Allegra's sides. The mare bolted off down the hill at lightning speed. Kleeton's horse fell in behind with Cyrus in a close third. The riders leaned low and flat over their mounts, bending to the wind. Kleeton overtook Julia when they came out of the second hill. Cyrus passed her a few minutes later. He set his sights on the back of Kleeton's tan jacket and dug his heels into Speed Demon's side, calling out praise as they soared through the field. Kleeton must have sensed his lead was in jeopardy because he pulled out a riding crop and whacked his mount several times on the hindquarters. Despite the bite of the crop, the white stallion slowed, as though he'd been ridden all out too early in the game and had nothing left.

Cyrus took advantage of the animal's distress, sailing past him, head low, knees in tight. He raced on for several hundred feet before glancing back to see how his competition fared. Kleeton had slowed his horse to a trot but Julia was still barreling forward in a valiant effort to finish the race. Pulling up on Speed Demon, Cyrus settled him into a light canter as he waited for Julia.

"My goodness," she called out in a breathless voice, falling into pace with him, "you certainly are a superb horseman."

"Speed Demon is a superb horse," Cyrus said. "That makes all the difference in the world." He glanced behind to see Kleeton gaining on them. Another thirty seconds and he would be bearing down upon them.

"You and Speed Demon are the perfect match!"

"Perhaps you're right, Lady Julia," Cyrus agreed. "But isn't that life? Finding the right match?"

"What do you mean?" She cast him a sideways glance, her golden brows pulled down in puzzlement.

"When a person finds his perfect match, he can do anything. A lame man with a lightning-fast horse can fly." He stopped his horse and faced her. She must have known he was referring to himself because she grew very still. "And an unworthy man with an honest woman can turn into the most trustworthy husband in the world."

He watched her face as his words sunk in. She looked stricken, her gray eyes wide, her face pale. "Not always, Mr. Mandrey. Not always."

He opened his mouth to speak but Kleeton was upon them. "That was quite a show, Mandrey," he said, assessing Cyrus with renewed interest.

Cyrus shrugged. "As I told Lady Julia, Speed Demon is an excellent horse."

Kleeton nodded. "Avenger and I are not in the habit of losing." He patted the big white stallion, and Cyrus once again focused on the gray leather molded to Kleeton's hand. Beneath the leather hid the truth, a truth that could either expose Kleeton as a criminal or pardon him as an innocent.

One way or the other, Cyrus would find out.

***

"And that I believe is checkmate." Cyrus moved his bishop to trap Julia's king.

"You win," Julia conceded on a sigh. "Again." Cyrus smiled at her. It was difficult to see the smile beneath all that hair, but she could hear it in his voice as it softened and lost some of its hoarseness. She rather liked it that way, though he didn't do it often enough. In the three weeks since his arrival at the manor, she'd grown accustomed to spending hours at a time with him. They rode horses every morning at eight o'clock, a concession for Cyrus's choice, which was six o'clock and hers, which was ten. Andrew Kleeton didn't accompany them on their early morning jaunts but was included in the afternoon ones. Evenings were quiet, simple affairs with dinner and card games or chess afterward.

Why did she feel so comfortable with this man who just a few short weeks before had been a complete stranger? Perhaps it was his unpretentious manner or his silent strength that enabled her to relax with him. He could sense her moods and anticipate her reaction, sometimes before she did.

"Would you care for coffee?" She remembered he preferred coffee to tea.

"No, thank you. I'm stuffed. I've never had such excellent lamb. And the cherry tarts were exquisite."

Julia laughed. "I thought you liked the tarts. How many did you have? Four? Or Five?"

"Six," Cyrus admitted. "Did you notice how pleased the cook was when I complimented her? She was ready to bring out ten more."

"She'll probably expect me to eat as many when you're gone. I'll be as big as a house if you don't stop with your compliments."

Their gazes locked, but Cyrus said nothing. Julia wished she could see his eyes beneath the wire spectacles he wore. Eyes were the conveyors of true emotion and her inability to see his put her at a true disadvantage.

"Perhaps you won't be dining alone after I leave."

"I suppose Holt and Sophie will visit from time to time. And of course Andrew would be invited."

Cyrus's bushy brows creased into a straight line. "I wasn't thinking of Kleeton."

The sharpness in his tone surprised her. "You don't like him, do you?"

"No, I don't."

He usually maintained neutral ground, trying to understand both sides of a situation with their accompanying consequences, but when the subject of Andrew Kleeton arose, Cyrus's opinions were harsh. She hadn't missed the subtle insults both men had been dropping at each other for the past two days. Andrew considered Cyrus a servant, who took far too many liberties in his limited position as temporary protector to Julia, and saw no reason why the man should follow them about when they went riding. Andrew maintained that his skill with a pistol, a sword, and if need be, his fists, would protect Julia from the invisible threat of a husband.

As for Cyrus, she didn't know what it was that made him dislike Andrew so, but she intended to find out. "Would you be so kind as to tell me exactly what you find so offensive about Mr. Kleeton?"

He took a sip of his sherry. "I dislike any man bent on seducing another man's wife. Especially if it's one I'm supposed to be protecting."

"How can you say that? Andrew is *not* trying to seduce me!"

"What do you call it?" he asked, folding his arms over his broad chest.

"I call it being a friend."

"Then he's trying to become an awfully familiar friend."

"That's absurd."

"Is it?" He stood and braced his hands on either side of the mahogany table, leaning forward a bit to close the distance between them. "Are the two of you not on a first-name basis?"

"Yes, but that is of no consequence," she answered, a bit intimidated by his closeness. His face, that which wasn't covered by hair, was much younger than she would have guessed. She'd thought him well into his forties but realized he was probably on the low end of thirty.

"It *is* of consequence," he bit out, revealing a set of even, white teeth.

He had nice teeth too. And two well-shaped lips. Sensual lips. *On Cyrus Mandrey?*

"Julia?"

"What?" What other secrets lay hidden beneath all that hair?

"You haven't heard a word I've said."

"Hah!" She jumped from her chair and glared at him. "You just called me Julia. *Not* Lady Julia. If I call you Cyrus, does that mean you and I are involved in a clandestine relationship?"

He shook his bushy head. "Of course not."

"Good." She smiled. "Then you may call me Julia and I will call you Cyrus."

"Don't change the subject. *Julia*." He leaned farther over the table, moving closer to her. "Does Kleeton not find every possible opportunity to touch your person?"

"No!" she denied. He was so close she could smell his spicy cologne.

"Does he not act as your personal footman, assisting you as you mount and dismount Allegra?"

"Yes, but—"

"Does he not clasp your arm as he walks you about, trying to locate the *perfect* spot in the field for you to sit?" Cyrus didn't give her a chance to respond. "And when he locates that perfect spot, does he not place his hand at the small of your back, guiding you to your seat, lingering just a bit longer each time?" His voice rose with each accusation until it became nothing more than a menacing growl.

"It's not like that," she whispered, a tiny thread of fear wrapping around her with each angry word he spoke. This was a side of Cyrus Mandrey she hadn't seen before. A violent, dangerous side.

"Look at me, Julia," he commanded.

She looked down, studying his large hands, splayed across the table. Strong, tanned, capable hands. With calluses. He didn't seem like a man who engaged in manual labor, but his hands belied that fact. Why hadn't she noticed this before?

"Look at me."

Julia squared her shoulders and raised her head to stare at his dark eyes through the lenses of his spectacles. The glass was so thick she couldn't make out the actual color of his eyes. Dark brown? Black?

"He caresses you with his voice," Cyrus continued. "In soft, low tones, so you have to lean close to hear him."

"Andrew speaks in the pleasant, cultured tone of a true gentleman. Unlike others I know, who shall remain nameless." She sounded cold and haughty, but Cyrus deserved it. He had no business making cruel insinuations about a man he barely knew.

"Kleeton is no gentleman, and you know nothing about him other than what he's chosen to reveal. For all you know, your Mr. Kleeton could be a thief. Or a murderer."

"That's absurd." Andrew Kleeton had been nothing but kind and considerate since the morning she'd met him. Like a brother.

"What I find absurd is how you can be so trusting of a complete stranger and so critical of your own husband," he flung back.

Anger bubbled through her, filled her soul with a fire that burned in her next words. "My husband doesn't deserve my trust." She balled her hands into fists, so tight her nails dug into the flesh of her palm.

"How can you be so certain?" he asked. "Perhaps there are circumstances that sent him away."

Something in his voice reminded her of the desolate winds of winter, whipping over the land, leaving it stripped and barren. She ignored the voice, ignored the feeling that Cyrus was the wind whipping over the land, alone, in pain and despair. She could think of nothing but closing the wound he was so determined to scratch open. If she allowed even the tiniest possibility that Jon had not *wanted* to leave her, then the great wall of anger that protected her from loving him might come crashing down, piling onto the ground like so much rubble. It would crush her and all the defenses she'd spent weeks developing. She'd be left alone, naked and vulnerable once again to the man who could strip away her pride with a single look.

He must have realized he'd gone far beyond the bounds of propriety because Cyrus stepped back from the table, cleared his throat, and spoke. "Please accept my apologies. My temper got the best of me and I spoke out of turn."

He looked so perfect, so proper standing there, his words cool and void of emotion. Julia rather thought she liked the heated version of Cyrus Mandrey much better than the lukewarm one he presented to the world.

"He's a *friend,* Cyrus," she said, wanting to make him understand and hoping to divert his attention from further talk of Jon. "I care about him like a brother, nothing more."

She thought those words would soothe him, but he was around the table, bearing down on her before she could say another word. "Andrew Kleeton is not your brother," he said, his voice darker than a moonless night. "And you are a married woman."

How dare he accuse her of impropriety? "I'm well aware of my marital status," she hissed. He stepped closer, his trousers brushing the hem of her gown. Julia inched backward.

"Then perhaps Mr. Kleeton needs reminding—" he leaned toward her "—so he will stop trying to get into your bed."

Julia's hand flew up to slap him, but Cyrus caught her by the wrist. They stared at one another as silence deepened the chasm between them like unbanked floodwaters.

Cyrus spoke first. "I won't apologize for speaking the truth. The man wants you in his bed."

He released her then and without another look, turned on his heel and left. Julia stared after him, her anger forgotten for the moment as she replayed the last several seconds over in her mind. She could have sworn Cyrus walked out the door with calm, purposeful strides and not a single shuffle.

.

Chapter 14

The house vibrated with tension. Everyone noticed it from the footman to the chambermaid. There were no raised voices. No slamming doors. No stomping feet. Not a single disagreeable word. Only silence. A silence so dark and deep it crushed any thoughts of smiles and laughter, smothered the very idea of lightheartedness. It began to eat away at the inhabitants of Glenview Manor, an insidious disease, gnawing at their souls, stealing their peace of mind. They avoided Cyrus and Julia as much as possible. Cyrus didn't blame them; he didn't much like his company these days either.

He should try to settle things with Julia so the household could get back to normal. But after three days, he was still furious with her. Last night as he lay in bed, staring into the darkness, he admitted his anger had little to do with the fact that Julia had tried to slap him. No, the red-hot fire in his gut centered on her unwillingness to believe anything bad about Kleeton. Or anything good about her husband.

He paced back and forth in the library, stopping occasionally to glance out the double-paned window. Julia knelt on the grass, her gloved hands covered with dirt as she separated a clump of herbs. She looked serene. Content. Cyrus cursed. How could she look so damned happy when he was so damned miserable?

And how could she honestly not know that Kleeton wanted to bed her? Couldn't she tell by the overblown praise he gave her? Did she really believe it when Kleeton told her she had hair the color of the sun, as though one hundred fairies had danced through it with their wands dipped in gold? Or that she was so exquisite she reminded him of a Greek goddess? What rubbish! He'd almost fallen off his horse when he'd heard Kleeton murmur those words. It had taken every ounce of willpower not to spring from Speed Demon and pummel the man.

Julia was an intelligent woman. Certainly, she could tell

when a man was feigning sincerity for ulterior motives. As in wanting to feel the silk of that luxurious golden hair running over every inch of his naked body, or finding out just how exquisite her body was minus clothing.

If Jon had made any of those ridiculous comments to her in the guise of a compliment, she'd have flung a chamber pot at him. Or jabbed him with a poker. But not Andrew. He was too perfect, too polished. Beyond reproach. It had been almost four days since the argument. They were becoming quite adept at avoiding each other whenever possible. Cyrus had received a note from Julia via Billington the first morning, informing him she was under the weather and wouldn't be taking her early morning ride for the next several days. Just as well, because Cyrus didn't trust himself to be alone with her for fear he'd wring her neck.

Meals were another somber affair. Cyrus tended to bury himself in the paper during breakfast and, other than a slight nod when she entered, ignored the beautiful woman at the other end of the table. He called forth his many tactical skills to elude Julia during the other meals by dining before or after the scheduled time. As for Kleeton and the afternoon rides, Julia gave those up as well, at least for the moment.

For all his apparent elusiveness, Cyrus knew where Julia was and what she was doing at all times. If she roamed about in the gardens, working among the herbs or wildflowers, which she seemed to do quite a bit, he watched from the library window. If she decided to stroll among the roses or walk the privet maze, Billington followed her. If Julia ventured to the stables, which she did every day, Cyrus trailed several paces behind. Henry Barnes was more than willing to report his mistress's comings and goings once he learned Cyrus didn't like Andrew Kleeton any more than he did.

Evenings stretched out long and lonely. There were no more after-dinner chess games or comfortable conversations. No more soft melodies drifting through the air as Julia's fingers glided over the piano keys. Only the echoes of silence rang through the manor, louder and more deafening than a crowded ballroom at the height of the Season.

"Sir?"

Cyrus turned from the window. Billington's measured steps advanced toward him, his lanky body moving with its usual air of quiet superiority. "What is it, Billington?"

"This, sir." Billington held out a plain white envelope with Julia's name on it. "It's from Mr. Kleeton."

Cyrus snatched the envelope and tore it open. He scanned the contents and said, "It looks as though I'm about to get a peek into Kleeton's lair. Julia's been invited to tea tomorrow afternoon. Isn't that nice, Billington?"

Edward Billington's upper lip twitched into a semblance of a half smile. "Very good sir. Very good indeed."

***

The carriage rolled along the dirt road, winding its way past rows of elm and ash, their leaves fluttering in the soft breeze like tiny jewels. Small clouds of dust kicked up around the wheels, partially obscuring the mosaic pattern the sun's rays cast on the ground as they filtered through the green foliage.

Cyrus stared out the window. He and Julia had been in the carriage less than ten minutes but it seemed like hours. The scent of her lilac perfume called to him. He stared harder. Her soft, even breathing floated through the carriage and wrapped around his body like a whisper, tugging at his heart. And his groin. He closed his eyes and blinked hard. A vision of Julia, naked and writhing beneath him, swept through his mind. Soft. Sensuous. His eyes shot open. Damn, but it was hot in this blasted carriage. He tugged at the knot of his cravat. This had been a mistake. He should have saddled Speed Demon and ridden alongside the carriage, a safe distance from the sight and sound and smell of Julia.

Casting a sideways glance at her, he noted she continued to stare out of the window, oblivious to his current state of distress or the fact that she was the cause of it. Her hair looked perfect, every golden lock in place under the pale-green bonnet trimmed in gold. Hands adorned in cream kidskin remained in her lap, resting on the neat folds of her pale-green gown. Julia appeared calm, cool, and unperturbed, unlike her husband, who was as wild as a tempest and as hot as the devil himself. Julia could do that to him. And it galled him.

He couldn't think straight when she was so close, which was the whole reason they were in their current predicament. He'd lost his temper, said things he shouldn't have, and all because whenever he looked at her, smelled her lilac scent, heard her soft voice, he lost his objectivity. Damnation! Never had he been on an assignment where he'd done that. He'd always prided himself on his ability to remain in character.

Until now. Julia made him feel things he'd never felt before and it was proving quite difficult to keep his cover because he felt anything but detachment from his wife. And because of this, he interfered with his own character. Jon kept creeping in, stealing an extra moment whenever possible, lingering on a word, fabricating excuses to spend time with her. Cyrus Mandrey would not have done that. Cyrus was here to do his job in a professional manner but Jon wouldn't let him, and now Cyrus Mandrey and Jon Remmington were intertwined, creating a dangerous, deadly situation.

Cyrus Mandrey would never have lost his temper or forgotten to shuffle along or spoken in Jon's voice. He would have completed his mission with as little emotion as possible and disappeared. That's what had always made Jon such a good operative. He possessed the ability to lose himself in whatever role he played. So much so, it was difficult to find a trace of Jon Remmington in any of his characters. Until now. Jon had seeped into the persona of Cyrus Mandrey, little by little, day by day.

It was time to get a grip on the situation and force Jon out of the picture, or at least control him before he made another mistake. If Kleeton were The Serpent, he'd be a trained observer, skilled at detecting the slightest incongruence.

Cyrus pulled his gaze back to the woman seated across from

him. Her eyes had fluttered closed, her head tilted back to expose the slender column of her neck. His gaze lingered on her chest, mesmerized by the slow, even movement of her breasts. He leaned against the velvet squabs and sighed. There was no way he could play the role of Cyrus Mandrey without Jon's thoughts and feelings taking over. No way at all.

***

Penworth was an old estate, older than Glenview Manor, with vine-covered brick walls and overgrown privet and arborvitae cowering along the pathways and main entrance. Clumps of overgrown grass and weeds crowded out the few spindly roses that fought through the thick greenery as they struggled for a hint of light.

Cyrus walked ahead of Julia, reminding her of a soldier blazing the path. Tiny shreds of guilt tugged at her. They hadn't exchanged a civil word in days. Longer than that since they'd laughed or shared honest conversation. She missed those times. He'd only been trying to protect her because he believed Andrew was a threat, but it hadn't been necessary. Andrew wasn't trying to get into her bed, for heaven's sake. Only one man had ever tried to do that, and he'd succeeded, with very little effort.

Jon was the cause for the rift with Cyrus. Everything always came back to that blasted man. If Cyrus hadn't tried to make excuses for Jon's actions, implying that he might well have had good reason for leaving, Julia wouldn't have lost her temper and this whole argument would never have taken place. Cyrus always seemed to rally for Jon, giving him the benefit of the doubt, making an excuse for his absence. She knew why he was doing it. She'd figured it out weeks ago.

Cyrus wanted to protect her feelings by fabricating forgivable reasons for Jon's leaving but there was no use trying to sweeten a bitter pill. Julia knew her husband for the uncaring rakehell he was, even if Cyrus did not.

"We're here to see Mr. Kleeton." Cyrus's low voice pulled Julia back from her thoughts. She looked up and gasped. A short, squat man with a black patch over his right eye stared straight at her. His good eye, if it could be considered that, was a rheumy faded gray. His sallow complexion matched the few strands of hair remaining on his head. He wore black from the ill fitting jacket stretching over his round middle to the boots on his small feet. He made no move to let them in, nor did he speak. His thin lips curved downward into a frown.

Cyrus cleared his throat and tried again. "Would you be so kind as to announce Lady Julia Remmington and Mr. Cyrus Mandrey? Mr. Kleeton is expecting us."

The man backed away from the door, an inch at a time. Cyrus took that opportunity to shoulder his way through, grabbing Julia's hand, and pulling her with him. The heavy wooden door clicked behind them. Julia turned to see the butler's pudgy hands pushing a heavy brass lock through the bolt. Thank God Cyrus was with her. She'd apologize for their silly little spat as soon as they were back inside the carriage headed home. And to think she'd almost tried to sneak away to Penworth without him. Julia clung to his arm as they walked down the hall. It was midafternoon, nearing the end of summer, yet Penworth gave off the feel of midnight in the dead of winter. Dark. Dismal. The butler stopped in front of a black double door and knocked.

"Come in," Andrew Kleeton called from the other side.

The butler opened one of the doors and stepped back to permit Cyrus and Julia entrance. A stale, sour odor reached Julia as she passed the strange creature of a man and when she sensed his rheumy eye on her, she moved closer to Cyrus.

Andrew Kleeton rose from an overstuffed chair and approached them. He was the one bright spot in an otherwise, gloomy room. The casual elegance of his coffee-colored, superfine jacket, cream breeches and snowy-white cravat were at odds with his dark surroundings. He was sunshine, and light, with his blond good looks and gleaming smile.

"Julia, how good to see you," he said, bestowing one of those smiles as he took her hand.

If she kept her gaze fixed on his summer-blue eyes, she could almost forget where they were. She glanced at the black brocade draperies that covered the windows, barring even a sliver of light from entering. The sofa, the chairs, the rugs were all done in matching patterns of black. What in the world was Andrew doing in a morbid place like this?

Andrew nodded in Cyrus's direction. "Mandrey."

"Kleeton." Neither man made an attempt to extend a hand.

"If there is no objection," Andrew said, "I had rather thought to share a quiet cup of tea with Julia."

"That's why we're here, isn't it?" Cyrus asked, his words laced with sarcasm.

"Alone."

"Why?"

Andrew's eyes narrowed just a hint, and then he smiled again. "I have some issues I wish to discuss with her. In private."

Cyrus crossed his arms over his burly chest. "My job is to protect Julia. Where she goes, I go."

"Are you still worried about Jon Remmington? You needn't be." Andrew strode to a brocade-covered window and pulled back the fabric. "Even your Mr. Remmington couldn't get through these." Black iron bars, set close together, ran the entire length of the window, blocking anyone from entering. Or exiting. A twinge of uneasiness gripped Julia. With each passing moment, Penworth reminded her more of a prison and less of a residence.

"Julia?" Cyrus asked, ignoring Andrew.

"Yes, I'll be fine," she said with more conviction than she felt. She looked about the room, from the huge sword displayed over the mantel to the flickering lamps that cast eerie shadows off the walls. What was Andrew doing here? It was the tenth time she'd asked that question in the ten minutes since she'd crossed the threshold of Penworth. He didn't belong in such morbid surroundings. Perhaps this was the décor of the previous residents, the duke and duchess of something or other.

Julia couldn't recall their names, but she would bet these hideous furnishings bore their stamp.

But what about the monster of a man behind her? She could still hear his thick, heavy breathing, still smell the sour cabbage emanating from his person. Was he a castoff from the duke and duchess as well?

"In that case, I'll be waiting right outside the door," Cyrus said.

Andrew addressed the butler. "Thank you, Charles, that will be all. Would you please send Mrs. Rothmore in with our tea?" He smiled at Julia again. "Oh, and have her see to Mr. Mandrey's needs."

The labored breathing diminished, as did the smell of something akin to a rubbish bin, signaling the butler's departure. As the door closed, Julia let out a long breath. "Andrew," she asked as she removed her bonnet, "where on earth did you find that man?" Dreadful, shocking, monstrous were more appropriate descriptions, but she didn't want Andrew to know how much one man bothered her.

"Charles? He's harmless," Andrew said, taking a seat beside her on the black sofa. He leaned back and crossed a booted foot over his knee. "Charles is the product of our country's illustrious prison system. When I found him, he was nothing more than a bloody, beaten piece of human flesh, his eye gouged out and his tongue ripped from his mouth. He'd been thrown in a fallow grave, left to bleed to death."

Prison. Beaten piece of human flesh. Left to bleed to death. Questions thundered in her brain, rolling over one another, fighting for the answers like the hooves of a hundred horses charging into battle. What was Andrew doing near a prison? Why was this man Charles beaten and left for dead? What crime had he committed? Why did Andrew's fine lips twist into a cruel smile, his eyes glaze, as though he relished the tale and wanted to say more? Perhaps expand on the hideous mutilation of the butler, describe each gory detail?

When Julia shuddered, Andrew's gaze snapped to hers, his

eyes warm and smiling, making her think she must have imagined the coldness in them a moment ago, must have dreamed the demonic curl of his lips.

He patted Julia's hand and asked in a voice the texture of brushed velvet, "Aren't you going to ask me what I was doing near Newgate?"

Julia nodded. How foolish and small of her to act so skittish about the tale of a man and his misfortune. She should concentrate instead on Andrew's valiant rescue effort and the fact that Charles was still alive, disfigured or not.

"It's a well-kept secret, but I'm something of an amateur writer. I've always kept journals of my travels, writing about everything, no matter how insignificant. Human suffering intrigues me. Exploring Newgate seemed logical. I wanted to understand the mechanisms of a prison from the dank, musty interior of the cells to the warped, sinister minds of the guards and the broken, hopeless spirits of the imprisoned."

"To fight the cause of the oppressed?" Julia asked, thinking him nothing short of a hero.

"To test the limits to which a human will go before he loses reason, blurs all sense of right and wrong, and is willing to compromise himself and his ideals," Andrew answered.

Julia frowned. She hadn't expected that answer. "But why is he compromising himself?"

Andrew leaned toward her, his summer-blue gaze pressing into hers. "Greed and power, Julia. It all boils down to that. Greed and power."

"Greed and power?" she echoed. "As in everyone has a price at which he or she will give over and perform in a particular manner?" Her voice rose. "Or, for the assurance of a certain amount of control, one can also be persuaded to surrender one's values? I most strongly disagree with you, Andrew. If one has true conviction, no amount of money or power will lure him from that conviction."

He laughed, a full and hearty sound that filled the air, lightening the somber mood. "Oh, Julia, of course, you believe in conviction and principle. That's what makes you who you are." His words were as gentle as the wind whispering through the trees. "That's why you are so very special. And you are, Julia. So very special."

She smiled, mistaking the heat in his voice for genuine brotherly affection. "As are you. Thank you for being such a good friend."

His lips tilted upward, a faint suggestion of a smile playing about his mouth. "Friends."

"Good friends," Julia said, her smile deepening.

"Ah, yes," he repeated. "Good friends."

A knock on the door signaled their refreshments had arrived. "Come in, Mrs. Rothmore." The door opened, but it was Cyrus, not Mrs. Rothmore, who bore the silver platter of tea and assorted cakes, cookies, and scones. He advanced, and without a word, placed the tray on the mahogany table.

"Your new duties suit you, Mandrey," Andrew said, nodding toward the silver tea service.

Cyrus ignored his words and addressed Julia. "Is everything all right?"

"Of course, Cyrus," Julia said, puzzled by his concern. "Everything is fine."

"I'll be outside," he said and turning on his heel, quit the room.

"He's the reason I wanted to speak with you in private."

"Cyrus?" Julia asked, holding her cup while Andrew poured the steaming brew for her.

"Yes. Mandrey. I think you should get rid of him. The sooner the better."

"I can't do that!"

"How can he protect you when he can't take his eyes off you long enough to notice the threat of danger?"

"That's absurd."

"The man's in love with you, Julia. Surely, you can see that."

"Cyrus is concerned for my welfare, nothing more.

Certainly nothing on a personal level." She sipped her tea, finding it odd that Cyrus had said the exact same thing about Andrew. She didn't believe either one. More likely, they were using her as a pawn, a prize to be won in their war against one another, for nothing more than the sheer sake of winning and besting the other.

She would have no part in their games.

"Julia, I tell you, I've been watching the man. He's in love with you," Andrew persisted.

"Funny, but Cyrus said the same thing about you." She met his blue gaze, her face somber, unsmiling. "The two of you have been at odds since the moment you met. I suggest you deal with one another on a private level and stop putting me in the middle."

Her words cast a shadow of gloom over the conversation, matching the dimness of the room. "Very well," Andrew said. "Perhaps that's exactly what we need to do. Settle matters in private."

"Good." At least one of these men was being reasonable. Cyrus had been about as easy to move as the stone fountain on the front lawn of Glenview Manor. But Andrew's next words made her realize he was just as stubborn as Cyrus, though in a more diplomatic, genteel manner.

"And when Mandrey is gone, I'll take over full protection of you against your errant husband, when and if he ever shows."

"Andrew—"

"Don't worry, Julia," Andrew waved a gloved hand in dismissal, "I can handle *ten* Jon Remmingtons."

***

The carriage pulled away from Penworth with Andrew's words clinging to Julia like a hot summer night, still and close, almost suffocating. *I can handle ten Jon Remmingtons.* There had been sincerity and conviction in those words. Determination, too. For the first time in all of her encounters with Andrew, Julia had detected a tenacity that heretofore lay buried under an air of gentlemanly civility. But she'd seen it today and it surprised and confused her.

What would happen if Andrew and Jon ever met one another? Though Jon could intimidate through sheer size and dark looks alone, Julia sensed Andrew would not fall prey to such tactics. Rather, he'd remain undeterred, employing craftiness and cunning to achieve his goal— whatever goal that might be.

The only bright spot in the whole situation was her relative certainty that Jon would not return. Seeing her again had most likely been a passing fancy—like their marriage. She closed her eyes and sighed. Jon was but a memory, and an unpleasant one at that. Everything would be fine.

"What the devil is going on?"

Julia's eyes shot open. They'd rounded the bend toward home where Glenview Manor sat several hundred yards ahead, in stately, vine-covered elegance. But the front lawn leading to the manor was anything but stately or elegant and this is where Cyrus's attention lay. Two men, one tall and skinny, the other built like a mountain, romped about the front lawn like children on a Sunday afternoon. They ran to the huge fountain and drenched their bodies with the water spouting from the stone angel's pursed lips. A third attempted to climb the privet hedge.

From the distance, their manner of dress appeared similar— breeches, loose-fitting shirts, jack boots. Most wore caps. Only one man stood out from the rest and Julia would have recognized his tall, lanky build anywhere. Edward Billington volleyed between the men like a black bouncing ball, his long arms gesturing to the house in choppy movements. He appeared to be trying to get everyone inside, probably to regain control and avoid a spectacle, as was the typical Billington style. Little did he realize he provided more entertainment than the men cavorting on the lawn.

"Damn them," Cyrus whispered under his breath.

Oh, but he did not look pleased.

Julia peered out the window in an effort to get a better glimpse as the carriage rolled around to the middle of the drive. The men stopped their play as all eyes centered on the elegant carriage bearing the Remmington crest. It was then that Julia saw their faces, young, old, stubbled, clean-shaven, familiar ones. Before Cyrus could stop her, she leapt from her seat and flung open the door, bounding into the waiting arms of *The Falcon's* crew.

Chapter 15

"I tell you, Miss Julia, er, I mean *Lady* Julia, the cap'n was dyin' without you." Big Tom's full lower lip pulled into a pout as he shook his shaved head. "Jest dyin'."

"Yep, it's true enough," Amos piped in, popping a piece of roast duck in his mouth and chewing it with great thought. His sun-weathered face resembled well-worn leather, creases and all. "The cap'n was miserable before he left. Ornery too." He shook his gray head and laughed. "He was a sight to be around, let me tell you."

"He's in love." All eyes turned to the red-haired youth who'd uttered the words. Jeremy's face turned five shades deeper than his hair. "It's just my opinion, is all," he muttered, bowing his head to stare at his plate.

Cyrus tapped his fingers on his glass of claret. When this was all over, he'd thrash every one of his men, starting with Big Tom and saving an extra one for Jeremy. Or two, perhaps. They were making Jon look like a weak-kneed spineless fool and there wasn't a damn thing he could do about it. From the moment Julia bound out of the carriage, he knew trouble was ahead, and he'd been right. For the last several hours, he'd heard nothing but what a sorry excuse for a man Jon had become since parting from his beloved wife. It was downright sickening.

"He'll come fer you now," Amos said around a mouthful of candied yams. "Sure enough, he will." The other men, mouths filled with samplings of roast duck, boiled potato, and candied yams, grunted agreement.

Was Julia worried for Jon's safety? Did *she* think he'd try to come to her? One look at her plate told him something was bothering her. She'd flattened her potatoes, topped them with smashed yams, and dumped shredded roast pork over the whole mess. And she hadn't taken more than two bites, though he couldn't blame her on that count.

Julia cleared her throat and glanced around the table. Her

eyes glistened with tears like stars on a cloudless night. Cyrus didn't miss the slight tremor in her hand as she smoothed back a stray lock of hair.

"Thank you, each of you. You've all been so kind, trying to make me feel better by telling such high tales about your captain." Her smile grew bright, too bright, as though it masked a pain buried deep in her soul where joy once dwelt before betrayal and despair blotted out its memory. "But," she continued with just the slightest quiver in her voice, "we all know there isn't a weak bone in Jon's body. He's proud and fierce, and—" she hesitated, stumbling over the next word as though her tongue refused to say it "—determined. You all know he's determined not to be saddled with a wife."

The men all started talking at once, their raucous voices drowning out Julia's protestations until a shrill whistle burst through the clamor, quieting the group in an instant.

All eyes turned to the man who'd issued the signal. Mac Judson patted Julia's hand and frowned at the misbegotten group that was more family than his own blood relations. He stroked his white beard with his free hand, a gesture the crew knew he employed when deep in thought. The room remained silent, waiting.

The oak chair squeaked under Mac's weight as he turned to face Julia, his paunch spilling over the ornately carved arm. His rough, reddened hand remained on her smooth, slender one, offering comfort and strength. It amazed Cyrus how this woman could make a man, any man, regardless of rank or station, want to help her.

"I've known Jon a long time, Lady Julia," Mac began, holding her gaze with his honest blue eyes. "As I told you before, he's a good man. When he left us several weeks back, he told me he wasn't returning until he had you with him. Those were his exact words." His voice grew soft and low, like the lapping of the tide on sun-weathered rocks. "I believe him."

A tear escaped and trickled down Julia's cheek. "But where is he, Mac? He's had plenty of time." The sadness in her voice ripped at his gut. Brave Julia. He wanted to stand up and rip off his wig, throw his glasses and beard on the ground, and end this cruel game. He clenched his hands to stop himself.

Mac's broad shoulders lifted. "Perhaps he's here. Somewhere." His blue eyes glanced over Cyrus, then settled back on Julia. "Have faith in him, Lady Julia."

"'E's the cause of it all," Big Tom said, pointing a sausage-sized finger at Cyrus. "We heard he was hired ta keep the cap'n away from Lady Julia. If'n it wasn't fer 'im, they'd be together already."

Julia shook her head. "Well, that's not exactly—"

"That's right," Amos cut her off. Scratching his gray head, he muttered, "Wot business is it o' 'is if the two of them git together or not?" He leaned forward, his faded blue eyes the color of the ocean after a storm.

"I agree." Jeremy's voice squeaked with feeling. "He had no business interfering with them. They would've worked it out. They-they—" he stuttered. "They love each other." His ears flamed but he kept his level gaze on Cyrus, challenging him to answer.

"Gentlemen, there's something you should know," Julia began.

"The kid's right," Big Tom said, hitting the table with a beefy fist.

"Right 'e is!" Amos seconded, his scrawny fist following suit.

Within seconds, the table resounded with shouts as the men pounded their fists on the hard oak, shooting venomous gazes at the man they now held responsible for their captain and his lady's separation.

Cyrus watched in amazement, moved that these men would remain so loyal to their captain. Or perhaps, it was his lady whose allegiance they now served. Either way, they were hell-bent and dead-set against Cyrus. It was time to settle things down before they pounded him with the same vigor they were attacking the table. He could ill afford another broken or bruised body part.

Slamming his fist down, he roared, "Enough!"

The room fell quiet, all eyes watching in startled silence.

Cyrus stood, his hands resting on the linen tablecloth. He eyed each man, holding his gaze until the other man looked away. Big Tom stared at his plate. Amos looked off to the right and scratched his ear. Jeremy turned several shades of red and planted his eyes on the ceiling. None of the other men were bold enough to hold his gaze.

Except Mac Judson.

Mac sat back in his chair, hands crossed over a stomach that reminded Cyrus of rising bread, expanding to twice its normal size. His blue eyes, usually warm and full of spirit, were staring with dead intent at Cyrus as though he could see behind the bushy wig and beard, behind the thick glasses and raspy voice, to the man who lay beneath the layers of extra padding.

Cyrus addressed the men before him. "You men may hate me and hold me responsible for the separation of your captain and his wife." This statement brought a round of low grumbles. "And I say—" he paused to give his next words added meaning "—if your captain truly loves Lady Julia, *no one* will keep him from her." He balled his hands into fists. "Not me, or Lord Westover. Or the devil himself. If he truly loves her, Remmington will find a way to be with her."

The men hadn't expected this backward rally for their captain. It was clear in the way they looked at one another, muttering low under their breath, scratching their heads, shifting their gazes between Cyrus and Mac Judson. Each man was prepared to hate Cyrus; he could see it in the way they narrowed their eyes on him, hear it in their harsh accusations, feel it in the tenseness vibrating throughout the room. They wanted to pounce on him for wreaking havoc on the lives of two people they cared about but now they couldn't, not after the words he'd just spoken. And that rubbed them raw.

Knowing his men, they'd probably want to get in a punch or two, just to work off some frustration. He didn't miss the glaze in Big Tom's beady eyes, which usually meant he was ready to launch an attack on some unsuspecting victim. Mac settled the matter, gathering his men around him to prepare for battle. He had the direction, the determination, the faith to lead his men and the wisdom to impart this knowledge to them. When Mac spoke, they listened. Only one man commanded more respect from these men. Unfortunately, Jon Remmington was hiding behind a wig and beard at the moment. Worse yet, the man he was posing as was the object of these men's ire.

"Listen here, men," Mac's quiet voice stilled the clamor in the room. "Mandrey's got a point. He's only doing his job, nothing more, nothing less. You have to respect him for that." Mac grinned. "And when Jon shows up—" his blue eyes twinkled "—and we all know he will, he'll only be doing *his* job when he trounces this unlucky gent."

"'E'll beat 'im to the bones," Big Tom said, nodding his head back and forth.

"Jon will string 'im up by his boots," Amos chimed in, cackling like a wild man.

"He takes care of his own," Jeremy said, his young voice trembling with emotion.

Cheers traveled around the room until Mac raised his hand to silence them. "You have one thing working in your favor, Mandrey," he said, stroking his long beard in casual speculation.

"Pray, Mr. Judson, what might that be?" These men had him all but buried. If one believed the roar of the crowd, the only advantage Cyrus might have against Jon would be a head start away from Glenview Manor.

Mac's lips turned up in a slow, easy smile as his gaze traveled over Cyrus's face. "I was just thinking that a few nicks and bruises would never show under all that hair." He tilted his head to the left. "And those glasses would hide a broken nose real well. Yes sir, Mr. Mandrey, you might just consider yourself a lucky man."

***

"I'm sorry, Mac, but I don't see Jon returning," Julia said as she poured coffee into his cup. They were sharing after-dinner coffee in one of Julia's favorite rooms. She called it the Cream Salon because everything from the thick Persian rug to the damask draperies, brocade sofa, and overstuffed chairs shone in various shades of cream.

Cream vases lined the fireplace mantel, each displayed in various sizes and shapes with oriental designs etched on them. A huge silk print of a dragon in white, gold and cream, hung over the mantel. Square cream pillows with gold tassels accented the sofa and chairs, and in the corner of the room rested a stack of four very large pillows of the same cream color and gold tassel design as those found on the furniture.

These particular pillows had intrigued Julia and when she was certain no one was about, she'd kicked off her slippers and crawled onto them. And toppled off. Apparently, sitting on them four high was incorrect. She had more success when she placed each one on the floor and chose one. Sometimes, she scattered them about and stretched her body on all four, which felt as though she were lying on a big, fluffy cloud. She'd done that a few times and fallen fast asleep.

Mr. Billington had caught her once and much to her amazement, made no comment other than to ask if she were comfortable, to which she pushed the tangled mass of hair from her eyes and replied yes, very much so. He'd bowed and left, and she almost thought she'd seen a shadow of a smile on his thin lips, which was impossible, since the man never smiled.

This room brought her peace, imposing a quiet serenity she often sought. She needed that feeling tonight, especially as she waited for Mac to bring up the one subject that could tear down her wall of tranquility.

Julia set the heavy pot down, making a production of preparing her own steaming brew. Two lumps of sugar, a spot of cream. Stir together, blend to a dark tan. Place spoon on side of saucer. Anything to avoid discussing her husband.

"He'll be here, sure as my name is Mac Judson."

There it was, the first words out of his mouth.

As confident as Mac was Jon would return, Julia was just as confident he wouldn't. Why would he when he had Desiree and Monique to warm his bed? Why should he when he'd been forced into a marriage he didn't want, with a woman he didn't love? No well-bred woman would discuss such delicate matters, especially with a man. But she wasn't just any woman; she was a woman with a mission.

She plunged forward. "Mac, you've known Jon for ages. Please don't try to spare my tender sensibilities. I know about his women. I saw the clothes or whatever you might call those wisps of material in his armoire. He's probably off on one of his adventures, lazing about in some port, too drunk on wine and lust to know or care where he is." Saying the words aloud shredded the last flimsy bits of hope she'd clung to into a hundred pieces of nothingness.

Mac shook his bushy white head. "You're dead wrong, Lady Julia."

She blinked. Why couldn't she discuss Jon without crying? Where was her calm? Why couldn't she say his name without a quiver in her voice, as though at any moment, she'd fall apart? When would it stop? *Breathe, just breathe, and think of nothing else.* But it was no use. The bitter truth dug its way out, clawing and taunting her with words she refused to believe. It would never be over. Not in one day or one year or one hundred years.

"No." She fought to block out the words swirling through her brain, teasing her with harsh reminders. "No," she repeated.

"Yes, Lady Julia. You're wrong about Jon." Mac's voice proved a soothing balm to her tense nerves, even if his words did not. "There have been no other women since the wedding. I'd wager there hasn't been one since the day he laid eyes on you." She wanted to laugh. Instead, she raised an eyebrow and scowled.

Mac held up a big, fleshy hand. "Now just wait a minute. I'm getting the feeling you think you're the only one who's unhappy with this marriage situation." He shook his head. "Not so. Jon was miserable the last time I saw him."

"Of course, he was miserable, Mac. I knew that." It was bad enough surmising his unhappiness and knowing she was the cause of it, but having someone confirm those thoughts was even worse.

"Sure enough he was miserable, but not for the reason you think. I went to visit him a few days before the wedding. Do you know how I found him? Do you know what he was doing?"

It would not have been ladylike to tell Mac she had a fair idea of how he'd spent his last days of bachelorhood. She wasn't supposed to know about *those* kinds of places so Julia kept her true thoughts to herself and simply shrugged.

"I'll tell you, little lady. I found him, drunker than a dog and more miserable than a bird without wings."

Because she'd clipped them.

"And all because he had to marry you and leave." His blue gaze searched her face. "He didn't want to leave you. He wanted to be a proper husband. A real husband."

The cup slipped from her hands, splattering hot coffee onto her blue gown.

Mac jumped from his chair. "I upset you. I'm sorry." He handed her his linen napkin, his big frame standing beside her as though to ward off further accidents.

"He—he *wanted* to marry me?" Hearing the words aloud sounded foreign, even to her, and she'd dreamed them a thousand times. Jon had wanted to marry her. He'd never indicated by even the smallest degree that he'd be amenable to such an arrangement. But then, she hadn't seen him until ten minutes before the wedding. And afterward, Julia blushed with remembering, there hadn't been more than a few minutes of talking before passion carried them away.

"I'm so confused. You said he wanted to marry me, but he had to leave. Why did he have to leave?"

Mac sat next to her, sagging the cushions with his weight. "I can't say, Lady Julia. I wish I could. All I can tell you is that he had good reason. You'll have to hear the rest from him."

She wanted to ask what kind of good reason could permit a man to desert his wife but decided against it. Mac was too loyal to divulge something he thought should come from her husband. If only she knew the truth. Memories of the last time they were together rushed through her and along with them, Jon's words, long buried, *No matter what happens or how circumstances may indicate otherwise, I will always want you.*

Oh, what could he have meant?

Julia sighed, resigning herself to the question she'd asked every night for the past several weeks. "How will I ask him when I have no idea where he is?"

Mac smiled. "You will. If I know Jon, he won't wait much longer. I'm surprised he hasn't come to you already."

"Well, it's not that easy, Mac," Julia said. "Cyrus Mandrey is here for the express purpose of keeping Jon away from me."

The old sailor threw back his head and let out a deep-bellied laugh. "Dear girl, do you really think one man is going to keep Jon from what's his?" He laughed again, clasping his big hands together. "Ah, well, time will tell. Yes, it will."

Julia was about to say more when a harsh rap on the door interfered.

"It's us, Lady Julia. Come to say g'night." Julia smiled at the rough, gravelly voice on the other side. Big Tom must be sending Mr. Billington into fits of apoplexy. She heard the butler's precise voice trying to persuade the group to wait, beseeching them to employ a little patience as the door burst open and in piled Big Tom, Amos, Jeremy, and Mr. Billington.

"We wanted to say g'night, but this bugger tried to stop us," Amos said, pointing a bony finger at Edward Billington. "Told us to use some 'reserve.' Wot's that?"

Big Tom screwed up his face and scratched his head with two beefy fingers. "Dunno. Jeremy, wot's a reserve? Is it like me mum's preserve? The strawberry kind?"

Jeremy crossed his skinny arms over his nonexistent chest.

"Hmm. I think it's something we do. Like...like..." his voice drifted as he tried to come up with a plausible answer.

"For your information, gentlemen," Mr. Billington's voice filled the room. "To practice reserve means to exercise self-restraint."

"Huh?" The three sailors looked at one another. "Exercise what?"

"I think what Mr. Billington is trying to say is that he wanted you to wait until you were invited to enter," Julia said in a gentle voice. "He was only doing his job."

"All 'e knows how to do is walk around like 'e's got a stick in 'is behind and a bunch o' lemons in his mouth," Amos said, casting the butler a disgusted look. Big Tom and Jeremy howled.

Mr. Billington straightened, long arms at his side, shoulders back, feet squared and centered. His mouth *was* puckered in a look of distaste as though he had a "bunch of lemons" in there.

Julia stifled a giggle. "Amos, he was only thinking of me. Isn't that what all of you have been trying to do since the moment you arrived?" She stood and walked toward them, stopping between the three sailors and the butler. "You've tried to protect me, worry over me, guide me. That's all Mr. Billington is doing and I have to admit, sometimes I make his job very difficult."

Julia threw Mr. Billington a sideways glance, hoping he'd play along with her explanation but he merely stared at her, the sour expression gone, replaced with open-mouthed confusion. It was probably as close to gaping as Mr. Billington had ever come. She gave him a small smile and turned back to her three friends. Mr. Billington thought her less than one step above this lot standing before him but she was offering him a way to save face with these men. All he need do was accept it by remaining quiet, which Julia knew, would prove very difficult for the ever-correct, self-righteous Mr. Billington.

"Maybe we was a little hard on 'im," Big Tom said, cracking the knuckles on his right hand. His beady eyes ran over the butler. "'E jest got some strange ways, is all."

"We ain't used to 'em. We ain't used to havin' a body look down 'is nose at us ever' time we fergit our manners." Amos puffed out his bony chest. "Captain never done that, and we met all kinds of royalty. All kinds," he repeated, taking a step closer to Billington.

Julia held her breath as Mr. Billington met Amos's hard stare. He offered no rebuttal, no dripping sarcastic commentary, though Julia knew his repertoire contained several. She thanked the heavens he chose this moment to hold his tongue.

"Big Tom and Amos said it all fer me. Nothin's left to be said." Jeremy grinned and punched Big Tom in the shoulder.

The burly man grabbed the young boy and hoisted him in the air as though he were one of the many cream cushions accenting the room. Amos let out a hoot and shouted, "Get 'im, Jeremy. Get 'im where it counts."

Jeremy thrust his fingers under Big Tom's armpits, tickling him until the giant let out a roar and dropped him on the hard floor.

Anxious to avoid another altercation between these three men and the butler, Julia stepped forward and said, "That will be all, Mr. Billington. Thank you."

He looked at her, his gaze hard and steady. Had a whisper of kindness passed across his face? Had she imagined those ever-narrowed gray eyes relaxing just a little, the tight lips smoothing out, the frown gentling? She couldn't say and before she could consider it further, he gave her a curt nod and exited the room.

"All right, *men*," Mac's commanding voice addressed the laughing, tickling trio who resembled naughty children more than seasoned sailors. "It's time we bid Lady Julia good-night. We need to be on the road by dawn. *The Falcon*'s got a schedule to keep."

The jostling, teasing gestures from the men died down and they approached their captain's bride. "Yer the most beautiful, kindest woman I ever met, Lady Julia," Big Tom blurted out, casting his eyes downward. "You got a heart o' gold an' the cap'n's gonna be back soon. 'E knows how to spot riches and yer a jewel." Heat colored his face, and she knew he'd just paid her a rare compliment.

She grabbed his beefy hands and planted a kiss on his cheek. The faint smell of cabbage reached her nostrils. Surprising, Mr. Billington hadn't lectured them on the basics of hygiene. It appeared he himself had exercised some "reserve" in that regard.

"Good-bye, Big Tom. Thank you." He smiled at her then, a wide, toothless grin that lit up his homely face and flattened the long scar on his forehead.

Amos was next. "Thank you, Lady Julia, fer lettin' us in yer home."

His faded blue eyes met hers, filled with wisdom that came from years of experience, situation, and circumstance. Life had been Amos's tutor, not the mere words found in books. "You treated us like the cap'n does, like friends." He nodded his gray head, the lines in his leathery face spreading like a fan as he grinned. Amos reminded Julia of an oak Jason had cut down years ago, its middle marked with a series of rings denoting its age. They'd counted fifty-seven rings. She wondered if the lines on this old sailor's face would outnumber the oak's. Julia kissed his sun-beaten cheek and whispered, "Good-bye, Amos."

Jeremy stepped forward. His face with its smattering of freckles was the same vivid hue as the scarlet roses on the front lawn. He twisted his hands a few times, his green eyes darting about the room, bouncing from the right to the left, up and down, before settling on Julia's chin.

"Thank you for coming, Jeremy," she said. He blushed an even deeper shade of red, the same vibrant color as the roses in the back of the manor. She tried again. "You all came to ensure my safety. Your captain would be very proud of such a noble act."

As the words spilled out, she questioned the truth of her own words. Would Jon really be pleased that his men had intruded upon his personal affairs? Bandied his name and emotions about, giving the impression he was a besotted husband who wanted nothing more than to reunite with his wife? She doubted he'd take kindly to *that* description.

"He'll come to you. I know he will." Jeremy's words rang with the innocent fervor of one who has never known the bitter taste of love's betrayal.

It wouldn't do to have him see her fall apart, better to do that in private where no one would bear witness to her pain. She hugged him and whispered, "Thank you, Jeremy."

The youth turned away, his face settling back to its pale pink hue. There wasn't more than a few years' difference in their ages, but it may as well have been decades. Jeremy still resided in a cocoon of naiveté where love prevailed above all else, while she'd been stripped of those beliefs the day Jon left their marriage bed.

A light touch on her arm reminded her she was not alone. She turned to find Mac studying her with quiet intent. "Oh Mac, what am I going to do?" Did she want Jon to return or didn't she? The words that spilled from her mouth said she never wanted to see him again, but the secret corners of her heart told a different story; they held onto some of Jeremy's fairytale beliefs of happily-ever-after.

"Jeremy's right, you know." Mac's soft voice wrapped around her like a warm blanket. "Jon will come to you. And then you'll have to decide if you'll listen to your heart or your pride."

***

Sleep would not come. The hours ticked by, creeping toward morning as Jon watched the dark edges of night give way to the gray shades of dawn. He lay on the bed, arms propped behind his head, staring out the window. Soon it would be time to shroud himself in a mass of bushy hair, don a pair of thick spectacles, and pad his chest.

Each day it became more difficult to pretend he was a trustworthy, nondescript, do-gooder named Cyrus Mandrey. It was becoming equally difficult to feign anything but polite interest in Julia when all he wanted to do was take her in his arms and bury himself inside her sweet silkiness. Her very presence made him a prisoner to his own senses. He heard her voice everywhere he turned. In his dreams, her golden beauty unfolded like an exotic flower, her lilac scent smothering his good intentions.

Julia wielded a power over him, like a sorceress casting a spell, making him want her as no woman ever had. Soon, he'd go to his wife and no one would stand in his way. Not Kleeton, or Holt, or even Cyrus Mandrey. Very soon, there would be nothing between him and Julia but skin against skin.

Things were moving too slowly. And what of Kleeton? Was he merely a quiet, country gentleman, harboring no darker side than a macabre taste in decorating? Or was he a ruthless killer, waiting to strike again? Jon sat on the edge of the bed and grabbed his breeches. Was the man's name Andrew Kleeton or Peter Crowlton? He splashed water on his face and reached for a towel. Gentleman or traitor? He opened a drawer and pulled out his wig and beard. Neighbor or nemesis? He strode to the closet where he removed a fresh shirt and jacket. Innocent or guilty? Grabbing his spectacles, he fitted them to his face and looked at his reflection in the oval mirror.

He'd created Cyrus Mandrey. Had Peter Crowlton created Andrew Kleeton? He thought of the calfskin gloves that Kleeton never removed. Crowlton could be Kleeton and there was only one way to find out. As he headed down the spiral staircase in the direction of the dining room, he plotted his next move.

The smell of bacon and fresh-brewed coffee reached him before his boot hit the bottom step.

When he entered the dining room, plates and utensils clanged against one another as *The Falcon*'s crew dove into piles of crispy bacon, sausage patties, fried potatoes, and eggs.

"This certainly beats young Jeremy's cooking," he commented as he took a seat at the head of the table. He reached for the silver pot and noticed all eyes on him. "Is something wrong?" He ran a hand through his full beard. Patted his hair and mustache. "What is it?"

Amos coughed into the silence. Big Tom cleared his throat. Mac's eyes narrowed. Jeremy's cheeks matched the strawberry jam on his knife when he spoke. "Pardon me, Mr. Mandrey, but how did you know I was the cook?"

Damnation! How indeed! He'd known because Jeremy had been practicing his sad culinary skills on the crew since he'd been hired on board *The Falcon* seven months ago. He'd known because underneath the hair and spectacles of Cyrus Mandrey resided the man who'd tasted every one of Jeremy's blasted meals from his lumpy porridge to his hard tack biscuits.

Cyrus cleared his throat and held Jeremy's gaze. He must not look away or appear flustered. "That's an easy one, Jeremy. I served a short time on a ship and the rule was the youngest member got kitchen duty. At the time, that was me. If the rule still applies—" he scanned the crusty lot of sailors "—you've got this room beat by at least ten or more years."

The boy grinned and nodded his red head. "Right you are. Big Tom is eight and thirty. Amos is...is...how old *are* you, Amos?"

The old sailor laughed and spat out, "Old enough to know better!" The crowd let out a whooping holler that put a twinkle in Amos's faded blue eyes.

"C'mon, Amos," Jeremy persisted. "Tell us how many years you been stomping on this ground."

Amos leaned back in his chair, scratched his stubbled chin, and looked at the ceiling. "Let's see." He counted on his fingers. "I was fifteen when I sailed on *The Tempest*, spent ten years with them, six on *The Runaway*, twelve on *The Lady*, and seven on *The Falcon.*" He paused, moved two fingers up and down, shook his head, raised three fingers, then two more. "Damnation!" Amos threw his hands in the air. "How the hell old am I, anyway?"

Big Tom grinned, the gaps between his teeth wide and uneven. "Old. Older 'n all of us put together."

"I am?" Amos leaned back in his chair and scratched his gray head.

"You're fifty," Mac said. "And full of more energy than the lot of this sorry group. Now eat up; we have a long trip ahead of us."

The rest of the meal passed in relative silence less the occasional clink of glass or scrape of silverware to plate. When the men finished, they bade Cyrus a hasty good-bye and left to gather their bags, leaving Mac and Cyrus alone.

"More coffee?" Cyrus offered, extending the pot.

Mac held up a hand. "I'm stuffed. My compliments to the cook."

"I'll see that she gets them."

The room fell into silence, laced with a fine tension that hinted of things unspoken.

"So you've sailed before," Mac said.

Cyrus nodded. "A few times."

"I've been sailing more years than I can remember. Used to be captain of my own ship until I met up with Jon." He leaned back in his chair and folded his hands over his rounded belly.

"Then you're managing quite well in his absence?"

Mac shrugged. "Well enough. Might as well get used to it. Once he and Lady Julia patch things up, he won't be back."

"Would that bother you?" *Seven years was a long time.*

"I'd miss him. Jon's like a son to me. Never had any children of my own."

"He must think of you as a father." *You were more of a father to him than his real father.*

"That would be a great honor." Mac held Cyrus's gaze.

"It would be an honor for him, too."

Mac said nothing for a full thirty seconds. "He's in love with her, you know."

Cyrus nodded, "I know."

"She loves him, too."

"Does she?" Hope pounded in his chest.

"She does," Mac said. "But she's been hurt and she's afraid. He better have a damn good reason for leaving her like that."

"I think he does."

Mac sighed. "Then they'll have to get past their stubborn pride, past the hurt and anger to find the love."

"Can they do it?" He asked the question as much to himself as to Mac.

"If their love is strong enough, if they fight hard enough, then they can."

Cyrus said nothing. There were no words left to say.

Mac pushed back his chair and stood. "I'd best be on my way before the men start trouncing the flowers again."

Cyrus stood and approached Mac. He held out a hand and said, "Good-bye, Mac."

The older man clasped Cyrus's hand with both of his. The eyes that studied him brimmed with unshed tears. "Good-bye, Captain," he whispered.

Cyrus's eyes widened. Mac smiled and squeezed his hands. "You're like a son to me, boy. I'd know you anywhere."

There was no time to respond as Big Tom's voice bellowed through the door. "All set, Mac."

Releasing his hand, Mac stood back and raised his right hand in a salute. "Good luck, my boy." One last smile and he was gone.

Chapter 16

Cyrus tapped on Julia's door once more, a little louder this time. He considered calling her maid to check on her but decided against it. If Julia were under the weather, he wanted to see her himself. Perhaps she had a case of the ague. What else would keep her in bed so long?

"Julia." He tried to keep his voice raspy but not too loud, which proved a difficult task. If he could just borrow Jon's deep drawl, it would have Julia throwing the door open posthaste. With welcoming arms or a poker in hand? Mac's words pounded in his head, beating through his thoughts like Holt's fist had beaten his body. *She loves you.* Was it true? Did she still love him, despite his desertion?

Cyrus heard a groan from behind Julia's door, followed by running footsteps and horrible retching sounds. Julia *was* ill! He threw open the door and burst into her chambers to find her huddled in a corner, kneeling over a chamber pot, her golden mane a tangled mass falling down her back.

"Julia." He knelt beside her, stroking her hair from her pale face. "Let me help you."

She shook her head and threw up again. Her forehead was warm and sweaty. A cool cloth might feel good. "I'll get you a cloth," he said, scrambling to his feet. By the time he had the damn thing ready, she'd been sick two more times. He knelt and pressed the cloth to her forehead.

Julia hunched over the chamber pot, her breathing quick and shallow. The cotton of her batiste nightgown clung to her in a white sticky mess. Cyrus rotated the cloth between her forehead and the back of her neck. Wisps of damp tendrils escaped the limp mass that Cyrus held in his hand. Long moments passed with nothing in the room but the sound of their breathing. When it seemed as though the worst had passed, Cyrus ventured a word. "Julia?"

Nothing.

"Julia?" he persisted. "What happened?" She didn't even try

to lift her head. Was she dying, right before his eyes? "Julia!"

"What!" She flung back her head and stared at him with wild eyes.

She seemed to be quite alive now, not on the verge of death as he'd feared a moment ago. Actually, she appeared almost angry.

"Are you all right?" She didn't look all right. Not at all. She watched him as though she wanted to pounce on him and scratch his eyes out. And then do some other bodily harm to him. "Julia?" He kept his voice soft and even, as though talking to a child.

Her brows creased into a straight line but she said nothing.

"Do you think you ate something that disagreed with you?" His words were gentle, patient.

"No." She looked away.

"Perhaps some sort of stomach upset?" He wiped her mouth with the wet cloth.

"No." Her eyes squeezed shut.

He was running out of possibilities. "You seem so sick. What could have made you so ill?"

No answer.

"I'll call a doctor."

"I don't need a doctor."

He shook his head. "You've been ill twice in the last five minutes. You're extremely warm and sweaty. You say you didn't eat anything that turned your stomach. Someone has to tell us what's wrong."

"I know what's wrong." Her words were faint, as though she couldn't muster the energy to speak them.

"Then dear God, woman, tell me. What's wrong with you?"

Julia closed her eyes and slumped forward. "I'm going to have a baby."

Cyrus stumbled back. *A baby?* He tried to make sense of what she'd just said, but the thought of Julia with child scattered his logic.

"A baby?" he croaked. *His baby!* He was going to be a

father.

"Yes," she whispered, burying her face in her hands.

"You're not...pleased...about the baby," he said. He had no experience in this area, none at all. Should he tell her that her husband would be thrilled with news of a child? Or should he not mention her husband at all? Or perhaps he should offer her another cool cloth and not say a word.

A huge sob escaped her. She looked up at him, eyes rimmed in red, tears streaming down her cheeks. "My baby has no father."

Cyrus rifled a hand through his thick hair. "Of course he has a father." To hell with watching his words. "And when he finds out, he'll be delighted. You'll see."

She shook her head, fresh tears spilling from her sad eyes. "He doesn't even want me. He'd never want a baby."

The words twisted his gut. *Did she really believe that?* "Do you want the baby?"

Julia swiped at a stray tear. "Of course I do."

He forced out his next words. "And do you love him?"

"That has nothing to do with it," she hissed.

"It has everything to do with it," he growled. "Answer me, Julia. Do you love him?"

She pushed the hair from her face and sat back on her heels, staring at him for a full minute before her head dipped a fraction of an inch. It wasn't a full nod, just a little movement downward and then up again, but for a man as desperate as he was for another chance, it was enough.

"You love him." The words spilled out before he could stop them.

"Cyrus! I really do not want to discuss this any further."

He had pushed her too far and forced her to admit something she probably kept locked away from everyone, even herself. He shouldn't have pressed her in her weakened state, but desperate men took desperate measures and he was well past desperate.

His heart lightened. He longed to take her in his arms and

pledge his eternal love. They needed to strengthen their fragile bond as husband and wife, before time and circumstance got in the way. He would shed his disguise along with his pride and go to her tonight. And then he would show her how much he loved her and their unborn child.

His gaze settled on Julia as she leaned against the wall, eyes closed, long lashes caressing her pale skin. He thought her the most beautiful woman he'd ever seen, even in her weakened condition. With great care, he scooped her limp body into his arms and carried her to the bed where he laid her down as though she were more fragile than the finest piece of china. Folding the covers about her shoulders, he traced a pattern along the slender column of her neck, ending at the delicate hollow of her cheek. Soon, very soon, she would be his again.

***

He pressed Speed Demon on, eager to set his plans in motion. Penworth loomed before him in the distance, cold and unwelcome. Not a splash of color anywhere; no flowers in the beds, no blooming trees, no shrubs on the lawn. Everything was the darkest green or the dullest brown. Drab. Oppressive.

Speed Demon trotted along the circular drive, ears perked, head high. A huge, darkly clad figure appeared from the side of the house and stopped several feet from Cyrus.

"I'm here to see Mr. Kleeton," Cyrus said, studying the big man. Big was not the proper term for this person. Neither was tall. Both were drastic understatements. The man staring at him as though he'd just as soon crush him with his bare hands rather than look at him was twice the size of Big Tom and several times meaner if the snarl on his face was any indication.

"Is Mr. Kleeton in?"

The giant crossed his burly arms over his chest, planted his feet, and remained silent.

Perhaps he'd had his tongue ripped out, too. Another prison escapee? What other creatures of misfortune inhabited the walls of Penworth? Before he could consider the matter further, the front door opened and Andrew Kleeton stepped out, dressed in black from cravat to boot.

"Ah, Mandrey," he said, smiling. "What a pleasant surprise." Neither the smile nor the words contained a hint of warmth.

"Did I interrupt something?" Cyrus cocked a brow. "Looks like you're headed for a funeral."

Kleeton ignored the question and posed one of his own. "Why is it when someone dresses in black, people think of death? Or evil? I find the color quite soothing to my senses, calming actually."

"Is that why the inside of your house looks the way it does?" Cyrus decided not to tell him Penworth reminded him of a dungeon he'd seen in Morocco once, cold and dark, a place where death lurked in every corner, waiting for the opportune moment to snatch its next unsuspecting victim.

"Penworth suits me," Kleeton replied without answering Cyrus's question.

Cyrus didn't ask for elaboration. If his plan were to work, he needed this bizarre man with the black-gloved hands to believe he trusted him enough to help him trap Jon Remmington.

"There's something I need to discuss with you," Cyrus said, his gaze darting from Kleeton to the monster on the lawn.

"But of course. Gerald, please take care of Mr. Mandrey's horse."

The monster approached Cyrus and waited for him to dismount. He said nothing as he took the reins and turned away. Cyrus noted a large chunk of his left ear was missing. "Was his tongue ripped out, too?"

Kleeton laughed as they entered the house and headed down the hall. "Hardly. Gerald, for all his size, is quite shy. He rarely speaks."

"Is he another prison escapee?" He'd bet his last coin on it.

They entered the study and Kleeton headed to the sideboard, his back to Cyrus. "Not actually an escapee. His time was up and he had nowhere to go. I happened to be doing research at Newgate and took pity on him." Kleeton poured two whiskies and handed Cyrus one. "He's very loyal, Mandrey. He'd kill anyone who tried to harm me."

"I'd say that's a little more than loyal. More like mad."

Kleeton smiled, his white teeth gleaming in obvious contrast with his dark attire. "Some still believe in 'an eye for an eye,'" he said, lifting his glass.

"Do you?"

He shrugged. "In certain cases."

Cyrus noted the slight flare of nostrils, the twitch on the right side of his jaw, the slow inhalation of breath. The man wasn't as nonchalant about the whole matter as he'd like Cyrus to believe. "What kinds of cases?" he pushed on.

Kleeton drained his whisky and headed back for another. Cyrus sipped his, curious about this man in black who shone like the radiance of the sun one moment and hid like the blackness of night the next.

"There's no formula, no exact rule by which one decides when retribution must be taken into one's own hands. It's a knowing that justice must be served in a certain manner without the protection of the law. Nothing will satisfy until the punishment is delivered because in these instances, the law is powerless, hiding behind its dictates, trying to preserve the rights of individuals who do not deserve to have those rights protected."

Cyrus eyed him over the rim of his glass. "You sound as though you speak from experience." *If he was Crowlton, he had more blood on him than a leech during a bloodletting.*

Kleeton's gaze narrowed. "Do you really want to know, Mandrey, or are you making polite conversation? Because, if we start to drag out our battle scars, things could get ugly and we'd both have to take off our masks."

Cyrus raised his glass in mock salute and drained his glass. The man might present himself as nothing more than a reserved country gentleman, but underneath the well-groomed facade,

Cyrus sensed the edginess and determination of a man with a mission.

"You said you had something to discuss?" Kleeton changed the subject with the finesse of one long accustomed to evading personal questions. Not that Cyrus would have pressed the issue. He hadn't missed the challenge in Kleeton's voice, warning him not to dig around in his past unless he wanted a few of his own skeletons unearthed—which Cyrus did not.

"I think Remmington has returned."

Kleeton raised a brow. "Oh?"

"I saw footprints beneath two windows."

"It could have been the gardener."

"Could have been," Cyrus agreed. *Plant the seed.* "But the figure running from the house at five this morning was not."

That got Kleeton's attention. "Did you follow him?"

Cyrus shook his head. "He disappeared before I got my second boot on but he couldn't have known I'd seen him." *Time to dangle the proverbial carrot.* "He'll be back."

"How can you be so certain?" Kleeton balled his left hand into a fist.

"He thinks our guard is down. All these weeks have passed without a sign of him. Remmington expects us to get careless. He's going to strike soon and take Julia away." Cyrus toyed with his empty glass, waiting for Kleeton's response.

"Then we'll have to get him before he gets her." Simple words, spoken as a vow.

Cyrus almost smiled. It appeared Kleeton needed little prodding to join the cause against Jon Remmington. If indeed he were The Serpent, then he'd waited years for this confrontation, living and breathing hatred and revenge as a form of daily sustenance.

"Good. I'll count you in." *Better to work with the enemy than against him.*

"What do you want me to do?" Kleeton asked.

"I need someone to monitor the perimeter of the properties. He might enter from your end, since Penworth is closer than any of the other properties." Cyrus rubbed the back of his neck. "I have to keep my eyes on Julia. Keep her close to the house. No more horseback riding, at least for the next few days."

Kleeton smiled. "She won't like that."

Cyrus shrugged. "I'm sure she won't, but she'll have no choice." He glanced at Kleeton. "You were in the military?"

The smile flattened. "For a short time."

"Do you know anything about surveillance?"

"A little."

"Good."

"I'll start tonight."

Cyrus nodded. "If you catch him, bring him to Glenview Manor. Immediately. Lord Westover will deal with Remmington."

"I can't guarantee his safety, Mandrey. Accidents happen all the time. Surely you know that in your line of business." The gleam in his eyes made Cyrus more determined to end this whole scheme as soon as possible. A gnawing in his gut warned him Kleeton was a powder keg waiting to explode at the hint of a spark. If he captured Jon Remmington, he wouldn't deliver him to Glenview Manor as ordered. At least not alive.

"He's not a criminal, Kleeton."

"That's a matter of opinion."

"You have no quarrel with Remmington. You don't even know the man."

"He's committed a crime against Julia. That's reason enough to want the man punished."

Cyrus ignored Kleeton's response and said, "I think it best if we don't discuss our plan in front of Julia. No need to cause her undue concern."

"Agreed," Kleeton said. "I'll begin my duties this evening."

Cyrus's lips twitched. "I see you're already dressed for the part." He gestured to the other man's black attire. Who was Andrew Kleeton? Predator? Enemy? Traitor? Murderer? Standing before him like a dark angel, a strange gleam in his eyes, Cyrus found it easy to believe he could be any or all of these.

***

The stone was cold against his fingers as he edged along the narrow passage. The lantern dangling from his hand provided a flickering pathway, permitting no more than a few paces of illumination before him. Just enough so he wouldn't stumble. It had been years since he'd explored this passage, with nothing on his mind but adventure and curiosity. Tonight, as he traveled the dimly lit path, all he could think of was his wife.

What if she turned him away? What if the hurt she'd suffered had frozen her heart? He ran a shaky hand through his tousled hair, glad to be rid of that damned bushy mop. He imagined Julia's fingers twining in his hair, sweeping that ever-errant stray lock from his forehead. Such thoughts proved tortuous because they elicited images that were carnal in nature and had nothing to do with the forgiveness he sought. He must push them aside.

But the floodgate of sensuality burst open, and Jon grew hard at the very thought of making love to his wife. It had been such a blasted long time. He tried to push away the vision of her sweet, supple body as it responded to his touch, writhing beneath him, above him, beside him. She was inside him, pulsing, teasing, and he could not extinguish her heat.

Jon reached the small door that led to the master bedroom. He fitted the key in the lock and rested a hand on the knob, waiting for his breathing to steady. Julia was a mere room away. So close. All he need do was step over this threshold and walk the ten steps or so to her door. How many times in the past several weeks had he wished she'd see him as her husband and not a bushy-haired protector named Cyrus Mandrey? Obviously, she'd grown quite attached to Mandrey, but he couldn't say she felt the same about her husband. He had the feeling she would have rather emptied her stomach again than profess her love for him, but he'd persisted and forced an answer from her. Not that a little half nod of the head was any great proclamation of love, but it was a start.

And then there was the baby. *His* baby. Strengthened by the thought of his unborn child, Jon opened the door and stepped into his chambers. Seconds later, his gaze fell on the small strip of light beneath the adjoining door.

She was awake. He stepped closer. The scent of lilac drifted to him and he pictured her unbound hair, her naked skin. Another few steps and he pressed his ear to the door. He gave a light rap and waited. Nothing.

Inching the door open, he peered inside. Julia was asleep, propped up with two pillows, an open book resting in her left hand. Her golden curls cascaded about her shoulders, a plump lock falling onto the swell of her breast. The white nightgown she wore was prim and proper, though the laces at her neck had come undone and revealed a glimpse of skin. Her breathing was slow and even. Peaceful. Perhaps he should leave her with her dreams and return tomorrow night. His thoughts and desires jumbled together, making it difficult to sort out the best course of action. Logic told him to leave. Emotion forced him to stay.

He had to get closer to her, had to touch her, breathe in her scent. Setting the lantern on the bedside stand, he leaned over and lifted a lock of her hair, caressing its silky texture as it spilled through his fingers like spun gold. He'd forfeit everything he owned to be with her again.

He laid gentle fingers against her cheek, drinking in the silkiness of her skin. He trailed a path from her cheek to her mouth, stopping to trace an outline over each full lip. God, but he wanted to kiss her and taste what she had once offered so freely.

Her lips moved, and he jerked his hand back. Was she waking? Her eyes remained closed, covered by a thick fringe of lash. He let out a silent breath as beads of perspiration peppered his forehead and he strained to detect the slightest change in breathing pattern or eye movement. Part of him wanted her to wake and find him standing over her; the other part grew petrified she'd do just that.

He placed a shaky hand on her belly. *His child*. A fierce wave of possessiveness washed over him for mother and child. But another feeling crept along his spine and wrapped its long tentacles around his heart. The emotion was foreign to him, for he'd experienced it not more than once or twice and it was long ago. Jon recognized it for what it was as it made his heart beat faster and jerked the breath from his throat.

It was fear in its most primitive form. Fear that the woman he loved would deny him a second chance. Would she deny him the baby, too? Jon backed away, one step at a time, so caught up in the maelstrom of emotion he didn't remember making a conscious effort to move. Another step backward and his booted foot hit the door with a dull thud. He could not face her tonight. He was too afraid.

He must come to terms with that demon before he went to Julia. Jon slipped through the open door, closing it behind him, and headed for the secret passage. Not until he was ready to enter the black opening did he remember he'd forgotten his lantern. *Blast it!* He stepped into the darkness and pulled the door shut. His fingers sought the cold, hard surface of the wall as he inched along the passageway. It was going to be a blasted long night.

***

Julia awakened early the next morning feeling quite refreshed. Her stomach didn't rumble or lurch in warning. Of course, she'd eaten nothing more than clear beef broth and a few wafers, but it was a start.

She recalled the terrible time Sophie had when she was pregnant. She'd almost had to carry the chamber pot with her for the first several weeks of her pregnancies. Everything upset her, from a drop of chicken broth on her tongue to a whiff of roast pork. Holt had remained by her side, worrying over her, ministering to her, loving her.

There would be no one to help Julia as she swelled with child. She thought of Cyrus and her heart warmed. Dear, sweet, dependable Cyrus had wiped her brow and carried her back to bed when she was too exhausted to move. He was the one who'd taken care of her.

But he was not Jon.

She'd dreamed of Jon last night, as she did every night, but this time it seemed so real. He stood over her bed, watching her with those deep-brown eyes, his full lips unsmiling. There was tenderness in his expression as he lifted a hand and trailed his fingers over her face and neck. She'd wanted to touch the slight crook in his nose, trace the small scar over his right eye, brush her fingers along his lips, but her hands wouldn't move.

Julia drew in a calming breath and detected a faint hint of spice. Her eyes snapped open. She inhaled again. The spicy scent filled her nostrils. Only one person wore that type of cologne. She shook her head, tried to rid herself of morning cobwebs. Last night had been only a dream, just like all the others. Hadn't it?

She threw back the covers, anxious to get dressed and out of her chambers before her imagination got the best of her. Next, she'd swear she'd spotted him beside her bed. Oh, but the man could wreak havoc on her emotions, even in sleep. As her bare feet touched the floor, she noticed a black and silver lantern resting on the edge of the bedside stand.

Had Jon been in her room? Had the touches been real? The questions bounced to and fro in Julia's head. What to do? Perhaps there was a logical explanation for the lantern. What would that be? Who would be so bold as to wander into her room in the middle of the night? Her heart answered—Jon.

She could not tell Cyrus. He was after Jon and someone might get hurt. For all of Cyrus's supposed training as a tactical expert or whatever it was he'd said, he would probably be the injured party. He lacked the ruthless tenacity she'd seen in her husband. On the other hand, Jon's guard might be down, and he could fall prey to Cyrus's patience. She would not risk hurting either man, which meant she'd have to deal with the potential situation herself.

She gripped the lantern and imagined Jon's hands on the handle only hours ago. If it had been him invading her chambers last night, she wanted no outside intrusion when he came again. As she clutched the lantern close, she knew he'd come to her last night and knew he'd come again. This time she would be ready. She opened the closet door, pushed aside several gowns, and placed the lantern on the floor behind a lavender and peach muslin. His secret was safe. For now.

Chapter 17

Cyrus avoided Julia the entire day. There were too many issues to address and seeing her would only take his mind off pressing matters. Such as the realization that he was a coward. Never in his entire life had he behaved like one. Could not even fathom the possibility until last night. Fear of losing Julia had driven him away as though he were chased by demons and he'd spent the rest of the night nursing his self-disgust along with a bottle of whisky.

He was in a foul mood today, blacker than the soot on a chimney sweep's cheeks. Lack of sleep and enough whisky could do that to a man. So could a woman. Cyrus swore under his breath as reminders of last evening's cowardice pounded in his head. Tonight would be different. He would not act the coward again. When the house fell quiet, he would go to Julia and ask her forgiveness. As her husband. Her lover. Her friend.

And she would accept it. Period. He hoped. Then he would lay his head on her soft, full breasts and let sleep take him. But, perhaps he wouldn't sleep right away. Provided Julia was amenable to the idea. He cursed again. Why shouldn't she be? They were husband and wife. She'd admitted she loved him. They'd been apart a very long time. She carried his child, for God's sake. Why wouldn't she be agreeable? *Why*, he ripped a piece of paper in half, *wouldn't*, he slashed at another with his letter opener, *she be agreeable?*

A knock on the door saved a third piece of ivory stationery from mutilation.

"Yes?"

"It's Billington, sir. You wished to see me?"

"Come in." Cyrus guessed it was time to apprise Billington of his plan, considering the plan was already in motion. He sighed and raked a hand through his hair. His fingers stuck in the tangled mess. He would be blasted happy when this was all over. Bad enough the mere sight of Julia made his objectivity sail out the window, but to have to deal with a matted mop on his head every day was a damn nuisance!

"Have a seat, Billington." He lowered his voice. "As I mentioned before, Lady Julia has a very bad habit of eavesdropping, and I don't wish to shout at you from across the room."

The butler's lips twitched. Almost a smile. "So you have said, sir, but I believe we are safe for the moment. Lady Julia is napping in the study."

"She is? Why?" Odd she didn't walk the short distance to the privacy and comfort of her own quarters.

Billington's mouth curved upward. Cyrus spotted a show of teeth. It was a definite smile. "Billington, is something wrong?" In all the years he'd known the man, never once had he seen him smile.

"No, sir," he replied, fighting to pull his lips into their customary straight line. "I believe Lady Julia is sleeping in the study because of the pillows."

"Pillows?" The man made no sense. Billington always made sense. It had to do with that damnable smile.

Clearing his throat, Billington flattened his lips and said in his most serious voice, "She's sleeping on them, sir."

"Sleeping on the pillows?" Cyrus repeated. Julia's chambers were equipped with two of the softest down-filled pillows at Glenview Manor. He'd made certain of it. "*Why* is she sleeping on the pillows, Billington?"

The older man lifted a bony shoulder. "It would appear Lady Julia is enamored with them. They're the rather large ones you brought from one of your excursions to the Orient. For the past two days, she's brought books in there after lunch." He leaned over and whispered, "She's fallen asleep both times. I made certain she was covered with a blanket so she wouldn't catch a chill."

"Very thoughtful of you, Billington. Thank you." Julia had gotten to the old man and melted a bit of that icy exterior. Poor Billington didn't stand a chance now. Next he'd be throwing down his jacket in puddles so she wouldn't get her feet wet.

"You wished to see me, sir?"

"Ah, yes, there is something I need to discuss with you. I embarked on a plan yesterday that involves our neighbor, Mr. Kleeton."

Billington raised a thin brow.

"I informed him I spotted Jon Remmington yesterday, running away from the estate."

"Did he believe you?"

Cyrus nodded. "He had no reason not to. The man may not care for me, but he wants Jon Remmington, and it has nothing to do with his misplaced loyalty for Julia."

"Are your suspicions concerning Mr. Kleeton proving correct?"

What he meant to ask was whether Cyrus felt Andrew Kleeton was the elusive Serpent. "I don't know. There's something about the man that reeks of deceit. It's in his eyes, behind all that blue. It's as if he's constantly assessing those around him; I can even detect it in his smile. If you look past the flash of white, you'll see nothing but emptiness, like falling into a deep pit."

"What of his hands?" Billington asked.

Cyrus shook his head. "He keeps them well covered in every color and texture imaginable." He clenched his fists, his next words sharp and fierce. "You can't know how tempted I've been to pin him down and rip them off. But since I can't do that, I've decided to include him in a little search for Jon Remmington."

"How so?"

A smile crept onto Cyrus's lips. "Kleeton will patrol his property and the surrounding estates in search of Jon."

"And never find him," Billington added, nodding approval.

"He'll find him all right, but not yet, not until I've had an opportunity to learn some of his secrets and test his skill. When I've done that, Jon will let himself 'be found' and if Kleeton is The Serpent, he'll waste no time striking."

A deep line furrowed Billington's shiny forehead.

"What is it?" He'd known the man too many years to not detect when something bothered him.

The older man sniffed twice, cleared his throat, and ventured, "It sounds dangerous."

"What did you say?" He could not have heard him right.

"I said, sir," Billington began, squaring his shoulders and sitting even straighter than before, "that the plan sounds dangerous."

"Dangerous?" Cyrus stifled a laugh. "This little event is *nothing* compared to what we've been through." He laughed again. "Surely you realize that."

Billington's gray eyes met Cyrus's. "Lady Julia was not involved then."

"What's she got to do with any of this?" The man was going soft on him. He liked him better hard and crusty.

"If Kleeton is The Serpent, he'll go after what Jon Remmington cares about most." His precise voice faltered. "And that would be Lady Julia."

Silence dragged Cyrus down under the threat of Billington's last words. Like sacks of sand, the words hung on his shoulders. He clenched and unclenched his fists and finally, grabbed the letter opener to still his hands. "If he touches her, I'll kill him with my bare hands." No one would hurt Julia. He would see to that.

***

Jon slipped through the opening of Julia's door, his eyes never leaving her face. She looked like an angel in sleep, her golden hair flowing about her, soft and shimmering. His chest ached as he moved closer. There was no turning back tonight. He would ask her forgiveness, pledge his love, and pray to God she took mercy on him. Lilac drifted to him, urging him closer. He leaned over, closed his eyes, and reveled in the sweet fragrance that beckoned him. Closer, closer, until wisps of silken tendrils graced his cheek.

He planted gentle kisses in her hair. It had been so long

since he'd touched her, so long since he'd kissed her. He opened his eyes and stared at her mouth, so inviting, like sun-kissed berries waiting to be plucked. He lowered his head, his mouth hovering mere inches from hers. His eyes drifted shut. Ah, but he was about to taste a slice of heaven…

Instead, a blow from hell landed square at the back of his neck. He jumped back, cursing as he rubbed the tender spot on his neck. "Damn you, Julia," he muttered, glaring at her.

"Stay right where you are," she said, backing up to the farthermost corner of the bed.

"Up to your old tricks again? What is it this time? Another pitcher?" Whatever she'd used, her aim was perfect. His neck hurt like the devil.

She shook her head and golden curls whirled about her breasts. Did she know he could make out her entire shape beneath that pristine nightgown she wore? The lamp shone just right and from her position on the bed, her charms left little to the imagination.

When she didn't respond, he asked again, "What did you attack me with, Julia?"

Her chest heaved and he spotted the hint of a nipple through the white material.

She swallowed twice. "One of those vases with the dragon on it," she whispered.

He raised a brow. "One of *my* vases?"

"It's fine. No harm done," she said, pulling a white and gold vase from beneath the covers.

"That's a matter of opinion," he said, massaging the muscles in his neck.

"Leave, Jon. I have nothing to say to you."

"Like hell." What was he doing? He'd come to ask her forgiveness, not engage in battle.

"Don't you dare come one step closer," Julia said, as she jumped from the bed and grabbed an old fire iron from the fireplace. She crawled back onto the bed and stood up, gripping the bottom of the iron with both hands, readying her swing.

If he weren't so damned annoyed and sore, the sight of Julia wielding a fire iron would have made him laugh.

"Leave, before you force me to use this thing," she said, swatting the iron through the air.

"For what, dear wife?" He cocked a brow. "Jousting?"

"For keeping you away."

"Ah," he replied. "I am indeed filled with fear."

"Not one step farther," she whispered, crouching like a hunter preparing for attack.

Jon met her gaze and took a step closer.

"I'm warning you," she hissed. "I'll use this thing."

He dropped his hands to his sides and advanced two steps. "You would maul me with it?" He glanced at the fire iron in her hands. "Scar me and beat at my head and body?" Her grip loosened and the iron slipped a fraction. "You would wish that for me, dear wife? You would be my attacker?" He took another step.

"No," Julia whispered. "I…don't want you…to be hurt."

He forgot about the dull ache in his neck and almost smiled. He and Julia were making progress, even if she didn't realize it. "Nor do I want you to be hurt. Especially by me," he finished, his gaze locking with hers. He had to keep his head about him, especially now, with Julia on the brink of catapulting into his waiting arms.

She swiped at her left eye, still keeping a grip on the iron with her right, but it was looser than before. "It's too late for that."

So much for catapulting into his waiting arms. Jon squeezed his eyes shut and pinched the bridge of his nose. He had to keep her talking. He said the next thing that popped into his head. "Why do you keep whispering?"

Her gaze shot to the door. "Cyrus might hear."

"Cyrus?" What in blazes did Cyrus have to do with anything?

Julia wet her lips, hesitated a moment, and plunged forward. "He's the man who's been hired to protect me." Her small chin shot up an inch. "From you."

"From me?" How to handle that remark? Humor and sarcasm. "Is he the hairy ape that's been following you around like a lost puppy?"

"He is not a hairy ape. For your information, Cyrus Mandrey is my friend and protector, which is certainly more than you ever were."

Jon winced. "You don't need that fire iron when you have a mouth like that for a weapon."

He could tell by the spark in her eyes that she was far from finished. She'd assumed her feet- apart, chin-up, hands-on-hips stance that told him she had much to say, and he would be the lucky recipient of her speech.

"Cyrus is a man of integrity, whose opinion I value. I trust him and his judgment." She raised her voice a hint with her next words. "*He* would never lie to me."

Jon raked a hand through his hair. Who would have thought he'd be competing with himself? "Then why don't you call your *hero* to come to your rescue? Surely, he'll save you from your cruel, wicked husband."

Her eyes narrowed to slits, her nostrils flared, and her hands tightened on the iron. Catapulting indeed. He'd be catapulting all right, straight into hell if he couldn't cool her temper.

"Uncaring," she hissed.

"Uncaring what?"

"Ruthless," she spat out.

"Julia." He took another step forward.

"Deceitful," she growled, raising the iron.

"Julia?" He held up a hand.

"My cruel, wicked, uncaring, ruthless, deceitful, arrogant husband," she said, taking a swing in the air. The iron whacked the bed, the force of the impact unbalancing her. Jon took that moment to dive toward her, throwing his arms about her waist and tossing her onto the bed. He wrested the fire iron from her with his right hand, pinned her arms behind her head with his left, and clamped a thigh over her lower body.

"Let me go, you beast." She glared at him, chest heaving, her breath coming in choppy gulps.

Jon was breathing hard, too. He'd forgotten how exhausting his wife could be, in and out of bed. Julia bucked underneath him, her knees just missing his groin. "Keep it up, Julia, and I'll take that behavior as an invitation."

She froze. Color seeped into her cheeks and spread down her neck.

"Now that we're both more comfortable—" he reached out with his right hand and brushed a stray lock of hair from her cheek "—why don't you tell me why you didn't yell for this Cyrus to come to your rescue?"

She looked away. "He is very skilled in tactical maneuvers."

He waited. Silence stretched in the room like shadows on the wall. "And?" he prompted.

"You would not stand a chance," she whispered.

"Would it matter?"

Julia turned toward him and opened her mouth but no words came out.

"Answer me, Julia. Would it matter?" *Dear God, please say yes.*

Her gaze flitted to his shoulder, his chest, his arm. Anywhere but his face. "On the other hand, you are quite a bit larger than Cyrus, and you might end up hurting him."

"And you wouldn't want Cyrus hurt." Anger spread through his body, one pulse at a time. How ironic that she would protect one man and condemn another. What would she say if he told her the truth about her dear Cyrus?

"Of course not." Three simple words, spoken with such conviction. Who would have thought they could wound so deeply?

"And me? You would not mind if I got a jab or two, would you? Maybe another broken nose?" Damn it, she was supposed to love him; she'd admitted it the other day. Had her feelings changed already? Had she only spoken the words so Cyrus would leave her alone? *Had she lied?* "Look at me." She buried her head further into the pale green of the counterpane. Jon closed his fingers around her chin and forced her to face him. "Look at me, Julia."

She turned her face to his and tears trailed down her cheeks. Unbidden, he was certain. Unwanted, most definitely. Were the tears for him or Cyrus Mandrey? He had to know. "You would care if something happened to me?"

Julia nodded. Just a little movement of her head, but Jon saw it. "But I wouldn't want to," she said, as though afraid to let him see her true feelings.

It hurt to hear the words but he could not blame her for her hesitancy. "Of course, you wouldn't want to," he murmured. "God, but I've missed you."

She stiffened beneath him. "It's not that simple, Jon."

Her words hit him like ten buckets of cold water. "There's much to discuss," he said. "Much I need to explain. But right now—" he ran a finger from her satiny cheek to the fine line of her jaw "—I want to know if you've missed me half as much as I've missed you."

Her eyes widened with longing before a cloud of indifference blanketed them. "Did you miss me just a little?" She shook her head. Jon ignored the dull ache in his chest. "Not even one little bit?" he coaxed, trying to strip away the fear that shielded the truth.

He waited as she opened her mouth to speak, and watched her lips move, though no sound came out. Sound wasn't necessary; he'd read her lips and seen the answer. She'd said no. Not merely no to his silly little question, for he knew she'd missed him. The answer had been in her eyes before she put up her guard, but her attempt to deny the truth told him she was saying no to a much larger question. There would be no second chances. All that and she hadn't uttered a sound.

"That's not true." She met his gaze, her eyes brimming with tears. "I did miss you. Very much." Her voice was hesitant, full of sadness and resignation.

Jon brushed his lips across hers, a soft, gentle balm meant to heal and comfort. "And I missed you, so very, very much," he murmured, a breath away from her lips. He dipped his head and placed a chaste kiss along the slender line of her jaw. "So very, very much." He trailed a path to her ear. Julia moaned and he buried his face in her hair.

"Why did you leave?"

Of course she'd want to know why he'd left and where he'd gone. He needed to be honest with her if they were to make a go of their marriage. Problem was, if he told his wife the truth, he'd betray his best friend. As for where he'd been these past several weeks, he couldn't tell her that either without risking her safety so he would have to settle for a half-truth until this whole mess was over.

"I can't say. Not yet."

Her mouth thinned to a straight line.

"Julia, listen to me. I *can't* tell you, yet. But I will. Soon." Desperation threaded his voice. "All I ask now is that you show patience a little while longer."

She turned her head away and closed her eyes.

"I had no choice. If you believe nothing else, believe that. I have dreamed of nothing but holding you in my arms every night. I have felt the pain of my leaving a thousand times, and it has been worse than any hell I could have imagined." He touched her hair, her cheek, her lips. "Please. Please, Julia. Give me your trust, just once more. I promise you'll not be sorry."

"You ask too much."

"Five days. Give me five days with no questions and on the night of the fifth, I will reveal all." He held his breath, waited for her response.

"You have three days to tell me the truth."

Three days wasn't much time. He'd have to force Kleeton's hand, but if Julia were willing to consider the bizarre arrangement, who was he to quibble over a few days? At the moment, he could think of nothing but the sound of her sweet voice and the feel of her soft body beneath him.

The tone of her next words reminded him that he might be in her bed but they were a long way from sharing any intimacy. "Will I see you every night until then?" she asked, her voice cool. "Or will you simply pop in whenever it suits you?"

"That will be up to you, dear wife."

"How did you get in here without Cyrus seeing you?"

Jon smiled. He'd wondered when she'd get around to asking that question. "That's a secret I can share. The library has a secret passageway leading into the master chambers. If you walk around the bookcases, to the left, you'll find a small door that will take you right into my room. My uncle had it built several years ago, though no one but myself and now you are aware of its existence."

"Whatever for?"

"Who knows? Most likely to amuse himself." Jon grinned. "We Remmingtons love a good intrigue."

"You're probably all crazy, the whole lot of you."

He gazed down at her lips. "You're probably right," he murmured, lowering his head to taste her mouth. Julia moaned as she parted her lips. Jon teased her bottom lip, tracing it with his tongue, savoring the sweetness before delving into her welcoming mouth. Their tongues touched, gently at first, reveling in the wonder of rediscovery. Soon, it wasn't enough. Jon groaned and thrust his tongue deep into her mouth, thinking he'd burst when Julia began to suck on it.

Without breaking the kiss, he settled himself between her legs and loosened his grip on her arm. He wanted her hands on his body, touching, pleasuring, exploring. He stroked her neck, trailed downward to the ties of her nightgown. *Flesh.* He loosened the ties and pushed the thin material aside, his fingers skimming her silky skin, trailing along a breast, tracing a nipple. Making Julia moan. He cupped her breast, then stroked a hard nipple in tiny circles until she whimpered.

She grabbed at his shoulders, her fingers traveling down his arms, moving to settle on his hips, where she pressed him further into the cleft of her womanhood. Jon lay hard and heavy between her, cursing the thin material that separated them. If not for that one little wisp of white, he'd be buried deep inside his wife right now. The thought made him pulse with anticipation and the knowledge that he needed her in a way that was so much more than pure physical desire.

He loved his wife.

Jon worked his hand along her thigh, brushing caresses down her leg as he pulled her gown up to touch naked skin. He stroked the creamy flesh on the inside of her thigh, traced a path from her knee to her ankle and up again. Julia moaned and moved her hips in a slow, sensual rhythm, like a dancer feeling the music in her soul.

Tearing his mouth from hers, he muttered, "You're driving me mad."

She laughed, a low, throaty sound that sent surges of desire through him. Jon lowered his head and took a nipple in his mouth, devouring the ripe bud with his lips, his tongue, his teeth.

"Love me, Jon," she whispered. "Love me. Now."

He pulled away and yanked open the buttons of his shirt with unsteady fingers. Nothing existed but his wife lying before her, her nightgown bunched around her hips, her long legs open and inviting. Jon tossed the shirt to the floor, kicked off his boots, and reached for the buttons on his breeches.

"Let me help you." She placed her hand over his, stilling his fingers. Her tongue darted out to wet her lips as her smile grew slow and sultry. His sex pulsed inches beneath her fingers, begging for attention. His hand fell away as he stood, mesmerized by the touch of her hand stroking his belly.

The buttons popped open, one agonizing moment at a time. It was heaven. It was hell. He sucked in a breath, his eyes glued to the nimble fingers working the buttons. When the last one popped, his sex sprang free. Julia closed her hand around him, her fingers gliding over his rigid flesh with even strokes. Blood rushed to his brain, filled his head, pushed out all thoughts save the need to be inside her.

Jon jerked in her hand, pumping once, twice, a victim to his desire. Her hands felt so damn good on him. Too good. If she didn't stop right now, it would be over before it started. "Julia," he said and grabbed her hand.

"You...you didn't like that?" she whispered, her face turning crimson.

Oh, he liked it all right. Every single stroke. Her eyes were on him, deep, soulful eyes that tugged at his heart. And his groin. The mixture of innocent and seductive drove him wild. Oh yes, he liked everything about Julia...

"Jon?"

What had she asked him? Oh, yes, she wanted to know if he liked her touch. How could he answer a question like that in words that would not offend her? Telling her the truth might scare her. After all, she was still a relative innocent where lovemaking was concerned. She'd only been with him a few times and there was still so very much to learn. Like how to substitute her mouth for her hands. Or lay on her belly with her legs spread wide while he entered her from behind. A groan of need and anticipation escaped him.

"Julia, you're driving me wild. Too wild, as a matter of fact." He wanted to tell her that a few more strokes from those nimble fingers would send his seed spewing all over her like a blast from a cannon. Instead, he opted for a more delicate explanation. "Sweetheart, you want me inside of you. Correct?"

She nodded.

"Well, three more strokes, and it would have been too late for that." She should be able to figure that out.

"Oh. I see," she said, pulling her gaze from his.

"No, dear wife, I doubt you do." He yanked off his breeches and knelt between her legs, enjoying the silken feel of her against his callused fingertips. "I want to see you naked. Take off your gown."

Julia shifted her weight, pulling the nightgown over her

head until she lay before him in glorious nakedness. "God, but you're beautiful," he murmured, lowering his head to mesh his mouth with hers. The kiss deepened, tongue mating with tongue, burning out of control, each touch more desperate than the last.

Reaching his fingers between their bodies, Jon found her swollen flesh and caressed it with a feather-light touch. Julia gasped into his mouth, her hips jerking off the bed. He worked his fingers over the sensitive flesh, stroking his way to her woman's heat. She was hot and ready, wet with desire. He probed a finger into her heat and her tightness closed around him.

She rose to meet the stroke of his finger. He caught her moans in his mouth, his tongue delving deep, showing her what he would soon do with another part of his body. The rapid, uneven movements of her hips told him she wanted more. "Now, Jon," she murmured against his lips. "Make love to me, now."

He pulled back and rose to his knees. Julia Remmington was his wife. There would be no more separations. He cupped her buttocks and leaned over her welcoming body. She was his. Forever. Her eyes turned smoky with passion as he entered her in one long, slow stroke. Her legs closed around his thighs, hugging him to her, drawing him closer still. When her nails trailed down his back, his hips, and his buttocks, he pumped into her, saw her smile, and pulled back. She lifted her hips to coax him to her and he pumped again.

With painstaking slowness, he eased out of her almost all the way, until she moaned. Three times, four, he repeated the sensual torment. When he reached six, his control burst, filling him with a wild need to bury himself deep in her hot, sweet body. He plunged into her, losing a piece of himself with each thrust. Julia matched him, thrust for thrust, nails clawing, legs high and snug over his back, mouth fused with his.

The desire to go on like this, to reach for the stars, the moon, the sky, warred with the need to find fulfillment as soon as possible, to float back to earth in peace and harmony.

Julia cried out first, her body rigid, her woman's heat sending tiny spasms along Jon's sex. She clung to him as he drove into her one final time before he called out her name and spilled his seed. He drew one last breath and collapsed, his body covering his wife's like a shield.

"I love you," he whispered. There. He'd finally said it. Jon closed his eyes and inhaled the scent of lilac mixed with the aftermath of their lovemaking. Very soon they'd put their stormy past behind them and start anew. Just the three of them. His heart clenched at the thought of his child. A real family built on love. The words waltzed around in his head as he drifted off. Real family...built on love. Love. Love. Something wasn't right. The words didn't feel right. Love. Understanding rolled over him like Speed Demon's hoof in his chest.

Julia hadn't said the words. Not once. There was no "I love you." No, "By the way, we're going to have a baby." Nothing. He only knew about them because she'd admitted those things to Cyrus, her friend and protector. Too bad she hadn't seen fit to make such an announcement to her husband, the father of her baby. The thought rankled, stirring a coil of anger and jealousy in his gut.

What the hell did she think she was doing by telling Cyrus Mandrey and not him? He wouldn't tolerate it. Absolutely not. Jon opened his eyes to find Julia staring straight ahead. So much for the slim hope that she'd fallen asleep and not heard his profession of love. She'd heard it all right, and she'd ignored it.

This was ridiculous. She loved him; he'd heard it himself. Well, in a manner of speaking he'd heard it. It was of little consequence that Julia had spoken the words to Cyrus. The fact of the matter was that she *had* spoken the words. And she would speak them again. To him.

"Julia?" Perhaps she just needed a little coaxing.

"Yes?" She did not look at him.

"Did you hear me a moment ago?" He tried to hide the hint

of annoyance from his voice. "When I said I loved you?"

She nodded.

"And?" *Just say the words.*

"Thank you."

"*Thank you?* I just told you I loved you and all you have to say is thank you?"

Her eyes darted to his chin. "I don't know what else to say."

Despair pounded in his chest. *Damn her*, she was not going to tell him. He'd opened his heart, and she'd replied with a thank-you as though he'd merely poured her a cup of tea? His eyes narrowed on her. "I assure you, any other woman would be dying to hear those words from me."

That got her. Her eyes darkened like a storm cloud about to burst, and her words spilled out in a downpour of emotion. "Then perhaps you should take your *words* and speak them to someone else."

"Fine. Maybe I will." Furious was too tame a word for his current state. He threw back the covers and stood. Where were his damn breeches? Lying on the floor with his shirt and boots and his tattered pride. So much for good intentions. Jon pulled on his breeches, the feel of Julia's gaze boring into his back. He had to get out of here before he said anything else he'd regret. He shoved his arms into his shirt and turned around.

One quick glance at his wife told him she was just as eager to see him gone. She clutched the counterpane to her chin, an act that infuriated him. "A little late for modesty, isn't it?"

"Get out of here," she hissed. *"Now."*

Jon finished the last button on his shirt and walked toward her, stopping inches from the bed. He leaned over and smiled. "You like that word, don't you, Julia?"

She pulled the covers closer. "I don't know what you're talking about."

His smile deepened. "A few minutes ago you were begging me to make love to you. *Now*."

"Temporary insanity," she spat out.

"I don't think so." He fondled a plump curl. She tried to jerk away but he trapped her between his arms. "You may not say the words," his voice remained soft and clear, "but there's no denying what happened in this bed, and we both know it." He released her and straightened. "And it will happen again. We both know that, too."

"Don't you dare come back."

Jon laughed. "Or what?"

Her eyes narrowed. "Or I'll have to stop you."

Her feeble words angered him more. "That's right, you have a *protector*." He cocked his head to the side. "Fair enough. By all means, you may inform *Cyrus* I will be returning tomorrow evening but if I may make one small suggestion," he lowered his voice, taking on the tone of a true conspirator, "why not wait until after you've had your woman's release? Maybe it will make you less cranky. What do you say?"

Julia scrambled off the bed and reached for the Chinese vase just as Jon opened the door to the master chambers. He cast one final look back as she prepared to launch her weapon. "I'll see you tomorrow night," he said, unable to resist one last jab before he pulled the door shut. Seconds later, a sharp thud hit the door, followed by a loud crash.

Jon shook his head and wondered, why, of all the women he'd known, he had to fall in love with one as impossible as this one.

Chapter 18

Julia finished tying a pale-green bow in her hair and turned toward the mirror. Everything looked the same. Same eyes, nose, mouth, hair. She squeezed her eyes shut. Who was she trying to fool? Everything was different now.

Her stomach lurched, and she pressed a hand against it to still it. Was she about to be sick? It had been two days since her last bout with the chamber pot and she prayed she could make it two more. Besides, the jumping in her stomach had been going on all night.

Well, most of the night. Ever since Jon left. Blasted man. She rubbed her temples. All she needed was a headache to go along with her riotous stomach. Not only had the man wreaked havoc on her emotions, battering down her defenses with little care or concern; now he was affecting her body as well. Double damn.

She'd been a fool to let him touch her again. She should have known better. She *did* know better. But it hadn't mattered. Not when he stood before her in all of his fierce, masculine glory, like a determined warrior come to claim her, eyes glittering with desire, mouth uttering soft, sensual promises of unexplored pleasures. She couldn't deny him any more than she could deny herself a breath of fresh air and that was the real reason for this morning's stomach problems.

Julia swung away from the mirror, disgusted with her own weakness. Her gaze fell on the bed and vibrant images of Jon's naked body moving over hers flashed through her, scorching the most private part of her body. Oh, dear Lord, she'd become a prisoner to her own sexual desires, captive to the holder of the key.

Last night, Jon had uttered the words she'd waited so long to hear, only to find that she did not trust him enough to believe them. Too many lies had passed between them, too much hurt, too much betrayal. He wanted her to speak the same words, but she couldn't, not when she had no idea where he'd been or if he'd be staying. He'd come back tonight, but what about the next? And the next? What would happen when she swelled with child and was no longer appealing?

And what of the day? Would he spend time with her, talking and laughing, even playing cards, as she and Cyrus had done on many a long night? Would Glenview Manor hold enough excitement to keep him here? *Would she?* The questions ripped Jon's words of love into tiny shreds, tossing them out as unbelievable and inconsequential. There was too much at stake. He must prove his love first. Then she would tell him her truth, the one she kept carefully guarded, even from herself.

She loved her husband very much.

When the time came, if circumstances permitted and God smiled upon her, she would pledge her love to her husband, but not a moment before. And then she would tell him about the baby. It was all quite simple to reason out without a certain pair of dark eyes boring into her. Her stomach growled. It didn't lurch, or jump, or even somersault. It simply growled, a natural response to a desire for food. Thank heavens, at least something felt normal. Smoothing her gown, she headed for the door, wondering what delicacies the cook had conjured up. Blueberry tarts sounded appealing this morning. Or perhaps a cranberry muffin slathered in thick, creamy butter. Then again, there were always poached eggs and toast, but she'd had a taste for a slice of cured ham, too, and a big bowl of fresh strawberries. It all sounded wonderful. How would she ever decide? Her stomach growled again. On second thought, maybe she'd have them all.

She was so preoccupied with breakfast she almost didn't see Mr. Billington coming out of the study. "Oh, good morning, Mr. Billington."

"Good morning, Lady Remmington," he said, with a hint of softness in his usually precise voice.

Julia bestowed a dazzling smile on the butler. Ever since she'd stuck up for him in front of Jon's men, he'd softened toward her, the crusty edges smoothing out, sometimes even disappearing. She rather liked this side of the man and took every opportunity to encourage more of the same.

"Is Cyrus in there?" she asked, inclining her head toward the study.

Billington shifted his weight to stand in front of the doors. "Cyrus?"

Julia smiled. Mr. Billington had a very good way of asking a question with a question, especially when he didn't want to answer it but she was on to his little tactics and could play the game almost as well as he could. "Yes. Cyrus," she said, crossing her arms over her chest. "You recall him, Mr. Billington. Tall, broad, bushy brown hair, beard, glasses. Does he sound familiar?"

Mr. Billington's lips twitched. "Quite."

"And?" she prodded.

"And?" he countered.

"Is he in the study?" Before Mr. Billington had a chance to answer, Julia detected Cyrus's raspy voice through the door.

"Ah, yes, Lady Remmington, Mr. Mandrey does happen to be in the study at the moment."

She gave Mr. Billington one of her I-already-knew-that smiles and waited for him to step aside.

He didn't move.

Julia sighed. The man might be softening a bit, but he still had a long way to go. "Excuse me, Mr. Billington, may I pass?"

The butler took a deep breath. "Mr. Mandrey is in a meeting at the moment and asked not to be disturbed."

"A meeting?" Who would he be meeting? As far as she knew, Cyrus didn't know anyone in these parts with the exception of Andrew and he couldn't stand the man. So who could it be? Had he found out about Jon and contacted Holt? She didn't like the odd look on Mr. Billington's face, as if he were trying to hide something. Or protect someone. Jon? *Was Jon in there?* "I need to see Mr. Mandrey. Immediately." If Jon were in there, she had to help him. He would be just foolish and arrogant enough to underestimate Cyrus because of his disarming appearance.

"But Mr. Mandrey—"

"I *need* to see him, Mr. Billington. Now." Her quiet persistence must have warned him it would be useless to argue further. Without a word, Mr. Billington stepped aside.

Julia bound through the door, words flying out of her mouth in an incoherent jumble. "I can explain everything."

Two pairs of eyes stared back at her, one with spectacles, the other a summer-sky blue.

"Andrew?" What was he doing here?

"Hello, Julia," he said, giving her one of his winning smiles as he rose from an overstuffed chair to greet her.

"Julia? Is something wrong?" Cyrus stood, too. She shook her head and drew in a deep breath.

She'd almost mentioned Jon's name. No matter how angry she was with him, she had to protect him, for her own sake as well as his. If he left now, his simple *I love you* would haunt her forever.

"What did you want to explain, Julia?" Cyrus asked, his voice gentle.

"Nothing," she blurted out. Her gaze swerved to Andrew. "Why are you here?"

Andrew's smile spoke of compassion and understanding. "Mandrey wanted my permission to scout my properties. He spotted your husband the other night."

"Kleeton."

Andrew dismissed Cyrus with a wave of his gloved hand. "Why not tell her, Mandrey? She needs to be aware so she can protect herself."

"That's *my* job," Cyrus shot back.

"You can't be with her every minute. And you won't let me stay with her, either."

Julia's gaze shot from Andrew to Cyrus. "Cyrus? Is what Andrew says true?"

Cyrus stepped away from the desk and walked toward her,

stopping when they stood face to face. His expression grew solemn, his voice quiet. "I found footprints beneath the windows the other night and saw someone running from the house. I'm assuming the man was your husband."

"No," Julia said. "It can't be him. He wouldn't come back." She looked away, afraid Cyrus would see the lie on her face. The situation was worse than she thought.

"We think he'll come to you, Julia. He's probably already tried." Andrew's words sliced through her.

"Have you told Holt?" Her chest hurt, like a large fist had landed flat in the center and stolen her breath.

"There's no need to alert him until the job is done," Cyrus said.

She bit the inside of her cheek to keep from showing undue emotion. It would not do to appear distressed. Cyrus watched her, his gaze intent, his mouth silent. He was only doing his duty. She understood that. As she was doing hers.

The four walls closed in, stifling her breath, choking her hopes with every word spoken. Julia needed to clear her head and formulate a plan to help her husband and she needed to do it now. She hazarded a glance at both men and willed her voice to remain steady as she said, "Well, then, gentlemen, it seems you have everything under control. I'll leave you to your strategies." She nodded and turned to leave. Her hand was on the knob when Cyrus's soft voice reached her.

"Julia, you will let us know at once if Jon tries to contact you?" It was a statement disguised in the politeness of a question.

"Of course," she said and quit the room.

***

Julia sat up in bed, two pillows propped behind her as she attempted to read. She'd been on the same page for the last twenty minutes. Her eyes flew to the clock. Eleven. She slammed the book shut. It was useless to try and concentrate. Nothing could hold her attention but the conversation she'd had this morning with Cyrus and Andrew. *Cyrus had seen Jon.*

Could he tell she was lying about having seen her husband? She'd tried to sound so convincing, but it was difficult to lie to Cyrus. He was such an honest, noble man that she felt guilty even though she had no choice. Jon needed her help, though he most likely would have a different opinion on the subject. The man was too bull-headed, too stubborn to see trouble when it stared him in the face and she was not about to let him get carted away before he proved his love for her.

She smoothed the French lace on the bodice of her silk nightgown. The nightgown she was to have worn on her wedding night. It was adorned with miniature satin rosettes and tiny seed pearls. The plunging neckline exposed ample amounts of flesh for an admirer's perusal. She told herself the only reason she wore it tonight was because it happened to be the first thing she grabbed and her cotton nightgown had a small tear in it from last night. Her cheeks burned as she recalled the way she'd flung the gown aside, eager to please Jon with her nakedness.

She jerked the bodice together with her right hand. This was ridiculous. What was wrong with her? Who did she think she was trying to fool, half-dressed in a flimsy swatch of material with a closed book in her hand and both eyes fixed on the door? She might have told Jon to stay away, even frowned and shaken her fist at him, but she wanted him to come tonight and one look at her half-naked body and he'd know it, too.

Throwing back the covers, Julia scrambled out of bed and yanked open her wardrobe. She must hurry. She rifled through layers of white cotton and found a simple nightgown, tied at the neckline, void of lace. If Jon decided to show up, she'd not have him thinking she'd taken extra pains with her appearance.

The soft click behind her told her she was too late. Julia froze, her back to the door, the gown bunched in her hands.

"Well, well," Jon's deep voice poured over her like fine brandy, "if it isn't my little wife." His footsteps moved toward her. "What a delicious surprise," he murmured. His breath was warm with a hint of tobacco as he stood behind her, almost touching.

Her fingers twisted the fabric she held. *She would not show him she cared.*

Jon touched her hair, a light caress, traveling from neck to back. His fingers trailed over the juncture of her hips, stroking her through the lace, heating her bare skin. She tensed and tried to ignore the desire pulsing through her.

"You wore this for me?" he asked, running his hands up the sides of her waist to the undersides of her arms, brushing past the swell of her breasts.

She shook her head and closed her eyes. His fingers outlined her breasts, circling them with callused fingertips, touching everywhere but the tips. She needn't look to know the peaks were hard and quite visible through the thin fabric. Perfect for his mouth, aching for his tongue. A small moan escaped.

"You want me as much as I want you," he said, his voice ragged and heavy. "Stop fighting it."

Julia tried to keep her wits about her, but Jon stripped away her convictions, one flick at a time as his thumbs worked her swollen nipples.

"We shouldn't be doing this," she whispered, leaning into the solid comfort of his chest.

His large hand moved down her body to cup her woman's heat. He pressed her against his thighs, her buttocks rubbing the hardness of his arousal. "We most definitely should be doing this," he murmured, lifting her nightgown to bury a finger inside her heat.

She rocked against him, trying to get closer to his touch. She reached back to stroke him. "I can't...let you..." She groaned, moving against his finger. "Hurt me...again."

"No. Not again. Never again," He tore open his breeches and his sex brushed against Julia's hand. She circled his shaft, ran her fingers the length of him, smiled when he growled low in his throat. He pumped into her hand, a slow, methodic rhythm that begged her to join in. Julia moved her hips, swaying to meet him.

"Jon," she breathed.

"Open your legs for me, Julia," he pleaded, running his hand along her inner thigh. She spread her legs, arching her hips in a circle. She pushed forward, straining to meet the gentle hum of his fingers on her. Pure, simple ecstasy. She leaned back and felt the slick, swollen tip of him, begging entry.

There was no denying him. "Yes," she whimpered. "Oh, yes."

He grabbed her hips and surged into her with such force she almost lost her balance. She felt him inside, warm and pulsing. Needing, just like her. Julia braced herself against the wardrobe, arching her hips and planting her feet.

Jon reached around to stroke her as he moved in and out of her with slow, even strokes. "Prepare yourself, my sweet—" he kissed her neck "—for pure pleasure, the purest you have ever known." His tongue circled a tiny spot on her shoulder, sucked the tender flesh.

"Yes...yes." His fingers skimmed and caressed her while his sex tortured her with measured restraint. "Yes," she groaned as a whirlwind of sensation grabbed her. "Yes!" she screamed, as she came apart and spiraled into ecstasy, one delicious stroke at a time.

Jon drove into her, hard and fast and deep, creating new waves of sensation with each stroke. Oh, but he had been so right about pure pleasure. Seconds later, he shouted her name, all signs of the controlled lover gone, and with one final plunge, he groaned and spilled his seed inside her.

She didn't know who moved first. Had Jon carried her to the bed and tucked her in with the tenderness of a loving husband or had she dreamed it? Had he made love to her a second time with such exquisite care she had sobbed? Fantasy meshed too closely with reality for her to tell the difference but how could she be expected to, when she'd dreamed it so many times it had become real? And was he lying beside her now, flesh and blood and warm male? There was only one way to separate fantasy from reality.

She opened her eyes and stared into a broad, hairy chest. It hadn't been a dream. He'd done all of those *things* to her, every one of them, and she'd done her share of *things* to him, too. How would she ever face him when she'd told him not to even try to enter her chambers or she'd boot him out? Well, not only had she not given him the boot, she'd welcomed him with eagerness and open arms. Julia winced. And open legs. He'd think her a wanton, no better than one of his mistresses in that lacy nightgown. That had started everything. If only she'd worn a serviceable gown, none of this would have happened.

"Julia?" Jon's deep voice ran over her like warm honey.

"Yes?" She stared ahead, right into his intimidating chest. Images of her fingers roaming over that chest, rubbing her bare breasts along it, feeling the tingle of crisp hair on her nipples flashed through her mind. She jerked her head down. That was a bigger mistake. The sheet rode low on her husband's hips, exposing another, much more dangerous part of his anatomy. She squeezed her eyes shut and refused to think about what she'd done with *that* body part.

"Julia?" There was a hint of amusement in his voice.

She kept her head low, eyes shut tight.

He chuckled. "Would you look at me, please?"

She shook her head.

"You have to look at me sometime."

"Not necessarily," she mumbled into the sheet.

He sighed, and she guessed he was trying to be patient. "I'm your husband. You've seen me naked before." He touched her shoulder. She flinched but he didn't remove his hand. "And I've seen you naked, too."

"It was the nightgown," she blurted out.

"The nightgown?"

"Yes. If I hadn't worn it, none of this would have happened."

"None of what?"

"This," she said, waving a hand in the air, but still refusing to look at him. "Me. You. Naked. Together. Doing *things.*"

"And *that's* what you're upset about?" He took a deep breath and let it out on a long sigh.

"I told you not to come back, and you did anyway."

"You knew I would," he said, annoyance clear in his voice. "And if I hadn't, you would have been even more upset."

She said nothing.

"Isn't that right?" he prodded.

"That's beside the point." It was, wasn't it? "I told you not to come and you did and if I hadn't been wearing that nightgown, none of this would have happened."

Jon remained silent for a full minute. When he spoke, his words fell over her like a caress. "You could have been wearing a sackcloth, and I would have done the same things to you. I like doing *things* to you, Julia. I like it a lot. As a matter of fact, there are a few *things* I would like to do to you right now." His fingers inched down her back, tracing circles on her skin.

"I acted no better than Desiree or Monique."

His laughter came out in gulps as though he'd tried to restrain himself and couldn't. "Really, Julia." He laughed again.

"I know." She shook her head in misery. "I acted no better than one of them."

The laughter stopped. Jon's strong fingers found her chin and forced her head up. "Listen to me," he said, his brown eyes blazing as he scanned her face. "You're my wife. We shared great passion in this room. If you deny everything else about us, for God's sake, don't deny that. What happened tonight had nothing to do with the damned nightgown or wanton behavior. It had to do with passion. And need. Don't apologize and don't be ashamed of it."

She saw the twitch in his jaw and knew she'd hurt him.

"I said nothing about love tonight because you're not ready to discuss it." He sat up and rifled a hand through his hair.

"You think I only want the use of your body."

The bitterness in his words stung, but she pretended they didn't bother her. "I told you, I won't let you hurt me again. You said this charade would be over in three days. That's tomorrow."

"I can count."

"Good." She bit the inside of her cheek to keep from crying. Who was this man who stared back at her with such coldness? How could he be the same one who'd made love to her less than an hour ago with such consuming passion? How was it possible to feel such closeness one minute and such distance the next?

"Let's get some sleep," Jon said. "We'll talk about this in the morning."

Julia grabbed his forearm. "Wait! You can't sleep here."

He shrugged her arm off. "I can't?" His words were soft, too soft.

"No, you can't," she stammered, feeling self-conscious and awkward. And very naked. She tugged on the sheet to cover her bare leg, but Jon's thigh weighed it down. She yanked at the counterpane and pulled it to her chin.

"Good night, Julia," Jon said, as though he hadn't heard a word she'd just said. He leaned over and snuffed out the lamp, casting the room in darkness, save the sliver of moon that slipped through the gap in the draperies.

"But, you can't—"

"I know," he sighed. "I can't stay with you tonight." He moved to his side and pulled Julia against him.

He wasn't going to leave. This just wouldn't do. What if Cyrus came knocking on her door in the morning? What if she were sick? Jon was too smart not to guess she was with child. She could tell him it was an upset from last evening's meal. Of course, that would be another lie but what was one more lie in the long trail that paved their relationship? Her stomach twisted into a knot. Lies. Would she and Jon ever stop telling them to one another? Was he lying to her now when he professed his love? She didn't know and it filled her heart with such overwhelming sadness that she ached.

"Good night, Julia."

He wasn't going to leave. *And* he was drifting off to sleep. The knowledge pricked every nerve in her body. Well, then fine, let him stay, but she'd see he got no sleep. "Cyrus saw you the other day," she said. That would rouse him.

"Hmm."

One mumbled half word was not the response she anticipated. "He's determined to catch you."

"Hmm."

"And he asked me if I saw you." There. Stew about that for a minute or two.

"Did you tell him you saw every inch of me?" The laughter in his voice was too much.

"You!" She tried to struggle from his hold but he held her down like a nasty pest. "Don't you care that Cyrus is after you? Could catch you? That I could have turned you in?" She maneuvered a few inches, trying to work her way to her side. Jon's arm went with her, landing on her hip. Her bare hip. She squirmed but he only pressed her deeper into his side. She froze when she felt the coarse hair on his legs brushing the inside of her thighs.

"You wouldn't turn me in." The certainty in his voice annoyed her. She didn't know what bothered her more, the fact that he was right or that he knew he was right. "As for Mandrey, I'll take my chances."

"You do that," she hissed, angry at his arrogance. "But you have one more day to end this charade and if you don't, I *will* turn you in."

"And see me hang by my ankles," Jon added, as though her threat didn't bother him one bit.

"Toes," she ground out.

"Toes?"

"I'll see you hang by your toes. Much more painful," she assured him.

Jon pulled her closer. "Dear wife, how will I ever get used to such unadulterated adoration?"

Chapter 19

Julia rolled onto her stomach, arms outstretched, uncurling one finger at a time as she shed the last layers of slumber. Her body felt warm and languid, like a rose gifted with the full bounty of sunshine. She sighed. Perhaps she'd drift back to her dreams a little while longer. Jon would be there, he always was, touching her with strong hands, watching her with dark, unreadable eyes, tasting her with full, firm lips. She smiled. Yes, she would dream just a little longer.

A rap on the door jolted her from her thoughts. "Julia, wake up. It's eleven o'clock. Are you planning to sleep all day?" Cyrus's voice rasped through the door.

"I'm…awake," Julia said on a yawn.

"It's a gorgeous day. I thought we'd take a walk if you're feeling up to it."

Julia buried her head under the pillow. She'd rather get back to her dream but Cyrus was much too persistent to leave her alone. Besides, dreams were just that. Dreams. She preferred to keep hers tucked away for midnight perusing or early morning wanderings. Throwing back the covers, Julia flung her legs over the side of the bed and called out, "Fifteen minutes, Cyrus. I'll see you then."

She heard him turn away, whistling as he went down the hall.

Twenty minutes later, Julia grabbed two buttermilk biscuits from the sideboard, tucked them in a napkin, and headed out the door. Cyrus waited for her by a bench near the maze.

"Good morning," she said, smiling at him.

"And good afternoon to you," he returned, smiling back.

"I guess I was more tired than I realized." And who wouldn't be with a virile, demanding husband like Jon Remmington?

"It's to be expected of a woman in your condition."

He was referring to the baby, of course. A pang of sadness struck her as she realized Cyrus knew about her unborn child but Jon did not. It wasn't time to tell him yet. She had to see if he'd keep his word and then she'd tell him. Within the next twelve hours she'd know if he'd betrayed her. Again.

Why couldn't Jon be more like Cyrus? Dependable, honest, trustworthy. "I'll miss you when you're gone, Cyrus."

"I'll miss you, too," he said as they rounded a corner of the rose garden and headed into the maze.

"What will you do when you leave here?" She hated to think of him alone.

He smiled. "There's a certain woman I intend to contact and if she'll forgive my stupid, selfish, uncaring ways and give me another chance, I'll be the happiest man in the world."

"You?" she gasped. "Are in love?" He nodded, and she was sure she spotted a blush beneath his bush of hair. "That's wonderful!" She let out a peal of laughter and gave him a quick hug. "I'm so happy for you. I had no idea."

He looked a bit sheepish. "Nor did I, to tell you the truth. But watching you made me do a lot of thinking. I left her without much explanation, and a lot of things unsaid. I don't plan on making the same mistake twice."

"I can't picture you being selfish or uncaring or anything but noble." *Unlike some men.*

"Love makes people do crazy things. Remember that. I wouldn't be surprised if your husband felt the same way."

The smile faded away. "Time will tell, Cyrus. Time will tell." Sooner than he thought.

***

He wasn't coming. It was eleven fifty-two and she sat alone, fully dressed on a high-backed chair in the corner of her room, staring at the cream-swirled wallpaper in front of her. All the promises, hopes, and dreams ticking away. Why couldn't he have left her alone? Why did he have to make her care so much that losing him a second time would prove almost unbearable?

Julia rested her head against the wall, wishing she could still her weary mind from the constant torment of loss and betrayal. She closed her eyes and tried to ignore the ache in her back.

After two hours in a wooden chair without a cushion, she longed for the softness of her bed. Eight more minutes. She would wait right here with every stitch of clothing on. Far from the bed. She must keep her wits about her so she could deal with his seductive charm. That's what he had and more than his fair share of it, too.

Something brushed her forehead, gentle as a summer's breeze. Julia murmured in half sleep, her head falling to the side. Another feather-light touch on the neck. She lifted her hand in silent protest and her fingers grazed something hard and scratchy. Her eyes flew open. Jon leaned over her, inches away, his stubbled chin stroked by her fingers.

She snatched her hand away and buried it in the fold of her gown.

"Why aren't you in bed?" he asked, his dark eyes as soft as warm honey. Her stomach jumped at the tenderness in his voice. He was doing it to her again. With no more than a few soft-spoken words, he'd blurred her judgment like raindrops on a window pane.

"I was waiting for you." She kept her voice even. Her gaze flitted across his face and she noted the weary lines of fatigue etched around his mouth and eyes. He looked older, tired, less self-assured. Something was wrong.

"You should be resting." His gaze darted to her stomach, settled there a few seconds, and then moved to her face. Almost as if he knew there was indeed a very real reason for her to be resting at such an hour.

Julia blinked that thought away. No sense in looking for complications, not yet, anyway. The sad, uneasy look in his eyes sent a shiver of foreboding through her. "You're not going to tell me what this is all about, are you?" She folded her hands in her lap, squeezing them so hard her knuckles turned white.

"I need a little more time."

Six words, that's all it took to crush her hopes for a life with him. Six small words. One sentence. Her future with Jon Remmington inked out before it started. "Then, there's really nothing left to say."

"I know what I told you, Julia. I thought I'd have everything under control by now, but I *need* a little more time."

She shrugged and tried to sound flippant. "Take all the time you *need,* Jon. Take a week, a month, a year, if that's what you *need.* But don't expect me to wait for you or welcome you back as my husband."

He cursed. "Can't you be reasonable? Can't you trust me just a little longer?"

"We haven't trusted each other since we met in The Fox's Tail."

"Then isn't it time to start?" He knelt on one knee and covered her cold hands with his strong, warm ones. "For God's sake, Julia, don't do this," he pleaded.

"Don't do what, Jon? Don't ask questions?" The right side of his jaw twitched. "Don't expect answers?" His nostrils flared. "Don't be difficult?" His eyes narrowed to brown slits. "Don't intrude on your plans?" His hands tightened on hers.

"Stop it."

"Stop what?" She disengaged her hands from his grasp. "Stop asking for the truth?"

"Yes, damn it! I mean no. No! Stop behaving like a child and be reasonable." He massaged the back of his neck. "Give me a little more time."

She folded her arms across her chest. "Sorry. Time's run out. Where have you been all this time?" She scanned his face. "Why did you leave me on our wedding night?"

He glared at her. "I told you, I'm not at liberty to say at the moment."

"And I told you, I'm not interested in excuses."

He stood and paced the room, plowing all ten fingers through his hair. "Damn you, Julia."

"Damn you, Jon," she shot back, a spurt of feeling pumping into her cold veins.

He gave her a dark look and a scowl before he rounded on her, stopping less than a foot away. She willed him to go away, but she knew with Jon Remmington, nothing was that easy.

"You're too upset to be rational right now. You're saying things you can't mean." He rubbed his jaw and studied her like a commander strategizing before battle, only this skirmish would hold no victory for him, only the bitter emptiness of defeat.

"If you say so." The man was persistent to the point of being downright exhausting.

"I know so," he said, enunciating each word with careful eloquence. And then came the dagger, twisting and gouging her heart. "I love you, Julia."

Those were the words she couldn't bear to hear. She didn't believe them, *couldn't* believe them, and perhaps that was why the pain seeped to her soul. A surge of anger made her want to lash out and make him feel her pain, hurt him as he'd hurt her.

"Words, Jon. Only words." What was love without trust?

"Believe what you will. One day, you'll know the truth." Julia kept her head bent, refusing to look at him. "I'll be back tomorrow night and then we'll talk."

Her head shot up and their gazes clashed. "Leave tonight and you'll be spared. Stay and I won't be responsible for the consequences."

"You would see me captured and treated like a common criminal?" He advanced a step, daring her to answer. She did not. He threw a hand in the air and said, "Do what you will. I'll return tomorrow night." With those last words, he stalked from the room, leaving Julia to stare after him.

When she was certain he was gone, she rose from the chair and moved to the bed. She lay on it and turned her face into the counterpane. Only then did she allow the tears to come.

***

Julia tried to hide the puffiness in her eyes the next morning but knew Cyrus noticed their swollen state. Thankfully, he was too much the gentleman to ask pointed questions. Unlike one particular person she knew. Brown eyes and a slow smile danced through her mind. That man was no gentleman. He was a scourge, a scoundrel, a rakehell. Her husband. She sighed. And the cause of so many tears.

"Kleeton should be arriving any moment," Cyrus said, cutting into her thoughts.

"Good." She patted a stray lock of hair into place.

"Why is he coming?" Cyrus asked, taking a seat beside her on the sofa.

Julia hesitated. She hated lying to Cyrus but couldn't very well tell him the truth, so she settled on a half-truth. "It's nice to have a visitor on occasion. Andrew is aware of our 'situation' and it's not as awkward inviting him to tea as it would be a new neighbor." She gave Cyrus a wistful smile. "After all, how would I explain your presence?"

Cyrus shrugged his bulky shoulders. "Soon enough, it won't matter. I'll be gone and you can invite the whole town if you want."

"Yes, soon enough it won't matter," Julia echoed, her gaze settling on the row of books harboring the panel that opened to the secret passage. She'd wanted to check the passage herself when Jon first told her about it, but hesitated, worried he might be hiding in its dark recesses. Now, she would not be undertaking any grand explorations for the fear of seeing Jon again was too real.

Last night as she lay on her bed, spent and exhausted from tears, Julia knew the pang of hurt and betrayal and vowed she'd never again let Jon close enough to hurt her. But when she woke in the gray dawn, crumpled and mussed in yesterday's gown, she remembered the heat in his eyes, heard the pleading in his voice as he begged for a little more time. *I love you, Julia.* His words rolled over her like waves beating against rocks, wearing her down a little at a time.

This morning she didn't know what she wanted to do. Didn't know which she'd regret more, leaving Jon or not leaving him. That's why she'd sent Andrew the invitation to tea. She needed someone to listen to her dilemma. Cyrus was out of the question for obvious reasons. Sophie was too far away and even if she weren't, Julia wouldn't risk creating a rift between her and Holt. Belle was touring the Continent with her aunt and Francie Bishop might create more havoc and uncertainty than currently existed. So, there really wasn't anyone left save Andrew.

He would know what to do. He'd been supportive throughout the entire ordeal, concerned only for her safety and best interest. He'd help her make the right decision. Now all she had to do was find a way to be alone with him, which meant fabricating an excuse to get Cyrus out of the room.

A single rap on the door signaled Andrew's arrival. Cyrus rose and opened the door. He and Andrew exchanged a few words, but their voices were too low for Julia to make out what they said.

"Hello, Julia." Andrew advanced into the room with a dazzling smile on his handsome face.

She returned the smile and placed her hand in his. "Thank you for coming on such short notice." She shot a glance toward Cyrus, who watched the exchange with mild interest. The sooner she got this over with, the better.

"It's always a pleasure to see you."

"Cyrus, would you mind very much seeing to tea? And would you speak with Cook about the lemon pastries and raspberry tarts I asked her to prepare? I've a sudden craving for them." Julia smiled at Cyrus, hoping he wouldn't realize she was trying to be rid of him.

His raised brow and tilted head told her he was on to her game, but Cyrus, being Cyrus, would comply with her request. He'd never embarrass her in front of Andrew. Unlike another individual, who would relish the very idea of it.

Cyrus gave her a slight nod and said, "I'll be back shortly."

As soon as the door clicked behind him, Julia turned to Andrew. "You must help me," she whispered. "I'm in a terrible mess, and I don't know what to do."

Andrew's summer-blue eyes shone with concern. He leaned toward her and adopted the same tone. "Whatever is troubling you, Julia?"

"It's Jon. He came to me the other night." Heat crept along her neck to her cheeks. "He told me in three days' time I'd know why he left and why he couldn't return. It seems it had nothing to do with Cyrus being here. It was almost as if there was another, much more serious reason he couldn't come to me." She rubbed her temples. "I'm so confused."

"Of course you are," Andrew whispered, soothing her shattered nerves as he took her hand in his. "Go on," he urged.

"Last night, he told me he needed more time." She hesitated, sucked in a deep breath. "I refused him. I said horrible things, Andrew. I just wanted to protect myself from being hurt again."

"And now you wonder if you did the right thing?" His quiet words voiced the uncertainty she'd felt since Jon had stalked from her room.

"Yes." She swiped her cheeks with the back her hand.

"How did he get into your room without discovery, Julia?"

"Oh—" her gaze shot to the bookcase "—there's a secret panel that opens a passageway leading to his room." What did it matter if she told Andrew?

"Where is this secret panel?"

Julia looked at Andrew, wondering at the sharpness in his voice, the keenness in his eyes. "It's behind the third row of books in that case over there," she said, pointing to several volumes of leather-bound books. Andrew let out a long breath as though he'd been holding it. What did he care if Jon harbored a secret passageway in his home?

"Telling me was the right thing to do," Andrew said, leaning back against the sofa and taking her hand with him. She didn't notice; her heart and her mind were tangled with thoughts and feelings, all centering around her husband.

"I don't know what to do. Part of me wants to hate him, but the other part won't let me. And I'm carrying his child," she murmured.

"Give it time," Andrew said. "Another day or so even.

Everything will work out according to a plan much larger than yours or your husband's. You'll see," he said, his gentle words a balm to her restless soul.

She gave him a tear-streaked smile and whispered, "I never knew you to be a religious man, Andrew. Thank you for your comforting words." She squeezed his hand. "I'll wait and let the Divine Plan follow its course."

Andrew smiled. "And so it shall be, Julia. So it shall be."

***

He had to make her see reason. Jon strode into the darkened library with nothing but a small lamp to illuminate his path. Damn, but the woman was bull-headed. He'd thought he'd be able to force Kleeton's hand in three days; thought the man would have slipped up in his overzealous endeavor to trap Jon Remmington. He hadn't missed the gleam in Kleeton's eyes when he mentioned Jon's name. He'd bet his entire wealth the man posing as a country gentleman was a notorious traitor and ruthless killer.

But hunches weren't enough. Not with stakes this high. Peter Crowlton had slithered away once before, hidden behind God knew how many rocks, escaping capture for years. Well, he would not escape again. Not if Jon could help it. Tomorrow, he'd force Kleeton's hand. He'd confront him, not as Cyrus Mandrey but as Jon Remmington, and he'd see what secrets lay beneath Kleeton's gloves.

Jon pressed the panel to engage the hidden door. He pushed it open and stepped inside, his thoughts once more on his wife. Why in the hell had she called a meeting with Kleeton? He knew damned well it was a meeting, not a social call as she would have Cyrus believe. What was she up to now? He turned to close the door when a sharp object lodged against his throat and froze him in his tracks.

"Well, well," a familiar voice said. "If it isn't the ghost himself."

"Crowlton," Jon rasped against the blade. "Traitorous bastard."

The blade dug into his flesh. "Watch it, Remmington. I've waited a long time to see you bleed. Seven and a half years to be exact." His breathing grew harsh and labored against Jon's ear. "I want to savor every minute of this. I want to feel the fear in your heart as I raise my knife in final revenge. See the helplessness in your eyes as I slit your throat. I want to remember *everything* for years to come."

"You can't remember anything if you're a dead man."

Crowlton laughed. "Always the hero, aren't you? You'll be no hero today. You'll pay dearly for what you did to me." He paused. "With your life."

Jon heard the bitterness in his voice, felt the fury as The Serpent's hand trembled against the blade, digging deeper, drawing blood.

"You did this to yourself. You wanted it all, no matter the stakes. It didn't matter who got hurt or killed, so long as you were in charge." If he were going to die, he'd make damn certain he had his say first.

The blow to the back of his neck was swift and sharp, placed with enough precision to drop Jon to his knees. The lantern fell to the ground but remained upright. Before he could recover, Jon suffered the toe of Crowlton's booted foot in his side. He slumped forward, groaning.

Crowlton snorted. "I did what I had to do. I had the power, don't you understand?" His words were fervent, demanding recognition. "I was in control, within two missions of absolute power." He towered over Jon, the tip of the blade glinting in his left hand. "Until you ruined everything."

"You...were," Jon rasped, sucking in air. "A traitor...to your...country and...fellow agents."

Another kick landed in his side. "I was a *businessman*. My allegiance was to whoever gave me the most coin. Turn around, Remmington. I want the satisfaction of seeing the life drain from your face when I slit your throat."

Jon tried to lift his head as nausea rolled over him. He grew dizzy and lightheaded at the same time. He had to gather his strength and his wits or he would soon be nothing but a lifeless pool of bloody flesh. Ignoring the pain in his side and the ache in his head, he rolled over and slouched against the stone wall. The coolness of the stone eased the pain in his head.

"I want you to see what you did to me." Crowlton yanked off his black gloves in two swift movements. "Look, Remmington. Look at what your fire did," he hissed, thrusting his hands forward in the dim light. His hands were gnarled extremities, covered with layer upon layer of thin white skin, stretched and crossed over one another, forming a grotesque pattern of human flesh.

Crowlton snatched his hands back. "You're the cause of this," he raged. "You! Would you like to guess how I came to be so disfigured?" He leaned forward, blue eyes glinting. When Jon didn't respond, he burst forth, "I tried to grab the files you torched. All those names, with dates, assignments, everything. All in flames. With a single match you stripped my power and turned me from the best espionage agent in the country to a wanted criminal."

"They were on to you, Crowlton," Jon said, meeting his cold stare. He had to distract him. Perhaps then he'd let his guard down and Jon could strike. Should he go straight for the knife or tackle him at the waist?

"Don't even try it." The words hit him like one of Crowlton's boots and knocked the wind out of his half-formed plan.

Crowlton was a master of many things—espionage, strategy, tactics, weaponry.

But he was human. Or as close to human as a traitor could be. What was his weak spot?

"I would have taken care of you sooner, but there were too many people after me," Crowlton said, tossing the knife from one hand to the other. "Too many tracks to cover. And then you were gone, disappearing for years. I decided to wait it out, certain that one day you'd return. Too bad I had to kill the old duke and duchess next door, but I needed their home and they refused to sell. Of course, their wastrel of a son had no choice, not after I bought up all of his markers and threatened to call them in. Poor dumb bastard. Most humans are such a pitiful lot, don't you think?"

Jon rested an arm on his knee, staring straight ahead, wondering at Crowlton's incredible arrogance. He didn't think he could ever be defeated. Not by anyone, least of all a man without a weapon.

That was his weakness.

"And then," Crowlton went on, "stroke of luck would have it that your beautiful wife arrived at Glenview Manor." He smiled. "Alone. Without her husband. That was a true gift and I will be forever indebted to you."

"Leave Julia out of this," Jon said, clenching his fists at his side. If he had a knife, he'd drive it right through the bastard's heart before he could utter another word.

"Oh, but I can't. She trusts me, or rather, she trusts Andrew Kleeton and has become such an important part of this whole, ah, shall we say, situation?"

Rage threatened to boil over and explode through Jon's body. He wanted to charge him, thought about it, but held back. He must be rational. "I don't know what you're talking about," he spat out, his eyes zeroing in on Crowlton's knife.

"Of course you don't." Crowlton gave a short, harsh laugh. "You weren't here, were you?" He tilted his head to one side and rubbed his smooth chin. "Well, not the whole time anyway." Reaching into his pocket, he pulled out a brown ball and tossed it to Jon. Before it touched his fingers, Jon knew it was Cyrus Mandrey's beard.

Crowlton threw back his head and laughed. "Very clever. They didn't call you The Chameleon for nothing." His smile faded. "But you're no match for The Serpent."

"I'm unarmed." What could he do to even the odds?

"That you are. Too bad for you, isn't it? Well, as I was saying, your wife will be my prize. I think I deserve something after ferreting you out, don't you?"

"Don't touch her." It took every ounce of strength not to lunge at the bastard.

"Don't touch her." The words rolled over Crowlton's tongue like velvet. "Is that a request or a demand? Either way, it seems you have little control over the situation."

Jon looked away, trying to fight the strong urge to wipe the smile off Crowlton's face.

Permanently. His gaze fell on the lantern, the sole source of illumination in this otherwise black passage. The flame flickered and danced within the confines of the glass. One sharp blow to the lantern would snuff out the flame, blanketing them in darkness. Evening the odds.

"I can't wait to touch your wife's creamy skin. Sink myself into her warm, wet heat." He paused, his voice little more than a whisper. "Again."

Again. The word pierced Jon's heart with more pain than any knife could ever cause. Julia and Crowlton? He refused to believe it.

"Did she tell you she's with child?" From the guarded look on Jon's face, it was obvious she hadn't. "I see." He flipped the knife in the air, caught it by the blade, and flipped it again. "Julia's going to have a baby, Remmington. My baby."

"Liar!" Jon roared, kicking the lantern with his right foot and lunging for Crowlton. Blackness covered them as he wrapped his arms around the other man, wrestling him to the floor. Jon was much larger, but The Serpent was wiry and hard to hold down. A slice of pain ripped Jon's side as a blade sank in, drawing blood. He reached for Crowlton's arm, missed, and suffered the slash of a blade on his forearm.

"Damn liar!" Jon hissed, slamming his fist in the area of Crowlton's face. The sickening sound of crushing bone filled the air, followed by a low groan. Jon punched him again. Harder. He swiped the air with his left hand, searching for Crowlton's arm. He found it, yanked it down over The Serpent's head, and banged the bastard's hand on the wood floor several times. "Damn liar," he rasped. The knife fell from

The Serpent's hand and Jon felt for it, grabbed it, and lodged it against his nemesis's throat.

"You lied." Jon trailed the knife along Crowlton's neck, pressing harder into his skin with each passing second. "Admit it." He waited for the confession, but the only sound he heard was Crowlton's labored breathing and mumbled groans. "Admit it!" Jon said, determined to force the words from his enemy's lips.

A slow gurgle filled the air. It was half laugh, half gasp. "Who do you think told me about this place? I win, Remmington, I win," Crowlton whispered. "My baby, not yours."

Jon sank the blade into Crowlton's neck, twisted it until pools of blood oozed onto his fingers. Then he twisted it again, trying to wipe out the words. Harder. Deeper. But it was too late. The Serpent lay before him, dead, his throat slashed. It should have been a welcome victory, but the win was cold and empty.

Jon dropped the knife and wiped his bloody hands on his breeches. He tried to stand, but the pain in his side kept him doubled over. He felt for the wall and edged along, one step at a time, his right arm bracing his weight. Blood seeped through his fingers from the deep gash on his side.

Had Crowlton told the truth? Had he seduced Julia as his ultimate revenge? Or had she gone to him of her own will and let him father her child? Is that why she hadn't told him about the baby? The questions teemed in his head, making him sick.

Jon took another shuffling step and thought of his wife's conversation with Cyrus the morning she'd been sick. She'd admitted it was Jon's child, hadn't she? But what else could she have said, under the circumstances? *She was carrying Andrew Kleeton's baby in her belly?* There had been plenty of opportunity for a distraught young bride and an experienced seducer to share a liaison before Cyrus showed up. *And* Julia had told Kleeton about the secret passageway.

Julia had betrayed him. Did she know Kleeton's true

identity? Was she in on his scheme? Perhaps waiting at this very moment for her lover to join her and inform her of her husband's demise? The pain of betrayal invaded every part of his body, from head to heart.

Jon reached the door leading to his room. He rested a sticky hand on the knob, hesitated a moment, and then pushed it open, thinking of Julia and her betrayal.

Chapter 20

She must have heard the door open because no sooner had he hobbled over the threshold than she ran to him, shock and surprise on her face. "Jon! What happened?"

Julia was a good little actress, he'd give her that. She actually seemed concerned about him, but he knew better. He settled into a large tufted chair, mindless of the blood he tracked behind and about himself. Leaning back, Jon pinched the bridge of his nose and rubbed his eyes.

Julia sank to the floor beside him and grabbed his free hand. Tears streamed down her face. God, but she was beautiful— beautiful and deceitful. "Kleeton's dead," he said, relishing the words. *Her lover, the father of her baby was dead.*

"What happened?" She held his hand with such force, looked at him with such concern in those smoky eyes, he almost believed she cared.

"Kleeton jumped me in the passageway and tried to slit my throat, but I beat him to it." That's all she needed to know.

A look similar to horror shadowed her face. "But why?"

Jon shrugged. "Perhaps he wanted you to himself." He pulled his hand away and rubbed his neck. "I need Billington."

"Of course," she mumbled, scrambling to her feet. "I'll get him right away." He tried to take a deep breath, but his side hurt too damn much. His head fell back against the chair and he closed his eyes, fighting the weakness that threatened to suck him under.

Minutes later, Billington was at his side. "Sir, you requested my assistance?"

Jon opened one eye and would have laughed if the pain weren't so bad. Ever the gentleman, even in a burgundy stocking cap and matching silk robe, Billington stood before him, not in the least perturbed by the sight of Jon covered in blood. But why should he be? Billington had patched him up on more than one occasion.

Before Jon could answer, Julia burst into the room, water

sloshing over the sides of the basin she carried. "Mr. Billington," she panted. "He's bleeding."

Jon wondered at her almost panicked voice. She needn't put on such a show for him or Billington. They'd seen it all before, the best plots of deceit imaginable. Julia clanked the basin on the floor and produced a cloth from the pocket of her robe. She dipped it in water and wrung it out, then moved toward him, holding the cloth.

He snatched it from her. "That's Billington's job," he snapped. He did not want her touching him, not after she'd lain with his enemy. His gaze shot to her stomach.

"Jon? I want to help." There was no need to look at her face to know there were tears in her eyes, but she would get no comfort from him.

"You've already helped enough. You almost got me killed." He ignored her gasp and turned to Billington. Holding out the cloth, he said, "Here. Do what you need to do."

Billington took the cloth but hesitated, his eyes darting to Julia. "Sir, perhaps Lady Julia could help."

"No. I said she's *helped* enough. If you can't do the job, then leave me the hell alone, and I'll do it myself." Billington clamped his mouth shut and within minutes he'd assessed the wound, applied pressure and a dressing. The other cuts were superficial and required less attention.

Julia sat a few feet away, her eyes never leaving him. Jon pretended to ignore her, but he smelled her lilac scent, glimpsed the cascade of curls trailing from her shoulders. He should hate her for her betrayal and part of him did, but a deeper part couldn't hate her, still wanted her, even now, in the hour of her greatest deceit, and he despised his weakness.

There was only one solution.

"Billington, in the morning I want you to send servants to help Lady Julia pack."

"Jon, what are you talking about?" Julia stood, hands on hips. "Where are we going?"

Jon forced himself to meet her gaze one last time as she

looked at him, a mixture of anger and confusion etched on her beautiful face.

"*We* aren't going anywhere," he said. "You, on the other hand, are going back to your brother's."

"What?" She took a step closer. Then another. "Why are you doing this? Last night you told me you loved me and today you won't even look at me."

He waved a hand in the air, annoyed with her questions. "Spare me the theatrics, Julia. It will do you no good. You know better than anyone the reason for my decision."

She inched closer, her small hands balled into fists. "Do I? Do tell, what *is* the reason? Is it because I couldn't trust you enough to admit my love for you before? Because I wanted to be certain you wouldn't leave again?" Her voice rose and he was certain half the household perched on the other side of the door. He cared less.

"Let it be. Don't embarrass yourself any further. Just leave. Tomorrow," he finished on a ragged sigh. Why did it cause him such pain to say the words?

"I will not leave, Jon Remmington. I love you and you told me you loved me," she half shouted. "I am not running away."

"Tomorrow, Julia," he repeated, his eyes burning into hers.

A tear trickled down her cheek. "I love you. I'm sorry I didn't trust you enough. Please forgive me," she whispered, bending to place a kiss on his forehead.

Jon jerked back before her lips touched his skin. Hurt and shock crossed her face but he'd do whatever it took to make her leave. His salvation depended on it.

She straightened and squared her shoulders, her gaze traveling over his face, from eyes to nose, to hair, to chin and back again as though she were memorizing it. When she spoke, he had to strain to hear her words. "I'm carrying your child."

"No!" he roared, half jumping out of his seat. The pain in his side forced him back down. "Do not," he bit out, "speak of your bastard child as mine!"

She gasped and stumbled back.

"The child isn't mine. It's Kleeton's, and I'll be damned if I'll be cuckolded just because he's dead."

"Andrew? No! It wasn't like that at all. We were friends, nothing more. How could you think such a thing after we...after we..." She shot a pleading look at Billington who'd faded to the far end of the room. "Tell him, Mr. Billington, tell him the truth."

"I don't want a goddamn testimonial from Billington. I heard it from your lover's own mouth," he said, the words bitter on his tongue.

"Why would you believe his words over mine?"

"You and I have never shared much in the way of the truth, but some people think honesty is a virtue, though I do doubt Kleeton was one of them."

"Yet, you choose to believe him." Her voice grew cold now, emotionless. "Well, if you won't listen to me and refuse to ask Mr. Billington, then let's find Cyrus and ask him. He'll tell you the truth."

Jon shot a sharp look at Billington, who coughed and sputtered into his hand. "Sorry. Can't do that," Jon said, clenching his jaw.

"Why not? Cyrus won't mind losing a little sleep. I'm surprised he hasn't woken up yet."

"I'm not," Jon said.

Julia's eyes narrowed. "What did you do to him? Did you harm him? Where is he?" Her voice rose with each rapid-fire question.

Jon shrugged. "Gone."

"Gone?" she echoed. She inclined her head, trying to get into his line of vision. Jon fixed his eyes on the Ming vase on top of the bureau. "He can't just be gone."

He raised a weary hand and signaled Billington. God, but he just wanted to be done with this whole mess. So many lies. No wonder he and Julia never stood a chance. "Billington? Would you care to enlighten Lady Julia?"

Julia's gaze flew to Billington. The butler cleared his throat.

Once. Twice. Three times before daring to speak. "Ah, Lady Julia, it seems as though Mr. Mandrey is no longer with us." He shot a reproving glance at his employer.

Jon scowled back. "Because?"

Billington straightened his shoulders. "Because..." he dragged the word out, "...he's been called away on an emergency." He finished in a rush, the words tumbling over one another in a blur. So much for Billington's preciseness.

"What kind of emergency?" Julia asked, taking a few steps toward Billington.

"Billington." Jon did not try to hide the warning in his voice. Or the exasperation. He needed to make a clean break from this whole business, and he didn't want Julia thinking her knight in shining armor, or in this case, her protector in hairy disarray, would rescue her. She might as well learn right now there was no such thing as charming princes or happily-ever-after. He'd been foolish enough to forget that for a short time and he'd pay for his error, for the pain of love, loss, and betrayal had seared his heart, scarring him worse than The Serpent's hands.

Billington's expression softened. "It seems there's been a bit of confusion concerning Mr. Mandrey," he began in a gentle voice. "Actually, quite a lot of confusion." There was a long pause as his throat worked but no sound came out.

What was wrong with the old crust? Had he gone soft after all these years? Of course, just one more sap ready to do Julia's bidding. Well, Jon would no longer be included in that number. "I'm Cyrus Mandrey," he said.

Julia whirled around. "You?" A choked laugh escaped her. "Where is he, Jon? What have you done with him?"

"He's me," he said, giving her a small salute. "I'm him. Ask Billington."

She turned to the older man, a question on her face. Billington nodded as though someone held a string around his neck, forcing him to respond.

"But you can't be Cyrus," Julia said, advancing on Jon.

"Cyrus is gentle and warm and caring." Jon stiffened but she didn't seem to notice. "He's honest and trustworthy. Filled with integrity." He heard the conviction and admiration in her voice and it irritated him.

"Of course I couldn't be him," he snapped. "How could I possibly know anything about those qualities? Nevertheless, I *was* Cyrus Mandrey. If you are so inclined, the wig and beard are in there," he said, pointing to the secret passageway. "But they might be a little bloody."

"Why?" The word was a mere whisper.

"The man you knew as Andrew Kleeton and I had a score to settle. I had to ensure your safety first, before I took care of him." That was as much as he would tell her about his past life.

"I see." Her voice wandered off. "This was like a play. The characters weren't even real." Her gaze moved to the butler. "And Mr. Billington?"

"Is not really a butler," Jon said, eyeing her.

"Oh." She looked at him then and he saw the hurt and torment in her eyes. "This was all an act, wasn't it?" she breathed.

She wanted to know if his words of love were real, if the passion they'd shared meant something or was merely part of a carefully thought-out script. His heart clenched, pounding against his ribs so hard it hurt. *He had to save himself.* The words stuck in his throat, but he pushed them out. "It was all part of the plan."

She gasped and turned away, running for the shelter of her room. The door slammed behind her, and he knew he'd been successful in shutting her out of his life. He rested his head against the cushions and gave himself up to the pain.

***

Julia scanned the chamber one last time. Nothing remained to indicate she'd ever been in this room, ever shared intimacies here with her husband that made her blush. Everything looked the same, but nothing would ever be the same.

Jon had stripped away every vestige of pride along with any

hope for a reunion. He'd done it with such callousness she found it hard to believe he'd ever looked at her with caring eyes or spoken words of love and devotion. But it hadn't really been him; that person was an actor, reciting lines from a script, not his heart.

Her bags and trunk were packed and waiting. It would be best to leave Glenview Manor as soon as possible. It appeared Jon planned to continue his life here, and he'd made it quite obvious she would not be part of it. Julia gathered her wool cloak and, with one final glance, left the room.

She'd declined a proper breakfast, preferring a cup of cocoa and toast in her bedroom. Her emotions were too raw to risk an encounter with Jon this morning, though he probably felt the same way.

She trailed a hand along the oak railing, finding comfort in the polished wood beneath her fingers. Glenview Manor had become her home and now she must leave it. Reaching the bottom stair, she pulled on her cloak, took one last glance behind her, and stepped outside into the brisk fall sunshine.

Of course, she knew Mr. Billington and Henry Barnes would wish her farewell and perhaps Cook and maybe even the shy young maid who changed her linens. She did not expect to find a line of servants peering at her from the top step to the carriage door. The entire household had come to send her on her way. Tears sprang to Julia's eyes as she worked her way through the gathering, hugging and exchanging words with the well-wishers.

"Best of luck to ye," Mrs. Connelly, the scullery maid, whispered, her bony hands clasping Julia's.

"We's heartbroken by it all, jest heartbroken," Cook murmured, the flesh under her chin jiggling with each shake of her head.

Mrs. Reeves, the downstairs maid, couldn't speak for the tears streaming down her face. Julia gave her a quick hug.

"Thank you," she said, fighting back tears. "I will miss you all."

She worked her way through the remaining servants, hugging and reminiscing.

"I ain't gonna git all teary-eyed, so don't go expectin' it," a gruff voice said in her ear.

"Mr. Barnes." Julia smiled.

Henry Barnes clasped her upper arms, shaking his gray, frizzled head. "He needs ya, the boy does. Too bad, 'e's too stubborn ta admit it."

Julia did not want to discuss Jon's shortcomings. He'd made his decision and from the line of sad faces surrounding her, they'd all pay for it.

"Take care, Mr. Barnes. Thank you for providing such wonderful care for Allegra. I'll send for her as soon as I'm settled."

A shadow fell over the groomsman's weathered face. "Take as long as ya need. No problem." Julia met his black-eyed gaze and saw sadness in its depths. She hugged him and stepped away, turning to the final well-wisher.

Mr. Billington.

He stood tall and erect, just as he had the first day she'd seen him, but that's where the resemblance ended. The gray eyes that were once cold and emotionless were now filled with warmth and compassion. The pinched, sour-lemon expression was gone, replaced with a softer, more relaxed visage. And sometimes, like right now, his lips actually curved into a semblance of a smile. Mr. Billington guided her away from the ears of the crowd. He cleared his throat, a habit she now knew signaled nervousness. "Maybe when he settles down, things will appear differently to him."

Julia shook her head. "I don't think so."

He shifted his weight from one long leg to the other. "You were caught in the middle of a very dangerous situation. Mr. Remmington could think of nothing but ending it."

"There's no need to make excuses for him, Mr. Billington. You were there. You heard what he said." She sighed, tired of thinking of Jon. "I have no great desire to know about his conflict with Andrew or whatever his real name was. Whether Jon admits it or not, the baby is his." She straightened her shoulders. "And that will be his loss."

"What will you do now?" Mr. Billington asked, searching her face.

"I suppose I have no choice but to return to my brother's for the rest of my confinement." She shrugged. "But after the baby is born, I'll seek a house for myself and the baby."

Mr. Billington nodded, opened his mouth to speak, and closed it again. Some things were better left unsaid.

Julia gave him a gentle smile and clasped his bony hands. "I will always remember you. Thank you." Her smile deepened. "For everything." Before he could see the devastation on her face, she hugged him and ran for the safety of the carriage.

Not until the wheels rolled down the cobbled drive, away from Glenview Manor, did she give herself over to the gut-wrenching grief in her soul and let the tears come.

***

Jon brought the bottle to his lips and let the amber liquid trickle down his throat in a slow, steady burn. He'd discarded his glass long ago, after the third drink, he thought. The past several hours blurred before him like a haze of jumbled words and vague images teaming with numbed emotions. He wiped his mouth with the back of his hand and set the bottle down.

Why the hell was he drinking anyway? He couldn't remember. Screwing up his eyes, he forced himself to concentrate. *Something had happened. What?* He looked down at his rumpled shirt. Torn, splattered with red. Blood. There'd been a fight. He'd killed a man. A glimpse of terror flashed through his mind. There was a face to go with the dead figure lying on the cold floor. Jon pinched the bridge of his nose. The image sharpened.

Another vision swayed before him. Julia. He pushed her sweetness away with another swallow and a curse. He would not think of her.

A light rap on the door disturbed his soulful musings.

"Come in," he said, his voice hoarse from lack of sleep and too much liquor.

Edward Billington entered, his expression more stoic than usual.

"Is she gone?" Jon asked, torn between pride and hope.

A slight nod of Billington's balding head told him more than he wanted to know.

"Good," he muttered, lifting the bottle again. Halfway to his mouth, Jon noticed Billington's gray eyes fixed on him. "What are you looking at?" The raw meanness in his voice echoed throughout the room.

"Nothing, sir." Billington took a step forward. "I was merely observing your choice of breakfast beverages."

Jon held the bottle back, squinting one eye, trying to bring the print into focus. "Damn, if I know what it says, but I know what it is." He held the bottle up. "Besides," he continued, his words slow and purposeful, "I haven't slept yet, so this isn't breakfast." He took another swig. "Whisky. Want a taste?"

"No, thank you, sir." Billington approached Jon and pulled a white envelope from his pocket. "This is for you, sir," he said, holding out the envelope.

Jon rubbed his stubbled chin. "Read it to me, Billington. I'm having a little difficulty focusing at the moment."

"Yes, sir." Billington opened the envelope and pulled out a single sheet of paper.

Jon sat back against his leather chair and rested his hands over his belly. "Just give me the gist of it, man. Don't bore me with the whole thing."

Billington scanned the paper. "Very well, sir," he said, looking up to meet Jon's bleary gaze. "It seems as though the entire household has resigned."

"Resigned? Resigned from what?"

"From your employ, sir," Billington said, clearing his throat.

"That's ridiculous."

Billington extended the paper. "They've signed their names,

sir."

"They can't resign," Jon barked, slamming the desk with his fist. "They're as much a part of Glenview Manor as the house itself." His eyes narrowed. "Why do they want to leave?"

"It seems they took a great liking to Lady Julia and sympathize with her."

"Of course," Jon said, his voice quaking with anger. "Everyone wants to rush to do her bidding. Fine. Let them feel sorry for her. See if it feeds their bellies. We'll replace every last one of them." He slashed his hand through the air. "Get on it right away, Billington."

The older man cleared his throat and coughed. "I'm sorry, sir," he said in a quiet voice. "I won't be able to do that."

Jon tilted his head to one side. "Why the hell not?"

"My name is on this list as well."

"You?" Jon sputtered. "You? Resigning?"

Billington squared his shoulders. "I'm afraid so, sir."

"Because of *Julia?*" He braced his elbows on the desk and rubbed his temples. *Billington couldn't leave.* "I thought you two didn't even like one another."

"We came to an understanding of sorts," Billington confessed. "I hold Lady Julia in the highest regard."

"I see," Jon said, but he didn't. He didn't see one damn thing.

Billington cleared his throat again. "Now that I am no longer in your employ, sir, I would like to make one comment."

"By all means, comment away."

A dull flush crept up Billington's cheeks. "Lady Julia loves you, sir. She did not betray that love. Crowlton knew she was your weakness, and he pressed his advantage, telling you a terrible lie. If you believe him, then he lives on, not in an unborn child, but in you, festering and growing until his hatred becomes your hatred. It will destroy you."

"She told *him* about the baby, not me," Jon said, letting the pain spill over his words.

Billington shrugged. "She also told Cyrus, but you didn't accuse him of fathering the child."

"That's absurd."

"No more so than what you're suggesting." Billington took a step closer. "But if you've a notion of putting matters right, you had best be on your way. Her carriage left over twenty minutes ago."

Jon sat slumped in the chair, his face buried in his hands. He didn't move, nor did he see Billington's lips twitch.

"She still loves you, despite what's happened," Billington said. "Though she did mention America again." He paused, tapping a long finger to his pointed chin. "Is it possible, sir, that Lady Julia would forgo her brother's house and set sail for America? In her condition? A pregnant woman, traveling alone?"

Billington's words swirled about the empty room, crashing to the ground in a careless heap. He turned just in time to see Jon bound out the door.

Edward Billington smiled and, for the first time in his adult life, threw back his head and laughed.

***

Jon flew down the road on Flash, hoping to catch a glimpse of the Remmington carriage. But as he rounded each bend, he saw nothing but a vast stretch of trees and road before him. Had he somehow missed her? Had she taken a different course? Panic squeezed his heart. Was he too late?

Billington's words echoed in every hoof beat. America. America. America. A pregnant woman traveling alone. Jon pressed on, harder, faster. The carriage should not be much farther ahead. Unless she'd decided on a different route? *One that did not lead to her brother's house.* Dread washed over him, frightening him with possibilities.

He was about to turn around and head in the opposite direction when he spotted the carriage. Urging his mount forward, Jon came alongside the black conveyance and signaled the driver to stop. He slid to the ground and grabbed the carriage door, flinging it open to find his wife, wide-eyed and open-mouthed, staring back at him.

"You're not going to America," he said. She may as well know he would fight to keep her and his unborn child with him.

"I'm not?" She stared at him as though he were a madman, which he might appear to be, given his current rumpled state.

"No. Unless you want to go after the baby's born." He paused, swallowing hard. "Then, if you'd like, we can visit my family and your brother."

She merely stared at him as though he'd come quite unhinged.

"Whatever you want." He climbed into the carriage and took her hands in his. "I love you, Julia. I've always loved you," he said, his voice ragged with emotion.

"You love me," she repeated.

"I do," he murmured, stroking her cheek. "With my whole heart. I've been such a fool. I almost let my hatred destroy us." He placed a hand on her stomach. "I want *our* baby. Very much." Jon leaned over and brushed his lips over hers.

She pulled away, her beautiful face blank as she said, "Yesterday you couldn't stand the sight of me. Today you love me. Pray, Jon, what will tomorrow bring?"

Her response unsettled him. He had hoped she might profess her love as well, but perhaps she needed reassurance before she risked the words again. He took her hand in his and said, "My dear sweet wife, I will love you tomorrow and the day after that and all the days that follow."

Her eyes grew bright and her lips trembled. "A day ago, I begged for those very words—" she withdrew her hand "—today they are too late."

A trickle of panic spread through him but he fought it, determined to drive it away. "Too late for what? I've admitted my love and my desire for our baby as well as my foolishness. What more do you want? Tell me and I'll do it."

The emptiness in her gaze made the panic spread. "I want nothing else from you. I shall return to my brother's to wait out my confinement."

She was leaving him. Even after he'd professed his love for her and the baby. "And that's it? We're finished?"

She swallowed hard and looked away. "We were finished before we started."

"You can't mean that." He grasped her hands, willing her to listen as the panic engulfed him. "Despite our past difficulties, we belong together."

She shook her head and said in a sad voice, "Lies and distrust kill love. We were never honest with one another, from the very beginning. How can love last where there is no trust?"

"But I *do* trust you. I was a fool. Please, Julia, I promise on our baby's life, I won't disappoint you." He would do anything for one last chance.

"I'm sorry, Jon, truly I am."

"Julia." He reached for her but she pulled away. "These past days have been a source of great upset, and I should like to put an end to them lest they harm the baby."

"I would never do anything to harm our child. I only want—"

"Then leave." She met his gaze and the cold determination in her eyes killed any hopes of reconciliation. "This constant upheaval is wearing on me and soon will affect the welfare of the baby. Please, Jon, just leave. When the child is born, you will be notified."

Chapter 21

Julia ascended the steps of Ellswood, anxious to be done with the inevitable questions and the gawking and the uncomfortable silence—not from the servants, but from her brother and sister-in-law. Upon her direction, Mr. Billington had sent word she was returning to them. There was no mention of the reason or the duration of the stay. That messy business would be taken care of face to face though once Holt and Sophie spotted the trunks and suitcases, they would guess the worst, and they would be right.

Jon was well and truly gone. She'd pushed him out of her life with words of fear for her child's safety, though the greater fear was irreparable damage to her battered heart. In the confines of the carriage, he'd spoken of love with such conviction and sincerity she'd succumbed to him. But she'd held fast. What future would they have if their foundation were built on physical desire and distrust? What would happen the next time an obstacle arose that appeared questionable, say, in the form of a handsome man? Would Jon accuse her of unfaithfulness? Would he turn her out once again?

Julia stifled a cry as she thought of Cyrus Mandrey, a man she considered honorable and filled with integrity—a man who did not exist. The extent of her husband's treachery shocked and pained her.

"Julia!" Sophie rushed down the steps and threw her arms about her. "I'm so very glad you're unharmed and that horrid man is gone."

Was she referring to Jon or Andrew Kleeton?

"Holt told me about him. Awful man and to think you never knew."

Indeed, she had not known about either man. Jon or Andrew. For that matter, she hadn't known about Cyrus. Or Mr. Billington. Perhaps Henry Barnes was the only man at Glenview Manor who was who he proclaimed to be.

Sophie pulled away and frowned. "Something's horribly

wrong. I can see it on your face. Where's Jon?" She glanced at the carriage, frowned. "And what are you doing with all of the trunks? Why, if I didn't know better, I'd say you were moving back...home."

"Yes, well, that is exactly what I'm doing." Julia paused and sucked in a deep breath. "But only until the baby comes. Then I shall find a home of my own." She squared her shoulders and proceeded up the stairs and past Pierce whose face resembled a cooked beet.

"Baby?" Sophie ran after her in a frenzy of concern and confusion. "Baby?" she repeated as though the word were foreign. *"What baby?"*

Holt chose that exact moment to appear. Of course. Tall, dark, and wearing a frown—his usual self. "What baby?" His eyes darted to her stomach and then back to her face.

"Mine, of course." She turned to Pierce, ignoring his open-mouthed stare and said, "Please see that my things are delivered to my room."

Holt closed the distance between them in three steps. "Julia, I wish to speak with you in private."

Odd, but he didn't intimidate her as he once had. Perhaps when one faced what she had, other fears were reduced to mere inconveniences. Her brother wished to speak? Well, she harbored the same desire. She nodded and proceeded past him with a casual, "In your study, please." He had no choice but to follow her and once inside, closed the door with a loud click.

"Sophie will not be joining us?" she asked. "I rather thought she might like to be part of the inquisition."

Her brother found no humor in her words. "What are you doing here and where is Jon? And what is this talk of a baby?"

She considered this and actually smiled at his confusion. Holt was not often perplexed and his current state gave her a small amount of satisfaction. "In answer to your first question, I think it obvious. I am returning to Ellswood but only until the baby arrives. Yes, I'm with child, oh, but that was your third question. As for Jon, why, I imagine he's at Glenview Manor."

She paused. "Where he belongs."

Holt's jaw twitched. "Which is where you belong."

She raised a brow and pretended surprise. "Indeed? You've reconsidered your thoughts on my union with him?"

The jaw twitched again and she noted a tiny flare of nostrils. "When my sister is pregnant with his child, yes, I have reconsidered."

Oh, he was indeed upset. Perhaps she would just add to it a bit, so he could understand her true situation. "Are you certain the child is Jon's?"

Holt sputtered, "Are you mad? What kind of idiotic comment is that?"

Julia took in her brother's countenance—a twitching jaw, flaring nostrils, mouth straighter than a line. Indeed, he was not pleased. "My husband did not think it an idiotic statement when he insisted Andrew Kleeton was the father."

"Kleeton?"

She shrugged. It pained her to recount Jon's accusation but she must if her brother were to understand the truth behind her departure. "Of course, he later apologized for the accusation but the harm was done."

"Julia." He clutched her hands. "People say things they don't mean in a fit of anger or jealousy."

"Yes, they do," she agreed, "but do they also dress up as other people and engage in various forms of espionage involving their wives and persons with dubious backgrounds? I think not. You were not there, Holt. You did not witness my husband as he drew me in and gathered my confidences. I told him things that were not meant for Jon to hear, and to think he knew this, knew *everything,* yet continued to plot and plan to trap a man he deemed an enemy." She shook her head and tried to still the memories. "It's unconscionable. The man flipped back and forth from Cyrus to Jon like a chameleon."

Holt gasped for air and rasped, "Never say that word again."

"What word? Chameleon?"

"Julia!" His gaze narrowed as he hissed, "Cease.

Immediately."

Holt could be such a bully but he no longer intimidated her. "Oh, for goodness' sake, why not?"

Her brother grabbed her arm and led her to the sofa. "Sit," he commanded. She only did so because his face had contorted into a visage not unlike a rabid dog she'd once seen. When she'd plopped on the sofa, he sat beside her. His features began to settle back into the Holt she recognized as he took her hand and said in a low voice, "What I am about to tell you is known by few. Not even Sophie is aware of it, but I fear if I don't tell you, then you may well blabber it about and cause great unrest for all of us."

"What on earth are you talking about?" She'd merely likened her husband to a lizard, and she certainly could have called him worse.

Holt cleared his throat, hesitated, and plunged forward, "Jon and I worked together years ago."

"At sea. But what does this have to do with me calling him a—"

"We were not always at sea. We had other," he paused, "missions as well."

"Missions?" Her lips twitched. "You make it sound as though you and Jon were—"

He clamped a hand over her mouth before she could finish. "Do not say the word."

Julia yanked his hand away. "What word?"

"The word you were about to speak."

She leaned close and whispered. "You mean, spies?"

"Julia!" He tightened his grip on her hand and said in a low voice, "Your husband was known for his ability to change—his appearance, his voice, his mannerisms. This garnered him the code name you used."

"You and Jon?" She could hardly believe it. They had been spies for The Crown? "What part did Andrew Kleeton play in this?" Mayhap he was a villain they'd been tracking years past.

Holt's expression hardened. "He was one of us until he

turned traitor. Good men died because of his treachery. There were files that had to be destroyed before he got his hands on them. We didn't know he was in the building when the fire started but we believe he tried to get the files and burned his hands badly. He spotted Jon from a window right before the building went up in flames. Everyone believed him dead, but Jon maintained the absence of a body meant he could still be alive." Holt ran a hand through his hair and sighed. "You can imagine Jon's panic when Kleeton appeared wearing gloves he never removed and sending an invitation with a particular creature on it that had been his code name."

"I assume his real name was not Andrew Kleeton?"

"No, it was not."

He offered no more and she didn't ask. It was an impossible story and yet, she'd seen the dark interior of Andrew Kleeton's home, witnessed the disfigured residents eyeing her as though they would relish squeezing the life from her. Even Andrew had on occasion studied her with such intensity it unsettled her. What a burden Jon must have carried, yet he'd told her nothing, which further marked the lack of trust in their relationship. "Had Jon told me, I could have helped him."

"You would have been about as much help as Mrs. Florence. Besides, the risk to your safety was too great."

Mere opinion and one she did not share. "I should have been told."

"Julia, we did what we thought best to protect you. Now that this is over, you need to return to your husband and patch things up."

She didn't miss the annoyance in his voice. Well, he wasn't the only one who was annoyed. "There is no patching, Holt." She removed her hand from his and stood. "The hole of distrust and untruths between us is too great to repair. I shall have this child, and then I shall seek my own residence." She did not add, *with or without your approval,* but the firmness in her voice left no doubt what she meant.

"Julia—"

"Please. Nothing you can tell me will change my mind. Now if you will excuse me, I should like to rest." She nodded and made her way toward the door, eager to reach the quiet of her room. Her brother could be so trying at times. Like now.

"What if I told you Jon was *forced* to leave you after the wedding?"

She swung around. "Why are you doing this? Can you not leave this alone?"

He stood and moved toward her. "It is not often I'm wrong but when I am, it does not sit well with me."

"Indeed?"

"Certainly not." He settled his large hands on her shoulders and actually looked contrite. "I've a grave confession to make. Jon's leaving is my fault."

"Yours? How?"

"I didn't think he had it in him to settle down with one woman, and I was not going to see my sister hurt. I called in an old debt and forced him to honor it by leaving."

Julia sucked in breaths of air as Holt's words swirled around her. "You forced him to leave? You watched me suffer and agonize over his disappearance and yet you said nothing." Her voice grew stronger as anger flared. "How could you?" And then, *"How dare you?"*

"I am sorry." He reached into his pocket and pulled out an envelope. "I should have given you this long ago. It's from Jon."

She eyed the unsealed enveloped. "You've read it." Of course he had. Wasn't that what constituted good espionage? Staying two steps ahead of the opponent?

He nodded.

She accepted the letter and stepped away from him. "I should like privacy."

He hesitated a moment and then said, "Of course." When he reached the door, he stopped and faced her. "I doubt I'll ever be able to make this up to you, but if it's America you want, I'll get you there."

"Thank you." The door clicked behind him, leaving Julia alone with Jon's letter. She lifted it from the envelope and began to read.

My dearest wife:

I miss you. Immensely. I never believed the depth of longing could be so great or all-consuming and though this feeling is not easy to admit, I will not deny it. I cannot deny it. You have captured my heart. Would that you might find it in yours to forgive my numerous lackings and grant me one more chance to be a true husband, I vow I will spend the rest of my days in honest endeavor.

Your faithful husband, Jon

Julia clutched the letter to her heart and whispered her husband's name. After all that had happened between them, did they stand a chance or was it too late? She reread the letter once more. After the sixth time, she knew what she must do.

***

Jon ignored the clamoring in the hall. He did not need to witness his staff packing up their carriages as they moved out of his home. They'd certainly wasted no time making their grand exits. He didn't blame them. Why would they want to be around him when they could look for a mistress with the charm and grace and beauty of his wife? They'd all be gone soon and with them the memories of Julia. Her smile. Her laughter. Her kindness.

Damn, he could use a drink right now but what was the use of dulling a pain that would never leave? He might as well get used to Glenview Manor minus its mistress. He pulled off one boot and then the other and opened the door adjoining the master suit. A faint whiff of lilac clung to the room. Just a hint but it was enough. Jon clutched the silver brush Julia had forgotten in her haste to get away from him and eased onto the bed. A few golden hairs had caught in the bristles and he pulled one out and closed his eyes. The pain in his heart was real and pure and like nothing he'd ever experienced before. He breathed deeply, willing the lilac to fill him and bring Julia back to him—if only in his dreams.

Moments or perhaps hours later, something brushed his forehead, then his cheek. He swatted at the unknown nuisance, desperate to fall back to dreams of Julia. Another brush, this time on his lips. "Damn it." He opened his eyes and found himself face to face with his wife. "Julia?" *How could it be her?*

She glanced at the brush in his hand and said, "You found my brush."

He cleared his throat and ran a hand through his mussed hair. "I did." He clutched the brush tighter. What was she doing here?

"Good."

Was that hope he saw in her eyes? *Dear God, let it be so.*

"What are you doing in this room?" she asked. He could save embarrassment and tell her he was overtired and couldn't make it to his own bed but that would be untrue. "It's where I feel closest to you." He avoided her gaze as he admitted the rest, "Sleep eluded me last night until I lay on this bed, surrounded by your scent and memories."

"Holt gave me the letter you wrote me shortly after our wedding." She touched his cheek, traced his lips. "I wish I'd read it sooner."

He nodded, tiny shreds of hope seeping through him. "I wish a lot of things had been different."

"They can be." She clasped his hand and moved closer. "I want them to be."

He crushed her to him, burying his face in her hair. "I don't deserve you but I can't give you up. You're a part of me. Please don't leave."

"I love you, Jon. I've never stopped loving you." She brushed aside a lock of hair and kissed his temple. "From this moment on, we must be completely truthful with one another. Agreed?"

He lifted his head and brushed his lips over hers. "Agreed."

"Completely," she repeated against his lips. "When I swell with our babe and ask if I resemble a cow, you must tell me the truth."

Jon pulled away and cupped her chin. "You will never resemble a cow, madame wife."

Her brows knitted as she considered his answer. "Even when I waddle to and fro and can't see my feet for the size of my belly?"

He trailed a hand from her neck, to her breast, to her belly, envisioning her ripe with child. "Most especially then," he said, tracing circles over her still-flat belly. "You will always be beautiful, Julia."

Her lips curved into a delicious smile. "Well then, I do believe I could grow accustomed to such *truthfulness*, especially when I'm waddling about."

"I've another tidbit of truth for you." He leaned forward and whispered in her ear, "I long to be inside of you. This very minute. Without pretense or—"

She flung her arms around his waist and pulled him on top of her. "I share your longing, dear husband. I have dreamed of this even when I dared not hope. Your beautiful nakedness inside of me." She wet her lips. "Deep and hard and oh, so very wonderful."

"I am ever at your service, sweet wife." He rather liked such truthfulness and looked forward to many more confessions beginning with all the delicious ways he could please her. He had one particular method in mind, involving his tongue and her—

"Come to me, Jon. Fill me and love me."

"Yes." He kissed her forehead, her cheeks, the tip of her nose. "Yes," he murmured as their lips met, forging unspoken promises, pledging truths, offering a glimpse of forever. Grasping freedom. At last.

The End

Many thanks for choosing to spend your time reading *A Scent of Seduction*. I'm truly grateful. If you enjoyed it, please consider writing a review on the site where you purchased it. (Short ones are fine and equally welcome.)

If you'd like to be notified of my new releases, please sign up at my website: *http://www.marycampisi.com*. Thank you once again for spending time with my characters!

About the Author

Mary Campisi writes emotion-packed books about second chances. Whether contemporary romances, women's fiction, or Regency historicals, her books all center on belief in the beauty of that second chance.

Mary should have known she'd become a writer when at age thirteen she began changing the ending to all the books she read. It took several years and a number of jobs, including registered nurse, receptionist in a swanky hair salon, accounts payable clerk, and practice manager in an OB/GYN office, for her to rediscover writing. Enter a mouse-less computer, a floppy disk, and a dream large enough to fill a zip drive. The rest of the story lives on in every book she writes.

When she's not working on her craft or following the lives of five adult children, Mary's digging in the dirt with her flowers and herbs, cooking, reading, walking her rescue lab mix, Cooper, or on the perfect day, riding off into the sunset with her very own 'hero' husband on his Ultra Limited aka Harley.

Mary has published with Kensington, Carina Press, and The Wild Rose Press. She is currently working on her next A Family Affair book as the saga continues...

website: www.marycampisi.com
e-mail: mary@marycampisi.com
twitter: https://twitter.com/#!/MaryCampisi
blog: http://www.marycampisi.com/blog/
facebook: http://www.facebook.com/marycampisibooks

Other Books by Mary Campisi:

Contemporary Romance:

Truth in Lies Series
Book One: A Family Affair
Book Two: A Family Affair: Spring
Book Three: A Family Affair: Summer
Book Four: A Family Affair: Fall
Book Five: A Family Affair: Christmas
Book Six: A Family Affair: Winter (2015)
Book Seven: A Family Affair: The Promise (2015)
Book Eight: A Family Affair: The Secret (TBA)

That Second Chance Series
Book One: Pulling Home
Book Two: The Way They Were
Book Three: Simple Riches
Book Four: Paradise Found
Book Five: Not Your Everyday Housewife
Book Six: The Butterfly Garden

The Betrayed Trilogy
Book One: Pieces of You
Book Two: Secrets of You
Book Three: What's Left of Her: a novella
The Betrayed Trilogy Boxed Set

Begin Again: Short stories from the heart
The Sweetest Deal

Regency Historical:

Young Adult: